C000261167

MICHAEL JOE

A Novel of Irish Life
by
William Cotter Murray

BRANDON

First published in 1965

This paperback edition first published in 1991
by Brandon Book Publishers Ltd,
Dingle, Co. Kerry, Ireland.

British Library Cataloguing in Publication Data
Murray, William Cotter
  Michael Joe.
  I. Title
  823.914 [F]

ISBN 0-86322-128-9

Cover design: The Graphiconies (Bartoli), Dublin
Printed by the Guernsey Press, Channel Islands

We tell you, tapping on our brows,
The story as it should be,—
As if the story of a house
Were told, or ever could be; . . .

From *Eros Turranos*
—EDWIN ARLINGTON ROBINSON

I

MICHAEL JOE MCCARTHY lived alone with his mother in a blue-washed, slate, two-storey house in the Main Street of Corrigbeg. It was a respectable house. He was the last of a family of three, two daughters and himself. The eldest daughter had run off with an English sailor, and Mrs. McCarthy promptly disowned her. Not because the sailor was English, but because her daughter did not get married in St. Joseph's church with Canon Lyons officiating and the people of the town present, watching. The other daughter joined the Poor Clares, and shut herself off from the world forever.

Michael Joe was Mrs. McCarthy's youngest. She kept him around her constantly as a child, going to the chapel, going for Sunday walks around Spanish Point, even doing her work around the house.

When he was five, she walked him up to the National School holding his hand, and insisted to Miss Flavin that she be allowed to sit with him all day. Michael Joe did not cry, and appeared to ignore the foolish figure his mother cut, sitting in the midst of the children. He kept trying to leave the desk where they were sitting to get up and go wandering off around the schoolroom, as if he were at home. After school she walked him home, still holding on to his hand. He asked her if he could go and play with some fellows who were kicking a football along the street ahead of them. 'No,' she said, 'they're too big for you.' He sulked, and kicked at the pavement. She tightened her hold on his hand. Then, when he seemed calm, she let him go. She was satisfied that she had exercised control over him.

The years of his growing up passed quickly for her. And, as he grew, she felt less and less able to command him, and make him obey. But she put on a brave front to the neighbours. A little bit headstrong, sure that's all he was. In her secret heart, she wondered what she had borne. Some kind of great man among men? Surely that must be it. She bore with him because of her private dream.

One morning, when he was fourteen, as Mrs. McCarthy was making young Michael Joe's bed, she noticed a large dried stain on the bottom sheet. She was shocked, panicked. What did it mean? Oh, she knew what it meant. Didn't want to think about it. Tore the sheet off the bed, and hurried downstairs and threw it in a tub of hot water, and put in a cupful of bleach. Then, put a clean sheet on his bed.

She said nothing to him about it. Then, a week later, there was another stain. She repeated the bleaching, and did not tell her husband, or question Michael Joe. Kept her secret until she could bear it no longer and had to approach the boy, one morning at breakfast before he went to school.

'Are you sick, Michael Joe? Is there anything wrong with you?'

With the instinct of a boy, he knew what his mother meant.

'No, Mammy. I'm all right.'

'Well, if you get sick in bed, you ought to go to the toilet.'

'I don't get sick,' he said truculently.

'Well, I like to have the sheets nice and white and clean,' she said. 'Don't you?'

He knew the male in him was being attacked, rejected.

'No!' he shouted. 'I want them dirty.' He ran out to school without being kissed. And Mrs. McCarthy never kissed him again.

When Michael Joe's father died of pneumonia and a weak heart, Michael Joe took over running the shop next door to the house. The house, a little bit of land, and the money remained in Mrs. McCarthy's name at the bank. When Michael Joe wanted money, he asked her, or took it from the till and told her. She never questioned how he spent it.

Michael Joe was twenty-one then. Medium height, large-chested, square-shouldered, dark-complexioned. 'Carried himself well', as the people of the town said. Took after his father's side of the family, who were dark. Mrs. McCarthy disliked the physical McCarthy strain in her son. A tinker or a gypsy strain. Spanish, maybe. Her own family, the O'Briens, were pure Irish. Going back to Brian Boru. A pure strain, and a pure temperament because of it. She tried to tell herself, though, that it was only in looks that Michael Joe took after the McCarthys. He had never since the day he was born given her any real trouble that she could remember, she'd say to the neighbours.

Michael Joe grew a moustache the spring after his father's death.

It came thick and black. Mrs. McCarthy did not like it. ' 'Tis a sight,' she said, the one time they spoke of it. 'You look like them pagan Turks.' 'I didn't think 'twas doing any harm,' Michael Joe said. 'Oh, it isn't the harm,' his mother said. 'What is it, then?' Michael Joe said. 'Botheration!' she said. Michael Joe shaved off the moustache to please her.

He hired a local boy to help him in the shop. A strong, quick-witted boy of sixteen who had been working for farmers since he graduated from the National School the year before. Michael Joe had seen him play football for the local minor football team. And liked the way he played. And hired him on that recommendation alone.

Michael Joe was able to leave the shop then, whenever he liked, once he had shown Vin Scanlon the ropes.

In the mornings, he generally hopped over to Dan Kerney's, with the *Irish Independent*, and spent an hour with the crowd debating the racing results from Leopardstown, or the Curragh, or Phoenix Park. He put a bob or two on for the day with Hogan, the bookie in Ennistymon. He did not tell his mother about his betting.

He bought a double-barrelled shotgun and kept it under the counter in the shop. On a fine Saturday he would take off for Mount Callan on his bicycle, with the schoolmaster, Tom Fitzgerald, or Seamus Larkin, the bank clerk, and spend the day shooting grouse or rabbits. He gave what he killed away because his mother did not approve of his shooting, and wouldn't clean his kill, and he had no wish to clean it himself. But the people he gave his kill away to were always honoured to get it. Meat was dear. No one in Corrigbeg was so rich that they could afford to throw away a gift of meat.

Michael Joe also joined the St. Joseph's Club in the Parochial Hall. On winter nights, if he didn't go to Blake's, or Rynne's, or Clancy's pub, he went up to the club and played nap or billiards with the bank manager, or Master Fitzgerald, or Ed Donovan, the auctioneer, or any of the local shopkeepers who happened to be there. He won several winter billiards championships.

During the summer he played full-back for the local senior football team, and when they were not playing, travelled anywhere in the county where there might be a good football match. And sometimes went even as far as Limerick, Tipperary or Cork, if there was enough of his own crowd to rent a car and go. He did not ask his mother any more if he could go. He told her where he was going, in a general way. When she asked what time he would be back so that she could have his supper ready, he said he did not know. It wasn't up to him. Whenever the other fellows wanted to come back he'd have to agree to it. But he'd be back.

She did not argue with him; he always came home. Sometimes very late, and staggering up the stairs.

As she lay in her bed in the darkness of her room, she heard him come in. She stopped counting her beads. She knew he was drunk from the noise of his stumbling around in the kitchen and his slow progress up the stairs. As he passed her room she said, 'Is that you, Michael Joe?' ' 'Tis,' he muttered. She whispered a 'thanks-be-to-God' to herself, and fell asleep.

This scene was repeated many times. She never berated him.

2

MICHAEL JOE MET Nell Cullen at a dance in the Parochial Hall given to raise money for the African Missions. Michael Joe was a good dancer. Carried his weight with ease and a smooth forcefulness. He led the woman firmly, drawing her close to him, and dancing head beside head. Never cheek to cheek. He spoke into her ear at first, and then, after he had established some kind of rapport, would let the woman draw back and have a look at him. Then he would press her to him again, and continue talking in her ear.

He was not a fancy dancer. Would rarely get up on the floor for a tango or rumba. The waltz, two-step, or slow fox-trot were his favourites. And he danced them slowly, keeping to basic steps, and getting by with a minimum of show and effort. Dancing was a means to an end for him. He never made the mistake of thinking a dance with a girl was an end in itself. And he always came late to a dance, having spent the evening at Rynne's, or Blake's, drinking with the fellows. As late as midnight, he would walk up to the dance and pay the full price of admission, though there was only an hour or two of the dance left. He would stand by the door, in a strategical position, from which he could get a good look at the girls sitting along the wall. Whatever girl happened to appeal to his fancy while he was making his survey—she was the one he decided he would take home that night. He'd ask her for the next dance, and wouldn't let her off the floor until the dance ended and she had promised to let him take her home.

Usually, he was successful. Not because he was a good catch, and a good match. His approach, a mixture of all-conquering Casanova and the contempt of Iago, appealed to some girls. He had an instinct for picking the right ones. He limited his field and played only where he was already a heavy favourite. He'd walk the girl home in the dark, after the dance. If she lived far out in the country, he'd get his bicycle and carry her on the crossbar.

His approach to love-making was as direct and as basic as his approach to dancing. A sod wall, a cabin, a hay barn, or a meadow —any place served. If the girl wasn't willing, he simply backed her against the nearest wall, and kissed her long and hard, and began feeling her up. If he got her excited enough, he would show her 'the tricks of the trade' as he called it. If she was slow, he would have to keep rubbing against her and feeling her up, until he satisfied himself.

He had never met a girl who would let him go all the way.

The night he met Nell Cullen, he had come to the dance with Tom Fitzgerald, the young schoolmaster, and Larkin, the bank clerk. He had been drinking with them all evening, and was medium drunk. He could walk without staggering, and talk with sense. He laughed more than usual, and the dark eyes were brighter. He came into the hall during an interlude in the dancing.

Nell was standing to the left of the bandstand surrounded by a group of girls. She was taller than most of them by half a head. Michael Joe did not pay any particular attention to her group as he let his eyes roam over the dance hall. Groups of girls clustered around the hall on the edge of the dance floor. The men were around the doorway.

A laugh rising clear above the talk drew Michael Joe's attention to her. She had pinned a piece of white paper on the coat of a man who had his back to her. He had turned around and caught her by the wrists. She laughed.

'Who's the one?' Michael Joe said to Larkin.

'Nell Cullen. Home from England. She was a nurse or something there,' Larkin said.

'Home for the holidays?' Michael Joe said.

'For good, I hear,' Larkin said. 'But you won't make out, if that's what you're aiming at.'

'That's what you think,' Michael Joe said. 'Watch this, man.'

He walked directly down the middle of the dance-hall floor in full view of everyone, to the bandstand where Nell was standing. Jack Madigan was blowing a few trial notes through his saxophone ... booooop, boop. ... The fiddler was tuning up, discordantly; and one of the band was picking a random tune on a banjo.

Nell Cullen was now looking up at the bandstand watching the band tune up. Michael Joe went up to her and said into her ear: 'How about the next one?'

Nell jumped away at the sound of a man's voice so close to her ear; then she turned around and saw Michael Joe. She laughed.

'Well? Is it a yes or no?' Michael Joe said.

'Yes or no what?' she said.

'Can I have the next dance?'

'Let me see now,' she said. She looked him over from head to foot. 'You won't step on my toes?' she said.

Michael Joe's eyes blazed.

The band began to play an old-time waltz.

'Can you waltz?' Nell asked him.

He took her around the waist and swung her out on to the floor.

She was so light on her feet, and adapted herself so quickly to Michael Joe's style of dancing, that he felt very little sense of holding a woman's body in his arms. Nell's head came almost to his face. As he swung her in the waltz, she seemed to be floating out of his arms in the swing. He held her close, in his usual style, and bent his lips to her ear. Paddy Jordan began to sing 'After the Ball'.

Nell drew back from him. 'Isn't it a hot night?'

For an answer, Michael Joe drew her to him again, and began to whisper in her ear.

'You're a grand-looking girl,' he began.

She drew away from him again. 'Am I, faith?' she said, and laughed. Her blue-grey eyes met his steadily.

He pulled her to him again. She gently pushed herself back from him.

'I don't like dancing close,' she said. 'You're a fine dancer, though. You can swing me all you like.'

Michael Joe decided to humour her a bit. He swung her clear a few times, and she leaned back on his arm and let herself sway.

'I love dancing,' she said. As she swung, her long, wavy, fair hair swung around with her. Paddy Jordan's voice crooned on over the microphone: ' . . . Many the hopes that have vaaaanished . . . After the ball. . . .' Nell sang as Michael Joe wheeled her. Her eyes were half closed.

'Listen to me,' he said. 'How about the going home?'

She opened her eyes and laughed at him. 'Can't you enjoy the dance?'

'Look,' he said. 'I haven't time to waste. Yes or no?'

The music stopped. They stood on the dance floor surrounded by other couples. Michael Joe stared at her as if he wanted to devour her. She looked around to see who else was on the floor.

'You don't even know me,' she said.

'You're Nell Cullen,' he said. 'You were in the Girls' and I was in the Boys' in school.'

'That was a long time ago. I'm not the same little girl I was in school.'

'I suppose they taught you a lot in England,' Michael Joe said. 'You're a big girl now.'

She laughed at him. 'What are you so mad about, all of a sudden?'

He decided to change his approach then. He wasn't going to let her make a fool out of him.

'A girl goes to England and then she comes home. And she thinks the country fellows like us aren't half good enough for her.'

'Ah, no. Sure that isn't true at all,' she said sincerely.

The band began playing again. Another medley of waltzes. Michael Joe tried to take advantage of the sympathy he had won.

'You'll let me have the going home, then?' he said.

'You don't ever give up, do you?' she said, as she was wheeled. 'Let me enjoy the dance, and I'll think about it.'

They danced together for the rest of the night until the dance was over. She never let Michael Joe hold her close. He never gave up trying. She seemed to have some knack of always being able to draw away from him. In spite of himself, he would feel his arm

7

letting her draw back. That made him mad at himself because he was giving in to her so easily. But he consoled himself by thinking that she would be going home with him anyway. And then he'd make up for lost time.

The band played 'I'll See You in My Dreams' for the last dance. A slow fox-trot.

'I'll get your coat,' Michael Joe said close to her ear. 'We'll leave before the crowd.'

'I want to dance this,' she said. 'I love it.'

He had to give in to her, and they danced to the slow, dreamy song in silence. Michael Joe did not talk. Paddy Jordan crooned; the lights were dim. The battle was won as far as he was concerned. Nell relaxed in his arms and made no attempt to push him away.

When the dance was over and the lights came up, he spoke again.

'Gimme your check and I'll get your coat,' he said.

'I'm not going home with you,' she said.

'You're codding.' He tried to kiss her, heedless of the crowd milling by them.

'You know that's no use,' she said. 'And don't be making a disgrace of yourself in front of everyone.'

That stopped him short. 'Give me a good reason,' he said. 'One good reason. I spent the whole night dancing with you. I ought to get some satisfaction.'

'I'm going home with a couple of girls,' she said.

'Girls!'

'Yes,' she said. 'Thanks for the dances. And good night.'

She left him before he could do anything to stop her.

He walked down home from the dance that night, in the dark, by himself, thinking of the time he had wasted with her when he might have gone after a girl who'd give him some satisfaction. He had a pain between his legs.

Seamus Larkin had watched Michael Joe dancing with Nell Cullen. He was glad when he saw that Nell kept drawing away from Michael Joe. Here was a woman, at last, who was a match for McCarthy. Seamus Larkin had never really liked the way Michael Joe had treated girls, as if they were cattle to be bought and sold at a fair. And the girls let Michael Joe get away with it. Larkin couldn't treat girls that way, himself. But this Cullen one,

8

Seamus Larkin saw, was putting a price on herself. Michael Joe was in for it. That gave Seamus Larkin cause for satisfaction.

3

OVER HIS EGG at the breakfast table in the morning, Michael Joe's mother inquired about the success of the dance.

'Was there a good crowd?'

'I don't know. Fair, I suppose,' Michael Joe said.

'Wisha, I hope they gathered enough for the African Missions after paying the band,' his mother said.

'Was the dance for the African Missions?' Michael Joe said.

'What did you think? Is it for the girls to be displaying themselves?' she said.

Michael Joe did not answer.

4

MICHAEL JOE MET Nell Cullen again at the eleven o'clock Mass the following Sunday. She passed by himself and his mother as they were walking down the middle of the Main Street from the chapel. Nell was wearing a light-blue coat and a white, knitted tam, and was walking with two other girls. Michael Joe stared at her in spite of himself as she passed by. She turned and smiled at him, taking a quick glance at his mother. Then she passed on, head bent. Michael Joe thought he detected a blush.

'Who's she?' his mother asked.

'One of the Cullens,' Michael Joe said. 'Home from England.'

Mrs. McCarthy stared after her, but asked no more questions. Michael Joe escorted his mother as far as the door of their house, and she went in telling him that the dinner would be ready in an hour. Michael Joe opened up the shop.

There was little business done on Sunday, but some of the fellows usually dropped in after Mass for a talk before going home to dinner. Seamus Larkin, the bank clerk, came sauntering in, sat up on the counter and lit a Player, and took a deep drag.

'God, the Canon kept us long, didn't he?' Larkin said.

Michael Joe looked up from the *Sunday Dispatch*. 'No harm kneelin' once in a week. Keep us in practice for better things.'

Larkin blushed. 'You have a dirty mind, McCarthy,' he said half seriously.

'What's on for the day?' Michael Joe said.

'Nothing much. A football match in Kilrush. We could get a crowd and hire Griffey and go.'

'All right by me,' Michael Joe said. 'As long as we're off somewhere.'

They were silent for a while. Larkin's cigarette filled the dark interior of the shop with smoke.

'Wasn't that Nell Cullen I saw at Mass?' he said.

'How would I know who you saw?' Michael Joe said.

Larkin glanced slyly at him. 'Did you get the going home?'

'What business is it of yours if I did nor didn't?' Michael Joe said.

'None at all. None at all,' Larkin said. 'I was only asking.'

A few customers came in. Michael Joe served them quickly, and passed a few words with each, and listened when they spoke, bending his dark head to them, and nodding in agreement with whatever they had to say. A girl from the Cottages asked for a half-pound of tea for her mother, and she couldn't pay for it till next week. Michael Joe let her have it, telling her slyly he'd take the price another way.

Larkin invited him down to John Thynne's for a quick one before dinner.

'I don't ever go there. And you know that,' Michael Joe said. 'The stout is two months in the barrel.'

'There might be compensations, this time,' Larkin said mysteriously.

'Hah!' Michael Joe said. 'Trying to put a fast one over on me. Well, come on then.'

They walked down the Main Street to Thynne's and after looking around to see that none of the guards were watching, they knocked and were let in by John Thynne himself. A few other fellows were in the dark pub. Larkin and Michael Joe ordered pints.

'Will we go in the kitchen,' Larkin said, 'and have a bit of quiet?'

'I have to be back for the dinner soon,' Michael Joe said.

They went into the kitchen. The wireless was on. Nell Cullen was sitting in an armchair beside it, listening to a dance band playing on Radio Eireann. Mrs. Thynne was putting a roast of beef in the oven.

'God bless all here,' Larkin said.

'On you too,' Nell murmured. And Mrs. Thynne murmured.

Michael Joe nodded coldly to Nell and sat down. Larkin began putting talk on her, asking her about being in England and what 'twas like over there. But sure a good-looking girl would make out anywhere, he complimented her. Nell answered politely, that sure 'twas like anywhere else, you meet the same sort wherever you go. Larkin was rebuffed, but went right on putting light talk on her, and she kept putting him off with short answers.

Michael Joe sat gazing at his pint without drawing from it. He made no attempt to get in the conversation, withdrawing himself completely in the contemplation of his untouched pint. Suddenly, he put the pint down behind his chair and stood up.

'You aren't going, Michael Joe?' Larkin said.

'I'll be late for the dinner,' Michael Joe said. 'The mother . . .'

Mrs. Thynne stood up from the oven. 'Ah, wisha, Michael Joe, it must be the company is not exciting enough for you.'

'Not at all, Mrs. Thynne,' Michael Joe said. ' 'Tis the mother. She hates me to be late.'

'And you haven't said a word at all to Nell Cullen there,' Mrs. Thynne said. 'Let me call John a minute.'

Before Michael Joe could stop her, or could decently make his getaway, she had shouted into the bar for her husband. John came running in. He saw Michael Joe standing up ready to leave.

'You're not going now, sure you aren't?' John said. 'Here, Nell, shove hether here, and sit by this dacent boy, and give him a chance to be acquainted.' He went over and pulled Nell by the arm off her chair. The dance band played on from the wireless.

Nell blushed. 'He mightn't want me to.'

'I can't stay, John,' Michael Joe said, backing towards the kitchen door. 'Some other time.'

'Since when have you come behindhand with the women?' John said.

'Let the man go, if he wants,' Mrs. Thynne said. 'We have Mr. Larkin here'll keep her company.'

John Thynne had dragged Nell out in the middle of the floor with a hand still gripping her arm, as if she was some sort of animal he was about to auction off at a fair. Nell avoided looking at Michael Joe, and kept turning back to look at the wireless from which music was still coming. Larkin was smiling, looking on. Michael Joe had backed to the door. With a wave of the hand and no good-bye, he left in a hurry.

He sat and ate his dinner in silence at home, while his mother tried to find out what had upset him. He did not finish his meat and potatoes. Ordinarily he had a ravenous appetite and just shovelled the food down.

'You aren't eating your dinner,' his mother said.

'The meat is too fat. And the potatoes aren't boiled,' he said, rising from the table.

'Wisha, wait a bit, and I'll cook them a bit more.'

'I'm going out,' he said, not telling her where he was going.

Mrs. McCarthy went to the window of the dining room and pulled back the curtains to watch what direction he would go in. He passed by the window out of which she was looking. 'On his way to the Hall,' she thought, 'thanks be to God.' She dropped the curtain, and pulled the black shawl tighter around her, and sat down and finished her Sunday dinner alone.

Seamus Larkin stayed on in John Thynne's pub. After Michael Joe left, the atmosphere there seemed more relaxed. Nell dropped her defensive attitude; she talked more openly to Larkin.

5

THAT AFTERNOON, IN Kilrush, Michael Joe sat in Foran's pub, in the darkness, and got drunk. He refused to go out to the football field with Larkin, to watch the match. Larkin wanted to know what had got into him. Michael Joe said there was nothing wrong with him that a couple of pints couldn't cure. Nothing wrong with him at all. He felt like having a couple of drinks in peace. And was there any harm in that? Larkin knew it would be useless to try and budge Michael Joe once he had made up his mind to do something. He left him sitting on a stool at Foran's pub, a big, dark pint before him.

Michael Joe drank alone, thinking of nothing in particular, just waiting until he felt the good mood coming over him from the drink. Usually, he got happy drunk, wild or singing, but never destructive, or fighting. His nature was easy-going; the drink expanded his goodwill towards the world. He'd stand drinks to every man in the bar and never want to be bought a round in return.

Larkin came back for him when the match was over, and found him sitting in a corner. 'You missed a great match,' he said. 'Kilkee won by a point.' 'Is that so?' Michael Joe said. 'Are you drunk, or what?' Larkin said.

'Stone . . . cold . . . sober,' Michael Joe said.

Larkin sat and drank with him. The pub filled up after the match. Fellows from the victorious Kilkee football team came in and got drunk quickly from the excitement of the match and the porter. An argument started between two middle-aged men, one from Kilrush and one from Kilkee, about the match. Tempers rose as sides were taken. A fight was in the making. Someone burst into song, and the tempers calmed as the fellows all joined in.

Michael Joe got up and asked the fellow who was singing if he would give them a bar of 'Mother Machree' and he'd buy him a drink. The fellow had a fine tenor, and put great heart into the song.

> There's a spot in my heart
> Which no colleen may own,
> There's a depth in my soul
> Never sounded or known. . . .

Michael Joe was a baritone. He shouted the song, as well as every other man, drunk or sober, in the bar.

'Songs like that will never die out,' Michael Joe said afterwards. He took a long drag from his pint.

Michael Joe and Larkin ate dinner at the Butler Arms, and Michael Joe paid for it under protest from Larkin. They went back to Foran's afterwards, and Michael Joe drank steadily until it was time to go to the dance. He got gloomier and gloomier as he drank, and began to criticize Larkin for coming to a small town like Corrigbeg, and being only a bank clerk. Larkin answered him with the soft word, and the laugh.

'No one in God's world would stop in a town like Corrigbeg, unless he had to,' Michael Joe said.

'Ah, 'tisn't so bad after all,' Larkin said. 'We're safe, anyway. And get paid. I know many that can't tell where the next meal is coming from.'

'You're a coward, Larkin,' Michael Joe said. Larkin laughed.

They went to the dance about half-past ten. Larkin latched on to a girl right away, and began waltzing her around. Michael Joe sat down on a bench, just inside the door, and stared bleary eyed at the dancers whirling before him. He felt dull and heavy and not very drunk. He dozed off, his head leaning back against the cold wall.

He woke up to find a woman on his lap, shouting at a couple of fellows who were laughing at her: 'Go on, ye blackguards! Can't lave a dacent woman alone.'

Michael Joe pushed her off, and gave her a once-over. She was in her fifties, with grey, stringy hair, curled in spots, and browned as if burning with a curling tongs. Her cheeks were scarlet with rose pink, and a flower-patterned cotton dress hung on her thin frame. The dress was two or three sizes too big for her, and obviously handed down to her by some respectable woman of the town. Her face was floury white from the thick powdering. She smelled strongly of sweet perfume.

'Come on for a dance,' Michael Joe said, grabbing hold of her by the thin arms.

Before she could answer, Michael Joe had dragged her on to the dance floor, and was pushing her around the floor, holding her hard against him.

She couldn't dance very well, and tripped all over his feet. But Michael Joe did not mind. The smell of cheap perfume rose from her up into his nostrils, and stimulated him. He grew excited, and held her harder and harder against him. She didn't protest.

'Come on for a walk,' he whispered down to her.

'I only just came in,' she whined. 'You're a grand dancer. I don't want to go out.'

'I'll give you ten bob,' Michael Joe said.

The woman hesitated, peering up at him from bead eyes, greedy and hard.

'They'll see us,' she said.

'I'll meet you outside the door,' Michael Joe said. 'Get your coat yourself.' He spoke in her ear, a deep, shaky whisper.

'If you'll come back and dance with me after,' the woman said.

'Of course I'll come back,' Michael Joe said. 'But don't let anyone see you going out now. And hurry up.'

He pushed the woman over to the edge of the floor; she stumbled over his feet. Then he left her and went outside, and waited for her by the dance-hall door, outside the arc of the electric light. A few local fellows were hanging around the hall door, not having the price to go into the dance. Michael Joe hoped they wouldn't see him.

The woman came out, buttoning up a black coat around her chin. It was too big for her. She looked around for Michael Joe.

'Here comes Biddy the Bag,' one of the fellows shouted.

'G'wan home to y'er mothers ower that,' Biddy shouted at them.

Michael Joe began walking down the pavement, hoping he couldn't be noticed by the fellows.

Biddy saw him, and set off walking after him. A couple of the fellows followed her at a distance.

She caught up with Michael Joe. 'What hurry are you in?' Biddy said.

'Come on somewhere,' he said urgently.

'Up here a piece. There's a lane. You'll come back to the dance with me after?'

'Trust me,' Michael Joe said. 'I wouldn't betray you for the world.'

They went down a dark lane, to the end, slipping and falling over the cobblestoned pavement.

'Here!' she whispered out of the dark. 'Over here!'

Michael Joe reached out and grabbed her in the dark, and backed her roughly against the wall. She whined at him to take it easy.

It was awkward against the wall. Michael Joe did not know how. They lay down on the road.

And he was no longer a virgin.

Then they heard steps running down the alley towards them.

'Holy Mother, we're caught,' he said to the woman. 'Run for your life.'

Michael Joe was hit on the back of the head by something rotten, an apple or an orange.

'They're pelting us,' the woman said. 'The blackguards!'

Michael Joe jumped up and buttoned. Rotten apples, oranges, sods of dirt—he didn't know what all—were flying past him, plunking against the wall behind him in the dark. He ducked low.

He reached in his pocket and took out paper money. On his hands and knees he crawled over the cobblestones searching for the woman.

'Here,' he said. He pushed the money into her grasping hand.

Then he stood up and began to run. Something hit him, and squelched on his chest. He did not stop until he was out of the alley and into the street, stumbling and slipping drunkenly, the steps running ahead of him. By the light of the street lamp, he could see his tormentors scattering.

He cleaned himself off as best he could, and went back to the dance hall to look for Larkin. A dark and destructive urge erupted in him when he heard the music and saw the dancers whirling around the floor. He wanted the roof to fall in on them, and on himself. Hatred and disgust filled him, for them and for himself.

He saw Larkin standing with a small, fat, blonde-haired, country-looking girl, with innocent blue eyes. They were laughing, and the girl was nervously twisting and turning and shifting her weight.

'Come on home,' Michael Joe said, breaking in on them. 'Get Griffey and the lads.'

'I will not, faith,' Larkin said. 'I'm having a good time, as you can see if you have a pair of eyes.'

Michael Joe looked full at the girl. She stepped back as if she expected to be hit.

'I'll be in the car,' Michael Joe said. He bumped against a dancing couple without apologizing, and lurched off the dance floor.

6

THE FOLLOWING WEEK Michael Joe abandoned himself to work.
He had never paid any particular attention to the layout of the
shop, and had left it very much as it was in his father's time. The
sacks of flour, Quaker Oats, maize, oats, barley, and meal were
standing piled in a random way to the right of the shop entrance,
and down the length of the shop, bulging like squat, fat men.
Opposite them was the counter, and behind it, on shelves, bags
of currants, raisins, tea, sugar and spices. Flitches of bacon hung
on hooks from the ceiling; the rasher machine was at the end of
the counter. Jars of marmalade and jam, and a few tinned goods
and butter were also stocked helter-skelter on the shelves. At the
end of the counter was a glass-enclosed cubicle where Michael
Joe kept his books. At the back of the shop, cut off by a partition,
there was a small room with a fireplace. Michael Joe had a fire
going there during the winter, and when business was slack, he
would sit there talking with any of the fellows who dropped in,
just as his father used to do.

Michael Joe was in the shop early Monday morning. Vin Scanlon
was surprised; he usually had to go inside to Mrs. McCarthy and
get the key from her to open the shop. Michael Joe pounced on
Vin immediately, and started giving him orders about moving
the sacks so that the flour would be in one place, the Quaker Oats in
another, and so on. Vin was used to a leisurely beginning of the
week on Monday. Michael Joe generally took off for an hour over
to Kerney's to discuss the weekend racing results. Vin had his
hands in his pockets while Michael Joe was giving him orders for
the day. 'Take your hands out of your pockets and stop scratching
yourself, man,' Michael Joe said. Vin took his hands out.

The sacks were heavy for a seventeen-year-old, and Vin stopped
working every once and a while to take a rest. Michael Joe stepped
down from the high seat in the cubicle where he was making out
accounts, and walked up and down behind Vin, saying nothing
but eyeing him.

Vin got so nervous, he put down a sack of flour too heavily, and it burst. Michael Joe swore at him. 'Christ, man. What have you? Butterfingers!' Vin had to get another bag and scoop the spilled flour into it, with Michael Joe spying on him through the glass in the cubicle.

Michael Joe complained about Vin's inefficiency when he went in home to his mother for his lunch. 'He'll never be any good,' Michael Joe said. 'I thought he would, at first. But now, I don't know. He hasn't a ghost how to keep things in order.'

'Wisha, he's only a young lad,' Mrs. McCarthy said. 'Give him a chance and he'll be all right.'

'And in the meantime I have to put up with his mess,' Michael Joe said.

He had not gone over to Kerney's all morning; instead, he worked at his accounts. He found out, going through his books in the morning, that he had a lot of outstanding accounts. That afternoon he was going to send out letters requesting something be paid on the accounts, and that they be paid up in full in a month.

Michael Joe did not linger at the table with his mother for the midday dinner. 'Take a little doze upstairs in your bed. 'Twas late in you were last night,' she said, trying to detain him. 'I have work to do,' he said, leaving her abruptly.

While Vin was in having lunch with his mother, Michael Joe inspected the shop. When Vin came back after his lunch, he told him every corner would have to be swept. 'The only place ever swept is down the middle of the aisle. There's an acre of dirt between them sacks.'

He hounded Vin the entire week until the front of the counter and the shelves behind the counter had been arranged neatly and efficiently so that you could put your hand on anything that was wanted without having to look like a spastic searching for it. All that week Michael Joe never left the shop except for lunch. The fellows stopped in to see if he was sick. He barely passed the time of day with them, saying he had pressing business to attend to. He went behind the glass cubicle. They raised their eyebrows. Over at Kerney's they satirized him by imitating his new efficient manner, and adding at the end: 'McCarthy's on the warpath. Watch out for the Injun.' Vin Scanlon spread gossip about him, after work. 'The boss,' he said, 'is acting strange, acting strange.' He'd point at his head. The fellows would nod, and then laugh.

Michael Joe did not go out to the football field or up to the Parochial Hall, or to any of the pubs, in the evening. He stayed at home, and sat with his mother in the dining room. The first night he was restless. He twirled at the wireless, but the music only bothered him. It made him nervous. He went to bed early, but tumbled and tossed for hours unable to fall asleep. He kept thinking about improvements that would have to be made in the shop. He fired himself up by imagining how he would surpass Johnnie Tom Pat, and Jackie Hynes, other shopkeepers. Their business would be only a drop in the bucket to what he would do, once he got going.

As he laid wild plans for the expansion and improvement of his business, images he did not want to see or think about pushed themselves into the forefront of his consciousness. The images came to him as sensations. He was being pelted again with rotton apples and oranges. With an effort of will, he put the images and the sensations out of his mind. They insisted. He saw himself down at Thynne's pub sulking at Nell Cullen. And Larkin making a fool of himself over her. Larkin was a clown. He took pleasure in thinking about his sulk. What did she think, anyway? She could walk on him? Who did she think she was? Queen Victoria? He'd show her there were some men in the world still she couldn't have at her beck and call. So he talked to his images. Then he was being pelted with rotten oranges and apples. He ducked. Suppressed the image. Then he heard his mother shuffling in her slippers around in her room, next to his. He tried to sleep, to sleep. To forget the images.

Then he'd see the shop again; and he would be safe for a while, imagining how the shop would look years from now.

The next night, he tried reading a book before going to bed. His mother had a copy of *Quo Vadis* in the cupboard. He tried reading that, but it was too unbelievable. He couldn't stretch his imagination that far back to the days of the suffering of the early Christians in Rome under Nero. It was one of the few books his mother had ever read completely through, and she thought it would be good for him to read it, too. He gave the book up after one night. He had a bad dream about lions devouring people who had no faces. He felt in his dream as if he knew well the people being devoured.

He came across a bundle of detective stories in the cupboard.

His father's. He galloped through one a night for the rest of the week, and slept peacefully.

Though he was irritated with Vin, and how the shop looked, and the fellows at Kerney's, he never spoke a cross word to his mother. He was constantly asking her if there were anything she wanted from the shop. He brought her in a jar of marmalade one night, and another night a jar of strawberry jam. He kept telling her she ought to have a servant girl in to do the heavy work around the house. Mrs. McCarthy bridled.

'What do I need a girl around the house for? Is it old you think I'm getting?'

'No, Mother,' Michael Joe said. 'You're too much on your feet. A sit-down would rest you. You're only wearing yourself out like this.'

'Ah, you're only dying to be rid of me. Waiting for the chance.'

'Don't talk nonsense,' Michael Joe said gruffly.

'No nonsense about it. Some day soon you'll be landing a girl into me here?'

'Ah, no, sure I'd never,' Michael Joe said weakly.

He felt that she was almost asking him never to marry.

That Saturday, after working hard all week, and after he had paid out the thirty bob to Vin Scanlon, and Vin had not even thanked him as he usually did, he decided to shut up the shop and go to Confession that night. He had made his Easter duty a few months before. Once a year to Confession and Communion had been his habit since he had started with his first girl at eighteen. The idea of going to Confession came on him suddenly. Out of the blue. What harm was in it? It wouldn't be the worst thing in the world to be seen at the rails more often than he had in the past.

He had steered clear of the priests, so far. He'd heard how they bawled out fellows for being after the girls, and how they followed courting couples around the country with a flashlight after dances on dark nights. Michael Joe privately vowed they weren't going to catch him. If they noticed you were the type to go to Confession and Communion often, or attend two masses on Sunday or during the week, they would pester you night and day for a contribution to this foreign mission, or that charity. Michael Joe let his mother take care of that end of the business.

Still and all, his going to Confession this Saturday night wouldn't bring him too much to their notice. He would go to Father Grimes, who had a reputation for being easy. He never asked embarrassing questions of detail. Sat with his head in his hands behind the lattice wire, as if he were bemoaning all the time the sins of the world, but wouldn't raise his head to protest. Gave the penance, and never looked one way or another to see whether it was man, woman, or child was there unloading sins.

Michael Joe told his mother of his intention. She decided to go along with him herself, though she had just been the week before. Some of the courage of his decision left Michael Joe then; but he humoured his mother by saying he would be glad to have her go along.

Father Grimes listened to him behind the lattice wire, and did not look at him. 'I sinned against the Sixth Commandment, Father.' 'How many times?' 'Once.'

Michael Joe was thankful that Father Grimes had spared him from going into details. And did not look.

'A rosary, Sorrowful Mysteries,' Father Grimes gave him as penance.

Michael Joe knew that if he stopped long enough in the chapel to say a rosary, his mother would suspect something. He knelt beside her in the darkness of the chapel while she lingered over her own penance—three Hail Marys. He put off saying his rosary until Mass in the morning.

He and his mother received Communion together at the rails next morning. A burst of fervour filled Michael Joe as Canon Lyons placed the white wafer on his tongue. A great good humour descended on him. He was not able, however, to speak to the Christ that had just united His body with his own. But he was in a good mood again. The Communion had put him into a good mood. And his mother, too.

That afternoon, a fine sunny afternoon, he borrowed Miko Hynes's pony and trap and drove his mother out to Ballard to pay a visit to his father's grave. His mother suggested it. 'Twas such a grand day, and she was feeling in top form. And the dead should be remembered amid the joy of the living. Michael Joe wanted to go to a football match with Larkin; but he could sacrifice one day for her. She was a great old scout, he thought sentimentally. Ah, he should go to Confession and Communion more often, it put him in such good humour.

At his father's grave, his mother cleaned the glass top of the artificial pot of violets, and weeded the grass beginning to shoot up amid the sea pebbles spread on top of the grave. She had brought a little trowel with her, and she dug up the pebbles exposing the underside to the sun, so that the grave looked fresh again. Michael Joe watched with curiosity for a while, not thinking to offer to help. Then he wandered around the graveyard leaving her to herself, while he read the names of the buried dead on the tombstones as he might glance at the obituary column in the newspaper. His mother was kneeling at the graveside when he came back. He knelt beside her, and muttered: 'May the Lord rest his soul. May he rest in peace.' He said the prayer without any true realization of whom or what he was praying for.

His mother rose off her knees, crossing herself. 'Ah, your father was a good man,' she said gazing at the freshened grave. 'Never spoke a cross word to me all our life together. Sorry I was to see him go.' She wiped away the tears. 'Said by me always, he was. Though, God knows, I was no shakes with the advice. Sure I never thought he'd leave me so sudden.' She cried a little. Michael Joe was embarrassed and looked away. She took his arm, and they walked back to the pony and trap. 'Thanks be to God he left me you to take care of me,' she said when they were settled in the trap.

'Hup, there,' Michael Joe muttered at the pony.

7

MICHAEL JOE LET up on Vin Scanlon and the work, the following week. The letters he had prepared to send out to his debtors he let lie in the cubicle until he'd have time to put them in an envelope and post them. He gave orders to Vin to wash down the front windows and clean the flag pavement in front of the shop. Then he left him alone, while he looked over the paper. Then he went across to Kerney's.

He was over there one morning in the middle of the week when Nell came in. Vin ran across the street and called him, and told him in front of the fellows that there was a girl wanting to see him in the shop. Michael Joe said: 'Let her wait.' But he hurried away a few minutes after Vin.

He entered the shop, and saw Nell.

'What can I do for you today, Miss?' he said, and went behind the counter.

'Isn't there . . . any place we can talk?' Nell said, looking at the sacks. Vin busied himself weighing sacks of flour.

Michael Joe came out from behind the counter and led her into the room at the back, letting her pass in ahead of him. She looked around at the snug, card table before the empty fire, chairs randomly around it, newspapers on the table. Pictures of dogs and horses on the walls.

' 'Tis you have the comfort,' she said lightly.

'If I knew you were coming I'd have lit the fire,' he said.

Michael Joe did not ask her to sit down. They were silent for a few moments, Michael Joe waiting, and Nell looking around, taking her time.

'I haven't much to say,' she said finally. 'Except I'm not the kind of girl you think I am.'

'Sure, I don't think about you at all,' Michael Joe said. 'What you do is your business. I'm the one that got caught. That's fair.'

'I wasn't trying to make a fool of you. I only wanted you to dance with me.'

'And not pay the price. What do you think I am?'

Nell coloured. 'I came in to say I'm sorry I gave the impression you got.'

'What's to be sorry for? You'd think *you* were the one insulted.'

'Well, I'll be going, if that's the way you're going to be,' Nell said, turning away.

Both of them had been standing just inside the door of the snug, Michael Joe closer to the door, which he had not closed. When Nell made as if to leave, instinctively he stepped closer to the door to block her path. Nell stopped, looked quickly at him, but did not ask him to let her by.

Both Nell's movement towards the door and Michael Joe's placing himself in her way were unconscious. Half movements. Small gestures in a dance. The camera of the eye flashed, and caught the movements; the impression was registered; and something had been decided, though neither of them yet fully knew, or would ever understand what or why.

'Hold on, there,' Michael Joe said, blustering a bit. 'You're not leaving me that easily. Getting off scot-free is it you think you are?'

Nell laughed. A release. During their conversation she had been taking Michael Joe in, with quick glances. Now, Michael Joe gave her a full look. Her face was large, V-shaped, tending to roundness about the small chin. She wore no make-up except for a light touch of lipstick on the full lips in a wide mouth. She looked serious, strained and intent when she first came into the shop. Now, she broke out in half-smiles, flitting and flashing in the eyes and mouth.

'I never thought of having to do penance,' she said, with light sarcasm.

Michael Joe was suddenly delighted with himself; no longer wanted to crush her. Felt like a little boy who wanted to have fun with the neighbour's girl. He moved away from the door and went to the empty fireplace, and sat down. Nell automatically went over and sat down opposite him.

'A grate without a fire looks lonesome,' Nell said.

'There's no need for a fire during the summer,' Michael Joe said. 'We're just as warm without it.'

'Just the same,' she said. 'I'd keep a fire in it.'

' 'Tis little you have to worry you, but fires.'

'Oh, I'm not worried,' she said. 'I notice the little things like that, somehow.'

He teased Nell, and she laughed readily and easily now. Did she truly go home from the dance with girls? 'Cross my heart,' Nell said. 'And what have *the girls* got that I don't have?' He pretended he didn't believe her. 'There was a fellow waiting outside the hall door for you. Don't be blinding me now. I saw him.' Nell explained easily that there was no fellow waiting for her that night. And there would never be.

'I suppose the fellows around here aren't good enough for you since you came back from England?'

'No. That isn't it,' she said. 'I'm not going out with anyone now. I came home for a rest.'

'Take a rest with me, then,' Michael Joe said with comic firmness.

Nell laughed. 'You're all the same,' she said. 'There's no rest for a woman when a man is around.'

He leaned toward her. 'Come for a walk up to the Puffing Hole with me next Sunday,' he said.

'What'll the town say if they see us?'

'Let them be damned,' Michael Joe said. 'What harm will we be doing to anyone? We're only going for a walk.'

Nell suddenly became quiet, hoping to make it plain to him that she did not want to go out with him. Michael Joe waited, leaning toward her, openly eager, almost boyish, except for the dark eyes bold and devouring, boring into her.

'It isn't you,' Nell said, breaking the silence. 'I don't want to be going out with any fellow.'

'Do you have one in England?'

'No. No, I don't.'

'Well, you can't go making a nun out of yourself.'

Nell looked quickly at him, as if he had somehow blundered into her deepest thoughts.

'No.' she said. 'I suppose I don't want that.'

'Look,' Michael Joe said putting a hand gently on her arm, 'I promise to be a good lad.'

She did not draw back from his touch, but did not look at him.

'Well, if you keep your promise, all right.'

They set the date for the following Sunday, in the early afternoon, at the White Strand, near the Puffing Hole. No one in the town was likely to be at the Puffing Hole. They would not be seen.

Michael Joe escorted her to the door of the shop. After she left, he felt extravagant. He looked around the shop; Vin Scanlon was weighing flour for old Mrs. Hynes. He put his hand on the counter and vaulted over it, inside. Vin and the old woman stared at him. 'Lord save us,' the old woman said crossing herself, 'but 'tis gone daft he is.'

Michael Joe locked the door of the cubicle, and revaulted the counter. 'I'll be back in an hour,' he said to Vin. The old woman crossed herself again.

He went over to the Kerney's and spent the best of two hours talking down the fellows there; he told dirty stories, to which the fellows listened without interruption.

8

THAT NIGHT, AT Griffey's where Vin Scanlon went to play cards, he casually dropped the information that Michael Joe McCarthy was doing a line with Nell Cullen. He imitated for the card players snatches of the conversation he had heard between Michael Joe and Nell.

'Who'd ever think of it? McCarthy hooked!' one of the fellows said when the laughter stopped.

9

MICHAEL JOE AND Nell met the following Sunday at the Puffing Hole. Michael Joe was there before Nell, and he sat down on the edge of the cliff hanging his legs out over, and watched the spray shoot up from the hole below, and the water recede with a soughing sound out of the hole before it came swelling in again with the force of the tide. A lone fisherman was fishing for pollack far out on the rocks. Michael Joe could not tell who he was. A cool breeze blew in off the sea. A ship was going by into Galway Harbour. The image of the ship struck Michael Joe in his romantic mood, and heightened it. He followed the ship until it passed the headland into the harbour.

As if he had eyes in the back of his head, he knew when Nell arrived. He turned to watch her cross the field to him. She walked with her head slightly bent, like a nun. She was wearing a bright-red summer dress with a white wool cardigan thrown over her shoulders.

'I can't stop very long,' she said coming up to him, nervous, tense, pulling at her cardigan.

'You're the boss,' Michael Joe said. 'Whatever you say.'

They stood a few moments looking over the cliffs and down at the rocks below, and the Puffing Hole. Spray shot up, and the sea soughed withdrawing. Nell shuddered and drew back. Michael Joe put an arm around her.

'None of that,' she said. 'Remember your promise.'

Michael Joe laughed. 'I forgot. The sight of you drove it out of my head. I was only trying to protect you.'

'I'll keep reminding you to be good, then,' she said.

They went for a walk along the edge of the cliff, moving away from the White Strand where the people from Corrigbeg might be spending a Sunday with their children by the sea. For a brief moment, when they met, it seemed as if the tone and mood might go wrong. But they soon fell into the teasing banter of their previous meeting in the shop. Nell established that tone, and Michael Joe was drawn into it again in spite of himself. He wanted to be serious.

They reminisced about their schooldays. Nell had gone to the Girls' and Michael Joe to the Boys' National School, with a year or two between them. They resurrected distant images of each other, though they could not remember having spoken. Nell lived just outside Corrigbeg, and never played with the town girls. She knew more about Michael Joe than he did about her. She remembered him as a bully who used to frighten the girls on the way home from school by pulling at their school satchels and trying to take them away, while the fellows cheered him on. Michael Joe said that sure that wasn't himself at all; she must have the wrong fellow entirely. He wasn't like that at all, at all. Nell said she could never mistake him for someone else.

They laughed often. The breeze was cool; the sky was blue; the waves swished and sprayed easily off the cliffs; seagulls soared and glided in the hot bubbles of air above the sea, and every once and a while gave off their wild, bagpipe cries. Brilliant green acres of grazing land stretched around the walking pair. They met no one from the town on the walk.

Nell was wearing a watch. 'My God, look at the time 'tis,' she said holding up her wrist to Michael Joe. He took her hand. She withdrew it quickly.

'We must be getting back. I told the girls I'd meet them at the Strand in an hour.'

'You're deserting me,' Michael Joe said. 'Leaving me stranded here all alone.'

'Oh, don't be putting on a little boy's face now. I said I couldn't stay long.'

On the way back, Michael Joe bullied her into another date.

'I'm not a bad fellow at all, you can see.'

' 'Tis easy to be good when you have no chance to be otherwise.'

They had come back to the Puffing Hole. Nell would not let him accompany her any farther, though he would gladly have walked back to the White Strand with her. Michael Joe continued to press her to meet him again.

'There's a dance in Lahinch next Sunday night, and I'll take you there if you let me?'

'I told you I don't want to go out with any one fellow. I don't want to get serious.'

'We won't be serious,' Michael Joe said. 'We'll be friends. Only give me a chance.' This was a new role for him to play.

She looked at him, to see if she could really trust him. There was no way she could tell. She heard the gulls bagpiping in the background, a wild cry. It disturbed her, but she did not know why. Lonely maybe.

'I might be there and I might not,' she said, and left him quickly.

'Good-bye till Sunday,' he shouted after her, confident he had won her.

She half-raised an arm without turning back to him.

Michael Joe watched her climb over the sod wall which separated the field from the road. She climbed with ease and grace, jumping off the top. He laughed to himself when he saw her jump, and thought of an angel. A white one. Floating from the blue sky. He smiled to himself at the ridiculous image. She was just a piece of skirt like all the rest of them.

He waited until he thought she would be back at the White Strand. She wasn't going to be an easy one, he thought, though he had enjoyed being with her. Not even a kiss did he get for his trouble. The fellows would never believe *that one* if he told them. But he wasn't going to let her get off so easily the next time. He wouldn't fail. Nell would have to be handled differently, not his usual approach. But he did not doubt that he would get what he was after in the end.

10

NELL WAS AT the dance in Lahinch the following Sunday. Michael Joe arrived a bit earlier at the dance than usual, after spending a few hours of the early evening drinking with Larkin and a few more fellows in Vaughan's pub. They wanted to stay in the pub until the dance would be well under way. Michael Joe was anxious to leave. But he could not show it. The fellows would get curious, and Michael Joe had no wish to let the real extent of his interest in Nell Cullen become known yet. He would have to take jokes and innuendoes. And maybe even direct questions about Nell. Was she fast? Did you get a tumble? Did she let you feel her up? All the way? In the past, he hadn't minded passing along information like that about a girl he'd been out with. He would do it quietly. Drop a hint. Leave a lot unsaid. But, as he sat in the pub, listening to the fellows talk, and trying to think of a way to leave without attracting too much notice, he realized if he was asked these questions about Nell, he might hit the asker.

Finally, he stopped drinking, Larkin asked him what was up. Michael Joe complained about the taste of the stout. Bottom of the barrel. Larkin himself thought he noticed it too. They left for the dance.

Nell refused to dance every dance with him. He got angry and made a play for an ugly-looking girl who could only be flattered and jumping over herself with his attentions. Nell saw what he was doing, but she did not bring it up when they danced together. This made Michael Joe even madder. He accused her of playing with him again.

'I'm nothing of the sort,' she said. 'You're very possessive. And I don't want that. I've told you before.'

Michael Joe repented, and said he was sorry, and that he couldn't help himself.

And so the dance went. Again, Nell would not let him take her home. And he walked away from her in the middle of the dance floor when she refused.

He picked up the ugly girl again, danced a few times with her in his usual fashion, and got the going home from her. He told Larkin that he wouldn't be bicycling home with him.

'You made out this time?' Larkin said. 'I didn't think she'd . . .'

'Mind your own bloody business,' Michael Joe said.

He took the ugly one home, carrying her on the bar of his bicycle. She lived out in the country. Halfway out, Michael Joe stopped and told the girl to get off. He left her standing in the middle of the road, and told her to walk home the rest of the way; she was too fat, he was tired of carrying her. The girl shrieked a stream of curses after him as he bicycled off.

Michael Joe wore himself out bicycling up the long Rineen hill, instead of walking it.

Next morning, Michael Joe did not even greet his mother when he came downstairs for breakfast. He sat with his arms folded on the table, and waited to be served.

His mother asked him a few of the usual questions. Was the dance good? Was there anyone there she knew? Michael Joe did not answer her. She tried to find out what was wrong with him. He stood up from his unfinished breakfast and walked out of the dining room, without answering.

Vin Scanlon had already opened the shop. Michael Joe passed through and into the cubicle. Vin watched him writing, tearing up sheets of paper, and looking in a dark mood.

He came out and handed Vin an envelope.

'Bicycle out to Nell Cullen with this,' Michael Joe said. 'And give it right into her hands. Mind what I say now. And don't breathe a word of this to a sinner's soul or you'll have no job.'

'Will I wait for an answer?'

'Of course you will, you amaudaun. Didn't I tell you that?'

'You didn't.'

'Hurry up with you then.'

The letter was simple and direct: 'Dear Nell, I want to meet you tonight behind the chapel at eight o'clock. I have something important to tell you. Michael Joe.'

When Vin Scanlon came back he told Michael Joe that Nell had said all right to what was in the letter.

'Did anyone see you talking to her?'

'No one that I know.'

'What was she doing?'

'She was outside in the back feeding meal to the pigs.'

'Feeding the pigs!' Michael Joe said.

'Yes, faith,' Vin said cheerily. 'She had on an ould smock, and a dirty apron, and a pair of hobnailed boots, and an ould straw hat on her head.'

'You're giving me my money's worth, aren't you?' Michael Joe said sarcastically. Vin did not understand. He thought he ought to be praised.

That night, at the fall of dusk, Michael Joe closed up the shop and went to meet Nell.

An old bog road began to the left of the chapel, ran behind it, and then twisted for a mile behind Corrigbeg, down to the Clonboney River, a small stream fed from a lake in the bog hills five miles away. The bog road was used only by town farmers to bring home and drive out their cows to the fields beside it. Since the cows were usually out before dusk, Michael Joe and Nell would not be likely to meet anyone along the road but lovers, who also wanted privacy and secrecy, and would not be likely to spread any rumours.

Michael Joe shaved and put on a clean shirt and tie to go out. His mother wondered, but said nothing after his bad humour of the morning.

The night was warm. Late June. It had showered a few times during the day, and a feeling of dampness and wetness was still in the air.

Nell was waiting for him in the shadows beside the chapel gate. He went up to her.

'Do you want to go for a walk?' he said. 'I can't stand being inside an evening like this.'

'I don't mind,' she said. 'I wanted to be out myself.'

They walked in silence down the bog road. On either side of them the hawthorn bushes were budding with clusters of green haws shining faintly in the dusk with falling dew. Nell noticed them, and said they were lovely. Silence again.

'Well, what do you want from me anyway?' Michael Joe finally said.

'I want nothing from you,' Nell said. 'Can't we just be friends?'

'Friends?' Michael Joe said. 'A man and a woman can't be friends.'

'You'll have to try if you want me to go out with you.'

' 'Tisn't natural.'

Nell did not answer. They walked on in silence again until they came to the end of the bog road, and the stream. A small bridge spanned it, leading across to a big grazing field where cows were lying down chewing the cud. The couple stood on the bridge and leaned over together watching the full stream gurgling below. Trout splashed in the shallows. A few swallows flitted through the air and over the surface. June nature was putting on a show.

'I can't stand leading me on and shutting me off,' Michael Joe said. 'I want you to go out with me.'

'I can't. I can't. A thousand times I have to tell you.'

'And why not? Gimme one decent reason. I haven't a disease, have I?'

'No. You're . . . well, I like you all right. But only for company.'

They went across the bridge and into the field, Michael Joe walking slightly ahead of her, as if by plan. Then they walked along the bank of the stream. It grew dark, a light darkness.

Suddenly Michael Joe turned and caught her savagely in his arms.

'No, I don't want that,' she whispered, raising her arms as he tried to kiss her.

'I'm fed up of the talk,' Michael Joe growled.

She kept twisting her head, so that he could not kiss her on the lips.

'Stop, or I'll scream for help,' she hissed.

Michael Joe kissed her neck, biting into it savagely. She moaned.

'You're a beast. Let me go! Let me go!'

They tripped and fell. He crawled on top of her, pinning her down on the wet grass.

Suddenly she lay completely still, and rigid. The whiteness of her face, and the sudden frozen attitude registered with Michael Joe, but did not stop him. He kissed her on the lips. No response. They were tight and cold. He bit them. Still no response. Her arms lay tight by her sides; her eyes were closed.

'Jesus Christ, stop holding back from me,' Michael Joe said, driven to more brutal biting, trying to arouse her from her coldness.

Then a voice shouted to them from across the stream.

'Go on home out of that, ye scamps ye! Or ye'll hear about it from the altar.'

Michael Joe scrambled to his feet. Across the stream he made out the form of a priest, a dark, hatted form, raising a stick in the air and shaking it.

'Go home yourself and say your prayers,' Michael Joe bellowed across at him in anger at being spied on, and interrupted. Nell stood beside him, and hid herself behind his back.

'Sinners! Ye pack of sinners! Violating the Sixth Commandment!' the shaky voice of old Canon Lyons screamed at them.

'Stop it, Michael Joe!' Nell whispered. 'Don't say anything to him. Come on.'

She began to pull Michael Joe away.

'Ye'll hear about this from the altar!'

'Ah, will you shove it . . .' Nell clapped a hand over Michael Joe's mouth. She kept pulling him along the bank of the stream, he looking back at the now shadowy figure, a stick high in the air, like a figure of doom. When they were out of sight, around a bend of the stream, Nell stopped and began to brush herself down. Michael Joe stood by her panting.

'Blast him, anyway,' Michael Joe said. 'Like an old hag, spying. Withered . . . a withered stick. That's all he is.'

'Don't add sacrilege to everything else.'

'Sacrilege! I'd puck his bloody face out if I got within an inch of him. Sacrilege! *He* committed the sacrilege!'

They began to walk. Nell did not complain about Michael Joe's attack on her. Michael Joe panted beside her. He ranted on about Canon Lyons. What sort of a man would go poking around the countryside looking for courting boys and girls? From condemning Canon Lyons, Michael Joe went on and condemned all the priests. All of them! They were all the same. They ran the country, and frightened the people with Hell and Confession. They poked into everyone's business. God, 'twas a terrible state the country was in with them. No wonder the lads and the girls wanted to emigrate by the thousands. He'd emigrate himself if this kept up.

'Sure he was only out for a walk in the evening,' Nell said. 'All the priests aren't that way.'

Michael Joe didn't answer her. They walked through the dewy fields in the light of a quarter moon, Nell not listening, Michael Joe raving on. The land around had changed into a shadowy, shapeless mass, and the sky had taken on a static quality, the clouds barely in motion; and few stars could be seen. Nell grew afraid in the dark.

They had walked through the fields in a half-circle, in the opposite direction from which they had started out, and found themselves in the Ennistymon Road, another road leading into Corrigbeg. Michael Joe had run out of talk. They stood on the road, neither one of them willing to make the decision whether they should walk back into the town together, or not.

'I suppose you don't want to see me again.' Michael Joe said.

'I'm tired,' Nell said quietly. 'And you're desperate.'

'I'm not sorry. You had it coming.'

'Walk me home. 'Tis dark. I'm . . . I'm not afraid of you any more.' She looked around and shivered.

Michael Joe softened. He took off his coat and wanted her to put it on over her wool cardigan. She refused.

'I hope you don't catch cold,' he said as tenderly as he could.

It was late. They passed a few people on the street. When they did, Nell hung her head, and Michael Joe looked straight ahead pretending to ignore the people they passed.

'I suppose either you or the Canon will have this all over the town by the morning,' he said sarcastically.

'I want to forget it,' Nell said. 'And 'twas such a grand night for a walk. You spoiled it.'

'Am I supposed to crawl on my knees and ask your forgiveness? I'll never do that. I'm walking you home, and that's all there's to it.'

They walked on in uncomfortable silence, side by side, as if they were almost strangers to each other who happened by accident to be walking together along the same pavement, on the same dark night, and one of them could not walk past the other, so they walked together. Michael Joe asked her, because he couldn't bear the silence, if she was going back to England. She said she didn't think so. She was going to stop home for a while and help her mother around the house and the farm. But she didn't know for sure what she was going to do. They were silent again.

As he was saying good-bye to her, at the gateway leading up to her house, he said: 'You're a strange one.'

She laughed briefly. 'Maybe I am.'

As she turned away from him to go in home, he was overcome with a sense of loss.

'Will you let me see you again?'

She turned around, surprised. And then she surprised herself.
'Yes,' she said faintly.
'Are you sorry for me? Is that it?'
'Go home,' she said.
'I won't touch you any more,' he said. And then left.

II

THAT WAS THE beginning of the romance between Michael Joe and
Nell Cullen. He pursued, and she gave no further sign that she
wished him to stop. Vin Scanlon became the go-between, carrying
letters out to Nell telling her where to meet Michael Joe. At first,
they met only on Sunday, and always outside Corrigbeg. If Michael
Joe was playing in a football match, he would tell her where to be
so that she could be picked up and ride in the car with himself
and the other fellows going to the football match. The first time
Michael Joe asked the driver of the car to stop at the Cross-roads
and pick up a girl there, the fellows in the car called him Lochinvar.

Michael Joe tolerated the name without protest. They saw the
earnest side of him for the first time. They stopped talking when
Nell came into the car. She had to sit on Michael Joe's knees. The
men were silent for a while because a woman was with them, but
then they got used to her and took her for granted, and talked
freely as if she weren't present at all. Nell and Michael Joe said
nothing to each other. He did not put his arms around her.

When the match was over, Michael Joe and Larkin and one or
two more of the better class of fellows would go off to the bar
of the local hotel of the town they were in. And Nell would go
along. The first time she wouldn't go without another girl with
her. She got a friend, and went. Larkin took up with her friend.
The men drank and talked. Nell sat and listened, and drank lemonade. Since Nell begun accompanying him Michael Joe had tapered
off in his drinking. Nell never said whether she minded him drinking or not. She never criticized anything he did. But Michael Joe
did not feel like drinking as much when she was with him. He was

quieter too, as if aware that her eyes were on him, and that she was listening and paying attention to what he was saying. The stories he told were clean. And the other fellows took their cue from him.

Nell and himself would always leave early for the dance. After they had left, the talk became a little freer, flowed more easily, and Nell's girl friend, left behind, laughed at the dirty jokes that were told.

At dances outside of Corrigbeg—in Lahinch, or Ennistymon, or Ennis, they sat together. Michael Joe danced with her, but not exclusively. And she danced with other fellows too. Michael Joe was not jealous any more. His early lust for her was gone; and new feelings, just as strong as the old ones, came. He was secure now. He knew that, in some way, he was important to Nell. When he danced with her, she wheeled about him, calm eyes lit up, a moment smiling, light-faced, swinging about him, fluttering or swaying as a girl might swing around a maypole. He was delighted by the sight of her untouchable image about him. Nell felt at ease when she saw that Michael Joe was no longer pursuing her in the male way. She gave free rein to her spirit of fun. And Michael Joe became her central figure of fun.

She sent him funny drawings when Vin Scanlon brought out notes to her. Michael Joe's burly figure was prominent in them. Or a big mouth making a pompous statement about the state of the world. Michael Joe was developing the critical habit, and a certain philosophical sense, as their relationship progressed. Women were a favourite object of his newly acquired philosophical habit. He despised most of them, and made no bones about it to Nell. Their double-dealing, their trickery, the way the local girls were acquiring the English and American fashions in dresses, and traipsing around the street half naked to the world. He was firmly convinced they had no sense of shame.

Nell tried to puncture these attempts to disparage her sex. Neither of them ever went beyond the bounds of good humour, or became serious. They played, using local happenings as their material, and never touched on personal matters, seeming almost to be unaware that they could be personal, or that there was anything of a personal nature between them to discuss.

They kept the romance as secret from the 'eyes of Corrigbeg' as possible. Michael Joe did not pay her way into dances at home. He met her inside the dance hall. Danced with her just enough, he thought, so that it wouldn't be said he was doing a line with her. She waited outside the dance hall for him after the dance, so that he could walk her home. They had never discussed whether they should keep their romance a secret or not. Both of them fell into the habit of making elaborate plans for concealing their dates by a sort of mutual instinct. They knew what open company keeping meant. That was practically an announcement of an engagement. To some, the old biddies who were self-appointed guardians of public morals, walking out together in public was as binding as marriage itself.

Nell never dared go into the shop after her first visit. If she passed Michael Joe at Mass on Sunday with his mother, she did not salute him. If they met in a crowd they barely acknowledged each other. If any of the fellows mentioned Nell in Michael Joe's hearing to bait him, he pretended no interest. And often the fellows made comments about her good looks, or what a match she would make, to draw Michael Joe out. He remained tight-lipped, though he knew they knew. Even if they did, and her presence at football games with him couldn't escape their notice, he would treat the matter as if it wasn't worth talking about. The casual approach. And indifference. Just another girl.

Both he and Nell accepted the conditions of the secrecy. If they were ashamed or guilty, they never acknowledged it to each other. To speak about carrying on the romance in any other way would be to bring up more serious matters. And neither of them wanted to talk about marriage. They were both satisfied with the way things were going between them now.

Michael Joe was becoming what the people of the town called 'sensible'. He had stopped betting on the horses, and started putting money in the bank. Larkin knew about the deposits on the Monday mornings. When Michael Joe came in with the bag, there would be a little embarrassment between them, at first, until Larkin, in his trained way, would make a sensible comment about the price of cattle going up, and the farmers having more money to spend in town. They had never exchanged a comment like that before. It smacked too much of business. But, there was an end to all good things. And Michael Joe, who had been always free with his money was becoming a saver, now. He used to buy drinks. Never passing up his round. Never wondering at all where the money came from.

The account was still in his mother's name. And Michael Joe left it that way, seeing no reason to change it, even when Larkin tentatively suggested that he might want to open one of his own. 'What for?' Michael Joe said. ' 'Tis all in the family, anyway.' He became careful with the books, and gave out credit with more reluctance than he used to. In the past, he never thought twice about giving out a pound of tea or sugar or a stone of flour to someone that needed it on credit. Now, he thought twice. And though he didn't dare refuse for fear of getting the name of a tightwad, still he now gave credit with bad grace.

He had never thought about becoming a rich man. But now, the thought of what he could do if he had a lot of money would often be lurking at the back of his mind. It would come out, and he would indulge in reveries.

He would take Nell off somewhere for a holiday. Maybe to a Billy Butlin Camp. Or to Ballybunion. Somewhere where they could be alone, without having to think about who was watching them.

He could leave Vin in charge of the shop. And take a holiday for a few weeks. Away from the 'eyes of Corrigbeg'. This kind of reverie, of Nell and himself having plenty of money, and free to go where they wanted, and for Nell to buy what she wanted— grand dresses, jewellery, gowns, shoes . . . anything she wanted, so she would be one of the most beautiful women in all Ireland, plagued him.

He never told Nell about those dreams. They were wild. Like the American pictures that they went to see in Ennistymon. Ginger Rogers and Fred Astaire on a happy honeymoon at a place by the sea. The rich man. In his sober moments, Michael Joe was ashamed of himself for the dreams. Celluloid dreams. But they would not leave his mind. They thrilled him when he had them, and made him forget everything else but himself and Nell.

He went on saving money. Became careful at cards. Cut down on the drink, and gave up the gun altogether. He made one or two big bets hoping to make a sweep, and began buying tickets on the Irish Sweepstake.

Summer passed, and autumn, and winter came. The romance continued, secretly, yet known and talked about behind the curtains of the dressmaker's shop, and in the kitchens in the morning when the old women visited and gossiped with each other, and read the

38

tea leaves in the bottom of the cup, to find what fortune was ahead for them.

Michael Joe's mother had heard about it. But she knew he had had girls before. She kept quiet to Michael Joe, but made inquiries about Nell in her own way. She waited, watching her son closely for whatever signs her motherly instincts would need to tell her that her son was seriously in the clutches of another woman. She noticed changes in her son. Sensible changes. He was quieter. More restrained. And given to sitting in the armchair in the dining room after his supper, smoking a cigarette and looking into the fire until he fell asleep, and then going to bed early, without going out. There was no trace of wildness about him. He was not restless. The McCarthy gypsy strain had not been aroused by the woman. So Mrs. McCarthy felt secure. Her blood was dominant in him. And he would never lose his head when her influence was uppermost. He even came home sober after he had been out at night.

As that Christmas approached, Michael Joe began to think of buying a Christmas present for Nell. He had never bought a present for any other woman before, except his mother to whom he gave a shawl, or cardigan, or bedroom slippers every Christmas. Usually something Mullins, the draper, suggested. For Nell, he was determined to buy something he thought of himself. Something from Mullins would not fill the bill. That he was certain of. The thought of buying her just something to wear like a cardigan or a sweater seemed somehow drab. Not exciting enough. Very ordinary. And his first present to her was going to be anything but ordinary.

The range of choice of gifts in Corrigbeg was small. After Michael Joe got the idea of buying the gift he began making casual surveys of the shops in Corrigbeg that might have something suitable in stock. He had nothing in particular in mind; only he knew that it would have to be something to match the person the gift was intended for. Nell wasn't just any girl. He hadn't looked at another girl, or even thought of girls in his old way, since he had started really going out with her. He had dreams occasionally, sexual dreams in which there was a woman whose name he did not know, or could not remember in the morning when he woke up. He got sexual relief from the dreams, and did not think much about them afterwards. In a strange way, he was glad of the relief, such as it was. It kept him faithful to Nell. Otherwise, he might have had to approach her in a way she had already rejected, or else go after another girl. Neither of these solutions would have been satisfactory to him, now. He bided his time hoping that Nell would come around to him in time. He would let her have the romance the way she wanted it.

The gift would be Michael Joe's way of letting her know how much he thought of her. He prided himself on his change of behaviour toward her. She must be aware of this change. The gift would clinch the matter.

But there was nothing suitable in Corrigbeg. P. J. Harley had a display of religious articles that Michael Joe thought might be fit for his mother. Mullins had nothing but the usual drapery items. John Nugent carried expensive boxes of chocolates. Michael Joe realized for the first time how truly small and dull Corrigbeg was. How could a man get rich, or of what use would it be to a man to be rich in a place like this where you couldn't even get a suitable Christmas gift for a superior girl?

He decided that he'd have to go to Ennis to look. And since he was going to Ennis, he might as well make a day of it with Nell. He dispatched Vin Scanlon out to her with a note. They could leave by train from Corrigbeg in the morning, and spend the day in Ennis, and come back that night.

Nell sent back a reply that said simply: ' 'Twould be in the *Clare Champion* next week.' Michael Joe sent Vin out again telling Nell that she could get in a different carriage to him at the station and then change in Lahinch. She agreed, adding a sarcastic touch: 'The pigs will miss me for the day.' Michael Joe laughed at that.

He told a lie to his mother. He had to go down to Lipton's to see about extra consignments of tea and sugar. She could keep an eye on Vin during the day and see he was minding the shop. 'There's no one going with you?' 'No,' Michael Joe said. 'You can't take a day out like that when you're doing business.' 'Wisha have some fun for yourself, too,' she said. 'You haven't stopped going this past half-year.'

Mrs. McCarthy sighed as Michael Joe bid her good-bye the morning he was going to Ennis. He was wearing the dark-blue topcoat, and the swarthy face was almost fair from the closeness of the shave. The dark wavy hair shone from brilliantine. He was a handsome figure entirely. She felt a tightness in her chest as she looked at him. He was not demonstrative toward her, and just said good-bye. She longed for the kiss on the cheek he used to give her as a little boy.

Nell was at the station in a sky-blue suit that went very well with her blonde hair. She was carrying a black umbrella. They ignored each other at the station in Corrigbeg.

At the stop in Lahinch, Michael Joe changed into her carriage. Nell was sitting by the window gazing out. A woman in black with a pig-tailed daughter was also in the carriage. The little girl stopped chattering when she saw Michael Joe. Nell turned and smiled, a quick half-guilty smile. Michael Joe beamed and sat beside her.

'A grand day,' Michael Joe said as if he were addressing himself to a stranger.

Nell made a face at him. ' 'Twill rain, I'm afraid,' she said. She glanced at the mother and girl.

The presence of the mother and girl spoiled the train ride for Michael Joe. The little girl kept staring at him. And he caught her listening whenever he tried to say anything to Nell. The mother began telling Nell a long-winded account of why she was going to Ennis. Her husband in the hospital with double pneumonia. Michael Joe couldn't muster any sympathy for her. Felt as if she were acting like the husband was dead already.

He spent two hours of misery until the train pulled into Ennis. Nell chatted sympathetically with the woman and her daughter.

'I thought that little one would never take her eyes off me,' Michael Joe said when they got off the train.

'You're handsome,' Nell laughed. 'Even the little ones . . .'

'Oh, is that it?' Michael Joe said. 'I'm glad the *little ones* think so.'

They walked from the station into Ennis. People stared at them as they passed on the pavement.

'Is there something wrong with us?' Michael Joe said.

'They can tell we're from the country,' Nell said teasing him. 'And they don't see our likes too often.'

'I'll show them what the country boy can do,' he said, patting his vest pocket where he kept his wallet. He drew himself up a bit taller. Though Corrigbeg could fit in one street of Ennis, Michael Joe wasn't going to let the big town throw him.

They had lunch at the Old Ground, one of the biggest hotels in Ennis. Nell wanted to go into Lynches' tearoom. Not Michael Joe! Steak smothered in onions and mushroom gravy for lunch. Michael Joe had a half-whiskey with it.

'And anything for the lady, sir?'

Nell whispered to Michael Joe that she'd like a glass of burgundy. Guiltily.

'A glass of burgundy for the lady.'

The half-whiskey went to Michael Joe's head right away. He talked extravagantly to Nell about what he could do if he was rich. He'd leave Corrigbeg. Open a shop in Dublin. Sure Corrigbeg was only a hole in the wall. And there was hardly any chance for a man there at all. Oh, he had great dreams of the life he'd lead in Dublin. Plays at the Abbey Theatre. Balls at the Gresham Hotel. Races at the Curragh and Phoenix Park. That was the life for a man.

' 'Tisn't like you think it is,' Nell said, on her second glass of burgundy, and feeling a bit melancholy.

'Ah, sure you're a woman. If you didn't like England 'twas because you hadn't the proper fellow to show you around.'

Nell was silent.

Michael Joe had a couple more of half ones. He was ready to conquer the world.

They went for a walk down O'Connell Street after the lunch. It began to rain. Nell put up her umbrella and they walked together underneath it. Michael Joe kept stopping at shop windows contrasting them with Corrigbeg. When they came to Maurer, the jeweller's, he stopped and took a long look. Neither of them spoke about the rings; most of the window display was of diamond and gold rings set in red velvet boxes.

Michael Joe tried to draw her out on what she liked.

'Ah, sure I'm not much interested in all that show at all,' she said.

'Wouldn't you like that brooch there?' Michael Joe said.

' 'Tis all right.'

'Come on in,' he said taking her by the elbow. 'I have to buy a Christmas present for my mother.'

They went in. Michael Joe went up to the small, bald-headed, dark-spectacled man behind the glass counter.

'I want to buy a Christmas present,' he said loudly to the little man, who looked up at him quickly and found out all he needed to know.

Nell had wandered off to another part of the shop.

'A ring?' the little man said glancing unctuously in Nell's direction.

'No. But you're on the right track,' Michael Joe said bending down and whispering confidentially.

The little man pinched his lower lip and thought. Michael Joe was looking at him anxiously. The man raised a finger: 'Ah! The very thing to suit!'

He showed Michael Joe a necklace made of gold-plated beads interspaced with little gold-plated leaves. Michael Joe knew the minute he saw the necklace that he had found his gift. He nodded at the man slyly, and then went over to Nell.

'Your man has a necklace over here, I want you to try on,' Michael Joe said to her.

Nell had a Swiss music box in her hand, and was listening to the tinkling of Liebestraum. 'Isn't it lovely?' she said to Michael Joe.

'Grand,' he said. 'Come on over here a minute.'

'Wait'll it finishes,' she said crossly.

Michael Joe stood with her while the little barrel rolled on, tinkling out the lullaby. Nell hummed. The mechanism stopped. 'Aren't they lovely?' she sighed, closing the lid and running her fingers over the Alpine village set in the snow-capped mountains.

Michael Joe took her by the elbow.

She didn't want to try the necklace on. Michael Joe told her it was for his mother. Reluctantly, she took it out of the box. The little man nodded, and nodded, and beamed. Michael Joe pretended nonchalance. 'They'll do,' he said.

Nell took the necklace off without glancing at it, and gave it back to the little man, who looked tenderly at her through his glasses. She went back again to the music boxes.

Michael Joe did not have enough ready cash on him to pay for his necklace, so he put a few pounds down and promised to send the rest when he got home. He gave his address.

'The intended?' the little man said.

Michael Joe tried to look enigmatic.

'Wait . . . . Gold. Will melt her heart, so it will, so it will,' the little man said, clasping his hands.

Michael Joe picked up Nell and they went back out into the drizzling rain. Nell put up her umbrella, and they walked on the pavement.

Michael Joe was feeling a little bit let down after his purchase, and would only rise to the heights again when the necklace was once more around Nell's neck, forever.

'What did you think of the necklace?' he said, not willing to give up the thrill yet.

'Oh, I'm sure your mother'll like it,' Nell said.

Michael-Joe laughed a belly laugh. People stared at him. Who would laugh in the rain?

'I want to see the River Fergus,' Nell said.

'In this kind of weather? There's a cowboy picture on. We'll be cosier sitting in the seats than watching a dirty river.'

'I'd like to,' Nell said. 'I don't want to be cooped up.'

'Well, 'tis *your* day out,' Michael Joe said magnanimously.

They went down O'Connell Street, passing the granite statue of 'The Emancipator' raised in the square.

'A soft day for your man to be out without a coat,' Michael Joe said, nodding up at the statue.

Nell laughed. 'I used to love him when I was in school. I used to think I was the servant girl who saved him that time in Dublin when the English put poison in his cup. "Oh, Daniel O'Connell, a dhiugeann thu Gaelic?" ' she sang.

They walked on in the drizzle, out to the bridge spanning the Fergus River, now full, muddy, and flowing strongly.

Nell leaned over the parapet with the umbrella over her head. Michael Joe she left standing bareheaded and unprotected. He glanced once at the flowing river, and then waited impatiently for her. The glowing mood was beginning to wear off him.

'Do you know that song from America, "Ol' Man River"?' Nell said.

' "Heay doan't say nathin' . . . He jus' kaaps rowlin' alaong", ' Michael Joe said, imitating Yankee nasality.

'Oh, stop it,' she said. 'You're murderin' it.'

'I'm getting wet,' he said.

Nell stayed leaning over the parapet a while longer, letting him stand in the drizzle. Then she let him in under the umbrella again.

'A little wetting won't harm you. A big, strong country lad the size of you.'

'You're always putting me off,' he said suddenly.

'I'm not,' she said. 'You're always putting on.'

'Don't be smart. You'd think I was a jackass or something. Pull the creature along. Give him a bit of a carrot now and then. A little'll satisfy him.'

They had stopped and were facing each other under the umbrella.

'I didn't ask to come here,' Nell said quietly. 'You asked me.'

'I know that. I know that, well,' Michael Joe said. 'And why did you come when you *were* asked?'

'I was bored at home alone,' she said simply.

'You'll never give me a swelled head from the compliments,' he shouted quickly.

'Shhhh,' she said. 'The whole town will hear you.'

Michael Joe calmed down as quickly as he had flared. They walked on in silence for a while.

'I'm giving you all I can give you,' Nell said. 'And that's the truth.'

'I don't know what's wrong with me at all,' Michael Joe said contritely.

Darkness was falling quickly, and the drizzle had turned into fog. Christmas lights were turned on and winking in the shop windows as the pair walked towards the railway station. The cathedral bell chimed the hour of four as they were passing it. They both looked at the Gothic limestone building, ghostly in the fog.

'Come on and we'll drop in,' Nell said. 'A prayer won't hurt you.'

'We might miss the train.'

'We'll only stop a minute. I feel the need. A Thanksgiving to make.'

She entered the dark cathedral, sprinkling holy water on herself and back on Michael Joe. Both of them knelt on the back pew. Nell bowed her head. Her damp, curly, blonde hair fell down over her face, and over her joined hands. Michael Joe did not pray, though he knelt. He looked around him at the church in which he could see nothing distinctly. The chapel, shadowed, haloed in candlelight, against a background of dark-toned stained-glass windows, filled him with gloom.

On the way out to the station, Nell tried to cheer him up by praising the golden necklace he bought for his mother. Michael Joe wanted to tell her it was for herself, wanted to put it on her neck that moment, gaze at her, his vision in the rain. He saw the scene in his mind, and for a moment actuality dimmed, Nell was inside him, more real. He was confused, and remained silent.

On the way home in the train Nell made a few attempts to

draw him into talk about local preparations for Christmas. The heart had gone out of the day for him, and the hollow and almost desperate note in Nell's voice threw him more into himself. They lapsed into silence. The yellow gaslight on the ceiling, over the ochre walls of the carriage and the dark velvet seats, completed the gloom. He left her in Lahinch and went into another carriage, glad to be away from her at last.

The following week Michael Joe tried to forget the trip to Ennis by keeping himself busy decorating the shop for Christmas. Business picked up, particularly in currants, raisins and spices. Farmers' wives came in from the outlying districts and spent what they had managed to save or beg from their tight-fisted farmer husbands during the year. Michael Joe often had to take the husbands out for a drink while their wives bought Christmas luxuries. It was a custom, and good for business. To stand a round of drink to the husband guaranteed his wife's business for the following year.

The custom of buying the drink was providential for Michael Joe this year. By the end of each day he was mildly drunk, and well on in the Christmas spirit. The constant good wishes for his health and prosperity in the coming year had their effect on him, too. He was easily warmed by expressions of good will towards him, and the atmosphere of good fellowship which was in the air. 'Peace on earth to men of good will.' Everywhere in the town signs of festivity, decorations, singing in the pubs, toys in the shop windows and children with their noses against the glass, reminded him of his own childhood. He had always liked Christmas as he was growing up—the barmbracks, the currant and raisin bread, the goose his mother cooked for the Christmas dinner, decorating the house with holly and ivy and Christmas cards, the toys.

It had seemed to him then that the festivities around the house were being conducted specially for him. He remembered his mother often saying to his sisters when the question of sharing or the ownership of a toy came up: 'Ah, sure he's the youngest, now. Let him have it.'

He had never had any reason to change his feelings about Christmas.

As the week went on, he began to fit his relationship with Nell into his general feelings toward the season. He began to look on his mood of the previous Saturday as being partly caused by the bad weather. It was no day for an outing. The thought of being able to give her the gold necklace became a way of asking her forgiveness, as well as making her a Christmas gift. Killing two birds with the one stone.

In the middle of the week he made out a money order for ten pounds and sent a letter down to Maurer's for the necklace. He had never spent that much on a gift before. The sum which he was willing to spend on the gift gave him further proof of the genuineness and greatness of his feelings for Nell. She couldn't fail to appreciate that when she saw the evidence. Spending that much money filled him with pride and self-satisfaction.

When the postman delivered the small oblong package, he brought it up to his room and opened it. The golden necklace lying in the velvet-lined case was exactly as he had remembered it. He took pleasure in it for its own sake, apart from the fact that it was intended for Nell. He left the box open on his dresser when he went out of the room, and it remained there open and untouched the few days before Christmas. He often glanced at it when he was in the room, until it began to take on in his mind the proportions of a sacred object, dazzling, with the power to influence the soul, and with the power to bind.

The day before Christmas Day he went over to Mullins, the draper's, when there was a lull in the rush, and bought his mother a black cardigan. Mullins was going to wrap it, but Michael Joe didn't have time. He brought it into her in the unwrapped box. She was putting a loaf of bread decorated with currants and raisins into the oven in the range.

' 'Tisn't much,' Michael Joe said to her. 'But Mullins said 'twas the warmest he had.'

Mrs. McCarthy wiped her flour-soiled hands on her apron, stared at the big box, and automatically reached for it.

'Ah, you shouldn't have bothered, Michael Joe,' she was able to say.

' 'Twas no bother. Well, I must be getting back out to the shop. We're almighty busy.'

Mrs. McCarthy went into the dining room, sat down in the armchair by the open hearth, and gazed for a long time into the fire, holding the box unopened on her knees. After a while she got up, put the box unopened on the sideboard, and busied herself preparing supper.

Though Mrs. McCarthy was in the late sixties, she did not show her age in her movements. She held herself straight, moved energetically and quickly about the kitchen, her heels beating on the flag floor. She seemed to have reached a certain point in growing old, and then her body had stopped showing that she was growing older. Her face was lean, bony, high-checked, and like yellow cream in complexion. Excess hair grew on her lower chin from dark-brown beauty spots. Her white-grey hair she had bound in a twisted knot at the back, but arranged in curls over her narrow, bony forehead. Jewelled horn combs kept the hair neat and in place always. The body was thin, and heavy-lidded grey eyes, large and shiny, were sunken under bony brows. Emotion or feeling no longer registered in her face. She had no mannerisms, which are often so pronounced in old people, to give clues to what they were like in their young days. It was hard to think of Mrs. McCarthy as having ever been young, as looking any other way than she did now.

She prepared a specially big supper for Michael Joe—sausages, rashers, and slices of the hot currant loaf she had just baked. She took tea and toast herself, sitting with Michael Joe watching him wolf down his food. She waited until he was nearly finished before bringing up her subject.

'The necklace on your dresser. 'Tis a lovely piece,' she said.

'Hummmm,' Michael Joe nodded. 'Grand.'

'Is it for someone I know?' she said, trying hard to keep her tone light, at the beginning.

'Ah, for a girl. The Cullen girl. You might have seen her around the town. She's a good-looking. . . .'

'Ah, yes. I remember, now. At Mass. That's the one, is it?'

'If you see her once, you wouldn't forget her,' Michael Joe said, proudly.

Mrs. McCarthy was silent for a while.

'It cost, I suppose?'

'Yerra, not much,' Michael Joe said.

'I hope she's worthy of it,' Mrs. McCarthy said. 'She's home from England, isn't she?'

'I think so,' Michael Joe said. He had finished, and was lighting a cigarette.

'Do you know why she came home?'

'I never asked her,' Michael Joe said. ' 'Tis none of my business.'

'Well, it might be,' Mrs. McCarthy said.

'Might be, might be. What's all the mystery about? Spit it out.'

'You're making a fool of yourself with your gifts of gold.'

'A fool of myself! Stop your damn nonsense.'

'She had a brat by a fellow in England. And came home because she lost her job.'

'That's a terrible thing to say about an innocent girl.'

'Innocent! She's been pulling the wool over your eyes long enough. Everyone in the town knows what I'm telling you but yourself.'

'I don't believe you. She isn't that sort. I know that.'

'How do you know it?' his mother said in spite of herself.

'A man knows,' Michael Joe said.

'A blind man wouldn't.'

'Where's the child, then?' Michael Joe said.

' 'Twas given out to an orphanage. Do you think she'd want her disgrace around here for everyone to see?'

'I'll ask herself, so I will,' Michael Joe said. 'You're all a pack of dirty gossips. Soiling a pure girl.'

'Are you calling your mother a gossip?'

Her question stopped him. He became flustered.

'I didn't mean it that way,' he said. 'I have to go to the shop.'

He escaped. His mother was jealous. He had been careless enough to leave the necklace out in his dresser in a place where she could see it. Nothing would have come up between them about Nell if she hadn't seen it. He began to think that her jealousy might have driven her to make up the story about Nell, thinking that he might accept it without question, believe *her*, and then give up Nell. He felt sorry for her because her strategy was so obvious, but he was irritated that she had interfered.

He had high hopes that this Christmas he and Nell might be able to reach some kind of more satisfactory agreement. What the agreement could be he had no idea. He wanted something from her, something more than she was giving him. What did he want? He did not know. It wasn't her body. Apples and oranges of the past. A dark lane. No. At first, yes. Not now.

He did not believe his mother. Nell had never let a man touch her. She wouldn't let him. Michael Joe. Had she let some fellow, once? He had to find out.

The Christmas spirit left him. He went out and shut down the shop though he usually kept it open late on Christmas Eve for last-minute shoppers. He threw a few pound notes at Vin Scanlon. 'Shut the shop.'

'Happy Christmas', Vin shouted after him.

Michael Joe was out of hearing.

On the way out to Nell's, his mother's voice kept sounding in his ears, and her accusation. Fool! Fool! Fool! Had he been a fool? A bastard baby Nell had by a stranger in England. And she wouldn't let him touch her. Hypocrite. All the sayings he had ever heard about women as deceivers going back to Eve, tossed around in his mind.

He thought he knew the deceiving woman. The fox. But Nell wasn't a fox. Or was she? But what did she want from him? Was she playing hard to get? He had never mentioned marriage to her. If he had? Was that what she was playing for? And if it was, was that what he wanted? Did he want to marry Nell? That thought had never occurred to him either. He accepted their romance within its present time without any thought of where it might or should lead to, or where he wanted it to lead to.

Well, he would find out where Nell stood. If it was marriage? Did he want to marry her? He was in love with her, wasn't he? He bought her the necklace for almost the same cost as a ring. He couldn't give himself a straight answer on whether he wanted to marry her or not. But he was inclined to think that he would marry her if she would have him. He'd wait and try and size up the situation when he met her. The thought of marriage to her didn't arouse any special excitement in him. He felt a bit desperate, almost as if he were forcing himself to admit something he did not really want to admit. But he kept telling himself he was in love with her. He must be. Or what was it then?

Halfway out to Nell's he remembered the necklace. He thought about turning around and going back home for it, but decided not to. He was in a hurry to see her. He could always make a date for the following day and give it to her then.

The Cullens lived in a roomy slate cottage about a mile outside Corrigbeg. In front of the cottage, Nell's mother kept a flower garden enclosed by a low sod wall. A small iron gate opened into a gravelled path that led up to the house. In the light darkness Michael Joe saw the white smoke curling up from the chimney. To the right of the cottage, he could see a huge rick of turf with a gap eaten into it from which the Cullens drew in their turf for the fire.

He knocked. A dog barked. A man shouted 'Lie down, Bowzer.' And a latch was lifted, and Nell's father in buttoned waistcoat, black tie and celluloid collar stood before him in the lamplight.

'Yerra, will ye look at who we have here?' he said.

'God bless,' Michael Joe said automatically. 'And a happy Christmas.'

'On you too. And many happy returns. Come in and don't be standing in the cold like that.' He took Michael Joe by the arm and brought him into the house.

The entire Cullen family were sitting down to their Christmas Eve supper. The house was decorated with holly and ivy and streamers. Lighted candles stuck in silver-papered turnip stumps were lighted in the windows. The table had been drawn into the middle of the kitchen, and the Cullens, four boys ranging in age from about fourteen to nineteen, and Nell were seated around it. Mrs. Cullen had the brown teapot in her hand and was pouring tea. The súgán chair at the head of the table was vacant.

'Draw hether a chair, Nell. Michael Joe will have a bite with us.'

'I won't be stopping. I never thought to break in on ye a night like this,' Michael Joe said, sincerely embarrassed at having broken in on a family during their Christmas Eve supper.

'Never mind that, now. Never mind. We always set an extra place, tonight, anyway.'

Nell had risen quietly and drawn up a chair for him, at the opposite end of the table, next to her mother. She was sitting on her father's right.

Michael Joe sat into the table. A huge barmbrack loaf was sitting in the middle of the table with slices already cut from it on a plate. Slices of goose were on another plate. Nell had a plate of slices of yellow Galtee cheese in front of her.

Mrs. Cullen put a plate with two thick slices of barmbrack and slices of goose in front of Michael Joe.

'Ah, not so much, please, there, Mrs. Cullen,' Michael Joe said. 'Sure I only just ate.' He could not refuse, but he had no real appetite.

'A big man like yourself needs to be stuffed. Eat up there and no nonsense.'

'Hold on there a minute, Mary Ann,' Mr. Cullen said 'Sure

I almost forgot. Come on down in the room a minute, Michael Joe. I have a word to say before you put that away.'

'Can't you wait, Dan?' Mrs. Cullen said.

Dan Cullen pulled Michael Joe away from the table and down to the parlour room. In the lamplight, he poured out a quarter tumbler of whiskey for Michael Joe before Michael Joe could stop him.

'Here. Put that below your belt. Once a year 'tis no harm.'

He poured the same for himself. The two men raised glasses. Slainte. Happy Christmas. Michael Joe drained his at one gulp.

The whiskey eased Michael Joe, and took away some of his embarrassment and nervousness. He was prepared to enjoy being part of the family when he got back to the table.

He glanced once or twice at Nell. She was looking down at her plate, eating.

Mrs. Cullen commented on the weather, the fine, clear Christmas, and no snow, though that might be a wonder to get, they didn't see it so often. Dan Cullen talked about the price of cattle, and the state of business. Michael Joe grew easy, and more easy. He directed a few questions to the boys about football. He teased them into a fight by asking which one of them was the best footballer. Mrs. Cullen intervened. The holy and blessed season! Can't even stop fighting this one sacred night of the year. Michael Joe took the blame for starting it.

He grew expansive from the company, the warmth, the obvious welcome they had for him, and the food. And forgot himself. He contributed his share to the flow of talk, humour, and argument. When Dan Cullen tried to be pontifical at the head of the table, Michael Joe turned him off with sly humour, a little dig at the farmers and their always complaining. Michael Joe heard Nell laugh often, but she never spoke herself. Mrs. Cullen kept order when things were threatening to get out of hand, and she quietly replenished the food on the table when it was running out. Even with all the talk, the food disappeared rapidly.

Michael Joe felt at home. Then, Nell got up from the table and said that she had to hurry in to Confession or she'd never get heard. There would be a crowd. Michael Joe remembered then why he had come. He pulled back his own chair and said he had to be off too.

While Nell was getting her coat, he thanked the Cullens for

their hospitality. They told him he was welcome any time. He detected no hint of pressure in their invitation. If they had a marriageable daughter they wanted off their hands, they did not betray their anxiety about getting her married off to a good match, such as Michael Joe. Mrs. Cullen asked after his mother, and sent her a happy Christmas. Then he and Nell left together.

'I'm sorry if all the shouting and talking bothered you,' Nell said. 'You're not used to it.'

'Ne'er a bit at all,' Michael Joe said. 'I couldn't have asked for better. That's my element. I could have stopped with ye all night.'

As they walked the road in darkness into Corrigbeg, neither one of them brought up the recent trip to Ennis. Michael Joe was now between two minds whether to bring up what his mother had told him. The gossip seemed even more far-fetched, after he had been sitting down at the Cullens' table, and shared their Christmas Eve meal with them. There was no sign given by anyone that there was trouble or a shadow over that house. The question of marriage to Nell didn't seem very important any more either. A sense of euphoria filled Michael Joe. Leave well enough alone. Yet, his mother's gossip kept nagging at him. To set the whole matter at rest as far as he and Nell were concerned, Michael Joe decided to broach the subject to her indirectly. He was so sure that there was nothing to the rumour, that he would be ashamed to bring it up directly. Nell would set his mind completely at rest. Then, he would let his mother have her rumours to herself, as long as she didn't bother him any more with them.

'I suppose Christmas in England is a lot different from what 'tis here?' Michael Joe said.

'They go in for New Year more,' Nell said. ' 'Twas always lonesome for me, though.'

'What part of England were you in?'

'London. I worked at Grey's Hospital. In the general ward.'

'That must be tough,' Michael Joe said. 'Dancing attendance on sick people is no bargain. Did you stop at the hospital?'

'Yes,' Nell said. 'They had nurses' quarters.'

'I suppose they gave you plenty of time off? You were able to have fun, I suppose. They couldn't jail you all the time.'

Nell was silent for a while. The countryside around them in the light darkness was still. The sky was bright with translucent clouds.

In the distance, they heard the soughing of the Atlantic against the cliffs, a sound always present over Corrigbeg, in winter.

'You're getting *at* something,' Nell said. 'You never asked me about England before.'

' 'Tisn't worth talking about,' Michael Joe said. 'My mother asked me what part of England you were in. And I had to say I didn't know.'

Nell stopped walking. Michael Joe went on not noticing. She turned around as if to go back home. Michael Joe faced her.

'Did you forget something?'

'You heard?' she said walking slowly back to him.

'Heard what, in the name of God?' Michael Joe said.

'About . . . about the baby. The baby I had.'

'There's rumours. But sure I don't pay any attention to gossip like that.'

' 'Tis true. True. I had to give my baby away.'

'True? You're coddin'. You'd never let a man. . . .'

'Yes. Once. I had a baby by a fellow I met up with. And he ran away and left me. And went in the army.'

'Jesus Christ! Jesus Christ!' Michael Joe said. 'You never told me.'

They had stopped walking and were facing each other, shadowy forms in the half-light.

'There was no need for you to know my shame.'

'That was a dirty trick. A dirty trick.'

'I wasn't tricking you,' Nell said. 'I warned you.'

'I didn't mean . . . do your father and mother know?'

'Of course they do.'

'And they don't mind?'

'They don't let on. You're the one that minds, I can see.'

'No,' Michael Joe protested. 'Honest to God! The whole town knows about you, I suppose?' he rushed on.

'I wouldn't be surprised.'

'And you're like that! And kept putting me off! Wouldn't let me lay a hand on you.'

'Like what?'

'You made a disgrace of me. A fool. I'm an eejit. My mother was right. Everyone knew but me.' He began to walk away from her.

'You don't have to walk with me,' Nell said.

'I will. I will,' Michael Joe said. 'There must be something you can say for yourself. Parading as a lily-white.'

'You poor amaudaun,' she said. 'I can see you're dying to start running.'

'Why didn't you tell me? Why?'

'I did. But you never took the hint. You have only yourself to blame.'

Michael Joe rushed back to her, took her in his arms and kissed her. To his surprise, she let him. His lips met hers roughly. No thrill passed between.

'There,' she said drawing away. 'Are you satisfied now?'

He spat into the darkness. Then he grabbed her by the arms as if he wanted to hit her. She could see only the lumps of his face in the darkness. His voice whipped over her.

'You let him do it. Took your knickers off for him. And opened your legs for him. And let him . . . oh, Christ, had you no shame?'

'He forced . . .' Nell began to cry. Then she controlled herself. 'I'm going to Confession. Let go of me.'

'I will. And go home and wash my hands.'

The blue-black outline of the church, the steeple rising to the dark sky topped by the vague form of the cross, loomed behind both of them. Shadowy forms of people were passing by them going in and out the chapel gate. He turned away from her and walked rapidly down the street.

The rest of the evening he spent going restlessly from pub to pub drinking half-whiskeys. He turned in at Jones's, the first pub on his way down after leaving Nell. For a Christmas Eve, there was nothing stirring there. A couple of old men were complaining in a corner that the Christmases weren't like they used to be at all. Jim, behind the bar, wasn't much for the talk, except business. Michael Joe left after two quick ones. He did not respond to any of the 'Happy Christmases'.

He continued dropping into pubs down along the Main Street; at Clery's there was a crowd of country fellows. From Clonboney. They had banded together the year before as a football team, and declared themselves independent of Corrigbeg. They were considered traitors. Michael Joe nearly got in a fight with one of them over whether Corrigbeg had power to have them thrown out of the Gaelic Athletic Association or not. Michael Joe wasn't drunk enough to go on with the fight. The other fellows reminded him of the Christmas spirit. Peace on earth. Even between Clonboney and Corrigbeg. The potential fight was turned into a laugh. And so he went from pub to pub, down one side of the Main Street and up the other, drinking whiskey, without water. Straight and quick. He met Larkin at Thynne's, and persuaded him to join him. Larkin had been to Confession and was drinking lemonade. They ended up at Blake's, at ten o'clock, just before closing. Nanno cleared the pub at ten, but tipped Larkin and Michael Joe the wink before they left. They came around the back way and were let in again. There was a crowd of about ten or twelve in the kitchen, girls and fellows, the privileged crowd that Nanno would let drink in her establishment after hours, any day of the week.

Michael Joe had been drinking solidly now for well over two hours. But he felt as sober as when he had started out. He continued to drink straight whiskey. Nanno took down the concertina and began to play. Michael Joe got up and danced a Clare set with a girl who was there, in from the country, from Cloon, visiting Kitty Falane, a cousin. The girl's name was Ann Shanahan. A mousy kind of girl, he thought, shy, timid, and not very talkative. The kind of girl who, if she were at a public dance, might be a wallflower.

Michael Joe, driven to play the clown, pretended he wasn't able to dance the set and stumbled all over the flag floor, bumping into other couples and generally making a shambles of the set for the other dancers. But it was Christmas Eve, and they all took it in good humour. Ann was embarrassed at the notice he was causing. She didn't like to have attention drawn to her. But she wasn't forward enough to tell Michael Joe to behave. She tried her best to smile her way past Michael Joe's antics. He staggered around continuing to make a clown of himself. He apologized to her often, just to see her struggling with herself, not to tell him he was making a show of himself, and saying that 'twas all right, sure the kitchen floor was crowded. Nanno Blake sat in the corner squeezing the concertina, eyes half shut, glancing at the dancers on the floor now and then, her shoe button eyes shining.

Michael Joe began giving Ann a line, telling her how beautiful she was, and trying to dance modern style to the Irish set. He told her she was the grandest looking girl he ever clapped his eyes on, and where had she been all his mortal life. He tried to hold her close and do a waltz.

'Will you look at McCarthy?' someone said.

'They're looking at you,' Ann whispered, trying to push him away.

'I'm mad about you, entirely,' Michael Joe said, drunkenly.

Mercifully, Nanno stopped playing, and the set ended. Ann disengaged herself from Michael Joe's bear hug, and scurried back to Kitty Falane at the other side of the kitchen. Michael Joe went back to Larkin, and had a few more half-whiskeys.

He began whispering dirty stories about women to Larkin.

'Ah, don't. Sure I don't want to hear,' Larkin protested. 'I have to go to Communion in the morning.'

'*I'm* committing the sin, not *you*,' Michael Joe said. 'Listen to this one, will you?'

Michael Joe told the one about the ould fella drunk coming home in the train from Ennis, and a couple a' women got in, and began talking about what they were going to have the next time. The ould fella couldn't sleep. He got up, and opened his fly in front of them, and took it out. And waved it at them. 'I'm going to have an elephant, and here's his trunk.'

Larkin thought the yarn was too raw for Christmas Eve. Christmas Eve was no time to go on like that.

'To hell with Christmas Eve,' Michael Joe said. He told a couple of more yarns to top that one. In the middle of the last one, a pounding came on the front door. Nanno went out.

'Who's there?'

'The guards. Open up in the name of the law.'

The crowd in the kitchen scattered like rabbits before a dog. The girls ran upstairs and sat at a table in the parlour, already set with cups and saucers for just such an emergency, as if they had visited the pub for a quiet cup of tea.

Michael Joe headed out the back way, stuffing the half-whiskey glass in his pocket. He began to run, stumbling as he ran. Around him he heard the other fellows running. Somewhere close he heard a guard's voice shout, 'Stop, halt, in the name of the Law!' The guards had come around the back in a pincer movement. Raiding on Christmas Eve. Canon Lyons must have put them up to it.

His head felt clear for a moment; he was excited at being chased by the guards. He felt like a little boy again, as he ran, when he and a gang used to rob an orchard, and send up and tell the guards they were going to, and then the guards came and chased the fellows all over the countryside. Michael Joe had never once been caught. And he wasn't going to be now either. As he ran in the dark, his legs began to give; he felt dizzy all of a sudden; he thought his heart had stopped. Up ahead of him a haystack loomed. He staggered towards it, and threw himself into the soft hay. He lay in the haystack, senseless, until the first light of the Christmas morning.

He awoke into blue light. His throat was dry, and his Adam's apple felt as if a snake was trying to squeeze it. Constrict it, and shut up his throat altogether. He did not know where he was for a few moments, and then only very vaguely he remembered how he got in the haystack. He tried to get on his feet, but began to vomit. After a while, he stopped, and then longed for water. He was able to stand up. In some backyard nearby, a cock crowed a couple of times. He staggered to a wall and tried to climb it to get out of the yard. He fell down. He began to vomit again, this time the dry heaves, until he thought his guts were going to come out of his throat. Finally, he was able to climb the wall and make it out into Ennistymon Road through a gateway in the next yard. He continued to dry heave as he staggered down the Ennistymon Road. A blue-grey light was dawning. The chapel bell rang for First Mass. No one was yet in the street this Christmas morning.

He pushed in the front door of his own house and left it open. As he was staggering through the kitchen, heading for the water tap, his mother spoke from the dining room.

'Is that you, Michael Joe?'

He stuck his head under the tap without answering. As soon as he drank water, he vomited it right back up into the kitchen sink. He began to moan into the sink.

Mrs. McCarthy came out into the kitchen pulling the black shawl around her.

'Merciful God, Michael, what happened to you, at all? Were you killed?'

He staggered away from the sink, and began to mount the stairs grabbing on to the banisters, and teetering as he went up.

'Michael Joe! Michael Joe!' she shouted from the bottom of the stairs. 'Watch out or you'll fall down.'

He was able to stumble to his room. He threw himself out on top of the bed. He continued to dry heave for a few minutes, and then fell into a half sleep, moaning. He heard the knocking at the door, and his mother's voice raised in a keen, as if he were dead and she was moaning over his corpse. She knocked, and knocked. He did not answer.

Time passed. Then she was bending over him, trying to raise his head to drink a glass of warm milk. She was muttering something at him in Irish. He did not understand. After a few sips of the milk, he slumped back in bed. He felt her putting a blanket over him. Whatever was in his throat was still squeezing, and squeezing.

He was alone then for a while. He lay there almost senseless. He felt nothing, knew nothing, remembered nothing, wanted to do nothing, and couldn't even if he had wanted to. He lay in a corpse-like trance, from which he awoke now and then and dry heaved. All images had been blotted out of his mind.

Some time later, his mother raised him again, and wet his lips with a piece of an orange. He bit into it. The juice seared his throat as it went down.

'I went to Mass and offered up my communion for you,' his mother said to him. 'Today is Christmas Day. The Crib is lovely.'

He did not want to speak, and did not even know if he could even if he had wanted to. He was able to eat almost a whole orange which she fed him, talking all the while about the morning Mass, and how good the choir was singing 'Adeste Fidelis' and 'Silent Night' and the Crib with the Christ Child lying in the Manger. He heard her, but could not listen.

Before she left him this time, she pulled down the blind, and the room was shadowed though not dark. After she left, he raised himself out of bed and began to undress himself. Wisps of hay still clung to his suit, and his shoes were caked with mud. He let them lie where they fell after he took them off. The hay scattered on the carpeted floor. He threw his clothes at the bottom of the bed, then crawled in between the sheets in his underwear, and gradually fell into a half sleep again.

The bell rang for last Mass. Footsteps on the pavement. Voices. He began to enjoy his state of being nothing, of hearing people moving by outside his window, and he not a part of that movement. Even the effort to turn from one side to the other was too much. He lay on the flat of his back sunk deep into the soft mattress. Then he fell into a deep, dreamless, imageless sleep.

He was awakened by his mother shaking him gently by the

shoulder and saying: 'Here, Michael Joe, I brought a morsel to eat. Try if you can get it down.'

She had turned the light on. He stared at her. She was carrying a tray with a glass of milk, toast, and a cup. She put the tray on the table beside his bed, and helped him sit up. Then she arranged the pillows against his back. He sat still until she pushed him back on them. Then she placed the tray on the bed and sat beside him.

He ate what she had brought without saying a word. The toast hurt, but the soft-boiled egg went down easily. She chatted to him.

'Jim Larkin came in and wanted to know where you were. He hadn't seen you at Mass. I told him you weren't going out today. Wisha, 'twas a nice day for Christmas. An awful crowd of people at the rails. Father Madden and the Canon giving out Communion. I didn't cook the goose. Sure 'twill hold. You'll be better tomorrow. Thank God 'tis St. Stephen's and you can take a rest. I'll keep the door shut and let in none of the wran-boys. There's plenty houses where they'll be welcome with their antics. A custom like that isn't civilized at all. The priests ought to put their foot down. The wrans are a nuisance, disturbing the peace and quiet of the holy season.'

She settled Michael Joe back down in bed again, and he willingly, will-lessly submitted to her fussing and attention. She turned off the light and left him in darkness. He tried to sleep again, but the food had restored energy to his body, set it in motion again perhaps, and he could not sleep. Images from the evening before began to filter back into his mind. Nell saying 'tis true. Then the awful image of Nell he had, that she somehow smelled like rotten apples. When she said 'twas true, he saw her with the man. Then, giving birth, the image of Nell expelling the baby from her womb. He had suppressed the image instantly, an image of blood and slime. As he tumbled and tossed in bed in the darkness of his room, the image came back. He suppressed it again. But he knew Nell would never be the same for him again. He would not be able to look at her without this image lurking somewhere in his mind and coming before him. Why was it? Where did it come from? Why did he see her now only as a creature covered in mud?

Then he remembered poor Ann Shanahan whom he had disgraced dancing up at Blake's. But that did not bother him too much. Even though he knew he had disgraced himself, he took sly pleasure in it, and smiled to himself in the darkness. But he got restless again when he thought of Nell. He despised himself. He didn't want to let her down like everyone else did, except her family. He wanted to go on loving her. She was a grand girl. What if she did have a baby by another fellow. Images of her having that sexual act with the other fellow surged back into his mind. He tried to put them away. Broke out in a nervous sweat. Became sexually excited.

Finally, as an act ungovernable, entirely beyond his will to control, partly out of hatred for himself, and out of frustrated love for Nell, he masturbated. Then he fell asleep.

In the morning, he felt physically much better, but completely without any feeling about Christmas Eve or last night. It was as if some chemical had suddenly entered his blood which made him immune to what he had done. He shaved calmly, and was even satisfied by the look of his face. He thought that he should look like a ghost after what he had been through. He saw in the mirror that the events hadn't left a mark on him at all.

Downstairs, a coal fire was lit in the range. He stood with his back to it, warming himself. His mother was probably at eight o'clock Mass. He would wait for her to come back so she could get him his breakfast.

He spent the early part of the day, after breakfast, loitering around the house reading old newspapers and listening to the wireless. The BBC had good light music on and it helped on the good mood he was beginning to feel. His mother asked no questions, beyond how he was feeling. He volunteered no information beyond the fact that he was feeling better. He was matter-of-fact. It would all be forgotten. Become part of the buried past. Nothing worth the mentioning had happened at all.

The wran-boys kept coming to the door all day, and Michael Joe let them all in, and gave generously to each group. He made them all perform in whatever way they were able—playing the mouth organ, dancing, singing, reciting. Sometimes he asked questions of the mummers, trying to find out the identity behind the masks. The young boys revealed themselves easily, tittering and laughing, and being a bit shy. The adult wran-boys could not be identified at all. A leader spoke for them, and he was completely masked, and would not be unmasked.

Mrs. McCarthy would not come out to see any of the mummers perform, though Michael Joe tried to persuade her. She cooked the goose she had not cooked on Christmas Day, and the two of them ate it for dinner in the dining room. The only Christmas decorations in the house were a few strands of ivy wound around a picture of the Sacred Heart before which a small red lamp burned on the mantlepiece in the kitchen. The dining room was not decorated at all. During the dinner, the wran-boys kept knocking at the door. Michael Joe kept getting up to answer. His dinner got colder and colder. Mrs. McCarthy registered a complaint, saying he shouldn't answer. Michael Joe said that 'twas only once a year, and he didn't want to get a bad name by not letting them in. And they amused him.

'Well, you're the boss, I suppose,' Mrs. McCarthy said. Michael Joe laughed.

After dinner, he went up to his room, took the box with the necklace in it, and went for a walk up to the White Strand. He saw no one on the way, except the gaudily decorated wran-boys, moving in groups from house to house, playing and singing in the cold December air.

The Atlantic was rough. Slate-grey waves topped by whitecaps swept high towards the cliffs, and pounded into spray off them; the land around shuddered. Michael Joe braced himself against the sharp, salt wind blowing in from the sea. The shiver of coldness running through his body delighted him. It was a challenge to keep warm. He stepped up his walking pace.

He threw the box with the necklace from the top of the cliff overlooking the Puffing Hole, which was spewing up foam and sucking the sea into the cavernous hole, with stormy energy. He watched the box fall in a shower of spray. It was sucked under. He drew a couple of deep breaths, looking at the wide span of swelling sweeping sea. Then he turned towards home, with brisk, energetic strides.

12

MICHAEL JOE FELL quickly back into the old pattern of his life before he had met Nell—the shop during the day, with a visit to Kerney's in the morning to talk over the news of the day in the papers, and the horses, midday dinner with his mother, and then the long afternoon in the shop and a gossip by the fire in the little snug at the back with whoever dropped in and wanted to talk; supper in the evening again with his mother, then the shop again until eight, shutting up, and then to the Parochial Hall to play cards or billiards, or to Blake's or the Central Hotel where his own crowd gathered for a drink until closing; then home to bed.

The subject of Nell never came up again between himself and his mother. She must have noticed that the necklace box was missing from the top of his dresser. But she never made any attempt, even indirectly, to inquire what he had done with it. It was gone; her son was back to normal; didn't even go out to a dance on New Year's Eve that he had never missed before since he had started going to dances at eighteen. He was eating heartily, so that whatever had happened on Christmas Eve had not affected his health.

Quietly and efficiently she went about paying him attention in the weeks following Christmas. She wasn't fully sure she had won her battle. She thought she might have from observing the regularity and almost openness with which he now began to behave. 'I'm going up to the Hall for a while,' he would say before going out at night. Sometimes after supper, he would even sit and turn on the wireless and listen to it, while she was doing the dishes in the kitchen sink. She'd sometimes call in from the kitchen: 'What was that, Michael Joe? What did the fellow say?' Michael Joe would re-report the item out to her patiently and slowly, so she could hear. She didn't mind giving him the impression that her hearing was going a little.

She made sure to cook the food he liked. He was especially fond of tapioca pudding, and had often said he could eat it three hundred and sixty five times a year. She made lots of it now. She kept him constantly reminded of his appearance. A clean white shirt, hand-washed, she ironed for him twice a week. He owned a tweed jacket and dark grey slacks which he wore with a diamond-patterned Argyll jersey, in the shop during the week, and a dark-brown double-breasted suit for Sunday. She persuaded him that he ought to buy himself another sports coat and trousers. The ones he now had were baggy. Not presentable, at all. Though Michael Joe was vain enough, he hadn't thought about buying himself anything new to wear. When his mother suggested it, he did. And enjoyed himself over at Mullins', picking out the sports coat and trousers. Mullins bought groceries from Michael Joe, so the move was good for business too. The sports coat he picked was an expensive Donegal tweed with a belted back. Mullins persuaded him to buy a cap, too. Michael Joe took a big size in caps, but Mullins had one. And so the dark, wavy-haired head began to be concealed under a checkered cap. The cap suited him, though.

'Ah, sure you're a man entirely, now, on me,' his mother said when he walked into her with it on. And it did indeed change the image he conveyed. He seemed less boyish, harder. The peak of the cap jutting out of his head, and the strong forward thrust of his jaw, gave him a more pronounced look now, of determined aggressiveness, where before he looked simply wild, with the focus on the black hair and the dark eyes. The cap gave him a strong, substantial look, as of a man impenetrable and strong. A firm, unmovable character, not easily given to wild passion, but a man who wouldn't let anything stand in the way of something he wanted.

He fattened too. He never paid much attention to food. Simply ate what was put before him until his plate was clean. His mother took advantage of this habit of his of cleaning his plate, to load it with more food than usual. She did not do this with the conscious intention of making him fat; she liked to see him eat, and so she gave him more, so that he would eat more. His face filled out, though he did not yet have the rotundity that he would develop later on. He drank plenty of milk, a tall glass of which his mother made sure always to have on the table for him.

As the months went by she began to be more sure she had triumphed. Her sources of gossip confirmed her. 'Twas rumoured that Michael Joe was no longer conveying out Nell Cullen. What had happened to break up the match? No one knew. The biddies didn't dare say to Mrs. McCarthy's face that they thought Michael Joe had jilted her. But that was what was whispered. He had let her down. Oh, the poor misfortunate girl. Another blow. But sure 'twould take a brave man to marry her with her reputation. The gossips confirmed Mrs. McCarthy's own private opinion that Michael Joe was well rid of her. And so they had another cup of tea, and read the leaves to find out would they have good fortune in the days ahead.

The shrewdest move Mrs. McCarthy made was to go down to the bank with Michael Joe one Monday morning and arrange the account which had up to this time been in her name only, so that Michael Joe could make out a bank draft in his own name. When she told him she was going to do this, he had answered that he didn't think there was any great need, sure things were going all right as they were now. But, if she wanted to, he wouldn't object.

Larkin helped them make out the joint account, after they had talked to the bank manager. Larkin was all efficiency, and never made a personal comment throughout the whole proceedings. He seemed cool and reserved. Michael Joe noticed but thought nothing of it. Larkin practically bowed and scraped all over Mrs. McCarthy. She thought he was a grand young man, and a good friend for Michael Joe to have, especially since he was working in the bank.

Michael Joe had little feeling one way or the other about the new authority he had to draw money out of the bank any time in his own name. It never occurred to him to thank his mother. He couldn't see that it was going to make any change in his life at all. He always took what money he wanted from the till, and then balanced the accounts at the end of the week and the month, deducting what he had spent from the profits. There was no need to tell his mother. The shop had always shown a profit; nothing very big, except over the big holidays like Christmas or Easter. But enough for them to live on comfortably, and for Michael Joe to have enough to spend without counting the pence. There was income, too, from the rent of a small piece of land they had outside the town. So there was enough and plenty of money always. He never had to ask his mother for it, though all the money had been deposited in her name. That never worried or bothered him. The change now did not impress him. It impressed his mother though.

'Well, you're free of me, now,' she said as they walked up from the bank.

He didn't know what she was talking about. 'Sure, 'twill always be your money,' he said not knowing what else could be said.

'No,' she said. 'You must take care of how 'tis spent, now. And if you're careful enough who knows what you'll be. Never despise the power of money. You could own half the town one of these days.'

Michael Joe laughed. 'And what in the name of God would I do with it?' he said looking around at the houses as they passed.

His mother said nothing about what good owning half the town would do him.

On the surface, Michael Joe appeared content with himself, absorbed his mother's attention, and grew stout. He felt no need for women. Though he still went to Sunday night dances, he went out of habit, and because Larkin and Ed Donovan, the auctioneer, and Tom Fitzgerald, the schoolmaster, went. He danced little, preferring to stand around with any of the groups of fellows who were not dancing, and observe the dancers gyrating around the dance floor. He grew in the habit of making satirical comments on the girls as they were dancing. 'Wouldn't she be better off footing turf in the bog?' 'Here's me nose and me arse is coming.'

He walked home from the dance with the fellows who weren't conveying any girl home. Sometimes they would pass a couple courting in a doorway. The fellows would make loud comments as they passed. Michael Joe made no comments; but he enjoyed the fun.

After coming home from a dance, he often dreamed that he was enclosed in some kind of metal contraption that fitted him like a tight suit of armour, and it was squeezing and tightening on him. Faceless women floated in and out of his vision; he was held in the contraption from following them. The contraption tightened on him. When he felt he was being squeezed to death, he ejaculated, shouting he could not remember what. He woke up, and lay awake for a while in the darkness of his room, feeling like he had felt on Christmas Day, as if somehow the world had come to an end for him. But he fell asleep again, and had forgotten his dream when he woke next morning.

Football started in late February. Michael Joe had never been a particular star at the game, practised the minimum, and was inclined to see the game as an opportunity for displaying himself before the girls. He was strong, and big, and had the height. Yet, he never appeared to exert himself too much on the football field, turning in reliable but lazy performances.

This spring, he began to take the game seriously, going out to the football field for practice every evening when it wasn't raining. At first, he winded easily because he was out of condition and growing fat. He began to run two-, three-, and four-mile races around the football field to get himself back in condition. And he gave up smoking. Larkin and Donovan and Fitzgerald played on the team also. He began to drive them to get out and practise, when before they always had to drag him out to the field.

His play became more aggressive, and rougher. He had always been a good-natured player. He never intentionally tripped, or elbowed, or kneed another player. He was known as a 'clean player'. Now, he deliberately played rough. He wanted to get the ball. If another player beat him for it, or took it away from him, Michael Joe gave him an elbow in the ribs or the back, the next time they went for the ball together. Since he began to play rough, the other fellows played rough with him.

He rarely came off the field without limping, or having a plaster over an eye, or cuts on his shins. A few times he started fist fights, which were broken up quickly before anything serious happened.

In one fight, he was tripped from behind and when he was on the ground, got a kick in the head. Corrigbeg was playing Quilty, a team made up mainly of fishermen from two or three families in the neighbouring village to Corrigbeg. If one member of the Quilty team was roughed, all of them wanted to fight. Michael Joe kicked a Quilty man accidentally, and then fourteen other men ganged up on him, before his own team could save him. That was when he got the kick in the head.

His head was bandaged, but the blood kept seeping out through the bandage. He would not leave the game, even though he could hardly see with the pain in his head. This was one of his greatest games, and Michael Joe was talked about in Corrigbeg for his heroics. 'He bate them singlehanded.' He took terrible punishment for the rest of the game. The Quiltonians were vindictive and savage, and not worried about injuring a man permanently, if he once had injured one of their own. The more punishment Michael Joe got, the better he seemed to play. Leaped higher, kicked farther, was instinctively where the ball was. The *Clare Champion*, in praising him the following week, hailed him as the hero of the match, saying 'he was all over the field'.

When he came in home after the match, Mrs. McCarthy was cooking his supper at the range. She put her hands to her chest when she saw him, streaks of blood caked on each cheek, and the bloody bandage around his head.

'What happened?' she said faintly. 'They tried to kill you?'

'Nothing. I'll go upstairs and wash it off. 'Tis only a scratch.'

'I'll send for the doctor. You need the doctor,' she said.

Michael Joe told her that there was no need for the doctor, that he could take care of himself. The only injury that showed was the one on his head. He was bruised on the thighs and chest, and had several cuts on both shins. He tried not to limp as he went upstairs.

When he was gone upstairs, Mrs. McCarthy threw a shawl on and went next door to Marrinans' and gave one of the young Marrinans sixpence to go out to Spanish Point for Doctor Healy.

When she came back she went upstairs and knocked on Michael Joe's room door.

'Are you all right?'

'Let me alone. I can look after myself. Tend your own business.'

She went back downstairs. She realized that she could do nothing directly for him any more. If she had won the battle over Nell Cullen, she didn't know what she had gained by her victory. But, at least, Michael Joe was in the house with her. It didn't matter in the long run how he treated her, as long as he came home every night and was there in the morning. He had always been distant and cold with her, anyway. She had, in her way, even encouraged him to be. He thought he did not need her. But she knew better. He would never realize it, or acknowledge it. But she didn't want that. He was a man now. Growing in ways she did not understand, and couldn't cope with. She couldn't make him do things any more. But still she had her faith in her own influence, working away somewhere in him. That faith sustained her now.

Doctor Healy came and patched Michael Joe up. After the doctor left saying that there was nothing serious, and Michael Joe was in good condition and would look as good as new in a couple of days, Mrs. McCarthy sat in the dining room and waited for him to come downstairs to eat.

During the supper she tried to persuade him to give up the football.

'They'll destroy you some fine Sunday,' she said. 'You'll be laying dead out there on the field with no one to help you.'

'Indeed and they won't,' Michael Joe said. 'Let them try their level best. I can give as good as I get. There isn't a man on the team has my strength. I'm able for the best of them.'

She got up from the table on some excuse, and went out to the kitchen so that he would not see the pride in her eyes. When she had control of herself, she came back in.

'For my sake,' she went on, 'give it up. I won't be easy till you do.'

'Yerra, sure the fellows would think 'twas a coward I was.'

'Am I to put up with seeing you come home like this Sunday after Sunday? Have you lost all feeling for your mother's wishes?'

He ate on in silence. 'We'll see,' he said when he had finished.

That night, Mrs. McCarthy went to devotions, and after they were over went up and knelt at the rails, and prayed for Michael Joe to the image of the crucified Christ, almost life-sized, hanging from the cross over the high altar.

13

MICHAEL JOE BECAME a local hero because of his exploits in football. Whenever he walked down the street, the young boys stopped their play and whispered as he went past, and stared at him. He ignored them; they were only young boys, after all, and didn't know any better. But when they asked him to referee a match between them out at the football field, he could hardly refuse. He was strict with them as a referee, blowing the whistle for every foul. The boys never argued with him, and played intense, earnest football, some of the better boys competing fiercely for his attention. He gave out praise sparingly, and was curt and domineering with them.

Whenever he himself played in a football match, there was

always a couple of boys fighting among themselves to see who could carry his football shoes and togs. He let them fight it out, and let the boy who was the winner carry his equipment.

From time to time one of the fellows would report to him about girls that were crazy about him. When he took up his position as full-back at a game, he always noticed a fair sprinkling of girls behind the goal. And when he made a good clearance, the cheers that rose highest were the high, hysterical screams of girls. He took the adulation in his stride, and ignored them. It made no difference to him if all the girls in the parish wanted to go out with him. He remained distant and aloof from all that sort of thing. Football was all that mattered to him, now.

He heard rumours that the girls said he had a swelled head. And he began to develop a bit of temperament. For one important match, against Kilrush, he let the committee know that he wanted to play centre half-back instead of full-back. The centre half needed to be faster than Michael Joe was, whose main asset was his strength and the long clearance he could give a ball. When the positions were announced, Michael Joe saw he was to play his regular position. He developed a sudden sprain in an ankle. Could he play? Ah, Jazus, he must. Sure they couldn't win without him. He'd be a great loss. Seamus Larkin knew there was nothing wrong with him. And told him to his face. 'Michael Joe,' he said, 'you only want us to beg you to play.' Michael Joe answered surlily that he had a sprained ankle.

However, he togged out for the match, and stood on the sidelines watching. When he saw the team was going to carry on without him, be began to run up and down the sidelines, exercising the ankle. Then he told Paddy Hassett, the trainer, that he thought he could play. He got a round of applause when he came on, limping slightly. The Corrigbeg team was beaten in the game, and there were some dark rumours that Michael Joe was to blame because he was playing too much to the gallery, and showing off with the ball instead of making quick clearances.

The defeat did not damage his image among the crowd. To them, he had played a star game, though his team had gone down in defeat. Seamus Larkin criticized him afterwards for not getting rid of the ball fast enough.

'Since when are you telling me what to do or what not to do?' Michael Joe said. Larkin walked away. A couple of fellows around thought there was going to be a fight. There was enough tension in the air, because of the loss, to start one.

At a few matches, Michael Joe saw Nell Cullen. Once, he passed by her when he was in his togs and jersey, the amber and gold stripes of Corrigbeg. Nell was with a group of girls, and they happened to glance at each other. Nell opened her mouth as if to say something. Michael Joe broke into a trot and went on by without saying anything. He played one of the roughest matches he ever played that day, and knocked out the full forward, a quiet thin lad who was quick and alert and a lot faster on the ball than Michael Joe and who wouldn't match strength with Michael Joe because he was cleverer than that and knew better. He made Michael Joe mad with his foxiness. Half deliberately and half unconsciously, Michael Joe gave him a knee in the groin as they went up for a ball together. The lad had to be carried off the field. Michael Joe felt sorry and claimed he hadn't kneed him deliberately. The referee gave a foul and a goal was scored. Michael Joe raged for the rest of the match. He knew the other team was out to injure him. He got kicked a few times, but he was so mad he did not feel any pain.

Michael Joe noticed that Larkin no longer palled around with him as much as he used to. He didn't stick around to go drinking or to a dance after the matches. He disappeared. Though they were playing football together, they hardly ever spoke to each other any more. Michael Joe wasn't worried. He had plenty of friends besides Larkin. And that was true. He had no particular friends, but there was always a group of fellows around him telling him about the great game he had played, and recounting the glorious moments of the match in which Michael Joe had figures as the hero, the star of the game. Michael Joe took the praise as his due. Larkin never came around and said anything. He must be jealous.

Early in May, Michael Joe learned another reason why Seamus Larkin had grown cool towards him. Michael Joe and his mother were at last Mass together. On the way out of the chapel he stopped to talk to a friend, who told him that he had heard for a fact that Nell Cullen and Seamus Larkin were engaged. Michael Joe left the friend abruptly, and caught up with his mother. He was silent for a while as they walked along.

'I just heard that Nell Cullen was engaged to Seamus Larkin,' he said casually to her.

'Are they, indeed?' his mother said. 'She has her man now, however she trapped him. But good luck to her, just the same.'

'Larkin isn't a bad match for her at all,' Michael Joe said. 'She could do worse. He'll have the National Bank behind him always.'

'But, sure she hasn't a penny. I wonder the bank manager didn't stop it.'

'Maybe he tried and wasn't able,' Michael Joe said.

'I hope for the best, for her sake. Sure she had a lot of trouble, the poor thing. And I wouldn't be the one to wish her any more,' Mrs. McCarthy said.

'I wonder how she did it?' Michael Joe said to himself.

The two of them walked down the middle of the Chapel Road, Mrs. McCarthy dressed completely in black, and Michael Joe looking handsome and virile in his sports jacket and cap. The crowd coming from Mass went by them; Mrs. McCarthy was a slow walker now, and Michael Joe had adapted his pace to hers. Nobody greeted them, not with any intention of slighting them, but they looked so private and apart, that a greeting might seem a rude intrusion into the privacy of mother and son, though they were in public. The people who passed by did not make a wide circle around them in passing, but they were definitely skirting them, so as to leave them by themselves in the middle of the moving crowd. Mrs. McCarthy would occasionally glance around at the crowd passing, but quickly withdraw her glance and stare straight ahead ignoring them, as if she would not be caught being guilty of curiosity. She did not take her son's arm, or look at him either. Michael Joe was as cautious as his mother about looking at the crowd. He took quick glances more often than she did, but returned to his aloofness.

After Mass, he opened the shop and waited for whatever customers would come in. A few young fellows came in to talk. They were shy in the presence of the hero, and spoke diffidently, and always for his approval. Michael Joe was reserved. The talk was mostly about football, past greats of the game. When the arguments got fierce, Michael Joe stepped in and resolved them with a quick judgment which the fellows were inclined to accept, and never directly contradicted.

Somehow, the talk got around to Larkin. A few disparaging remarks were made about his ability as a centre forward. Missed chances in every match. Michael Joe stayed aloof from that tack.

He got the point. They were letting him know they were on his side, in case there was any trouble ahead. After all, they knew that Nell Cullen had been his girl. Larkin was an interloper. A Dublin jackeen who was in Corrigbeg only because he was working at the bank. He wasn't one of their own. Michael Joe was. Bred, born and reared in Corrigbeg. No boyo coming in from outside could steal their girls. All this was implied in the talk about Larkin. Michael Joe did not take part in it, at all. They didn't expect him to. But as long as he did not tell them to shut up, they felt they were on safe ground, and expressing sentiments that he was in agreement with.

Since Michael Joe gave them no sign to stop the talk, they even went so far as to hint a few things about Nell. At this point, Michael Joe said: 'Enough is enough, there.' And went off to serve a customer who had come in.

That afternoon, the team was not playing a game, so they met at the football field for practice. A friendly match was picked. While the players were loitering around waiting for the match to begin, Michael Joe walked up to Larkin, who had been avoiding him, and congratulated him.

'The best of luck, there, Seamus,' he said extending his hand magnanimously. 'You're getting a grand girl, I can tell you.'

Larkin gave him a quick handshake. 'Thanks, Michael Joe,' he said. 'I know that well.'

Some members of the team were watching the little byplay. Michael Joe tried to give Larkin a playful shoulder.

'You're a better man than I am, Gunga Din,' Michael Joe said, laughing.

Larkin was built physically on the light side, and easily side-stepped Michael Joe's clumsy attempt.

'I hope we'll be friends, anyhow,' Larkin said.

Michael Joe straightened up a bit embarrassed after he had missed the shoulder. 'There's nothing on my part,' Michael Joe said. 'The past is the past. And 'tis all over as far as I'm concerned.'

And he meant that; he would be a good sport, take his medicine. After all, Nell Cullen was nothing to him any more. And Larkin and he used to be friends, and Michael Joe would want him as a friend still, in spite of the fact that he was going to marry Nell. But Larkin was afraid of him. Wasn't that a peculiar idea? Michael Joe wouldn't harm him. The poor bastard. Did he know what he was getting? A piece of damaged goods. The poor bastard Larkin.

Michael Joe was sorry for him. Felt paternal. Maybe he ought to caution Larkin. Warn him about what he was getting into. He'd think about it.

They played a friendly practice match that afternoon, and Michael Joe found himself taking the friendly match seriously. Once, Larkin appeared in front of him, hopping the ball, driving in for a score. Michael Joe instantly drove blindly at him. Larkin danced, sidestepped around Michael Joe charging, and went in to score.

Paddy Hassett, the trainer, came up to Michael Joe.

'Play the ball, McCarthy, and not the man.'

Michael Joe was insulted. 'I wasn't playing the man,' he retorted.

'We have eyes, we have eyes,' Hassett said.

Michael Joe walked away. To think of it. Why would he want to injure Seamus Larkin. Sure, poor Larkin himself was harmless as a fly. Michael Joe could fight him with one hand tied behind his back, if he wanted to. Michael Joe could eat him, if he wanted to. But he didn't.

To prove it, he invited Larkin to have a couple of drinks with him after the match. But Larkin refused. He had work to do at the bank that night, and the drink would only muddle his head for the figures.

Michael Joe felt rebuffed. But that couldn't be. What did Larkin have against him? Michael Joe had no further interest in Nell. Larkin must know that. Why was he avoiding him, then?

The following week, Michael Joe made several attempts to get Larkin to have a few drinks with him. But Larkin always had an excuse. Michael Joe saw the light. A poor sport. A damn poor sport. If anyone should hold a grudge, it should be Michael Joe. After all, in the eyes of Corrigbeg, Michael Joe had lost Nell Cullen to Seamus Larkin. Little did they know who was the loser. But Michael Joe would be generous. He could afford to be. Look at what poor Larkin was getting. He had no grudge against either Larkin or Nell. He was beyond that now. Glad he had escaped.

He waited for a chance to show them that he had only feelings of friendship towards them. He heard that Larkin was going to be transferred out of Corrigbeg because he was marrying a local girl. A Bank of Ireland regulation. That was Michael Joe's opportunity to show his good intentions. He set about organizing a petition to be signed by all members of the Corrigbeg Gaelic Football Club, to have Larkin stay in Corrigbeg after his marriage. That would show the town that Michael Joe harboured no grudge. They would see his generosity. A man wouldn't want people he held a grudge against living next door to him for the rest of his life.

He buttonholed Tom Fitzgerald, the schoolmaster, on his way down from school, and brought him into the room at the back of the shop, and put the proposition to him. Fitzgerald could write up the petition. Michael Joe had the ink and pen and paper all ready. Fitzgerald pointed out that a meeting of the club would have to be called to make the whole thing official. A petition from Michael Joe alone would be no good. He could present the petition in the form of a motion at the committee meeting and then a vote could be taken on it. Michael Joe thought that that would be the slow way of doing it. But if that was the way it should be done, he would go along, though he thought they should call a meeting right away. Fitzgerald was the secretary, and promised to have a meeting by the end of the week.

Michael Joe spent the rest of the week drumming up support among the members of the football club for the petition. Over at Kerney's, the fellows were interested but not half as enthusiastic as Michael Joe thought they should be. Larkin wasn't that much of a hero that they should go to that much trouble. He was a good footballer, sure enough, but there were those just as good.

'He's the fastest man on the team,' Michael Joe argued. 'And can drive a ball between the uprights from any angle inside the twenty.'

The fellows argued with Michael Joe that Larkin never marked his man. They admitted though that he was a brainy player. Michael Joe argued with them for not responding with his own enthusiasm, and seeing the great loss. 'Ye wouldn't know a good football player if it was Mick Callaghan himself,' Michael Joe said, naming a great star of the last decade. 'Ye're all blind as bats.'

'We thought you'd be the other way around about Larkin,' Dan Kerney said as he sowed away from his perch above in the bench.

Michael Joe stopped his blustering. The fellows eyed him waiting for his answer.

'Nell Cullen and myself were only friends,' he said. 'There was never anything serious between us.'

'That wasn't the way I heard it,' Dan Kerney perused him from his perch looking down at him from over his rimless spectacles.

'Would I be behaving this way if I was mad at Larkin for stealing her? She never meant anything to me, only another piece of skirt to go round with.'

Michael Joe left.

This gave him a view into the way the town was seeing the whole affair. They suspected his intentions were not good. They were suspicious of his sudden affection for Larkin and Nell. He'd show everyone they were wrong. He wasn't interested in Nell any more. He didn't care who she married.

One evening, after a practice match, he buttonholed Larkin. He whispered that he wanted to talk to him. He had something important to tell him. Would he stop behind and walk in from the football field with him. Larkin hesitated. He was ill at ease with Michael Joe's large hand placed in a friendly way on his shoulder.

'All right, Michael Joe,' he said. 'But I can't stop long with you.'

They walked in together, Michael Joe followed by a young boy who was carrying his football shoes and togs.

'I want yourself and Nell to know I wish you only the best,' Michael Joe began.

'Sure I know that, Michael Joe,' Larkin said. 'Let the past be past.'

'I have a lot of experience myself of the women. You know that. And let me give you a bit of advice from the horse's mouth . . . you're getting a grand girl . . . one of the finest. There's a lot of them that aren't. All they want is to get a man to kneel and crawl to them. Then when he's down, they kick him. But Nell isn't one of those, though.' He was making his supreme effort at generosity and forgiveness.

'I know she's the best,' Larkin said. And began to walk faster. He did not want to talk to Michael Joe about Nell.

'You don't know much about women, yourself?' Michael Joe said.

'I'm no innocent.'

'Well, 'tis better not to know too much. They're not all Holy Marys. No shame in them. None of the higher things. Always faking that. When they're in heat, like the bitches, they'll let any mongrel rise on them that comes along.'

Larkin began to sweat. They were nearing the Central Hotel where he stayed. He was dimly aware of what Michael Joe was trying to do to him.

'You're wrong, Michael Joe. They're the true spirit of the world,' Larkin said fiercely. He hurried on ahead of Michael Joe, and entered the hotel door.

Well, Michael Joe thought, Nell had him well trained already. He was a woman's man, God help the poor so and so. Nell had picked herself the right one.

Michael Joe then dropped up to Blake's for a drink, though he knew he shouldn't because he was in training; but he couldn't sit still at home, or listen to the wireless or read the paper. It was a week night. The pub was quiet. He sat in the kitchen drinking a pint. Nanno Blake was sitting in an armchair putting a patch in some trousers. She inquired after his mother. And then went on reminiscing about the old days, and the Troubles. Michael Joe listened with half an ear. He was restless even here.

By and by, Kitty Falane came in with Ann Shanahan, the girl Michael Joe had danced with on Christmas Eve. Michael Joe got a pang of guilty conscience on seeing her again, and remembered vividly how he had tried to make a fool of her dancing that night, and ended up making a fool of himself. He said 'hello' to her, and she answered him shyly, as if she too had remembered.

'Are you in from the country?' Michael Joe said, putting talk on her.

She answered reluctantly, as if she was afraid to talk to him. 'For a while,' she said.

'Who's milking the cows at home?' Michael Joe said under the impulse to make quiet fun of her.

'Ah, wisha, leave the girl alone,' Nanno Blake said. 'You smart alecky townies think you know it all.'

Michael Joe laughed. Ann laughed nervously, too.

'I have a couple of brothers that take care of the milking,' she said seriously.

'Will you be stopping long with us?' Michael Joe said.

Ann looked at Kitty Falane, her cousin.

'She can't stop away from the town,' Kitty said.

'There isn't much excitement for a good-looking girl out there in the wilds of Cloon,' Michael Joe said to Ann.

Ann hung her head and blushed, as if her preference for living in the town over the country where she was born and grew up, was something to be guilty of.

'We'll be seeing a lot of you, then, I suppose?' Michael Joe went on.

'Don't listen to that rascal,' Nanno Blake said to Ann. 'He'll only be putting notions in your head.'

'And what of it?' Michael Joe said. 'She's able to have notions as good as the next one.'

Ann's face and features were small and pinched, as if they had been arrested in their full development; they still retained the contours and half-grown shape of a child's face. She looked quickly at anyone who spoke to her, as if she was surprised, or expected a blow instead of a greeting from them.

Michael Joe could not resist poking fun at her. But he found her strangely attractive tonight. She obviously wasn't good-looking. But being with her aroused him sexually, as he had not felt aroused for a long time. He couldn't deny his own blood. So he pursued his interest.

'Do you come in often?' he asked.

'I bicycle in every Sunday,' she said looking at him, and wondering at him, and his interest in her, because he was a handsome man, a good match, and lived in the town, and 'twas gossiped could have any girl he wanted to just for the asking. And what would he be doing interested in a girl like herself?

'And you're stopping up with Kitty there, tonight?' he said bluntly.

'Yes,' she said.

Michael Joe let the talk drop for a while. He tried to think of a way to get rid of Kitty Falane so he could walk Ann Shanahan home by herself. Finally the girls got up to go, and he rose himself.

'I'll walk a bit of the way with ye,' he said.

'No one invited you,' Kitty Falane laughed.

'I won't take a bite out of either of ye,' Michael Joe said, going out with them.

They walked up the Ennistymon Road, Ann taking the inside, keeping Kitty between herself and Michael Joe. The night was bright and cool. Michael Joe persuaded them to come for a walk with him up as far as the White Strand. He talked mainly to Kitty Falane on the way up, teasing her about Tom Healy, the doctor's son; she had been courting with him off and on for many years. It was one of the great local romances. No one knew how it started. No one knew how long it would go on. Tom Healy was wild. Kitty was patient. He had money. She had nothing. She wasn't good enough for his family. Nothing would come of it. Or would they marry? The gossips talked.

Kitty knew that Michael Joe wanted to be alone with Ann, and when they got to the White Strand she left them to go for a walk along the strand.

'I'll go too with you,' Ann said.

'You'd only get your shoes wet,' Kitty said. 'And what would your mother say to me if you caught a cold. Stop here with Michael Joe and he'll take care of you. I won't be long.'

'Don't be in a hurry back,' Michael Joe said.

When he and Ann were alone, he suggested they take a walk by the path running up to their left. The night was bright enough to see. Ann looked quickly around her. There was no escape for her but to go along with him. The soft shishing of the waves breaking on the strand below broke the quietness of the night.

They walked in silence, Michael Joe waiting for the right moment. Ann stumbled. He caught her, and backed her against the sod wall.

'No, no,' she said trembling.

Michael Joe tried to kiss her. She hung her head, and kept it down.

'No, no. Don't,' she kept saying. ' 'Tis a sin.'

'A sin!' Michael Joe said. 'What's a sin, in the name of God? A kiss won't hurt you.'

'I'd have to tell it in Confession,' she said. 'No.'

Michael Joe had to use brute force to get his kiss. He tried to slide his tongue into her mouth, but her lips were shut tightly, and she was rigid against him. He released her with a laugh.

'Can't you see 'twon't harm you?' he said. 'I'm not going to take a bite off you.'

She was silent, and kept her head bent.

'Well, come on then,' he said.

They walked on up the path. Michael Joe tried to kiss her again. But with the same result. He was boiling with excitement himself, and pressed himself hard against her. He felt her trembling, but she resisted him with a helpless doggedness. He kissed her in the neck, behind the ear, and squeezed her tightly against him, but she wouldn't let him touch her lips. He tried to make her caress him where he liked, but she kept pulling her hand away.

'You're only bashful,' he said finally. 'You'll be all right when you get rid of that. You don't have to be shy with me.'

'What'll I do, at all?' she said. 'I'll have to tell it in Confession.'

'Tell what? You did nothing,' Michael Joe said, feeling the pain beginning between his thighs.

'I want to go home,' Ann said.

'You're a peculiar one. But . . . you're the boss,' Michael Joe said.

They went back down the path, Ann scrambling ahead of Michael Joe, stumbling over the rutted path in her eagerness to get back to the strand.

Michael Joe spoke only to Kitty Falane on the way home. He found her more of a match for him, and tried to size her up to see if he could make out with her. He had taken the wrong girl walking along the path.

'You're not a bad piece of skirt, yourself,' he said to Kitty. 'You'd give me a run for my money, I suppose.'

'I pity the girl that gets a man like you,' Kitty said.

Michael Joe was satisfied with himself when he went in home. Though he hadn't got very far with Ann Shanahan, still she was the first girl since he had broken up with Nell. And he was proud of himself that he still had the old interest. After breaking up with Nell, he often had the feeling that he would never be interested in another woman. And all desire for them had left him. Though Ann Shanahan wasn't much, still she must have something to bring his interest back. He was under no illusion that he was in love with Ann, or could ever be. She was a bit too quiet for him. She had no go. And he liked girls with some go in them, he thought.

14

THOUGH MICHAEL JOE suspected that Larkin did not want to stay in Corrigbeg after his marriage, he went ahead organizing support for the petition to the bank manager which would let him stay. He said nothing about the petition to Larkin who, he thought, wouldn't know what was good for him anyway. A meeting of the Corrigbeg

Gaelic Football Club was called on a Friday night. Michael Joe bullied Tom Fitzgerald, the schoolmaster, into calling it. The meeting would be held to vote on the petition, and to authorize presenting it to the bank manager. He would know that there was Corrigbeg sentiment behind it if it came from the club. Tom Fitzgerald tried to dissuade Michael Joe from going on with the petition.

The laws of the National Bank of Ireland weren't going to be changed for Corrigbeg. It might be a good thing if Nell and Seamus Larkin left, taking everything into consideration. Tom Fitzgerald was circumspect.

'Taking what into consideration?' Michael Joe said.

'Yerra, you yourself knew well what the town says about Nell Cullen,' Tom Fitzgerald said.

'About the child,' Michael Joe said. 'Maybe this will be a lesson to them not to be small-minded. What matter is it to them? They ought to learn to be more generous. 'Twasn't the worst crime in the word she was guilty of.'

'Now, I don't pay any mind on the gossip myself,' Tom Fitzgerald said. 'But look at it from Nell's point of view.'

'She can face the town,' Michael Joe said. 'She isn't the sort to want to run away, anyway. She has great pluck. The courage of ten men.'

'Well,' Tom Fitzgerald said, 'and what do you propose to say in the petition.'

Michael Joe was so far gone in his hypocrisy that he did not know whether he meant what he said about Nell or not. He dictated the petition to Fitzgerald while he took it down. It was eloquent with praise for Larkin. How well liked he was. Would be missed in football circles, in particular, by a host of friends. A popular young man in every sphere of Corrigbeg life. Had, in addition to his talent as a footballer, played a prominent part in local theatrical productions, winning acclaim as an actor. His transfer would be an irreparable loss to the parish.

'I never knew you had that much in you,' Tom Fitzgerald said. 'You should be correspondent for the *Clare Champion*.'

'Larkin deserves it. He's a brave man,' Michael Joe said.

He presented the petition at the committee meeting in the Parochial Hall. The meeting was well attended, though not crowded. Michael Joe was disappointed that there wasn't a bigger turnout. He was called on by Tom Fitzgerald to read the petition, and he did in a strong, firm and sincere voice.

Then a vote was called for. Larkin stood up at the back of the room and requested the chairman if he could say a few words.

He was hesitant and nervous, and kept putting his hands in his pockets, and pitched his voice too high. He was trying to express his gratitude.

'Ladies and gentlemen,' he began though there were no ladies present. 'I want to extend my gratitude . . . my heartfelt gratitude. I don't want the petition to go to a vote. Accept my humble apologies. I haven't done anything to deserve this gesture. And my humblest thanks to Mr. McCarthy for making the proposal. Plans have already been made for my transfer to Silvermines in Tipperary.' He sat down abruptly.

There was silence for a few moments.

'That closes the matter. Any other business?' Canon Lyons said.

There was no more business. The meeting was dismissed.

Michael Joe buttonholed Larkin on the way out of the meeting.

'You saw the support you had,' Michael Joe said. 'The whole parish wants you to stay. Are you blind?'

'We're going, Michael Joe,' Larkin said, 'after the wedding.'

'And Nell wants to go? Are you sure of that?'

'She says she does.'

'Ah, sure a woman never knows her right mind,' Michael Joe said.

'Whatever she says I believe,' Larkin said.

Michael Joe stopped and looked at him. He wanted to call him a fool, a big amaudaun. But he checked himself. He wondered how Nell would ever want to marry a man like Larkin. It was a great comedown for her. But, he supposed, beggars couldn't be choosers. If she couldn't have himself, she wanted a man at any cost.

He invited Larkin down to Blake's for a drink. Larkin made an excuse, and left him, walking up the Chapel Road in the direction of Nell's house. Well, Michael Joe supposed, Nell had him well under her thumb. She had captured him, and she'd cage him. Like a good little boy, he was going out to her with the news that the petition had been dismissed, and Michael Joe McCarthy put down.

Only then did Michael Joe see the idiot he had made of himself. He had blundered along in all good faith. Wanting to be generous.

Nell and Larkin were two foxes, out to trick him with their cleverness. Wouldn't accept his generosity. Behind Larkin there was Nell, moving and manipulating him. Somehow, before the pair of them left Corrigbeg Michael Joe would have his revenge.

He went down to Blake's and began drinking. Kitty Falane and Ann Shanahan came in. He manoeuvred so that he was able to get Ann for a walk, alone, she, half willing because Michael Joe was persuasive, and not willing because she was afraid of his persuasion. He was just as brutal with her as he was the night before. She protested; he ignored her protests; but she did not submit. Tears and trembling stopped him. He felt sorry for her.

Ann Shanahan slept in the same bed with her first cousin Kitty Falane when she came into Corrigbeg for a visit from the country. Coming back after the walk with Michael Joe, she was worried about being out so late and that the door might be locked. They went to bed early in the country. Her father bolted the door of their cottage every night at half-past ten, and turned the men out then if anyone had dropped in for a talk. Tadg and Mary, Kitty's mother and father, were still up, Tadg reading the newspaper and Mary darning, when Ann got back and let herself in.

'I'm sorry to be out so late,' she said to Tadg Falane.

He raised his head from the paper. 'Wisha, girl,' he said, 'that's nothing to be sorry for. You come and goes as you like in this house.'

'Is Kitty out?'

'No. If she had your excuse to be out, she would be though, you can be sure.'

Ann blushed.

'Leave the girl be,' Mary Falane said to her husband.

Ann went upstairs. The bedroom was in darkness. She turned on the light, and Kitty woke, and sat up and stared at Ann. Ann undressed herself in silence.

'Aren't you going to say anything for yourself after being out with the best match in Corrigbeg?' Kitty said.

Ann was in her slip and ran across the room, and dived under the clothes and hid her head in the pillow.

'Whoa, there,' Kitty said. 'Did he do something to you?'

Ann did not answer, but kept her head buried in the pillow, gripping it with both hands.

Kitty pulled her by the shoulders. 'What did he do to you?' she said with a restrained excitement.

'He tried to kiss me,' Ann said. 'And something else.'

Kitty laughed. 'That's all. He did *nothing* to you. Nothing! Only tried. I think 'tis he has the right to cry,' Kitty said.

' 'Tis a sin,' Ann said.

'There's more committing it than not,' Kitty said.

' 'Tis awful,' Ann said throwing herself back against the pillow.

'You don't like it? Well, if you want to catch a man like Michael Joe McCarthy, you'll have to put up with a lot.'

'Is he nice?' Ann said.

'If you don't know, I can't tell you,' Kitty said.

'Is that the way they are?'

'Is that the way what are? Men?'

Ann stared at Kitty wide-eyed. Kitty was smiling at her.

'Michael Joe McCarthy is the best catch in the town of Corrigbeg. Outside my own fellow. And I'll never get *him*. But, sure, what the matter? That's a different story from your case. Michael Joe has a good business. You'd have a house in the town. You don't want to live out in the country all your life, do you? Stuck out there.'

'No,' Ann said.

'Well, there's your passport to freedom,' Kitty said. 'His ould mother won't live long more. You'd have that house all to yourself. If you have to put up with a few things into the bargain. You can't have butter on both sides of your bread.'

Ann sighed. 'He's very good looking, isn't he? There must be a lot of girls after him?'

'You have a chance as good as the rest of them.'

'Ah, no I don't,' Ann said. 'What would he see in the likes of me?'

'He must have seen something in you or he wouldn't go to the trouble of manoeuvring you into a walk by yourself tonight.'

Ann touched her hair. 'I'm not beautiful, am I?'

'You'll pass muster,' Kitty said. 'You can never tell what men see in us. Would you like to marry him?'

'No,' Ann said throwing herself back on the pillow. 'I don't know. I might. If it wasn't for . . .'

'Botheration to that,' Kitty said. 'You'll get to like it after a while, maybe.'

'I'll say my prayers,' Ann said. 'And ask God for guidance.'

She turned her back to Kitty and joined her hands before her small breasts, and her lips began to move in prayer.

Kitty got up and put out the light.

15

MRS. McCARTHY HEARD through her gossips of Michael Joe's attempt to keep Seamus Larkin in Corrigbeg after his marriage to Nell Cullen. She managed to control herself in front of the gossips, who put the matter to her as if to show how generous-hearted her son was in the light of everything. No one in the town knew for certain whether it was Michael Joe who jilted Nell Cullen, or Nell who jilted him. But they suspected that Michael Joe had done the job. Wasn't it he that had the big heart now, that took pains for her to stay, when another man might want her out of his sight altogether?

Mrs. McCarthy was of this latter mind. Nell Cullen had come too close for comfort to making Michael Joe marry her, she thought. And the farther away she took herself now, the better Mrs. McCarthy would have liked it. And that poor unfortunate boy who was marrying her. She wished she could do something for him. His own mother would do it if she was there. But Mrs. McCarthy was sensible enough to know that she should keep her nose out of the whole business now, once she had her own point won. But she couldn't resist reminding Michael Joe of his foolishness which she attributed to some small spark of the former flame that he was still carrying for Nell Cullen.

'I hear that that one of the Cullens is leaving after the marriage,' she said to Michael Joe one evening during supper. 'And good riddance to her.'

'Good God, Mother, haven't you any charity at all?' Michael Joe said. 'I don't want to hear any more about them.'

'Charity, is it?' she said. 'And you making a fool of yourself trying to show off your big heart.'

'I haven't anything against either of them,' Michael Joe said.

'Put her out of your mind, once and for all, for God's sake, before you make a worse fool of yourself than you have already,' Mrs. McCarthy said.

'I'm not making a fool of myself. I'm trying to be decent.'

'Make sure. Make sure. She's going to be another man's wife. She's better off out of Corrigbeg altogether, where you won't see her. I declare. Wanting them to live here. You must have lost your senses altogether.'

He stood up from the table and banged his fist down on it, making the silverware and dishes jump.

'I don't want to hear another word in this house about herself or Larkin,' he said. 'Not another word. Do you hear?'

'The poor fellow ought to be warned about her,' Mrs. McCarthy said.

'Shut up. Shut up,' he said. 'I never thought I'd hear such low-down talk.' He left.

Mrs. McCarthy realized she had gone too far with him. He had never shouted at her before. Though he had tantrums as a child, she had never seen his anger as a grown man. It frightened her. He would do anything if he was in a fit of anger, and she would have no power to stop him. His voice was like a blast of a storm sweeping straight at her. As if she were nothing. Nobody. Not his mother, even. *That* she had counted on his never forgetting. She saw that he could forget her. This was a shock. Here was a new force she had to contend with, a force beside which Nell Cullen was almost insignificant. She did not know what it was. Nell Cullen was a woman like herself, and could be brought to do certain things because of certain pressures she was subject to because she was a woman. Mrs. McCarthy thought she knew what made a girl like Nell Cullen tick. So she was an easy opponent for her.

But Michael Joe's anger was something intangible until it suddenly flashed out, threatening to destroy everything in its way. A temper. He has a temper, she kept saying to herself. That explained him. If he was crossed in anything, he would trample everything before him like a mad bull.

Her husband, Michael Joe's father, had been a mild-mannered man. She herself was not noted for her temper. Where did Michael Joe get it? As a child, he never seemed to have more than his normal share. Now, as a man. Ah, that was different. This was some force in him that was beyond her control. All she could do in the future was to try and not arouse it. But what brought on his temper, and what did not? It would be like living on the side of a volcano, for her. She had won him from Nell Cullen, and was in danger of losing him to God knows what devil inside himself. The temper. The temper.

Mrs. McCarthy began a novena to St. Joseph, the model saint for mild-mannered men, beseeching his intercession in Heaven for the cause of her son, Michael Joe, to give him self-control and divine grace to govern himself on all trying occasions. She prayed that her son would seek St. Joseph's guidance in all things, and choose him as a model of behaviour, who submitted his will to the Almighty God.

16

MICHAEL JOE RAGED quietly now in his double disgrace. Nell had betrayed him. That was the worst. A private disgrace, man to woman; she had blinded him, and almost brought worse things on him. He would never forgive her that. The privateness of their war made the outcome more bitter. He would never forgive her. The other disgrace, the public one, when she and Larkin undermined the petition by simply refusing to have it sent to the bank manager, rankled but did not hurt as much as the other. Michael Joe had only been trying to show his generosity and open-mindedness by organizing the petition.

He blamed Nell, not Larkin, for refusing the petition. She was behind Larkin, and had put him up to it. Michael Joe supposed that she had also warned Larkin to steer clear of himself, and that was why Larkin had been avoiding him. And of course, being a good little boy, he had obeyed her. Nell had good reason for wanting to leave Corrigbeg. Maybe that was why she was marrying Larkin. He was her release from the prison of the town. *That*. And the money. Larkin was a bank clerk. Someday he would be a bank manager. Nell would be mistress of a bank. That would suit her. She would be able to shut up all talk about her, then. She would buy her way out of her disgrace with Larkin.

Michael Joe thought the worst he could think about her. She had fallen to a new low, for him. Marrying for the lowest of reasons —money. Poor Larkin! Michael Joe wondered if he knew what he was getting into. Blinded by Nell's beauty he probably didn't. Controlled by her devious mind she was making a monkey out of him.

Michael Joe began to feel that he would have to protect Larkin from her witchery, in some way. He saw the cause of Larkin's protection as a male cause. In the war against women, men had to stand shoulder to shoulder. Larkin, poor man, had to be protected from Nell because he couldn't protect himself. That much was clear to Michael Joe. But how to go about it? He still had a trump card to play if he wanted to. Larkin didn't know about Nell's past. How could he? She surely didn't tell him. She wanted him as blind as she wanted Michael Joe. But Michael Joe was her match. Larkin wasn't. Michael Joe saw that clearly.

He reasoned that since no one would protect Larkin from Nell, as Michael Joe himself had been protected, he'd have to take the responsibility on himself.

One night, soon after the presenting of the petition, Michael Joe went down to the Central Hotel where Larkin was staying and asked the maid if he was in. The maid said he was above in his room. Michael Joe paused. He would have preferred to say what he had to say over a quiet drink in the bar. But then, the nature of his message to Larkin might demand more privacy. He got the number of Larkin's room from the maid.

'I'll go on up,' he said, giving her a wink. He pinched her as he went by. She gave a little 'ouch!' Michael Joe laughed heartily.

He knocked at Larkin's door, and Larkin's high tenor called: 'Come in.'

Michael Joe entered. Larkin was sitting at a desk with a book open before him. A table lamp gave the only light to the room. Larkin looked at Michael Joe filling the door. For a moment, his jaws tightened, and the nervous, thin, long-fingered hands stroked the pages of the book he had been reading.

'I thought I'd drop up and see you for a minute. I didn't have time to talk to you the other night after the petition,' Michael Joe said swaggering in. He clapped Larkin on the back. 'You can't say but I did my best for you.'

'There was no need to go to the trouble, Michael Joe. The regulations are there. Unalterable.'

The only chair in the room was the one Larkin was sitting in. Michael Joe plunked himself down on the bed.

'What's that you're reading? A book?'

'Yes,' Larkin said. He pulled at his long, straight nose. '*Dubliners*. By an Irishman. James Joyce.'

'Who?'

'He was a Dubliner,' Larkin said. 'He's well known.'

'Ah, well,' Michael Joe said. 'We wouldn't have heard much about him this far down in the country.' He shifted in the bed, and looked around the dark room. 'I wouldn't care to be cooped up here for too long,' Michael Joe said.

'When you're in my line of business you can't afford a palace,' Larkin said. Then he stopped, letting the silence indicate to Michael Joe that he should state his business.

'Men have to stick together,' Michael Joe said abruptly as if the silence bothered him. 'Through thick and thin. And sometimes when one man sees another going downhill, he has to try and stop him.'

Larkin's pale brow creased. He had an arm draped over the back of his chair, and was half-turned to Michael Joe, and half-turned to his book.

'I came to warn you,' Michael Joe sighed. 'You're in grave danger.'

'Am I?' Larkin said, giving him no help.

'Can't you see it, man?' Michael Joe said, jumping off the bed and coming into the arc of light. Larkin tensed. 'Can't you see it staring you straight in the face? Or has she you that blinded altogether?'

'I'm not blind,' Larkin said.

'She's done it to you, too,' Michael Joe said. 'You can see nothing. There's a war on between men and women. You and I are soldiers fighting. As one soldier to another—you're being stabbed in the back.'

A muscle in Larkin's jaw began to work. That was his only indication of tension. He kept his lips closed tightly.

'You don't know what I'm talking about. You haven't the

faintest clue. Ah, God help you.' He paused. 'Nell had a child by a fellow in England,' he said quietly.

Larkin remained sitting. He gazed down at his hands lying on his thighs, and then spoke in a calm even voice.

'I know that,' he said.

'You know it! You know it! And you're letting yourself be led on. Like a heifer to the slaughterhouse.'

'I wouldn't put it that way.' Larkin got up. 'Look,' he said. 'If that was why you came here, I don't want any of your filthy tales.'

'Call off the engagement, man, before she makes an absolute disgrace of you.'

Larkin looked at him levelly. 'You're mad,' he said. 'You ought to see a doctor.'

'You're going to marry her?'

'Of course I am,' Larkin said, trying to keep himself under control. He was afraid if he lost his temper that anything might happen. In the close room, Michael Joe could kill him in a fight, at such close quarters. And he had that fear that men have when they are in the presence of another man who is dangerous, dangerous enough to explode and kill.

'You're a bigger fool than I thought. You know what she's like. And you want to marry her.' He grabbed Larkin by the lapels of his jacket. 'Why, man, why?'

Slowly Larkin pried Michael Joe's hands off him, and Michael Joe gave way.

'If you don't know, I can't tell you.'

All the tension seemed to leave Michael Joe then, and he gained some measure of control over himself.

'I'm sorry for you,' he said walking out of the room.

One evening, a few days later, Tom Fitzgerald dropped in to Michael Joe's shop on his way home from school and solicited Michael Joe for a contribution for a wedding present the football club was getting up for Seamus Larkin and Nell Cullen.

'Whose idea was that?' Michael Joe said sarcastically.

'A couple of the lads. Larkin has served the football club well. Always played his best. We ought to show our appreciation.'

Michael Joe saw that his sarcasm had missed with Fitzgerald. Then he did a quick reversal.

'Why wasn't I in on it?' Michael Joe said.

'You will be if you contribute. We're going to give a dinner at the Central Hotel and make the presentation at it.'

Michael Joe went behind the counter and took a pound note from the till, and handed it to Tom Fitzgerald.

'God, you don't have to go that big,' Tom said, looking at it. 'No one gave this much.'

'G'wan,' Michael Joe said. 'Take it. Put me down as an anonymous donor.'

'Faith, I won't,' Tom said. 'I'll make sure they know where it came from. And they'll appreciate it all the more, I expect, coming from you.'

'Have ye decided on the present?'

'No. Nothing yet. Something for the house, I suppose.'

'A clock!' Michael Joe said. 'A mantelpiece clock. Something with musical chimes in it. Nell likes didoes like that.'

'We have to satisfy Larkin too,' Tom said. 'But the clock sounds fair enough. I'll convey your idea to the lads and ask what they think.'

After Tom Fitzgerald had left, Michael Joe sat behind the counter on a tall stool. Then he got up and went and stood in the doorway of his shop looking up and down the street. It was an early June evening. Boys were playing marbles on the pavement; young girls were skipping beyond them. There was no other sign of life on the street.

He watched the young boys and girls at their play, and remembered when he too used to bowl marbles. He was a champion at it as a young boy, and had a big tin of marbles he had won, buried somewhere out in the backyard. He had forgotten to dig them up one spring. The spring when marbles seemed no longer enjoyable to play. He remembered the cache now, as he watched the boys.

One of the little girls reminded him of Nell, and he admitted to himself, for a moment, the great sense of loss he would feel if Nell left. He thought now that their breakup had been hasty. They should have talked it out. Maybe what had happened to her had not happened the way he thought it did. But he knew it was useless to think that way. He couldn't alter the fact by imagining it any different from what it was.

And what if she had a child by another man. Here were children playing in the street. What was there wrong in having a child?

But the thought of another man fathering Nell's child filled him with uncontrollable jealousy.

'G'wan, get away from my shop. Play yeer marbles somewhere else,' he roared at the boys.

They eyed him in disbelief. He had always let them play in front of his shop door.

'G'wan. Ye'er stopping the customers from coming in.'

They picked up their marbles without saying a word. Then they ran, one of them calling back at Michael Joe: 'Bully! Bully!'

He went back into the shop and shouted at Vin Scanlon to get the lead out of his backside and do what he was paid for.

He couldn't accept tainted goods. That was the truth of the matter. He would have to face that. No matter how much he was still in love with Nell, he would never have married her, even if Larkin had not interfered. And why didn't Larkin feel as Michael Joe himself felt? Michael Joe would like to find out the answer to that. He would not be satisfied until he did. He couldn't imagine a man knowing about Nell and still wanting to marry her. That was too much too expect of any man who thought anything of himself. Larkin had no respect for himself? Marrying a woman with no respect for herself, either. God, were they all worms?

A few days later, Tom Fitzgerald came into the shop again, and told Michael Joe that they had decided on the clock, and it had already been bought down at Maurer's in Ennis.

'We'd like you to make the presentation at the dinner,' Tom said.

'Me!' Michael Joe said. 'Ah, no I can't. It wouldn't look right. I used to do a line with Nell Cullen. We were great once.'

'I thought you were all over that,' Tom said.

'I am. Indeed, I am,' Michael Joe said. ''Tis water over the dam. But maybe *she* mightn't be, can't you see?'

'Oh, that's all in your head. She hasn't had an easy time of it with all the rumours and gossip. This would be a good chance to show her we think well of her. And what better man than yourself? An old flame! All is forgiven between ye. And they'll be no sour feelings.'

The peculiarity of the situation he would be in suddenly appealed to Michael Joe. He saw himself presenting the clock to Nell and Larkin. He'd even wind it up and let the chimes ring. It would be a gay and sentimental occasion. Bitterness, and hate, and jealousy would disappear. He wouldn't mind any more that she was marrying Larkin. She would see at last that he was willing to forgive and forget, and she would know that he was calling on her to do the same. He did not consider what he had to forgive her for. But the chance to see her again, especially in this kind of situation, of celebration and congratulation; and he himself in the role of presenter of the gift—a token of their reconciliation, and he, the Grand Master, in the grand gesture of forgiveness, presenting the gift—this image pleased him immensely.

Seamus Larkin and Nell Cullen's wedding was to be held in mid-June in the Corrigbeg parish church, Canon Lyons to officiate. The dinner honouring them was held in the dining room of the Central Hotel, the Saturday night prior to the wedding. It was a 'by invitation only' dinner. Tom Fitzgerald, who was head of the dinner committee, went around and personally invited each guest. He had to know the exact number so that the food could be prepared. He dropped in on Michael Joe again to make the invitation official, and to give him the mantelpiece clock in its box, which Michael Joe would present at the dinner.

'Are you bringing anyone?' Tom asked him. 'Maybe your mother might like to come.' The suggestion was indirect but full of meaning.

Michael Joe considered. 'No. I don't think she'd be up to it. Are we to bring someone?'

'No. But 'tis a social occasion. And we don't want to have too many of the boys standing around by themselves gawking at one another not knowing what to say.'

'I'll bring my own girl, then,' Michael Joe said on the spur of the moment.

'Your own girl?' Fitzgerald said.

'Ann Shanahan. I don't know if you know her or not. But she'll come. Put me down for two.'

'They'll be about fifty altogether,' Fitzgerald said. 'We'll have a little money present over and above to give them beside the clock there. No one refused to come. You never know how popular a man is 'till he's leaving you.'

Michael Joe felt as if the whole town were in league against him. Pushing him into playing a role he had no real heart for playing. He would like to forget he had ever met Nell, or known Larkin or tried to be friends with him. But he was in the affair up to the hilt now, and couldn't back out. The whole town knew about Nell, and here they were turning out to honour her. And himself among them. The élite would be at the dinner. How could Larkin and Nell be so barefaced as to allow it to go on? A quiet affair might be all right. You'd think they would want to be married quietly in another town, and then go off quietly somewhere, without creating a fuss. Hadn't they any shame? And the people who were coming to the dinner. Didn't they know they were honouring a girl who had . . . well, who had a bastard child? Well, if *they* didn't care, he didn't. And he was willing to go along with them.

The inspiration to invite Ann Shanahan to come with him was a godsend. Everyone at the dinner would remember that Michael Joe had once done a line with Nell, himself. Ann would be his guarantee against their thinking he was carrying around a broken heart. Not a man like Michael Joe who had women falling all over themselves for him!

When Michael Joe's mother heard about the dinner, she took off on a harangue against the whole town.

'They're out of their senses. Don't they know what they're up to? A dinner for that slut.'

'I thought I said her name wasn't to be mentioned in this house,' Michael Joe said ominously. His mother shut up for a while but began again. This time he didn't stop her. They were sitting in the dining room, she darning a sock, and Michael Joe trying to read instead of going out.

'And you have to make the presentation. A conspiracy, that's what it is. A conspiracy to disgrace you. How can they dare? I wouldn't do it for them. I wouldn't do it,' she said.

'I'll have to show them I'm a good loser,' Michael Joe said ironically.

'A good loser? Sure 'twas you that jilted her. Don't they know that?'

'No, they don't,' he said. 'And I'll never tell them.'

'Well, I'll make sure 'tis known where I go,' she said.

'The less said the better,' Michael Joe said.

'I won't stand by and let them shame you.'

'No one is trying to shame me,' he said. 'You don't see the whole of it at all.'

His mother aggravated his sense of martyrdom, but he would

not let on to her. She talked on, and compared her son to Larkin, a 'little weasel' in comparison to Michael Joe. Sure a good puff of wind would blow him away. And the Cullen one was getting what she deserved. Michael Joe did not really want to listen to her, but he did. He was feeling sorry for himself in his new role of loser, victim and martyr. He could not escape the commotion that was being caused by the impending wedding. His mother's praise was solace to his smouldering pride. Though he listened to her, at the same time he was aware he was not completely the man she thought her son was. A hypocrite now, even to his mother. And she did not see. He had rejected Nell. But he had loved her, and had still some feeling left for her. He wasn't really sure that he had done the right thing by jilting her. Here was Larkin marrying her. Here was the town planning a dinner for herself and her intended, treating the marriage as if there was nothing peculiar about it at all. As if Nell were a bride to be, as pure as the driven snow. If he himself had become engaged to Nell, he wondered if the town would have acted the same way. And what would his mother say? It would have killed her. She never would have been able to live through it. The situation was too much to think about. It was better to go along and pretend everything was all right.

He did not tell his mother he was taking a girl to the dinner.

When he asked Ann if she would go to the dinner with him, she refused at first, and he had to persuade her. They were alone in Falanes' back room where Kitty had left them, after he had come up, dropped in casually, pretending he only wanted to sit and talk with Tadg Falane by the fire. But arrangements were quietly made to leave Ann and himself alone. He asked her if she'd come to the dinner.

'No,' she said, immediately, 'I don't think I'd like to.'

'They won't serve you up on the plates,' Michael Joe said. 'Are you afraid?'

' 'Twill be a grand affair. And no place for a girl like me.'

Michael Joe burst out laughing. 'You little oinseach. They'll be no one there but the football team. Fellows like ourselves.'

'Are you sure?'

'Of course, I'm sure.'

Ann sat across the hearth from him with her two hands joined tightly together in front of her on her lap. She never looked at

Michael Joe, not even when she spoke to him, but kept her eyes on the fire. She looked neat, and clean, her short, light-brown hair with each curl perfectly in place. She wore no make-up, except for a faint trace of lipstick. Her skin was a delicate white. She spoke hardly above a whisper, as if she were terrified at being alone in the room with Michael Joe. His voice and laughter boomed across to her. He laughed a lot when he was with her.

'*I'll* be beside you. And I'll hold your hand all the time if you like,' he said.

She looked up with a childlike smile on her face. 'Stop, now,' she said, 'I'm not a child entirely.'

'Well, come then.'

'You used to do a line with Nell Cullen, usen't you?' she said after a short silence.

' 'Twas nothing more than friendship, ever,' he said. 'So that's what's wrong with you. Jealousy. You have no call to be jealous. I wouldn't be going myself if she meant anything to me still.' Michael Joe never knew now when he was telling a lie or a truth. Certain things he wanted to believe so badly that he thought they were true when he said them on the spur of the moment.

'Will I have to dress up?' Ann said.

'Come in your shift for all I care,' he said.

Then he saw he had hurt her. 'Wear your best dress,' he added quickly. 'And show them you're the belle of the ball.'

'Will Kitty go? If Kitty goes I'll go.'

'You're one to beat the band,' he laughed. 'You won't trust me even in public without someone along for protection.'

She said nothing; just sat looking into the fire insisting on her point with her silence. Michael Joe talked himself out. 'If that's the way you want it, I'm agreeable. If Kitty'll go I'll have her, too. It won't look so bad for me to be seen there with two women in tow.'

Ann went out of the room in search of Kitty to ask her. She found her lying down upstairs.

'He asked me to go to the dinner with him,' Ann said showing the excitement in the presence of Kitty that she had inhibited before Michael Joe.

'And you accepted, of course,' Kitty said.

'No, I didn't. I said if you'd come I'd go too. I won't go without you,' she said, protesting sudden loyalty to Kitty.

'My fellow wouldn't go,' Kitty said. 'Too much trouble to dress up. He'd just as soon get drunk in his working clothes.'

'Kitty, you'll have to! You'll have to,' Ann said coming over and kneeling beside the bed, in a pleading attitude. When she was not lying in a bed, she was kneeling beside it, praying.

Kitty propped herself up on an elbow and gazed with a half cynical smile at Ann.

'You have him hooked? The dinner is important to you? That much!'

Ann buried her face in the quilt. 'Don't say it like that. I don't know. I'm afraid. If you come with me, maybe I'll know better. I like him,' she confessed.

'Well, if it helps you get a chance to capture him, I'll go,' Kitty said. 'Come on now. Don't let him see you're so glad. We'll go down and face the bull.'

Michael Joe pretended to be annoyed at having to take the two of them. 'One of ye is bad enough,' he said. A quick look of disappointment appeared on Ann's face. She did not see through his small irony. 'Take us as we are or you'll have none of us,' Kitty shot back at him.

Michael Joe laughed at her in a very challenging, masculine way. Ann was smiling politely.

The night of the dinner was a warm June night. Michael Joe spent a long time getting himself ready, stropping his razor to a fine edge and taking as close a shave until the dark complexion had taken on a faint lightness. His mother had a clean white shirt ironed for him, and grumbled when she gave it to him, that it was a waste of her work to be ironing a shirt for such an occasion. She grumbled again when he asked her for a white hanky to put in his breast pocket. He tried to arrange it himself, but was clumsy. She did it for him, and stood back to admire him after she had fixed it in a spearhead.

'You're a knockout, entirely,' she said in a rare flash of humour. 'The girls will faint when they see you.'

'Stop talking like that,' he said. She had shined his low, black shoes until they shone in the kitchen light.

He left without bidding her good-bye. She sighed after he was gone.

He felt a strange excitement running through him as he walked to Falanes' to pick up the two girls. He could not attribute it to either of the two girls he was going to pick up. Kitty Falane was beyond him, fatally in love with Tom Healy whose family would never let him marry Kitty, because she was beneath him. They both knew it. The love affair would drag on for years, and finally die. And Ann. He was not excited over her. She was a child. She made him feel paternal at times; he secretly took delight in mocking her.

He admitted to himself that it was the chance to see Nell again that so aroused him. He didn't try to fool himself, this time. He wondered what would happen when he saw her. They had not met since that Christmas Eve night he had walked away from her outside the chapel gates, except for glimpses at football matches.

The two girls were not ready so Michael Joe had to wait. He talked to Tadg Falane about the new potatoes, the cutting of the hay, and the weather.

When the two girls did come downstairs, Michael Joe saw that Ann was the better dressed of the two. Kitty had given her a white organdie dress with a full bodice, that she had got from a cousin in America. It was a bit too big for Ann's thin body, but the dress gave her an unearthly paleness which somehow suited her. She had a rosebud corsage pinned to her shoulder. Kitty was dressed in a plain red dress without ornament.

'Look at the job I did on her for you,' Kitty said to Michael Joe.

'You're wasting your talents ... here in Corrigbeg,' Michael Joe said. 'Come on. We're late.'

He walked between them, chatting mainly with Kitty, with whom he suddenly felt very sympathetic. Tom Healy was off somewhere drinking when he ought to be taking her to the dinner. She wanted no sympathy though. And gave Michael Joe a few digs about Nell Cullen, humming a few bars of 'The Girl I Left Behind Me'. Ann was silent all the way.

Seamus Larkin and Nell were just inside the door of the lobby in the Central Hotel, with Tom Fitzgerald and Canon Lyons, greeting the guests as they arrived. Everything blurred that instant for Michael Joe. He tried to introduce Ann to Nell but forgot Ann's name. Nell passed it over with a laugh.

'There's a man with a lot on his mind. Watch out for him,' she said in a kindly way to Ann, who smiled faintly. Larkin laughed nervously beside Nell. Michael Joe moved on into the lobby and forgot to shake hands with him. The lobby had been laid out with a long table because the dining room was not big enough. There was a bar off the lobby.

'Ye can take care of yeerselves for a minute,' he said to Ann and Kitty. 'I have to see a fellow within here about a horse.' He ducked into the black recesses of the bar. It was crowded with members of the football team. They greeted him loudly. He could hardly believe it. They had all turned out in force and full style for Larkin and Nell. There wasn't a man of them wasn't wearing a clean shirt and tie.

He had two quick half ones at the bar, by himself, refusing to drink with a couple of the fellows who wanted to buy him one. He used the women waiting outside in the lobby for him as an excuse. He had to hurry back to them. The whiskey heightened the excitement he was already under. He went back out and stood with Ann and Kitty, and talked a blue streak to them about what a grand occasion it was, and how the dinner couldn't be given for a better cause. He covertly watched Nell and Larkin greeting people at the door as they came in.

'Did you ever see such a spread in your life?' he said glancing at the long table shining under a white tablecloth and gleaming silverware. 'Fit for a king and queen. And, God knows, I suppose they are. No one can take it away from them tonight.'

'They're a handsome pair,' Kitty Falane said glancing over at Larkin and Nell.

'They are that, surely,' Michael Joe said. He was caught. Had to play his role to the hilt.

'She's lovely,' Ann said. 'Lovely looking. He's like . . . a saint.'

Tom Fitzgerald came up and whispered to Michael Joe.

'Great God, I forgot,' Michael Joe said clapping himself soundly on the forehead. 'I'll be one minute. 'Tis at home. I'll be back in a jiffy.'

He had forgotten to bring the mantel clock which he was to present to Larkin and Nell as a wedding gift. On the way he had to pass by Nell. She was talking in a group of girls. She glided away from them seeing Michael Joe about to leave.

'You're off home early?' she said. Her tone was bright and casual.

'I forgot something. I'll be back. I wouldn't miss this for the world.'

'I never expected it,' Nell said. 'Isn't it grand. And I'm glad you came. In spite of everything.'

'We're giving it mainly for Larkin,' he said. ' 'Twas the football club's idea. He's very popular with the lads.'

She looked at him for a moment, and then quietly turned away, leaving him standing there. He rushed out and up home to get the clock.

He did not know why he could not leave well enough alone. He would not admit he was jealous. He did not want to marry her; and he was twice the man Larkin was, in his own opinion. Then her physical image flashed into his mind. She was by far the best looking girl there. He liked the powder-blue dress she was wearing, and the string of pearls around her throat. Ann would not hold candlelight to her, he thought. Nor Kitty. There she was tonight, calmly and coolly accepting the night as hers. To look at her greeting the guests, standing by Larkin, smiling and talking in the lilting, musical voice that he could hear in any crowd, you would think that she was as innocent and as pure as the Blessed Virgin herself. Poor old St. Joseph . . . Larkin. Did he know what he was letting himself in for? Not only that, but she spoke to Michael Joe himself as if there had never been anything between them. She never gave away by word, expression or gesture that the past meant anything to her. When he had met her at the door, he had expected something to happen between them. A recognition. When they looked at each other Michael Joe felt as if he had never known her. Her clear blue eyes had gazed steadily at him, giving nothing away. Michael Joe did not know what he expected. He wanted to see some sign that he was still the man she loved. Was that what he was looking for? And had been so excited all evening anticipating. He could not believe that she had forgotten, so easily and so quickly. It was only four months ago. And did she compare Larkin with himself? She must know what kind of man she was marrying. But Michael Joe had observed her hovering over Larkin, bending to him, listening to what he said, smiling, never really laughing as she had with him. He could detect nothing between them that gave any indication that she thought Larkin was inferior in any way.

He had locked the clock in a drawer in the shop. If he had brought it in home, he knew his mother would see it. There would be questions. She had been bitter enough as it was without giving her more ammunition. They were making a fool of him, again. The third time. As he walked back down to the Central Hotel with the box under his arm, the excitement he had felt at the beginning of the evening was gone. He began to see Larkin and Nell as two of his bitterest enemies who had to be outwitted at any cost. Larkin he dismissed as an opponent not worthy of his attention. He was directed entirely by Nell. Nell who was bent on getting her own back because he had rejected her. The rejected woman, turning her viperish fangs on her rejector. What was the old saying—Hell hath no fury? He would beware. He would arm himself. He had been too generous entirely, not really knowing to what lengths she would go to get her own back on him. She was even marrying Larkin to show him up. He began to be convinced of that. There could be no other reason. Michael Joe could not conceive that when she did not love *him*, she could love any other man.

She greeted him at the door when he came in. The guests were sitting down to the dinner.

'I'm glad you came back. 'Twouldn't be worth sitting down without you.'

Well, if *she* could say things like that, *he* could. She seemed to have forgotten and forgiven his little dig before he left.

'No matter who the dinner is for,' he said, 'I'm here because of you.'

'Oh, go on with you. Come on. I put you between Ann and Kitty.' She glanced at the box. 'What have you there?'

'A little bomb. To keep the excitement up if it lags.'

She glanced quickly at him as if she half believed him. Then she laughed, relieved.

'I wouldn't put anything past you.'

She led him to the table, gently touching his arm. He drew back.

He could not believe her. She was the absolutely, consummate actress. How many eyes had been slyly glancing at them as they walked down the length of the lobby to his seat at the dinner table? For a moment he half wished that the box he carried did have a time bomb in it.

'Here he is,' she said to Ann.

Michael Joe sat down, shoving the box under the table.

No drink was served with the dinner. Canon Lyons was sitting at the head of the table, flanked by Nell on one side and Larkin on the other. Ed Donovan and his girl were next; then the bank manager and his wife; and then Kitty, Michael Joe, and Ann. She nudged Michael Joe, who was talking to Kitty.

'What fork do I use?' she whispered. He stared at her in dumb amazement then held up his own.

The conversation was strained. It was not a family dinner, though Canon Lyons often ate at the bank manager's, and so was able to keep up a conversation to which all the others at that end of the table listened. The talk was on politics, business, and the state of the world. Larkin got in a few words here and there. Quietly, incisively. Michael Joe drew more and more into himself. Nell was diagonally across from him, so he could not help but catch her eye every so often. She smiled. He was confused. He attacked his food with ferocity. Ann tried to say something to him once or twice about the food, but he only grunted at her. He wished he had something to drink. The effects of his two quick whiskeys were wearing off. But Canon Lyons was against the drink. Michael Joe wondered if the dinner was for the Canon, or to celebrate an engagement. There was laughter from the other end of the table where the regular members of the team were. Michael Joe wondered what they were laughing about. If they knew what he was thinking, they wouldn't laugh. He had made a fool of himself again by even being present at the dinner. His mother was right. He shouldn't have come.

Once, toward the end of the dinner, Nell got up from her place and came over behind Ann, and spoke to her. She hoped Ann was having a good time. Michael Joe's gorge rose. He saw it as a deliberate hint to himself to pay more attention to Ann. He turned to her.

'What did *that one* say to you?' he said. 'Trying to turn you against me?'

'No,' Ann said. 'She's lovely. She wanted me to have a good time.'

' 'Tis little you know about her one way or the other.'

After the cake and tea was served, Canon Lyons rapped on the side of his cup, and called for attention. He made a brief speech complimenting the young couple and invoking the blessings of Christ on them in the stupendous undertaking they were about to embark on. But tonight was not the night for reminding them of the serious side of their stupendous adventure. He came down hard on the word 'stupendous'. He loved the word, and was nicknamed locally 'stupendous' Lyons. He glared around him and down the table, as if daring anyone present to contradict him that marriage wasn't a stupendous step to take. But tonight was a night for celebration. He introduced Joe Devitt, a heavy baritone, to render a song.

Joe rolled out his all-time favourite: 'Sitting on the Bridge Below the Town'. He invited everyone to join in the chorus. And they did. All except Michael Joe. Even Ann beside him sang, high and off key.

The bank manager made a short speech praising Larkin. A very efficient worker. He would be sorely missed. Popular in social circles in the community, he could see from the large turnout.

Then Michael Joe's turn came to make the presentation. He stood up intending to get it over with quickly.

'On behalf of the Corrigbeg Gaelic Football Club, I wish to present you with this mantel clock. May it keep time for you always.'

He had to bend down under the table to get the clock after he had finished the speech. He was so bulky that Ann and Kitty had to draw back their chairs so that he could get under the table. It had somehow been kicked far in. He had to crawl under the table among the feet. Everyone was silent at the table waiting for him to come up with the box.

'Are you there, Michael Joe?' one of the fellows shouted at the end of the table. 'Send out a search party, lads.' That broke the awkward silence. Michael Joe came up with the box, his face dark, and handed it across the table to Nell. There was a round of applause. She was surprised that he had handed it across to her, and almost dropped it as she reached.

'Speech, Michael Joe!' one of the fellows shouted. 'Speech!'

Michael Joe looked down the table. 'You know as much about the bride there and her intended as I do,' he said. 'A speech of mine wouldn't add or subtract a hair from one or the other of them. The bride is well known in the parish.' He stopped and sat down abruptly, glancing across at Nell. She had hung her head, and gripped the box. Michael Joe could not see Larkin at all. There was no applause for his ungracious presentation.

Canon Lyons stepped into the gap, rising hurriedly and throwing a dirty look at Michael Joe.

'Will you open it, young lady?' he said to Nell. She raised her head and shook it.

'Open it! Open it!' cries came from down the table. She looked down and smiled, and began to pull the package apart. Larkin rose from his chair and went over to help her.

The clock was a plainly wrought, mahogany piece, Roman numerals on a gold face, and black hands. Both Nell and Larkin stood back and admired it. Nell wound it up, and set the hands so they would chime. It had a deep, musical chime. All the table had to be quiet so they could hear the chime.

Something struck Michael Joe. He did not know what. Something from the past. A noise from the past. Music from the past. The chiming of the clock aroused a desire in him to upturn the whole dinner table. The urge came on him suddenly with the first few chimes of the clock. And he was barely able to control it. He could not leave the table. He was caught. He could barely control his impulse to do something destructive. He had to stick it out. Listen, listen, as each deep, soft, melodic chime chimed out. Eight o'clock. A definite time. He gripped the side of the table and squeezed hard, trying to keep control of himself. Listen to the chime.

Larkin, on behalf of himself and Nell, thanked the people present who had contributed towards the gift, and for their thoughtfulness. The clock would be installed in the place of honour in their new home. All were invited to the wedding.

The dinner broke up soon after. There were a few more songs, a tune on the piano, and Jackie Fox played the melodeon. Then the Canon gave a blessing on all present. 'Match against Quilty tomorrow,' he said. 'All go home early.'

Michael Joe made for the bar as the crowd broke away from the table. He was the first into the bar, and drank a half-whiskey, and then another, drinking at the end of the bar. The fellows trooped in and avoided him. He had another by himself. Larkin came in, and went up to Michael Joe.

'I know how you feel,' he said. 'And I'm sorry you were put on the spot. I hold nothing against you. A night like this everything should be forgotten.' He held out his hand.

Michael Joe turned and hit him square on the jaw, putting into the blow all the pent-up frustration and wounded pride of all the weeks since he had first heard that Larkin was engaged to Nell.

Larkin fell back against a table, but recovered quickly, and advanced back to Michael Joe with his fists raised. Michael Joe had not followed up his first blow. Now that Larkin advanced, he put up his fists, and rushed at Larkin.

The fellows in the bar jumped on him from behind and pinned his arms.

'Take your medicine like a man, Michael Joe,' someone said to him.

'If he wants a fight he'll get it,' Michael Joe roared. 'I'd take on ten like him. Let me at him.'

He lunged, but was held back. Larkin had dropped his guard and was staring at Michael Joe as if he was in the presence of a raving lunatic whose lunacy and its cause were beyond his comprehension.

'He insulted me. I'll teach him to insult a McCarthy,' Michael Joe roared.

Nell had come in. She went immediately to Larkin, and put a hand on his arm, staring at Michael Joe, the wavy black hair falling over his face, being held back by the fellows.

'Let him go,' she said to the fellows. They did. He shrugged them off and glared at her.

'I expected it of you,' she said. 'To strike. To rape everything you touch.'

Michael Joe rubbed his jaw as if he had been hit, then strode out of the bar.

'Ye'll remember me, anyway,' he shouted as he left. Nell stepped aside to let him pass, keeping Larkin between herself and him.

Ann and Kitty were waiting in the lobby, Ann holding on to Kitty's arm.

'Come on,' Michael Joe said. 'This bloody place is like a grave-yard.'

He walked quickly. The women had trouble keeping up with him.

'Did you hit him?' Kitty said. 'Aren't you the bad little boy.'

'I did. Once. They held me back. I'd have slaughtered him if they didn't.'

' 'Twas just as well to get it out of your system. You can forget about it now. They'll both be leaving and you can forget them.'

'I will,' Michael Joe said. 'I won't give either of them another thought. That's the end. And that lunatic Larkin. He said I should see a doctor. I'll doctor him.'

'Was he hurt?' Ann said fearfully. 'Did you hurt the poor fellow?'

'Isn't you're soft-hearted for him. Since when did he win your sympathy?'

'Thanks be to God!' Ann said. 'He didn't get hurt.'

Michael Joe laughed, a deep throaty laugh. A satisfied laugh. 'He'll remember me, though. I gave both of them cause.'

17

MICHAEL JOE'S SATISFACTION with himself did not last very long. He stopped in at Blake's that night for a drink on the way home. None of the fellows there had yet heard about the fight. He expected that word would have gone around fast, and that the whole of Corrigbeg would already know about his famous deed. No one was talking about it in Blake's. Michael Joe wished they were. He wanted to know what was thought about the incident. He sat brooding over a pint wondering when some one of the fellows would broach the subject of the fight to him. He was in the kitchen. The wireless was blazing out Sousa marches. Most of the talk was about a football match that was to be played tomorrow against Corrigbeg's arch rivals—Quilty, the neighbouring town. Michael Joe knew that it didn't look good for him to be drinking in a pub the night before an important match. That was why the dinner at the hotel had broken up early.

No one spoke to him, and he was dying to talk to someone. He went outside in the dark bar, and stood beside a fellow from the country he hardly knew, and bought him a drink. Michael Joe brought the subject around to the fight he had with Larkin. The country fellow listened. 'I nearly slaughtered him with one blow,' Michael Joe said. 'Jazus,' the fellow said, 'and did you?' 'I did. But they saved him in the nick of time. But for they held me back I'd have killed him.' Michael Joe bought the fellow another drink. He leaned close to his ear, pouring out his exploit. 'What do you think of that, now?' 'I'd have backed you up if I was there,' the country fellow said. 'He deserved it. He had it coming to him, anyway,' Michael Joe said. 'And more,' his companion nodded. Michael Joe bought him another drink.

Michael Joe exhausted his tale soon. His listener was unsatisfying.

He didn't know the background of the case, and his approval of Michael Joe's actions was the approval of a man who always liked to hear of a fight no matter what it was over, or whether there was a right or a wrong to it. Michael Joe grew silent, finished his pint and left.

At eleven o'clock Mass next day, Canon Lyons gave a sermon on one of the deadliest of all the seven deadly sins—anger. 'Originator of *stupendous* destruction and ruination among mankind!' (Pounds the pulpit). 'And not only among nations. Don't cast your eyes across the water and say they, those over there, are the guilty ones. Right here at home, in our own very parish, before our own very eyes we can see the rack and havoc caused by this sin that likens us again to the ravening packs of wolves that once roamed our country before the coming of St. Patrick. This is our second greatest sin, in the eyes of the world. Anger. We're the laughing-stock of the Continent for it. And Amerikay.

'I won't mention names. There are those among you whose ungovernable tempers have already wrought *stupendous* havoc, and will continue to do so. Those who are not fit to live in civilized communities. Blackguards, and ruffians! The seeds of Christianity were sown in this country long ago to lift us above the pagan state. We were savages before St. Patrick. There are those among us who are still in that state. Instead of turn the other cheek 'tis raise the two fists, symbols of man's bestiality and drive to kill and ruin. Those that live by the fist shall perish by the fist, to paraphrase Isaiah.' (Pounds the pulpit). 'Amen.'

Michael Joe sat with his mother listening, and knew the sermon was directed against him. Everyone who saw the fight last night would know. The Canon had left before it broke out. But someone had brought the news to him, in time for him to compose the sermon on it.

Michael Joe began to shake. He could have stood up and reeled off a string of foul names at the lean, emaciated man thundering in a high, effeminate voice from the pulpit. But he had to control himself. His mother was listening to and approving of every word the Canon spoke. And Michael Joe could not forget he was in church. No matter how angry he was with Canon Lyons, still the chapel, with all its symbols of religious devotion and authority, exercised its influence over his mind, and restrained him from standing up and shouting back at the thunderer.

Michael Joe pushed out of the pew leaving his mother staring after him. Outside it was a warm June day, with a breeze blowing in from the sea. He walked down the middle of the deserted Chapel Road, the peaked cap pushed back from his forehead, and the dark hair bunched underneath. He walked freely, swinging his long arms, striding more than he ordinarily did. He held himself erect, and did not glance either right or left of him.

He went down and opened the shop as an act of defiance, and stood in the door, waiting for the people to begin coming out from Mass. Suddenly, he remembered the day he and his mother had been to the bank and she had said to him that he might own Corrigbeg some day, and he had laughed at her. The idea did not seem too far-fetched to him now, for some reason, as he glanced up and down the deserted streets. He had some vague idea that if he did own Corrigbeg, he would be able to strike back at Canon Lyons. He felt like striking out now, in all directions. That blow at Larkin had been the first. Now he wanted to strike again. But what could he strike at? The Canon. Though he was on the verge of madness with rage, still the thought of striking a priest brought him up short. He would have to be far gone to do that. Yet, he had been hurt again. The whole parish would know at whom the sermon had been directed. Michael Joe felt alone. Fighting the battle alone. And all because of Larkin and Nell. The town had stuck up for a stranger. The Canon was backing Larkin and Nell. A stranger, and a whore. Yes, that! It was peculiar for a representative of the cloth to be backing a pair like that. He could count on no one in this battle. Very well. He'd fight it himself. Himself against the world. Somehow, he would get his chance to strike back at them.

The people came down from Mass and passed by him standing in the door. Those he knew, nodded to him, and he nodded back as if nothing was wrong. He would be two-faced if they could be.

When he saw his mother coming, he went back inside the shop. She came in after him.

'Were you sick that you left the Mass?' she said to him.

'I couldn't stand that fellow above in the altar with his preaching.'

'Oh, Michael Joe. Don't say such a thing about your own parish priest. Every word he spoke was the truth.'

Even she was against him. 'He's a dictator. A Mussolini. No one has to take it from him. Who does he think he is?'

'He wasn't talking about you, sure now.'

'It makes no matter. He should say his Mass. That's what he's paid for.'

Mrs. McCarthy looked up at him from underneath the brim of her black hat. 'I don't know what's come over you at all,' she said. 'You used to be so easygoing. And never bothered by anything.'

'A man has to grow up sometime,' he said.

'Will you be in for your dinner?'

'We're playing a match in Quilty. I'll eat when I come home.'

He turned his back to her, and went behind the counter. She put both hands around the big black prayer book she was carrying, and raised it before her, as if she was invoking all the prayers that were in it to cure her son of whatever it was that disturbed him and changed him from his old self.

After she left, Ed Donovan and Tom Fitzgerald came in. After some casual conversation about the match to be played that afternoon, they got around to the reason for their visit. Would Michael Joe apologize to Larkin, and the matter wouldn't go any further. For the sake of good feeling among the team. If they were fighting among themselves, the Quiltonians would disgrace them. The fellows on the team were not entirely in Michael Joe's favour. He had struck the first blow. Without warning. When Larkin had come to him in friendship. Be a man, and apologize.

Michael Joe refused point-blank. The matter was between Larkin and himself. He saw no reason for anyone else to be concerned in it. It was no business of the team. Or of the Canon's either, for that matter.

'I'm not altogether sure you're right,' Tom Fitzgerald said. 'We'd like to have peace in the ranks today meeting those barbarians beyond. 'Tis always a fight with them, always, you know that. We'll patch up our differs. And play a clean game.'

'No,' Michael Joe said. 'Stay out of this. Between Larkin and myself 'tis. And no one can make me say I'm sorry to him.'

Donovan and Fitzgerald saw it was useless to try and persuade him. A charge could be brought for assault and battery, they reminded him. He said to tell Larkin from him, to go ahead with the charge if he wanted to. Michael Joe had a few accusations to make himself, that wouldn't look too good in the public eye.

The two fellows left warning him to play a clean game that day. They wanted no fights during the match.

The games against Quilty had always been noted for their bloodshed. No game had ever been played between the two teams without several members on both sides being injured, and the game constantly having to be stopped because of fights. Once or twice, championship games had to be called off because the spectators from both towns had invaded the football field, and a minor battle had taken place, with the local guards of both towns being unable to stop the combat for a couple of hours. The Quiltonians were fishermen, hardy, hot-tempered and rough. Many of the team members were either brothers or cousins. And the families, even to the fifth and sixth removed, watched the match from the sidelines, waiting for one of their own to be injured. Then they swarmed on to the pitch, yelling battle cries, and war began. The Corrigbeg team had a reputation for playing a quiet, clean type of football, clever and methodical, rather than rough. The meeting between the two teams was a meeting between opposites.

Michael Joe togged out in a corner by himself, avoiding the other players, and thinking murderous thoughts of what he was going to do when he got out in the football field. He would show them the kind of man he was. Able to fight his own battles. They thought he was a fool. Wrong to hit Larkin. Wrong at the dinner when he presented the clock and made no speech. He would go out and play so that they would realize they couldn't do without him. In tough battle, it was a man like himself, and not Larkin, the team needed.

He was the first of the team out on the field, and immediately began aggressively pursuing the ball. Before the throw-in of the ball for the match to begin, Paddy Hassett, the trainer, called him to one side.

'I want no dirty play, now. You know what kind of a team we're up against. Holy war could break loose if you play dirty. If you make trouble they'll be down on you like a pack of wolves. For the sake of the team, play clean.' Michael Joe pranced up and down on his toes, hardly listening. He was longing for the physical contact of the game, and never felt stronger or more anxious to play.

From the start, it was clear that this was going to be his best game. He played like a man possessed, and, strangely enough, played his cleanest game. He ignored the man who was marking him, and leaped for the ball every time. When he had possession, he charged through the opposing forward line and cleared the ball, jostling the men aside. He never passed the ball off to any of the other members of his own team, but cleared it himself.

The Quiltonians soon saw that Michael Joe had to be knocked out if they were to win. From the sidelines came shouts of 'Gut him, gut McCarthy,' when he had the ball. And they went after him physically, since they saw they could not beat him for the ball. He was tripped, shoved, elbowed, and kneed in the back and the groin. The more the opposition attacked him physically, the better he played. He never once felt any of the blows that landed, though, by half-time, his body was a mass of bruises, and his shins were bleeding from cuts where he had been kicked.

At half-time, Paddy Hassett put iodine on the cuts. It pierced. Michael Joe stood there in his amber and gold jersey, patiently suffering the piercing pain from the iodine. Hassett rubbed embrocation into the bruises.

'Jazus, the bastards, they're out to get you. You're playing a star match. And they know they can't get past you.'

'Let them try their level best,' Michael Joe said. 'I can take whatever they hand out. And give better back. They're not playing against a bunch of ladies' men.'

Because Michael Joe had ignored the several attempts to maim him and knock him out of the game, there had been no fights so far. He was feeling very satisfied with himself, and was even more satisfied when Donovan and Fitzgerald came over and inquired how he was.

'Holding me own,' he said laughing.

'We'll do our best to keep them off you. Pass the ball out. Don't be asking for trouble.'

'I'd take on all fifteen of them.' Michael Joe flexed both arms.

They looked at him, a little bewildered. Michael Joe was not noted for taking punishment without giving it out, too. If he once tried to get his own back on the Quiltonians, the fight was on.

' 'Tis up to you,' Donovan said. 'God knows you have enough reason to strike back. We'll be behind you if you do. Hold out if you can though. If you don't fight back, they can't start it.'

'I won't start anything,' Michael Joe promised them.

Larkin was having a bad day. They were not playing his type

of football. In fierce man-to-man football with close marking, he was not very successful. And when the play was as rough as it was this day with the Quiltonian fishermen, he got more knocking about than he cared to take. He was not a glutton for punishment, like Michael Joe. If he could avoid getting a jarred shoulder, he sidestepped it; he never mixed it up in the ruckle when four or five men from either side kicked and elbowed and pushed, fighting for possession of the ball. He waited outside for the loose ball to come out. Today, there were few loose balls. And he was caught in the ruckle a few times, before he could skip clear. He was jarred, and had a slight headache. That put him off his style and accuracy. He missed a few scores. The forward attacking line was bad.

But the defence, led by Michael Joe, was holding up. Michael Joe saw Larkin missing a few easy shots, but said nothing. All his efforts at defence were wasted if the forwards did not score. He couldn't complain if Larkin missed scoring chances. Not after what happened last night. That he might be to blame! But Michael Joe didn't think that was it altogether.

Michael Joe also found himself now in the position of holding the key to whether the match would end up in a fight, or would be played to the end without incident. He was determined to keep the peace. He would not lose his head; whatever physical punishment the Quiltonians dealt out to him, he'd take peaceably. The role of the suffering martyr was balm to his spirit. He rose to new heights of football in the second half. He could almost see the *Clare Champion* reporter writing that he was 'in the thick of the fray at all moments' and 'all over the field, until it looked like there were fifteen Michael Joe McCarthys instead of the one stalwart full-back.'

Midway in the second half the Quiltonians mounted a strong attack on Michael Joe's goal, and pressed hard in a mêlée around the goal. There had been no score so far in the game. Michael Joe got possession of the ball, and, holding it close to his chest, tried to bull his way through the mêlée. He was tripped and as he fell, three or four Quiltonians piled on him and began to kick, elbow, and fist him. The referee blew the whistle frantically. But the players paid no attention. They kept piling on top of Michael Joe. The ball squirted loose. Michael Joe lay flat on the greensward, writhing in pain, and trying to roll himself up on his feet. He fell back again on the grass. Donovan and Fitzgerald ran to him. Other members of the Corrigbeg team ran up, and surrounded him forming a protective circle around him. But there was no need. The green-shirted Quiltonian men were walking away. They had accomplished their mission. Paddy Hassett ran out. Michael Joe writhed on the grass, and moaned in pain. His right arm lay limp and useless from his side. Paddy Hassett came running in and saw that a doctor was needed. One was called from the sidelines.

The doctor examined Michael Joe. His right arm was out from its socket. He called the ambulance. It whined on to the field, and Michael Joe was lifted into the back on a stretcher, moaning.

'We'll get them, Michael Joe, we'll get them for you,' Donovan said.

Michael Joe moaned on. On the way into Corrigbeg in the ambulance, Michael Joe was in great physical pain. But he didn't really mind, now. He knew he had played a great match. He remembered the way the lads on the team had formed the circle around him while he was down. Half the team must have lifted him on to the stretcher, and stood around the back of the ambulance door. Donovan and Fitzgerald had lifted the stretcher on. They had murderous looks on their faces, to a man, as if they were all ready to go back on the field and avenge Michael Joe. These little images of his own heroism and his team's concern for him, floating and flashing through his mind, eased his pain. Doctor McMahon, just out of medical school in Dublin, sat beside him, as they rode back to Corrigbeg to inform his mother that they would go on to the hospital in Ennis to have the shoulder properly looked after. The young doctor was concerned. He had nothing to kill Michael Joe's pain until they could stop by his house for his bag. He kept asking Michael Joe if the pain was getting worse. And Michael Joe kept telling him that he had hardly any pain at all.

'You played a great match,' the young doctor complimented him.

'Do you think we'll hold out and win?'

'From the looks on the faces, I think murder is about to break loose.'

Michael Joe smiled, and held back a wince because he had moved, and a stab of pain went through him.

'Lie still,' the doctor commanded him.

Michael Joe stayed quiet. He began to feel lonely. He wished a couple of fellows from the team had come along so that they could talk to him about the match. He began to relive moments of it, those moments when he had the ball in his hands and went charging through the ruck, feeling the Quiltonians bouncing off on him, and then kicking the ball with all his force down to the other end of the field. He remembered that Larkin was not among the players who had surrounded him when he was hurt.

The ambulance stopped outside his own door in the Main Street. A crowd of young fellows and old women had gathered outside. He could hear the voices. The doctor went in to see his mother.

In a few moments, she was kneeling beside him, bareheaded, staring down at him in the little cot. She put out a hand and touched a bruise on his fleshy face without uttering a word.

'Michael Joe?' she said, then.

'There's nothing wrong with me, at all,' he said roughly, embarrassed by his mother's peculiar attention. If she had screamed a fuss, he would not have minded. 'They'll fix me up down at the hospital.'

'I'm not letting them take you. I've sent out for Feidlim McGuire.'

The young doctor crept into the ambulance. 'Mrs. McCarthy, you're doing a dangerous thing. McGuire has no knowledge of bones. He's ruined as many as he's healed.'

Mrs. McCarthy turned and stared at him out of her cold, grey eyes.

'He has the gift.'

'Oh my God,' the young doctor said. 'Will ye never give over *that*.'

'I want him out of here, and up in his own bed. His own bed, do you hear?'

'Very well. On your own head be it. I'm not responsible for him. But he has some say himself.' The doctor turned to the cot where Michael Joe was stretched.

Michael Joe was afraid now. His mother. She put fear into him. He thought she might make a scene, and when she didn't, he began to be afraid. It was an undefinable fear. The savage and barbarous attacks of the Quiltonians on the football field had not made him afraid. He delighted in struggling with them. His mother made him afraid, now. Afraid for himself; and for her. For her. And because it was for her, he himself was afraid too.

'I'll do what she says,' he said to the doctor.

'God, ye'er all half daft in this town,' the doctor said. 'Ye have no use for doctors or hospitals at all. Only quacks.'

He went out and got a few men to help the ambulance driver to take Michael Joe out of the ambulance.

The trip off the ambulance, into his home, and upstairs to his own room and bed, was a long journey of torture for Michael Joe. None of the handlers of the stretcher was skilled at it, and so he bounced around in the canvas, his right shoulder searing pain through him. He tried not to moan. His mother walked beside. It was no good frightening her. But the moans escaped. She took his hand.

'There, now, a leanbh,' she murmured. 'Whist, asthore, whist, you'll be better soon.'

Michael Joe was in agony. His mother, muttering again to him as if he were a child, comforted him in his pain.

She made one of the men stop in the bedroom and undress him for bed, and went outside and tried to pay the doctor.

'You wouldn't let me do anything. Why should I take pay for it?' he said angrily. 'I wouldn't be surprised if that quack maimed him for life.'

'He's my son, doctor. I'll care for him.'

'God help him,' the doctor said, getting into the ambulance with the driver.

Mrs. McCarthy turned around. A crowd of children had gathered around the hall door.

'Be off home with ye. Off now, do ye hear,' she said in a quivering voice.

Silently the children straggled away, throwing sidelong looks at her as she stood there, a black-robed figure, with a knot of white hair bound with jewelled combs, giving her the look of one of those tall, masculine, Irish queens, who fought and led men in battle in ancient times.

She hurried upstairs. Michael Joe had been put to bed. He had sense enough to demand that no pillow be put under this head. Now that he was resting again, the pain had dulled. He was dozing.

Mrs. McCarthy sat herself beside his bed and stared at him for a while. She knew he was not asleep.

'What happened that you let them do that to you?' she said.

'I was tripped in the ruck. When I went down, they got me.

They had it in for the whole match. I'll get them again, though. They're not through with me yet.'

'Weren't your own there to help? Couldn't they save you?'

'I can fight my own battles,' he said. 'I don't want their help.'

'They could have killed you. Then where would I be? Your father's gone from me. You're all I have left.'

'I know that. But a man has to go out and fight for himself at some point.'

'Do you have to get youself nearly killed? I don't want anyone crucifying my son. And I don't want him going out getting *himself* crucified either. Do you hear?'

In her fear, she was attacking him. She did not know what she was doing, but if she had given in to tenderness it would seem like despair. In fighting with him this way, injured and helpless though he was, she did not have to think about the possibility of losing him entirely.

After her outbursts, there was silence between them. She got up and went downstairs, and out to the front door, where she stood waiting for McGuire, the bonesetter, to come.

The bonesetter came without bag or instruments. His gift was in his two hands. That was all he needed. She welcomed him, and brought him upstairs immediately. She wanted to stay, but he told her she would be no help, and having a woman around when he worked only made him nervous. And it was only a simple matter to put the collar-bone back in place. She left.

When he was finished with Michael Joe, he came back downstairs and told Mrs. McCarthy that Michael Joe was right as the mail and would need only a week or ten days of rest to give the arm a chance to set back in its socket. He refused the offer of money for his services. His gift was given to him by God. He couldn't charge for it. She promised to send a load of turf out to his cottage. Then she went back up to Michael Joe.

He was lying with his arm slung in a black scarf improvised for the occasion. The right shoulder was bared; the empty space bebetween collarbone and arm was filled up again. She was relieved when she saw it that way. She thought he might be maimed for life and the ugly hole would always remain in his shoulder.

'He's made you handsome again,' she said. She felt no longer compelled to attack him. She was relieved, and could tease him now. 'You won't even have a battle scar.'

'Did you hear who won the match?' Michael Joe said.

' 'Tis little I care who won the match.'

'I care. I got this for them.' He glanced down at his arm in the sling.

Mrs. McCarthy's face lost the lightness that had been on it for a few moments.

'I want you to give up the football, Michael Joe. Give it up. For my sake. I asked you before. And you wouldn't.'

'What would the lads think of me? Just for a little thing like this.'

'The next time it'll be something worse. I know. They're bent on your destruction.'

'I was helping them win the match. There was no destruction.'

'What's that?' she said looking at the injured arm.

'I'm not going to give up playing. Let that be the last of it. I'll fight them again, another day. They got me today. I'll get them tomorrow.'

Mrs. McCarthy stood up and went over and looked out of the window. A motor-car went by with a crowd of men in it, cheering and waving the gold and amber jerseys of the Corrigbeg football team through the window.

'Let down the window, Mother. I heard them cheering.'

'I'm no use to you any more,' she said. 'No use to you. Except to nurse you when you come home killed.'

'They must have won the match. Let down the window, Mother.'

Mrs. McCarthy did not let down the window. She saw more cars pass on the Main Street and from the side of the window she could see all the cars stopping in random places around Canada Cross, and the footballers come piling out screaming and roaring, still in their togs, jerseys and football boots. Doors opened that had been shut for the Sunday, and people began to appear standing in them, looking up towards Canada Cross. Mrs. McCarthy moved over to the side of the window to get a better view.

'What are they doing? Are they stopping at the Cross?' Michael Joe asked from the bed. He half rose, winced, and settled back again.

'The oinseachs,' Mrs. McCarthy said with contempt. 'Making a show of themselves before the whole town. And you in there, the worst of the lot. Going out to get yourself killed. For what? All for the screams of the crowd. They'd turn on you just as soon as they'd cheer for you.'

'Stop that, Mother, and open the window. I want to hear them.'

'You want to hear them! You want to hear them! Living Mother of God, ye'er all mad.'

'I'll get out of the bed and open it myself if you don't.'

She turned back to him. He was making attempts to get up in bed.

'Don't hurt yourself worse. I will. I'll do as you say.'

Old men, children, middle-aged men, men who used to be footballers and now played only in their imaginations and their talk, went running up to Canada Cross to surround the victorious footballers, slap them on the back, inquire about the great moments of glory and who made them in the winning of the victory. And the women came too, the women who hated the football because it maimed their men, sapped their energy, usurped the love of their men, but who later learned to take their own pleasure in the victories of their men, though it sometimes meant their own loss. All traffic was stopped around the crossroads. The lazy, summer afternoon in the small town exploded.

Mrs. McCarthy unlatched the window and lifted up the lower half. A soft summer breeze puffed in, and with it the roaring of the crowd.

'What are they doing? Tell me,' Michael Joe said.

'The footballers are parading around like pluming roosters down in the street.'

Michael Joe smiled.

'They're forming in a march . . . I declare . . . they're marching down the street . . . someone has a drum.'

Michael Joe could not hold himself in bed any more. He edged out of the bed, wearing only the bottom of his pyjamas, and padded over to the window beside his mother.

'Jesus, Mary, and St. Joseph, protect me. You're mad! Go back to bed this minute.'

'Not till they pass.'

The marching line of lightly clad footballers, surrounded by the townspeople and children of all ages, stopped in front of McCarthy's house. Someone saw Michael Joe and his mother in the window. Mrs. McCarthy played nervously with her hair.

'There he is. There's McCarthy,' someone shouted. 'Three cheers for McCarthy!'

The crowd gave three thunderous cheers. Michael Joe waved his good hand. He was so excited he began to sweat.

'Up Corrigbeg,' he roared down to them, and made as if to lean out of the window. He staggered with the pain. His mother caught him.

'Back to bed! Oh, my God. Back to bed,' she whispered to him. He felt suddenly weak, and leaned on her. Though she was ageing, her wiry body stiffened itself, and bore his weight as they crossed the room; then, she eased him back into bed. She rushed out of the room and came back in with a glass full of brandy.

'Take this.'

She held the glass to his lips as he lay flat on his back. The crowd still went on cheering for Michael Joe below the window. She made him sip the brandy slowly. When he finished, she wiped his sweating forehead with her silk handkerchief. Then she went over, closed the window, and drew the shutters and bolted them.

She sat beside the bed while Michael Joe fell asleep, worrying over Michael Joe's madness, and what he would do when she was gone. She took out her rosary beads and began to pray.

18

AND SO MICHAEL JOE began his confinement to bed with a broken collar-bone, suffered playing for the glory of Corrigbeg against the neighbouring town, Quilty, mortal enemy in the playing field. He did not mind in the least the pain and the suffering. Lying in bed, whenever he moved even slightly, he ached all over, and the stretched tendons in his shoulder stabbed pain through him again. But he never once felt that his suffering had been in vain. Corrigbeg had won the match. He was the hero. He was able to play football with the Quiltonians. Not many men could do that. They put the fear of God in every team they played. Fishermen who fought the sea the year long, were never afraid to fight other men. And Michael Joe had stood up to them. And all for Corrigbeg.

Of course, his own team appreciated him now. As he lay in bed, his thoughts constantly kept returning to the crowd underneath the window giving three cheers for him. He thought it was decent of them not to forget him. And he was glad they hadn't. He had played his heart out for them. And well they knew it.

He lay in bed reliving his triumph, and sometimes thought about the dinner and the blow at Larkin, or Canon Lyons' sermon on anger. That was all water under the bridge. It seemed to him, in the rare moments he remembered the incidents, that they must have happened ages ago. Or never happened at all. It was easy to lose a sense of the proportion of time lying in bed all day, half dreaming, being waited on hand and foot by your mother. Breakfast, dinner and supper in bed. That was the way to treat a hero. A read of the paper. And a doze. And before you knew it, morning was evening, and then night. And a couple of the fellows always came to see him and sit with him in the evening for an hour or two. They talked to Michael Joe about the match, going over in detail the recent victory. Michael Joe's play came in for discussion and admiration. He remained silent. 'God knows, Michael Joe, sometimes you went up for the ball and took it from five of them, and they hanging off you like flies on a round of beef.'

Michael Joe was very restless after their visits. Between the physical pain, and the excitement caused him by their praise, it was often late in the night when he could fall asleep. And even then only fitfully. And he could not turn and toss or change sides. He had to lie out straight. That was also a part of his delicious torture.

Vin Scanlon ran the shop, and came up every night after he had closed it to present Michael Joe an account of the day's business. He told him who had been in to buy, and what. And who got credit, and who paid cash for what they bought. Michael Joe wasn't very interested. He wanted to know if anyone had been asking for him, in the shop. Vin said that everyone who came in missed him, and wondered how he was getting along, and when he would be down in the shop again. Michael Joe told Vin to tell them that he wouldn't be long in bed, if he could help it.

He was bored after the first few days. Some of the charm of lying in bed and being visited and waited on, was wearing off. The soreness of his body was almost gone, and the shoulder bothered him only occasionally, when he moved. He wanted to be up and about, down in the shop meeting and talking with the customers who came in.

Mrs. McCarthy saw his restlessness. He became irritable about the food and complained that his bed had not been made. Mrs. McCarthy was afraid to let him get out of bed, to make it. In an effort to quiet him down, and to bring about a reconciliation between himself and Canon Lyons, she tried to persuade him to go to Confession and take Communion while he was in bed. She had found out about his fight with Larkin, and put two and two together in regard to Canon Lyons' sermon on anger. She suggested to Michael Joe that he ought to do his Easter Duty. She'd ask one of the curates to come down some morning, hear his Confession, and give him Communion.

Michael Joe refused to have it. She asked for a reason. He hadn't done his Easter Duty, had he? No. But he'd do it in his own good time. He wasn't a child any more to be bullied into going to the rails. She saw she was upsetting him, and gave in, before a serious argument developed between them. She wouldn't be able to stand that. She wished he would give up the football, and become a little more religious. She made a novena for that intention. She was afraid now, most of the time. She knew she would not lose him. He would not go away. But he was becoming stubborn. Ignored her wishes. There was something bothering him. Driving him to assert himself more than he used to when she thought of him as being her son. My son, Michael Joe. Or simply, my son. She did not know what was wrong with him.

One morning, he insisted that she make the bed if he was going to lie in it all day, and he edged himself out of bed, and padded over to the window and looked down on the street with his back to her, while she made the bed. She made it quickly and nervously. She didn't like making it with him in the room with her, even though he had his bare back to her. She began to feel her age as she hurried through making the bed. She did not linger over it. Pulled the sheets tight and smoothed out the wrinkles quickly.

'Are you through yet?' he said.

She hurriedly and carelessly threw the eiderdown over the blankets. 'Yes.' She left the room.

Feidlim McGuire, the bonesetter, had recommended that Michael Joe stay in bed for at least two weeks, to give the shoulder a rest and a chance for the tendons to strengthen and the bones to set back properly. On Saturday night, at the end of the first week, while his mother was at Confession, he got up, dressed himself with difficulty, and painfully, and came downstairs, and went out to the shop. Vin Scanlon was busy serving a few customers. Michael Joe had swung his jacket, cape fashion, across his shoulders, leaving the arm still in the black sling. The business of the shop stopped for a few minutes, while the customers crowded around him. They were mostly young married women buying groceries for the week. They had heard about his injury. They admired the arm in its black sling, and commented solicitously on the pain he must be having, and sure he shouldn't be up out of his sick bed at all. Michael Joe said he was better, and moved away from them and behind the counter.

He was glad he had come down. Though he was shaky on his feet, he felt his spirits rising to be in the shop. And the sympathy of the women, though he scorned it, yet it didn't go entirely against his liking.

His mother missed him when she came down from the chapel, and came running into the shop, one of the few times she ever came in there, and saw him sitting behind the counter, talking to Vin.

'Oh, my God, on your feet! You're driving yourself to death. Vin can take care of the shop. Come on in home, now, like a good lad.'

He stopped in the middle of a story he was telling Vin about the match.

'I'll wait till the shop is shut, I think.'

'Have you any control over him?' she said desperately to Vin.

Vin laughed. 'Yerra, he's all right, Mrs. McCarthy. I'll watch out for him.'

'You'll watch out for him. Dear God, what'll I do with him?' She stamped her foot. She looked pathetic in her gesture. It would have looked right once for her. She was still well preserved, but the gesture lacked energy and real authority.

Michael Joe got up and went to Mass with her next day, Sunday. She made the best of it, fussed over his appearance, combed his hair, and arranged his jacket over his shoulders. He cut himself shaving, and did not get all the soap off his face. She attended to him, putting a slight daub of iodine on the cuts. It pierced. 'God knows!' he fretted, 'as if I haven't suffered enough!'

After Mass, a crowd of the footballers met him outside the chapel gate, and he left his mother, and went for a drink with them. They wouldn't let him buy a round, and would have kept him drinking all day, if he didn't use his mother as an excuse to get away. He was serious and quiet, and they were jolly and loud. He relaxed, taking his full pleasure in their admiration. They protested when he said he had to go. He promised to come back.

He had waited for someone to mention Larkin's name. No one had. Since he had been injured the week before he had not heard the name, and there was no trace of strain in the relationship of the fellows with him. It was as if his injury had somehow exorcised the presence of Larkin and of Nell because if he could forget Larkin, he could forget her, out of his mind, and out of the minds of everyone else. Had they been married and left Corrigbeg already? No one had said. If they were still around, he did not know. And it did not matter, now. He had been reinstated in the esteem of the town. He was the local hero. He admitted that fact to himself. He took quiet pride in it. Larkin and Nell were insignificant. He hardly spared them a thought. With his reinstatement in the goodwill of the town, he considered his relationship with them of no more importance. He had some satisfaction from the blow he struck Larkin. He would remember that with pride for a while. And the sight of Nell trying to protect him. If the fellows hadn't held him back, God only knows what he might have done to Larkin. And Nell wouldn't have saved him, either. But that was over and done with now. He could afford to be generous. He would forget about them.

On the following Monday morning, Michael Joe was back in the shop for the whole day, though his arm was still in a sling. He did not attend the customers, leaving that to Vin Scanlon, but sat in the little snug at the back of the shop where Vin had built him a small fire in the grate because the late June had turned rainy and chilly. There he sat reading the *IrishIndependent* and then the *Irish Press*, interrupting himself only when he heard a voice in the shop, and going out to pass the time of day with whoever had come in. He spent an hour or two in the morning over at Dan Kerney's talking over the race results. He made a few bets for the day with the boy who was going up with the bets to the bookie in Ennistymon—there was no bookie in Corrigbeg.

There was little talk about the football match that had been played and won the week before. There was another just one week away against Kilrush, footballers who played the same style of clever football that Corrigbeg usually played. Michael Joe wouldn't be able to play. He'd be missed, the fellows said. Then one of them made a smart crack at Michael Joe's expense: 'Another martyr for ould Ireland, eh, Michael Joe?' The fellows in the tailor shop laughed. 'I'll play with my arm strapped as it is,' Michael Joe said, trying to make light of the remark. But he was irritated that he should become an object of fun, now. The fellows played a different tune a week ago.

Feidlim McGuire dropped in one day during the week to have a look at the shoulder to see how it was mending. It was doing fine, but he told Michael Joe he wouldn't be able to play football again for a long time. 'Twould be too dangerous. If the shoulder was put out again, he would risk danger of infection, and might end up getting TB of the bone. That frightened Michael Joe. The enthusiasm for playing the hero had worn off to the point where he began to consider his own skin again. Sometimes, looking back on the game against Quilty, he frightened himself with the thought of how reckless he had been, and how close he had come to really being maimed. But he told no one about those thoughts. He had no wish to tear down the image of the hero he had built up. He was a bit ashamed of himself for having those thoughts because he believed in the image himself. When Feidlim McGuire told him he couldn't play for a long time, he was half pleased, and half panicked. The team couldn't do without him. They'd have to, Feidlim said. It was either that or risk a serious injury that he might have the sign of for the rest of his life. 'They'll think I'm a funk,' Michael Joe said. 'Let them,' said Fiedlim.

He told the fellows what Feidlim had advised him, and swore up and down he would play anyway, in spite of the risk. The fellows advised him against it. He'd done his bit for Corrigbeg. More than his bit. God knows. But he raved on. 'The only bloody way they'd keep me off the football field is to tie me hand and foot. I can take care of myself against the best of them. Ye saw I could.' They nodded sympathetically.

When the list of the team members was posted down in Tom Fitzgerald's window the following Friday, Michael Joe's name was not on it. He raged to Tom about it. And then to Ed Donovan. They tried to calm him down. He was going to go to the game anyway. He had done enough, they told him, and nothing more was expected of him.

He went to the match against Kilrush, and stayed with Paddy

Hassett the trainer, advising him on the strategy of the game. Paddy paid little attention to him. Corrigbeg lost. Michael Joe got a secret satisfaction out of the defeat. If he had been in togs . . . and spear-heading the defence . . . Larkin had played a bad game again. He had become too careful of himself, even worse than he used to be in the past.

He met Ann Shanahan and Kitty Falane at the match. He had seen neither of them since the night at the dinner for Nell and Larkin. He stopped and passed a few words with them. He noticed Ann staring at his arm which was still in its black sling. Kitty asked how he was.

' 'Twasn't half as bad as the fuss that was made of it. Were ye at the game?'

'We were. And you covered yourself with glory, as the paper said. Didn't he, Ann?'

Ann nodded, and dropped her eyes from Michael Joe when he looked at her.

'Did you faint when they carried me off?' Michael Joe said, teasing her.

She looked up quickly at him, shocked that he would make light of a moment when she herself had felt fearful for Michael Joe.

'No,' she said seriously. 'I prayed for you. I said prayers.'

'That's why I was cured so fast. That's it, by God.'

'I thought she was going to die herself when they put you in the ambulance,' Kitty Falane said.

'Oh, Kitty, stop!' Ann said.

'She didn't sleep for a week. I had to go down every day and ask your mother how you were, for her. She wouldn't dare go down herself.'

'That's a lie,' Ann said. 'Stop your lies.'

Michael Joe laughed. Larkin passed by in his togs, and did not salute them.

'Getting married in a few weeks,' Kitty Falane said.

'Are they?'

On an impulse, Michael Joe invited the two girls to a dance that night, and Kitty accepted for both of them. Michael Joe spent most of the night dancing with Ann. She was not a very good dancer, but the more he danced with her, the more she softened up, especially since he had the use of only one arm. She began to cling a little to him as the night wore on.

He teased her about his helplessness, saying that she was no longer afraid of him. She just smiled, and kept her arm lightly on the elbow of his injured arm as they danced, as if she were protecting it.

19

ONE DAY THE following week, Michael Joe was sitting in the snug at the back of the shop, reading the paper, when Vin came in a bit flustered and announced that there was someone outside who wanted to see him. Michael Joe went out to the shop. He was still wearing the sling around his arm, though there was no longer any real need for it. But his mother insisted. And he told himself he was doing it to please her.

Nell Cullen was standing at the counter, with a long-fingered hand resting on top of it, nervously tapping on it as if the counter was a piano.

'I'd like to talk to you,' she said seeing him and then glancing around the shop. Vin Scanlon pretended to be very busy sweeping the floor.

The past he had thought buried swept back in a sudden upsurge. He forgot that she had deceived him. She looked lovely. She wore a light cotton dress, with a purple and green flower motif. Irises. A slight breeze coming in the shop door stirred the dress around her bare legs. There was a hint of light perfume. She wore strapped sandals. Her fair hair was long, wavy, and loose around her shoulders, parted in the middle and pinned with two small jewelled combs on both sides. She carried herself tall, direct, and faced him calmly, watching for his reaction.

'Come in here,' he said withdrawing inside the snug to be away from her sight for a few moments so that he would have time to recover his self-possession. He wondered if Larkin had told her about the talk in his room that night. If he had . . . .

'I won't keep you a minute,' she said coming in. 'I want to try and patch up your fight. I don't want to leave with it on my conscience.'

'Your conscience . . . ?'

'You hit Seamus. I said some hard things to you.'

'The past is over with. Forget it. That's what I'm going to do.'

'No one can forget the past,' Nell said deliberately. 'That's too dangerous.'

'I'm forgetting it. Let sleeping dogs lie, as the saying goes.'

'You didn't once. You remembered my past. *That* you couldn't forget . . . . But I didn't come in to fight. There isn't any need any more. I'm all right now. I'm happy. And I want you to be. I can't forget we went out together. I'm glad we did. For a while I thought I might be able to fall in love with you. You're very handsome. And the best of company, sometimes, when you're yourself.'

'You must be mad,' he said. 'Coming in here like this . . . are you asking me to forgive you?'

'I'd like you to come to my wedding. You aren't in love with me. You never were. You only thought you were. Don't be tormenting yourself. I want to be reconciled to you, and you to me.'

'Come to your wedding! Do you take me for the world's greatest blithering eejit? You're just turning the knife another twist. That's what you want. The spite of a scorned woman.'

She continued to look calmly at him. He had retreated into a corner of the snug, next the fire, and spoke across the room to her from there.

'You can't insult me,' she said. 'And you didn't jilt me. We never got to that point at all, if you remember rightly. I was through too much before you left me in the lurch, as you might think you did.'

'And what did you want with me? Why didn't you leave me alone?' Michael Joe said. 'You didn't have to go out with me. Why did you torment me? To make me small?'

'I was lonely. You kept after me. I thought we might be able to get along.'

'So, I'm to blame, now. Not you. I'm the guilty one. 'Twas all my fault.'

'There's no blame. I didn't come in to rake up the past.'

'Well, *I* want it raked up. You said no one can forget the past. All right. What was wrong with me? What was wrong with me?

127

I'm ten times the man Larkin is. Why wouldn't you give *me* a tumble?'

She turned away as if to leave. 'I thought you might be reasonable. You want to hurt me and you're only hurting yourself.'

He could not let her go. He realized fully that if either of them should feel injured, it should have been Nell. He had walked out on her. But here she was offering him forgiveness, and here he was attacking her as if it had been she that had rejected him.

'I'm sorry,' he said coming out of his corner. 'Don't go awhile. Sit down. I lost my temper.'

'You're very good at that,' she said.

He pulled a chair up to the fire for her. 'I'll behave myself if you sit down a minute.' He went over and shut the door.

Any sign of gentleness on Michael Joe's part had always softened her. She went over and sat down. They were silent for a few moments.

'You hated me for walking out on you?'

'I half expected it sooner or later, when you found out.'

'But you have to hate me. You have to!'

He calmed himself. He wanted her to tell him about himself. He had to hear what she thought. His own image of himself as a local hero was falling apart. And he must hear from her the truth about himself. He attributed great powers of understanding and insight to her at that moment.

'How did you know I wasn't in love with you?' he said.

'I know myself. I was hurt once, you understand. You learn a lot that way.' She began nervously looking around now as if the conversation had taken a more personal turn than she wished. 'I knew I was not what you thought I was. You had some idea of me in your head. I don't know. I don't know.'

'An idea in my head of you? And I loved that?'

'Yes,' she said. ' 'Tis queer, isn't it. I'm no idea though. England woke me up. What happened to me there. I'm not one of your innocent local girls, any more. Who's willing to hang on to a man, and glad to get him at any price. And be his little slave. I have rights of my own. If I'm a sinner, I want to be loved in spite of that. Because of it, maybe. You couldn't love me. It would be too humiliating to you.'

Michael Joe could not follow her. She was talking about herself and not him. He wanted her to tell him what *he* was.

'You learned a lot in England,' he said lamely. Then he said 'Larkin knows.'

'Yes. He does. I told him early on.'

'You didn't tell me. You let me go on being deceived.'

'That was different. You'd take advantage. You took advantage. Seamus doesn't. For some reason, he doesn't. He was upset, at first, like you were. But he got over it. He's very different from you. But I like you still, though. And that's why I dropped in. In spite of everything.'

'There's something wrong with me then, I suppose, because I couldn't . . .' He almost went on and called her a name.

'I don't know. Maybe you're just selfish. Spoiled maybe. That sounds like I'm making a child of you. It isn't that simple any more. You have to be catered to. I saw you at the football game the other Sunday,' she said, 'when you got injured. I was glad,' she confessed.

'You hate me, then?'

'No. Sometimes, maybe.'

'I must be a terrible monster entirely,' Michael Joe said. 'Am I?'

'That isn't the point,' Nell said regarding him. 'You can do nasty things. At the dinner, you did. And you can be dangerous. To other people. And yourself. I suppose I'm afraid of you,' she said.

'And Larkin you're not. He's a lamb.' He could not conceal contempt.

'Yes,' she said. 'Seamus is a lamb. I'm not ashamed to admit it.'

Nell stood up. 'You'll come to the wedding, then? As a token. An important token.'

The tone of her voice triggered Michael Joe, gave him a warning, a caution. And he forgot her gesture of friendship.

'No,' he said. 'I won't. I wouldn't be seen dead at it. You came in here trying to show your superiority to me. Forgive and forget. I'm not a bloody fool entirely. The runner-up for the hand of the ravishing Nell Cullen attends her wedding. I can hear them saying it now. Go back to your little lamb that you can do what you like with.'

Nell listened to the harangue in disbelief.

'I'm sorry for you,' she said. And left him.

After she left him, he was ashamed and guilty, but still un-repentant enough not to use her dropping in to see him as an excuse to build up his pride. He despised her because she was paying a price no woman should pay for what she wanted. It would be gossiped around the town that she had come in to see him. What would the people say in the light of what they already knew about her? She had done a dangerous thing in coming to see him. Could it not be that she was still in love with him? She had humiliated herself and her lover, Larkin.

But, Michael Joe also felt defeated. She had taken the initiative away from him, shown her willingness to forgive and forget, when it was he that should have gone to her. She had not blamed him for what he was, nor condemned him, nor despised him. She wanted only to be friends. Her offer of friendship and reconciliation made Michael Joe despise himself a little more. He had rejected her again.

20

NELL CULLEN AND Seamus Larkin's wedding was held on a Saturday morning in mid-July. Michael Joe did not go. When he came out of the house in the mid-morning to go into the shop next door which Vin Scanlon had already opened, he noticed the cars parked above around the church gate, and the flocks of children running around them tying canisters to the rear ends. He knew immediately what the cars meant. No one had told him that this was the day of the marriage; he had not seen the announcement in the papers, and Nell had not told him during her visit the date of her marriage. Yet he knew, the minute he saw the scene outside the church gate, who was getting married. He did not linger long looking, but hurried into the shop. Vin Scanlon was reading the *Irish Independent*, having it spread across the counter.

'Get the lead off your arse,' Michael Joe said to him. 'What did I hire you for?'

'Jazus, Michael Joe, I was only taking a read of the paper,' Vin said.

'Don't give me any of your smart alecky back gab. Get to work.'

Michael Joe went into the back room and tried to read the paper. But he couldn't sit still. He went out of the back door and took a short walk down the back way. Birds were singing in the blossoming hawthorn trees along the wall in the yard. Rambling roses flushed a delicate red. Somewhere a cock crew from a dunghill. In the distance, he could hear the faint roar of the Atlantic. A blackbird trilled in the bushes. Ironically he thought she had a grand day for her wedding.

On an impulse, he lined three or four old bottles up on the stone wall and began pelting stones at them. When he had smashed the bottles he came back into the shop. He had not done that since he was a boy. Then he tried to read the paper again, but could not concentrate. Finally he went across the street to Kerney's. Dan was by himself sitting cross-legged on the bench, sewing away at a suit he was making. Michael Joe asked for news. Dan said there was nothing strange. Then there was silence between them.

'Why aren't you above?' Dan said looking at Michael Joe with shrewd eyes.

'Is it an eejit altogether you think I am? Marriage is for fools. I'm not one.'

'Well, the better man won,' Dan said, needling him.

' 'Tis little you know of it,' Michael Joe said, and left in a huff.

He went back to the shop and sat there trying to do the crossword puzzle in the paper until it was time for the midday dinner. 'Have you my football togs washed?' he asked his mother when he came in for the dinner. 'There's a match tomorrow. And I'm playing.'

She put a plate of potatoes and mutton chops before him without answering.

'Have you?' he said.

'No, I haven't. And you know why. I won't help you to destroy yourself.'

'I'll do them myself then. I'm playing tomorrow or burst.'

The football team was scheduled for another match tomorrow. Michael Joe's shoulder was well set by now, but he had not yet gone back to playing football. In the evenings, he had sometimes gone out to practice, but merely to watch, never togging out. The urge to play again came on him this morning.

After dinner, he hunted up his playing togs in the cupboard. They were caked with dry mud from the game against Quilty, not having been used since then. His mother eyed him as he held them up to inspect them.

'I'm warning you. I'll take no part in this,' she said.

'Very well. I'll wash them myself,' he said.

He washed the togs, scrubbing and scrubbing on the washboard trying to get the mud out of the togs. His injured shoulder pained him, but he went on scrubbing. His mother watched him, silently ashamed that he was doing the work of a woman, but she would not help him.

He went out in the backyard and hung the now fairly white togs out to dry on the line.

'I wouldn't make a bad washerwoman, at all,' he said to the togs waving on the line.

He went back into the shop, and stood in the door. He noticed that the cars from the wedding were now parked down the street, outside the Central Hotel, and there was a crowd outside the door. He was glad he had missed the honking of the horns and the clattering of cans when the wedding passed down the street to the hotel.

He was back in the shop only a few minutes, when Ed Donovan and Tom Fitzgerald sauntered in. They were in their Sunday clothes. They chatted with Michael Joe for a few minutes about the game tomorrow. He told them he wanted to play. They thought maybe he could go in for a while and give the arm a test and see if 'twould hold up. He insisted it was perfect and he was fit as a fiddle and bursting to go. There was a lull in the talk.

'I'm wondering,' Tom Fitzgerald said, 'if you wouldn't let bygones be bygones, and come down to the hotel for a drink with us.'

'To the wedding reception! Are ye mad. I couldn't go down there.'

'Come on. Don't be holding a grudge.'

Michael Joe saw that they thought that Nell had let him down and picked Larkin over him. He would reveal the true story to them. It was high time he made an attempt to put himself right in the public eye.

' 'Tis *they* have reason for the grudge, and not me.'

'Is that so?'

'*I* stopped going out with *her*. It wasn't the other way around. Like it might appear to an outsider.'

132

'What matter which way it was. There's bad feeling on your part, or else you wouldn't have struck Larkin. Come on down now, like a good man, and make it up.'

'It isn't that simple,' Michael Joe said. And then he saw that his public position was very weak after they had not been impressed by the true facts of his relationship with Nell. He could not tell them that the wound was deeper. They did not know of his visit to Larkin's room at the hotel, or that Nell had come into the shop to invite him, herself. It wasn't as simple any longer as apologizing to a man for hitting him. That would have been easy to do. But he knew he was in deeper than that.

Yet, now that the wedding day was here, he wanted to see Nell as a bride. When Fitzgerald had made the invitation, he was glad. To go down to the hotel, and actually see for himself Nell as a bride. Married at last. Out of his life forever.

'I'll go,' Michael Joe said. 'But I won't shake hands to anyone. Ye hear. And don't make me.'

Michael Joe knew he had no business going down to the wedding reception unless he went in a spirit of friendship. But he was not going like that. He was driven only by the morbid curiosity to see this woman he had once loved, marrying a man whom he despised. And he had to see her in her wedding dress. It would be the physical image that would really impress him, purge her image out of his mind forever.

He walked down between Fitzgerald and Donovan, they thinking that he was going out of some sort of friendship.

'Would you swap places with Larkin?' Michael Joe said to Tom Fitzgerald.

'She's a lovely girl, Michael Joe.'

'Would you marry her?'

'I don't know. 'Twould depend.'

'Depend on what?'

'How much I was in love with her, I suppose.'

The foyer of the hotel was jammed, packed. Somehow, Michael Joe was pushed, with Fitzgerald and Donovan on either side of him, through the crowd, through the foyer right to the end, where there was a table on which was the iced-layer wedding cake, already well sliced into. To one side of the cake, Seamus Larkin and Nell were standing. Nell was in a satin, white gown with a wispy veil thrown, now, off her face. Larkin was in a dark-blue suit and had a white carnation in the buttonhole. He and Nell were talking, she looking directly into his boyish face, and he looking to one side or the other of her as if he could not bear to look into her face.

Michael Joe saw the scene in time to have avoided it if he wanted to. But someone behind him in the crowd was pushing him on and up to the table. He was half-mesmerized, and did not resist too much. Then he found himself a few feet from the table, watching them together. They had not seen him yet.

'Look at that. Married an hour and they can't stop mooning at each other since,' Tom Fitzgerald boomed out.

Nell turned and saw Michael Joe. Her face lit up with real and sincere pleasure. She was standing a little behind the table with Seamus. She put her arm into his, and came forward with him to the edge of the table beside the wedding cake.

'We're glad you could come, after all,' she said. She glanced at Seamus. Though he looked extremely nervous and pale, he seemed to steady himself under her glance. He extended a hand across the table to Michael Joe.

'Welcome, Michael Joe,' he said firmly.

Dumbly, Michael Joe took the offered hand, and mumbled something. He vaguely felt the presence of Donovan and Fitzgerald behind him, as if, had he not taken the proffered hand, they would forcibly have made him. He had been driven into this gesture. Driven. Tricked into it.

'You'll have a piece of the cake,' Nell said picking up a plate.

He muttered some excuse about coming back later, and pushed off back into the crowd.

That was all he could stand of the scene. He was glad too many people hadn't noticed him. 'Twas a wonder they didn't have a photographer from the *Clare Champion* there. Well, it would be all over Corrigbeg soon that he had come down to the wedding and congratulated the groom and the bride. He would be the goat, again. Once more he had let himself in for it.

She looked lovelier than he had ever seen her. She was calm, as if she had everything under control and was at perfect peace with herself. How could she do it? Michael Joe was amazed. She must know her situation. Half the town was there in the lobby, and they all knew her past. Wearing white. Great God! Didn't she have any shame. And Larkin bravely stood beside her, facing the public out, putting on a brave front, as if nothing was wrong at all.

It was a mystery to Michael Joe. He would never have gone through with it. No matter how good-looking Nell was. Neither of them showed any sign that the day was other than happy for them. And there was something about the way they stood together and were talking that told Michael Joe, more than any words, that they were easy together, even under a tense situation such as this. They weren't pretending. He knew that. He was alert for the slightest giveaway on that score. Both of them seemed glad to see him there, in spite of what he had done and tried to do to both of them. That galled him.

Did he expect to see them hiding away in a corner of the hotel as if they were ashamed of what they were doing? Michael Joe didn't know. He couldn't understand them. Maybe it was that neither of them had a sense of shame. Nell had said some bitter things that day in the shop. She was a mystery to him. She was cold and hard sometimes. And a little girl. When he first met her, that night at the dance. And then frightened, another time. And then, now, cool and calm in a situation which terrified most girls.

Michael Joe hooked up with a few fellows and went to the bar and got drunk. He brooded for a while, taking only a small part in the loud talk going on in the bar. He had to face the fact that Nell seemed happy in choosing to marry Larkin. And Larkin himself must be a bigger man than he thought he was. Or else an amaudaun altogether, and Nell had pulled the wool over his eyes so much that he was willing to humble himself to any lengths for her. That kind of love Michael Joe couldn't understand. A man had to have his pride. Well, Larkin didn't have any, as far as Michael Joe could see; or else he was of such a forgiving nature that Nell's past didn't bother him at all. But who could believe that? Michael Joe couldn't. There would be some little worm gnawing at Larkin in the time to come. It wouldn't be all peaches and cream for him.

He knew it wouldn't be for Nell. She was disillusioned with the world. He knew that. At times, she showed it; at times, she didn't. But her past would always be there for her, reminding her of what she once was, and did. She would never be totally happy, no matter how much of a brave face she had put on today.

This thought gave Michael Joe a peculiar satisfaction, and lifted him out of his brooding mood. She was a haunted girl. She couldn't escape that. He felt some pity for her; but he could not deny that he was glad. He began to blame her for making him look like a fool in the past. Herself and Larkin. He did not think at all that it was he who had injured her, had failed her. In the light of the clown she had made of him, people thinking that it was she who had rejected him and not he, her, she was getting what she deserved. The thought lifted his spirits. He did not feel guilty about his feelings.

He sat on in the bar. Singing broke out here and there among the crowd. A piano was being played. Someone had gone out and got Willie Fox. A melodeon joined the piano. Then céilidhe dancing started. Michael Joe went out into the foyer to watch, for a minute. He was feeling in good spirits now.

On the edge of the crowd watching the dance he met Ann Shanahan.

'What drives *you* here?' Michael Joe said. 'You should be home helping your mother dig the spuds.'

She looked up at Michael Joe and blushed, and didn't ask him the question she might have asked him.

'Nell sent me an invitation. Isn't she lovely looking? I had to come. To see her. She's a . . . a . . . queen.'

Michael Joe began to tease her. 'You're not lagging behind yourself there, I'd say you were as good-looking as your . . . queen.'

'Stop codding me,' she said seriously.

'I'm not. I mean every word of it,' he said laughing. 'I wouldn't tell you a lie for the world.'

Ann blushed and hung her head. The melodeon and the piano struck up an old-time waltz. Michael Joe asked Ann to dance. He held her close, and firmly, in the old way. The floor was crowded, and they weren't able to move around very much. Once, they bumped into Nell and Seamus Larkin dancing cheek to cheek. They drew apart. On an impulse, Michael Joe walked out of Ann's arms and cut in on Larkin, who let him, with a smile. And Michael Joe danced a last dance with Nell, while Larkin danced with Ann.

They danced without speaking, and apart. No one seemed to be taking any particular notice of them. Michael Joe held himself stiffly, dark head high, and looking off into the crowd. Nell watched him, a serious and concerned look on her face.

'I'm glad you changed your mind and decided to come. Aren't you going to wish me well?'

'I'll pray for you every night,' Michael Joe said cynically.

'You could do worse,' Nell said. 'We all need it. Well, I'll wish you good luck. And be gentle and kind to her. *That* can make up for a lot.'

'Gentle and kind?' Michael Joe did not know what she was talking about.

'It won't come easy to you. You could make her very unhappy.'

'Who are you talking about?'

'Ann.'

Michael Joe laughed, 'Me? And Ann? You're not pulling my leg?'

'Don't be cruel to her. She's not strong enough for you. Forgive her.'

The music stopped and Nell went back to Seamus Larkin and Ann. Michael Joe danced with Ann again. In the middle of the dance, he stopped.

'Come on,' he said. 'The two of us are going someplace.'

'I can't. I have to stop at the wedding.'

'Ah, it isn't that at all, man. We're going out to see your father.'

Ann blushed a blush that suffused her face and neck in a peach red. She could not say anything, and just looked at him while the blush remained on her face. He took hold of her arm, ignoring the blush, and pulled her through the crowd.

'Get your coat,' he said releasing her arm.

Ann knew what he meant when he said he was going out to see her father. There was only one reason. Marriage. The thought stunned her, and left her unable to think. *See your father . . . see your father . . . see your father . . .* The phrase kept shouting itself inside her mind, excluding any thought of whether she wanted to marry Michael Joe or not, or whether she should refuse him now, at this point before the affair went any further. But she went and got her coat. She didn't know what to do, so she did what Michael Joe told her, as if he had cast a spell on her.

Michael Joe waited for her by the hotel door. An hour ago he would have thought it preposterous that he would be standing like this waiting to take Ann out to see her father to ask him for her hand in marriage. A sudden careless good humour had come over him as he danced with Ann. He had thought of Nell's advice. If she was so certain that he was going to marry Ann, then Michael Joe supposed a lot more people must be in on the secret that most concerned himself, but that he didn't know. Since everyone was so certain of the match, why should he let them down? There was nothing wrong with Ann Shanahan as a wife. She was obviously in love with him. That was good enough to start with. She was no beauty. But she was quiet. As innocent as the days were long. The thought of her innocence made Michael Joe smile. He began to feel warm towards this child of a woman that he was thinking of marrying.

She came up to him, and bent her head shyly when their eyes met. He put an arm about her, and led her outside. He was smiling broadly.

'You won't be afraid, now,' he said. 'There's nothing to be afraid of. People get married every day of the week. And if your father has no objections, we'll give it a go ourselves.'

That was the proposal. Ann submitted. She was swept along in his decisiveness, and his sudden kindness overwhelmed her. He was not now, as they walked along the street in public, his arm around her, as formidable as he had been. She was suffering mortification that they should be seen so intimately in the street, together, and, much as she wanted his arm around her to give her the courage she needed desperately, she made him take it away.

'They'll all be watching us.'

'I don't give a rattling damn who's watching us. They'll know soon enough anyway.'

But he took his arm away, to please her.

They went up to Mickey Honan, who had a Model T Ford he hired out as a hackney car, and Michael Joe got him to drive them out to Ann's house, about eight miles to Cloon. In the privacy of the motor-car, Ann let Michael Joe kiss her. It was a tender kiss, short, and without any real passion. Ann gave herself to it nervously, and trembled all over afterwards. Michael Joe was smiling.

'That wasn't bad, was it?'

Ann would not look at him. She moved over to the corner of the car and looked out at the hilly countryside now in full summer bloom, the tall grass waving in the meadows, waiting for the scythe or the mowing machine to be cut, and some meadows already cut and farmers and their families already shaking out the hay to be dried in the sun.

Michael Joe moved over beside her impelled by some vague desire to protect her, she looked so lost in the corner of the car. He put an arm around her. She stayed looking out at the fields. He felt her trembling again, and gave her an encouraging squeeze. He let down the window of the car. A breeze blew in the smell of new-mown hay. Michael Joe took a deep breath. ' 'Tis a grand day.'

'Aren't they lovely?' Ann said.

'What?'

'The cowbells. They were growing on the side of the road. Oh, they're lovely.'

The next time Michael Joe noticed a patch of the flowers, he made Mickey Honan stop the car, and got out and picked her a bunch. She almost cried when he gave them to her. He became even more tender, and he kissed her again, a little more passionately this time. Just as his passion began to arouse she drew away with a sigh, and buried her nose in the purple cowbells.

When they arrived at Ann's house, a long, one-storey, slate cottage farmhouse, the door was locked and all was quiet inside.

'They must be out saving the hay,' Ann said, a bit embarrassed.

'Well, come on and we'll find them.'

'I'll go and get them,' Ann said.

'You will not. I can talk to your father in the meadow just as good as anywhere else. And we won't be spoiling the day for the work.'

Ann would much rather have gone out and fetched her parents from the fields. She didn't want Michael Joe to see them working as they were. She was caught in an embarrassing fix. She should have known they would be in the meadow. Why hadn't she thought ahead. Michael Joe could come at night when they would be in out of the fields, and have the cows milked and be sitting around the fire. Oh, why hadn't she thought?

She led Michael Joe over the fields to the meadow where she knew her father, mother, and two brothers would be working at saving the hay. She suffered physical pains of embarrassment as she walked ahead of Michael Joe trying not to let him see her face. She had already developed the peculiar notion that he knew everything that went on inside her mind. What would he think of her people? In the fields. Working in the fields.

Michael Joe praised the land. The grass was knee high, and the garden to his right was turning golden with thick wheat. He wanted to know what her father sowed. She didn't know. How many cattle did he keep? She didn't know that either. She knew nothing about the farm.

'I'm disappointed in you,' Michael Joe said, faintly mocking her.

John Thomas Shanahan was in the meadow with his wife, Mary Ann, and their two sons, tossing golden, dried hay into thick beds, before making the hay into tall trams. He was dressed in a striped cotton shirt open all the way down in front, showing a hairy chest. His sleeves were rolled up almost to his shoulders, displaying thick, black arms.

Michael Joe moved ahead of Ann as they came up to the family working.

'God bless the work,' Michael Joe said.

They all stopped working. Ann's father answered.

'On you too.' He wiped the sweat off his forehead.

Ann introduced Michael Joe, and then went over to her mother, who, barefoot and in a dirty straw hat, was leaning on a pitchfork, watching Michael Joe. The two brothers had taken advantage of the time out to light a cigarette, and had thrown themselves on the grass.

Michael Joe praised the weather, the hay, the look of the garden beyond. John Thomas Shanahan agreed with pride. He was not modest about his property, and its fertility. He owned about fifty acres, all of it good except for about ten acres of bog.

Michael Joe praised the land more.

'You wanted to see me, I suppose?' Ann's father said, moving away a bit from his family so that if the matter was private Michael Joe would be able to state it out of everyone's hearing. He stuck his pitchfork into the earth before he began to walk. Michael Joe took the hint, and went with him.

'I want to marry Ann,' Michael Joe said, deciding to come to the point and not waste any more time.

John Thomas Shanahan stopped and looked at Michael Joe. He was a dark-complexioned, big-chested man, who carried himself very erect, and was of imposing physical presence even now, unshaven, with hayseeds and hay ribs in his tangled black hair, and wearing trousers that were patched and torn and tied with a rope around his waist.

'You're a son of old McCarthy, aren't you? The Lord have mercy on him. A decent man. Your mother was one of the O'Briens. A fine family.' He paused, bent and picked up a rib of hay and put it between his even white teeth, and began to chew on it, while he meditated.

'Ann is a quiet class of girl,' he said. 'She won't come to you empty-handed. She'll have five hundred pounds with her.'

'That'll be fine,' Michael Joe said, just as direct as her father. 'She suits me. I'd like a quiet woman.'

'She'll bring no land. I have two sons.'

'I'm satisfied,' Michael Joe said. 'I have a bit of land myself.'

The two men stood facing each other under a bright early July sun. Physically, they were remarkably alike, though Michael Joe was the taller of the two, finer and less brutal-looking in appearance, less dark because he had not been weathered, softer and fleshier about the face from the shopkeeper's life. Their manner of holding themselves, the outward thrust of the jaw and the dark heads held high, the way they faced each other to talk, in this they were alike.

They spoke like men making a bargain. It was not that Ann was being sold. But practical matters were first to come into her father's mind. He knew Michael Joe's family background, but very little about Michael Joe except that he was a shopkeeper, and the shop seemed to be doing a good business. That was enough and more than enough of qualifications, as far as he was concerned, for a son-in-law. Other matters were not his concern. Questions of love were outside his responsibility. He would provide his daughter with a dowry. Pay some of the expense of the wedding. He was not sentimental about losing his eldest daughter. She was going into Corrigbeg. That was a good match for her. To marry some fellow from the town.

Michael Joe did not expect much of a fuss to be made. He knew his man the moment they met, and he was at ease with himself talking to him in the terms that he did. As if they were making a bargain. If the father had asked him if he was in love with his daughter, he would have been stunned. He had asked to marry her. That was enough. And Michael Joe saw that it was enough for the father.

The business of the engagement having been agreed upon, and a date set for legal matters, the two men returned to the family group.

Michael Joe was beaming; Ann's father looked serious. But he was the kind of man who rarely smiled. Because talk seemed in order, they were once again discussing the crops, the weather, and the price of cattle on the English market. John Thomas came up to his wife, who had taken off her straw hat to let the sun dry her head and hair.

'We're agreed,' he said to her.

She looked at Michael Joe. 'You must stop for a cup of tay. 'Twill only take a minute to make.' She prepared to leave the meadow.

'Don't let me stop the work,' Michael Joe said. 'They'll be plenty time later on.'

Mrs. Shanahan looked at her husband to see what she should do.

' 'Tisn't often we get a day as good as this,' he said, looking up at the sky.

Ann did not have enough presence of mind to offer to make the tea herself, and did not want to be alone in her own house with Michael Joe.

'We'll leave you to yeer work,' Michael Joe said. He took hold of Ann. 'God bless, now.'

As they left the meadow, Michael Joe heard the two brothers skittering and laughing behind him.

'What's funny with them?'

Ann blushed. 'They have dirty minds,' she said, and hung her head.

Ann did not invite him into the house. They stood awkwardly on the flagstone in front of the shut door, she with her hands joined in front of her midriff, and avoiding Michael Joe's eyes.

'I'll bicycle out tomorrow, and we'll set the date and make arrangements,' Michael Joe said to break the nervous silence. Then he hopped in the waiting car without kissing her. She half expected him to kiss her, wanted it, but in the open, and was disappointed, her small face registering it plainly in dumb appeal, when he did not kiss her good-bye. But the car had sputtered off carrying him away. She went out of the yard to the road and watched it disappear. Then she went into the house and down to her room where she examined herself in the mirror.

In the ride back into Corrigbeg, Michael Joe had time to realize fully what he had committed himself to. He was engaged. How had that happened? He wasn't swept away by passion for Ann. Nothing like that made him decide. He had danced with her. And as he was dancing it struck him it was high time he got married. He knew Ann would have him. And she wasn't such a bad-looking girl. A bit shy. But he would soon cure her of that.

Was it as simple as that? He felt even casual about it. What was all that rubbish about taking the fatal step? What was fatal about it? 'Twas simple. He had just demonstrated how simple it really was. He had gone ahead and acted as if he were going about a piece of business that was part of ordinary, everyday events.

But now, sitting in the car, he began to have a let-down. He insisted to himself that getting married was simple and easy. But the doubts began. How would he tell his mother? He remembered the way she had acted when she found out that he was going with Nell Cullen. At least she could have nothing against Ann. Poor Ann had no past, to speak of. She was the opposite of Nell Cullen in almost every way you could see. Not as beautiful or as well spoken, and without much experience of life at all. She had a lot to learn. Michael Joe felt soft when he thought of himself as her protector. Nell Cullen would need no protector. Not her, she wouldn't.

For some reason, he began to feel very angry at Nell Cullen. It was a quick anger that rose into his mind and consumed him in a flash. From anger his feeling developed quickly to hatred. The image of Nell came into his mind in conjunction with Ann. And, for some reason, he began to imagine that Nell was trying to show her superiority to Ann in every way. He remembered the night at the dinner when Nell had come over and spoken to Ann. Patronized her! Then, inviting her to the wedding. Another stroke in a planned campaign of showing off. And then the conversation Nell had with him while he danced with her. Be kind to her! She's not able for you! Patronizing again.

He began to plan some way to get his own back on Nell in one final stroke, before she left the town. It was all clear to him. It was almost as if Nell had tricked him into marrying Ann. But he wasn't tricked. Ann was twice the woman Nell was, underneath. She hadn't the showy qualities. And she hadn't the past!

Driven by his hatred, a grotesque scheme entered his mind for getting his own back on her. He would have to strike through her past. Bring it to mind vividly for her. He knew where there was a perambulator in the hotel. It belonged to the wife of Gent Marrinan, the owner. He would wheel it into the room where the wedding reception was taking place. Everyone would know what the pram meant. Michael Joe would pretend it was a joke. A symbol of his good wishes that the marriage would be fruitful.

He would shame them, as they had shamed himself and Ann, for he now saw himself and Ann fighting the same battle against the malignant figure of Nell. She was not a better woman than Ann, who was innocent and quiet and shy, and not able to fight her own battles. But Michael Joe would fight them for her. The pram would say all for him. And publicly. All that needed to be said.

He was thrilled with his own evil, though he did not think of it as such. Getting a bit of his own back, he thought. In the excitement of planning his counterblow to end all blows, he forgot once more to think about the irrevocableness of the step he had taken. In fact, the championing of Ann's cause, as he thought of it, only convinced him of the right choice of wives that he had made. It bound him to Ann at a moment when he had some doubt. It built the image of Ann up in his mind. He was her prince charming, defending her against a woman who had tried to make her look small and cheap in the eyes of the world. The world of Corrigbeg.

Mickey Honan, the hackney driver, dropped Michael Joe at the hotel. He went in to take a look around before going ahead with his trick, making sure the stage was set. But Nell and Seamus Larkin had already left for the Lakes of Killarney, and their honeymoon.

The maids were cleaning up the tables. There was drunken singing from the bar.

'They're gone?' Michael Joe said to one of the maids.

'And God speed them,' she said. 'They were a grand couple.'

Michael Joe could have struck her. He went into the bar.

For the rest of the evening, until closing time, he sat in the bar getting drunk. Vin Scanlon came in around supper time and asked Michael Joe if he was coming home for his supper. Mrs. McCarthy had sent him down to find out. Michael Joe told him to clear out and mind the shop. That was his business.

It was a brooding drunk for Michael Joe until he gradually drank himself into stupefaction. He tried to sing ballads with the fellows who had remained after the wedding but he was more seriously intent on drinking than they were. They were interested mainly in the companionship and carrying the festivities of the wedding on as long as they could. Michael Joe was not interested in celebrating. It did not occur to him until he was very drunk, that he had something to celebrate. He told the fellows he was engaged, and set them up in a round of drinks. They stood him. Stories about the first night started. Dirty stories. Michael Joe told his filthiest, and revelled in them.

They celebrated Michael Joe's engagement with more drink, and more dirty stories. Michael Joe sank in his own and their obscenity.

Vin Scanlon came down again, and said his mother wanted him to come home. Michael Joe swore at him. Vin ran out of the bar.

At closing time, Michael Joe had to be lifted out of his stool and helped up home by two fellows in the bar. He refused to be helped at first, but he fell against the counter unable to walk, and only able to hold himself up with support of the counter. The two fellows babied him, and he let them take an arm, telling them that McCarthy was always able to get by under his own steam. He was tellin' them, wasn't he? McCarthy under his own steam. No one going to lay a hand on him. They kept telling him he was a great man. Reminded him of the game against Quilty and his heroics in it. He let them help him.

As they were helping him inside the hallway of his own house, Mrs. McCarthy came out with a shawl around her. The two men stopped when she confronted them; Michael Joe lurched forward out of their arms, but they caught him before he would have fallen at his mother's feet.

'You're a disgrace,' she hissed at Michael Joe.

He looked at her stupidly and bleary-eyed, half smiling.

'Get him inside,' she said to the two men.

They carried Michael Joe into the dining room and dumped him into an armchair by the fire, where he slumped down already half-asleep. Mrs. McCarthy thanked them, shortly. They left in a hurry, afraid that she might accuse them of being a bad influence on Michael Joe and of leading him to the drink.

She bent down and shook Michael Joe.

'You're a disgrace, do you hear! A disgrace to your poor mother! And the memory of your father.' She was finally driven to anger at him.

Michael Joe pulled himself together for a moment. He tried to focus on her bending over him.

'I'm . . . I'm getting married,' he said.

'What's . . . what's that you say? What's . . .'

Michael Joe could not make the effort to tell her again. He had slumped in the armchair, and began to snore.

'Oh, merciful Mother of God. What'll I do?'

She shuffled slowly to the armchair opposite Michael Joe, and sat for a while and stared across at him. Her long lower jaw began to fall open, as if she were gradually losing control of her ability to keep it shut. Her parchment face sagged; the tension was going from it. She had always been well preserved, had aged with that clear, white skin, delicate and veined, of the once beautiful woman ageing well. Even the lines were but delicate cobwebs on her face. They deepened now, as she watched her son, slumped drunk in an armchair, snoring himself drunkenly into deep sleep.

She got up and put a few sods of turf on the fire. Then took out her black rosary beads and began to say her rosary, whispering the prayers to herself above the snoring.

She pulled the black shawl tightly over her shoulders, as if the new-made fire was not keeping her warm enough. She repeated the prayers by habit, but her mind was thinking on what she had done wrong to deserve this from her only son. She had done her best to make him grow up a decent, respectable man. He had been an obedient boy. Images of him as a child came back to her. He would let no one else hold him. She had left him once with a maid, when he was only nine months, for a few minutes. He had cried and cried. For three weeks after. Almost constantly. And would only shut up when she gave him the breast. The doctor said there was nothing wrong with him. Missed his mother.

Gradually, with her feeding, he quieted down. What could she do? What would any mother do? He would not quiet down for his father! Or anyone. Only herself.

Here he was now. A drunkard. And getting married. What business did he have getting married? Taking care of a wife when he did not know how to take care of himself. Who would take care of him? Who? Who? Her poor drunken child.

She sat all night with him, herself awake, remembering his childhood, his youth, his manhood. The fire died and she did not renew it; she sat in the cold room, praying for a time, but forgetting the prayers as one image after another succeeded themselves in her mind of her past life with her son.

21

MICHAEL JOE WOKE up in the early morning and went up to bed without saying anything to his mother. She did not question him as to who he was marrying. She had no idea. She knew he had not been going out with anyone special since he stopped going out with Nell Cullen. He had taken her completely by surprise. She did not know how to stop him from marrying. She could argue with him that he wasn't ready for the responsibility yet. But that tack might lead only to bad feelings. She would have to tell him that she still thought he was a child and not ready for such a big step.

During the night, she had half come to a resigned acceptance that he was going to go ahead and bring a woman into the house. Another woman in the house! The wife of her only son. She watched him dumbly in the morning as if he might tell her that it wasn't true, that he was going to do this to her. When he said nothing but went upstairs, she grew even more resigned to the fact that he would marry. He had not been raving in drunkenness last night. If she had any faint hope left that he might be telling a lie just to make her mad, the stubborn, quick look, bleary-eyed from the dark McCarthy eyes, he threw her, and the silence—that was enough to convince her.

She went to seven o'clock Mass herself, ate breakfast alone, dismissing an impulse to try to wake Michael Joe, and then went to ten o'clock Mass again. She dropped into Mag Reidy, the dressmaker's next door, in search of gossip. She did not reveal to Mag the announcement of Michael Joe's forthcoming marriage. She manipulated the conversation with Mag hoping she might stumble on something. But if Mag knew anything she gave no hint. Mrs. McCarthy did not know what to think. Was Mag clever enough not to talk of what she really knew? Was there a conspiracy on to keep her from finding out the name of the girl? Who was the girl? Who could she be? What was she like? Mrs. McCarthy would like to have asked the direct questions. But she was too proud for that. That would reveal too much of her business.

She had to go home in doubt. And she began to torture herself by calling up images of this unknown girl who was to enter her house and displace her as its mistress. She imagined that she was tall, beautiful and clever. A queen. She would have to be a queen to make her son want to marry her. Oh, and what would herself do in the presence of such a one. The new woman would despise her. Crush her under her heel. Make a servant of her. Other thoughts, more shocking to her still, came into her mind. This new woman would be in the same room with Michael Joe. In his bedroom, that no woman but herself had ever entered up to this. She couldn't think about this. Though she tried to keep herself busy around the kitchen, her thoughts would not let her be. And she suffered in her age, and was defenceless except from time to time she was able to make short ejaculatory prayers: Christ have mercy on me . . . holy Mother of God pray for me now and at the hour of my death. Amen.

She heard Michael Joe getting up, and prepared his breakfast. He ate hurriedly so that he would catch the half-eleven Mass. He did not look at her, but sat at the table with his dark head between his hands. She poured black hot tea.

'Would you take an Aspro?'

'No.'

She put the teapot back on the range in the kitchen, and came back in determined to find out at least the girl's name.

'Who is she?'

'A girl named Ann Shanahan. You don't know her. She's from out the country.'

'A country girl!' A certain pride, haughtiness and disgust came into her voice.

'Yes,' Michael Joe said. He finished his tea and boiled egg, and hurried out, muttering on his way that he would not be back for dinner.

The information Michael Joe had given her only aggravated Mrs. McCarthy's self-torture. She abandoned her first image of the girl Michael Joe had chosen as his wife, and substituted for it the image of some barefoot country slattern with streelish hair and loud laugh who would bring disgrace on Michael Joe and herself with her bad manners and poverty. How could Michael Joe pick a woman like that? A countrywoman! In from the bogs without style or grace or charm. And a flock of country cousins the living image of her ugly self. How could Michael Joe do it! Did he know what he was doing at all? He was driving her mad in her old age. She would never be able to bear up under it.

So she continued to torture herself all that Sunday. At times, she felt as if her heart were going to give out. Then, it became hard for her to breathe. She lay down. But her body's rest gave her mind no ease. The image of the country girl, a girl she did not know and had never seen, haunted her. Who were the Shanahans? No one had ever heard of them. There was nothing distinguished about the name. Oh, my God, he's going to marry a pauper. She'll spend everything he has on dresses. Countrywomen went wild when they came into the town, and saw the civilized amenities for the first time. Mrs. McCarthy regretted that she had signed over control of the money to Michael Joe. She could have that changed. She would. She wouldn't leave him a penny. Or that country strap he was marrying. Would drive them all to the poorhouse!

When she could stand being inside the house no longer, she dressed in her black going-out clothes—wide-brimmed black hat ornamented in the band with a sprig of wax purple fuchsia; a plain-cut heavy black coat with fox fur around the collar, which she buttoned to the chin; black high-buttoned shoes, and a black umbrella. She had bought the complete outfit after her husband had died, and had worn nothing but these mourning clothes when she went out, ever since. That had been almost eight years ago now.

She walked up to the White Strand by herself this bright, late July day. A forbidding figure in black whom the neighbours out walking saluted, but did not engage in conversation. Occasionally, groups of boys and girls, young men and young women, passed her, bicycling in groups, shouting, laughing, showing off by performing tricks in the middle of the road with the bicycles, all of them dressed lightly for the summer. She noticed them and felt that someone ought to report their conduct to Canon Lyons or the guards for creating a public nuisance.

Michael Joe did not come home for supper, so she ate alone again, and afterwards went to the chapel for evening devotions, sitting as close to the altar as she possibly could, and keeping her eyes raised to the scene of the crucifixion modelled in bas-relief above the high altar. She said her rosary gazing up at the cruci-

fixion scene, and knew a moment of peace when the priest blessed
the congregation with the Blessed Sacrament, the living presence
of the crucified Christ . . . *benedicat omnipotens Deus* . . . *Pater* . . . *et
Filius* . . . *et Spiritus Sanctus.*

22

MICHAEL JOE HAD gone to the half-eleven Mass, and afterwards
bicycled out to Cloon. Before going out there, he went out in the
backyard and took his white football togs off the line, and brought
them in and shoved them into the cupboard. He would not go to
the game. As he was bicycling out to see Ann, he decided that his
football days were over. He would never play again. He had more
on his mind now to occupy him. He had got himself engaged to be
married. He was going to be serious about it. He would devote
himself to Ann. When it came to making his choice as to whether
he would go out and see Ann or to go the football match, Ann won
without any struggle.

He felt no special thrill of anticipation at seeing Ann again, but
he thought that to go out and see her was the thing he should
do. He was engaged to her now. He owed her his loyalty. She
would come first with him. After all, herself and himself had both
suffered at the hands of Nell Cullen and her husband, Larkin.
Of that he convinced himself easily. The feeling that they had been
united in a common cause helped ease any uneasiness he felt about
the engagement. By the time he had arrived out at Ann's home in
Cloon, he had wrought himself up to a pitch of excitement at the
prospect of seeing Ann, which convinced him that he was really
in love with her.

The feeling carried over when he met Ann. No one but John
Thomas was in the kitchen when he came in after knocking. He
was sitting by the fire reading the *Irish Press*, the Fianna Fail party
paper. He had opened his waistcoat and taken off his collar and tie,
but still had on his good navy-blue Sunday trousers. He was shaven.
The dark moustache was trimmed. He welcomed Michael Joe

without rising from his chair, and then called down to the room for Ann. Michael Joe heard some whisperings and shufflings from behind the partly opened door. Then Mary Ann Shanahan, Ann's mother, came out followed by Ann. There was some resemblance between the two women. Michael Joe had not noticed yesterday because Mrs. Shanahan looked anonymous in her meadow clothes and against the background of the meadow. Both women were small and thin, though the mother was tanned and wiry as against the blanched, powdery look of the daughter. Mrs. Shanahan had the look of a wire stretched taut and alive with nervous energy. She welcomed Michael Joe profusely and then set about making tea.

Ann was dressed in a plain, cotton, canary-yellow dress with white high-heeled shoes. She looked airy and bright. She stood not knowing how to welcome Michael Joe. Her father shouted heartily at Michael Joe to take a seat by the fire. Ann went to her mother to help her set the table.

John Thomas Shanahan expounded on Fianna Fail politics, and how bad the Fine Gael government was under Costello. The price of cattle had fallen. Michael Joe wasn't interested but he listened, nodding his head from time to time, and beginning to feel the need for a drink. But only tea was forthcoming. It occurred to him that John Thomas wasn't the kind of man who would waste money on drink.

The tea was strained and polite, with Mrs. Shanahan fussing around apologizing for the inadequacy of the meal and sorry they hadn't more to offer, but it had all come on them so sudden.

'Will you whist, woman,' John Thomas said once, when he could no longer stand her nervous chattering. 'The lad is content with dacent hearty food.' Michael Joe had little appetite for the griddlebread, but drank several cups of tea which eased the headache from the night before.

He wanted to get out of the house. There was something close and confining about it. Dark. Flitches of bacon hung from the black rafters. Michael Joe thought of death.

Finally, he rose from the table in between a lull in the orations of Ann's father. He looked at Ann.

'I must be off.'

Ann sat at the table looking up at him, not knowing what to do.

'Convey the lad a piece of the way,' John Thomas ordered his daughter.

Ann blushed and got up. Mrs. Shanahan fussed over Michael Joe and hoped the tea wasn't too weak for him.

He and Ann were finally able to get away.

They went for a walk in the countryside around. Ann brightened as they walked over the fields, and began to talk freely, telling Michael Joe about the neighbours around, the boundaries of the various farms; she named trees, flowers, grasses and herbs for him, and picked a bouquet of buttercups for herself. Michael Joe softened out of the gloom that the house had brought him. He began to enjoy Ann.

This was her countryside. The scene of her childhood play and rambles. She knew every field. She took him down to the little stream where she had often played with her brothers, and helped them try to catch trout with bare hands. She took off her shoes and waded into the cold water. Michael Joe would not go in with her. He watched her play and delight herself, taking pleasure in her delight. After that, she took him to the hazel wood, where she used to collect hazel nuts as a girl. They were ripe. Michael Joe picked some for her. The whiteness had left her face, and a bright burn had come on her cheeks. Her grey eyes had grown slate-dark and soft. He plied her with questions when she seemed to be running out of things to say. His own interest in the country was mild. He was town-bred and born and reared. He grew up with the attitude of the town man for the countryman—contempt mostly, but with a sort of grudging respect in some matters, especially when it came to buying and selling. He had no real feelings about the countryside. But he indulged Ann, and pretended interest for her sake. The more she talked, the more she forgot about him, and was her natural simple self.

After leaving the hazel wood, they wandered through a meadow that had not yet been cut. Ann stopped Michael Joe, and pointed to a meadowlark hovering close above them, and trilling urgently. She made Michael Joe bend down, and they crouched in the thick meadow grass, Ann observing the bird. The bird dived, and the song gave out.

'Shhhh,' Ann said, and began to creep along the meadow. The meadowlark flushed, and rose into the air with a nervous song. Ann searched and found the nest. She beckoned Michael Joe. There were four speckled birds in the nest, orange beaks opening and shutting begging for food.

Michael Joe bent to take one of them up.

'No, no, no,' Ann said. 'Don't touch them. The mother'll never feed them again. She'll smell your hand on the nest.'

'That's all country piseóg,' Michael Joe said. 'A bird has no smell.'

'Whatever it is she won't come back if you touch them.'

Michael Joe didn't. Ann remained crouched over the nest talking to the little birds, telling them their mother would soon be back. Michael Joe took her around the waist and pulled her back into the thick grass. He could feel her body tensing, though she did not protest. He kissed her. She remained unresponsive, taking his kiss but not returning it. He began to caress her legs, and to move his hand under her dress.

'Nooooo, nooooo,' she muttered. 'We're not married yet.' She sat up, and arranged her hair.

'We'll get married right away,' Michael Joe said. He was feeling passionate and wanted badly to make love to her. 'We'll do it in a couple of weeks. I'll talk to the Canon first thing tomorrow. And we can be married in a couple of weeks.' He tried to drag her back in the meadow grass.

'No,' she said, resisting. 'That's too quick. I don't know.'

'Don't you love me?'

'Yes, I think I do.'

He kissed her. She did not respond, but she let him draw her down on the grass. Be gentle and kind, gentle and kind. But he was full of passion, and he could barely control himself. She lay still, while, with great restraint, he kissed her gently, her face turned away from him into the grass. He began to feel her again, but the moment he touched her breasts, she caught his hand and sat up again.

'We're not married yet,' she said again, looking away.

'A month from next Saturday, we will,' he said.

She turned around to him. Her eyes had a strange, burning look, as if they were trying to burn their way into him to find out what he was, and what he wanted of her.

'I will,' she said, 'if you'll do one thing.'

'What is it?' Michael Joe was willing to promise anything now.

'Make the pilgrimage to Lough Derg with me.'

'Make a pilgrimage to Lough Derg?' he laughed. 'Of course I will. That isn't much to ask.'

'I always wanted to do it before I married. Make the pilgrimage.'

He put his arms around her and kissed her.

'On my Bible oath, we'll do it.'

Then she surrendered to him, falling back on the grass in a mild ecstasy. She would not give herself completely, but let him do almost everything he wanted, while she remained still.

He was able to achieve some satisfaction.

They sat in the grass afterwards, Michael Joe telling her when the wedding would be, and she agreeing to everything he said, but insisting that the visit to Lough Derg would have to come before the marriage. Michael Joe agreed that they would make the pilgrimage to Lough Derg two weeks from then, and two weeks later be married. Ann seemed bemused with the suddenness and quickness with which this man wanted to be married.

'I'd like to stay here forever,' she said lying out on the grass and looking up at the sky. She had lost some of her fear, now.

Michael Joe looked around. 'I'd say 'tis a lonesome place to want to be. Nothing but fields, and birds and cattle.'

' 'Tis lovely just the same.'

23

THE NEXT EVENING, Michael Joe went up to the parish house, to talk to Canon Lyons about making the necessary church arrangements for the marriage. He had given no more information to his mother than he had already given her, telling her, when she inquired at breakfast, that she would know all about the marriage soon enough. He sensed that she was ready to make an all-out attack on Ann, or himself, to try to prevent the marriage. But he would not let her get the chance, so he simply stopped talking to her. He knew she was suffering, but she was not going to stop him this time as she had before. He never really had forgiven her for telling him about Nell, though she had been right. He could feel her accusing him of deserting her, now, again. But he had to make his move on his own.

So he had been short, and surly, and silent most of the time, when she tried to talk to him. He was cruel, he knew. But he had no choice. And in a strange way, he began to take delight in his cruelty towards her. He would defy her to break up this marriage. And he would go through with it before she had time to do anything.

He wanted to get the marriage over with from the fear of what his mother might do if he went into a prolonged engagement. He thought of himself, too, as the type of man who, once he had made up his mind to do a thing, went ahead and got it over with quickly. He had decided to get married, so he *would* get married. Without the traditional long engagement. The marriage would take Corrigbeg by surprise. There had never been any gossip about himself and Ann. So much the better. The marriage would create a stir.

He was ushered into the Canon's library by Mary Harty, his dry, bent, old housekeeper, who spoke to him in whispers as if the human voice should not be raised in the Parish House, the dwelling of the Canon.

Michael Joe spoke loudly to her, even laughed. She put her fingers to her lips, and ushered him into 'The Presence'.

The Canon was seated behind a desk littered with papers and open books. He was writing, and did not look up. The housekeeper retired, closing the door noiselessly, leaving Michael Joe, cap in hand, standing uncomfortably in front of the desk.

The Canon went on writing, and after a few minutes, looked up and blinked as if surprised to see a man standing there. He frowned and rubbed a pale, long-fingered hand over his forehead. Then motioned to Michael Joe to sit down in a stuffed chair beside the desk.

'And what is it you came to see me about, young man?'

'I want to get married, Canon.'

Michael Joe said it defiantly, louder than he had intended.

'Keep your voice down, like a good man. You're not at a fair.'

There had never been any personal contact between the two men beyond the present one. Oh, Canon Lyons had caught himself and Nell that evening long ago, and interrupted their lovemaking. And then he had made that sermon directed at the sin of anger, in general. But Michael Joe and the Canon had never really come face to face before over any issue. If they had met in the street, Michael Joe had saluted him, and went about his business.

But the Canon knew Michael Joe, as he knew each and every one of his eight hundred parishioners. A constant supply of the gossip of the town flowed to him through his housekeeper, and through the confessional.

He bent again to his letter, and let Michael Joe sit.

'I'm in a hurry, Canon,' Michael Joe said after a while, waiting.

The Canon looked up at him, and brushed a shock of grey hair off his forehead.

'Any man approaching the holy sacrament of matrimony cannot be in a hurry.'

Michael Joe and Ann had decided yesterday that they would be married in Corrigbeg, and have a nuptial mass, and hold a reception afterwards at the Central Hotel. Michael Joe didn't care one way or the other where they were married. Ann did. He nsisted, though, that they would go to Dublin on their honey-imoon. The thought of spending two weeks in the city lifted his spirits considerably after Ann had talked about the ceremony in Corrigbeg and the nuptial mass.

As Michael Joe sat there now, before the Canon, he had a sudden change of heart. He would not be married in Corrigbeg. He'd be damned if he'd be married by the Canon.

'Is there trouble?' the Canon said, darting a sharp look at him. 'I expected it. You aren't a model of good behaviour. I've had my eye on you for a long time.'

'There's no trouble, Canon,' Michael Joe said trying to hold his temper, antagonized but not cowered by the priest.

'Your past isn't exemplary. You have a reputation . . .'

The Canon had dropped his pen into the inkwell, and joined his hands, elbows resting on the desk, before his face. He rhythmically began to tap the tips of the fingers of both hands against each other, peering out at Michael Joe between taps. He was a lean, hollow-cheeked priest, with skin as smooth and unwrinkled as fresh parchment. His fingers were almost skeletal.

'I'm not here about my past, Canon. About the future. My marriage, I came to see you about.'

'Ah, yes, marriage.' He paused, tapping the fingers. 'And I suppose you think you can turn over a new leaf all of a sudden.'

Michael Joe was getting irritated. 'To what are you referring, Canon?'

'We won't mention any incidents. For the sake of the other party involved, you understand. Who is happily married now, thanks be to God. Marriage is a *stupendous* responsibility. A Christian responsibility. Instituted by Christ, not for pleasure. Not for pleasure. But for the begetting and upbringing of children in His name.'

'I learned my catechism, Canon,' Michael Joe said sulkily.

'Mr. McCarthy, some men never learn it well enough. You are not undertaking this sacrament with the expectation of your own pleasure, I hope?'

Michael Joe remained silent. He understood the Canon well. The nice word 'pleasure' was as far as the Canon would go in mentioning what was between them. Michael Joe had never considered his sexual appetite a matter for guilt, one way or the other.

'The carnal appetite has no place in marriage.'

Michael Joe began to feel hemmed in. As if this dry, faded man, with the intense, cutting voice was trying to penetrate into his very veins and draw out the blood. Or to freeze it in his body. Stop the flow.

Michael Joe stood up and began to pace back and forth in front of the desk, compelled to assert his own motion before a man who would inhibit it.

'Sit down, my good man, and control yourself.'

Michael Joe sat down. He had no choice, and knew well that he should not antagonize this man more than he already had.

A little struggle had started between them, here in a small, cramped study, lined with leather-bound books, lit with a small desk lamp, and dark velvet curtains drawn over the only window. The air had a peculiar musky smell, that Michael Joe had casually noticed at first, but now it contributed to his sense of being oppressed. But he was in the control of the priest. He could not get married without his permission. The birth certificate, the calling of the banns.

'Who is the girl?'

'Ann Shanahan. From Cloon. We're going to be married in the church there.'

'Not in your own parish! Hmmmmm . . . ashamed. They know too much about your shenanigans around her, eh?'

'No, Canon. Ann wants to be married in her own parish.' He told the lie to achieve the slight victory. And he did not mind.

'Humph!' He was silent for a while. A clock ticked somewhere in the dark study. Tick . . . tock . . . tick . . . tock. A mantel clock. Michael Joe shifted in his chair and rolled his cap between his hands. The Canon took his hands away from his face, and leaned slightly over his desk towards Michael Joe.

'I pity the poor girl. And if there was anything I could do to prevent this marriage, I would.'

Michael Joe stared at him. The priest had gone beyond the bounds of what Michael Joe considered his duty, and was attacking him personally. He was no longer a parishioner, who had come merely to get permission to be married. To the Canon, he was some kind of evil force that had to be cut down to size. Now, Michael Joe was really aware of the personal attack. His instincts sensed it from the moment he had come into the study. Now, his blood began to rise. Was the Canon trying to make him lose his temper? He was insulting him, baiting him. Michael Joe calmed himself. He would not be trapped.

'Might I ask why, Canon?'

'You are a menace. A danger to pure womanhood. I read destruction and ruin in your face. God help that poor girl. She doesn't know what kind of an animal she's getting.'

The priest spoke coolly, never letting his voice rise in variations of tone. He was abstract, impersonal, and precise, even casual.

Michael Joe got up. 'Is that all you have to say, Canon?'

'Yes. I have to make the arrangements since you asked.' As Michael Joe reached the door, he heard the Canon say in a slightly raised voice: 'I'll remember you in my Masses.'

Michael Joe ran down the carpeted stairs, and past the housekeeper who was waiting to let him out, and out into the dark windy night. He cursed the Canon, letting go a stream of obscenities out aloud, into the darkness, as he went by the chapel. What he remembered most about the Canon's attack was the veiled references to the incident with Nell. Cheap, dirty of the Canon to throw up the past in his face. As if he himself, Michael Joe, had been doing something filthy dirty, instead of only trying to love Nell. What sort of a man, priest or no, would go around the countryside peeking at lovers in the night? It was he that was dirty and not Michael Joe! And of course, he said nothing about Nell at all.

Keeping her name out of it. Blaming it all on Michael Joe. Was the whole world in a conspiracy against him? Had Nell, during the time after he had jilted her, poisoned everyone's mind against him? Had she gone to the Canon, in this very same study that Michael Joe had left, and confessed all to him, and asked his forgiveness for her sins? A vivid image of Nell on her knees before the Canon, tears dropping down her white face, streaking it with dirt, her wavy hair dishevelled and her head bowed, rose in Michael Joe's mind. And in a wailing voice she was imploring this old man for forgiveness, as if, somehow, she had soiled him. The image drove Michael Joe into a fury of walking. The Canon laid his hand on her head, and spoke softly to her. Mary Magdalene. Let him who is without sin.

But the Canon would lay no hand on him. Michael Joe would not kneel. Be led like a lamb, driven, and made to obey. The Canon wanted to humiliate him, to make him feel ashamed of his past. That was why he brought it up. To remind Michael Joe he was a sinner. Michael Joe would not be reminded. He would not be ashamed of himself.

Michael Joe began to run. Down the Chapel Road, up the Ennistymon Road toward the White Strand and the sea. He was out into the open country beyond the town, and kept running, having settled down from his early pace into a dogged, determined gallop, as if he was running a road marathon, and might keep on going for the rest of his life.

When he arrived at the White Strand, he stopped. The night was dark, and a stiff breeze, feeling faintly of rain, was blowing in from the sea which broke, roaring below him on the sand. He was hot, and breathing heavily. He ran down the rocks, slipping and falling, and banging his shins, until he came out on the soggy sand. Then he stripped naked and went for a swim in the rough sea, swimming in the darkness, out, out, until the final animal caution, calling in his ear, screamed at him to turn back. He did, and then lay exhausted on the wet sand.

24

ANN WAS VERY upset when Michael Joe told her that the wedding would have to be performed in Cloon chapel, in her own parish. She wanted it in Corrigbeg chapel, at St. Joseph's. It was a bigger and more impressive chapel than the little one at Cloon, which was just a country chapel. Hardly fifty people could fit into it. Oh, she was very upset. Michael Joe would rather have the ceremony in Corrigbeg too, he told her, but then, he thought a nice small wedding in the country would be better. If they held it in Corrigbeg, it might look like they were competing with Nell Cullen and Seamus Larkin, coming so soon after their wedding as their own would. Ann could find no consolation in that line of argument. She wasn't the type of girl to see things in a competitive light, or to think that people would remark on a comparison at all. But Michael Joe insisted that that was the way it would have to be, without giving her the real reason. Ann hinted that he might be ashamed to be seen wedding her in the town. Michael Joe came out strongly in favour of the country. She herself had extolled its wonders of field and farm and nature to him, but a short Sunday ago.

He wouldn't be marrying her if he didn't have the greatest respect for the country. The girls in the town didn't know which end was which of anything. Their heads were scatterbrained. Could be turned by the least little whim. Give him a solid, sensible country girl to those town flirts, any day. One that had her head on her shoulders. He kissed her, and did not try to make love to her. But was gentle, and paternal. And gradually she came to accept the idea that the wedding in the country church was maybe the best after all.

But, she had imagined a wedding something like Nell Cullen's, in the town. With a lot of people there. And a nuptial mass. With the Canon and his two curates. And Michael Joe and herself receiving the Holy Eucharist. And a choir singing Latin hymns. And then a reception after it at the Central Hotel. But no drink. No drink. Only mineral waters and the wedding cake.

The reception, as the plans stood then, would have to be held in her own farmhouse. It was almost the destruction of all her dreams. Her wedding reception held in the house she was born in! A farmhouse! Again, Michael Joe had to bring all his powers of persuasion to bear on her. He didn't want either the wedding ceremony or the reception held in Corrigbeg. He wouldn't give old Canon Lyons the satisfaction. But he couldn't mention his quarrel with Canon Lyons to Ann. What she didn't know wouldn't trouble her.

He invoked her sense of the romantic in persuading her that holding the reception at her own house would be just the thing. A hotel! Sure there was too much the touch of business about it. There was no nature in having a wedding reception at a hotel. Like holding a public dance. Sure they might as well charge admission, if they went that far.

Ann surrendered her point unwillingly.

'I don't know, I don't know,' Ann kept saying.

'You don't know what? Sure I'm absolutely right, I tell you. Our wedding is between yourself and myself. We don't have to be showing off to half the county.'

Michael Joe so overwhelmed her with the passion he put into his argument that she did not have enough presence of mind to ask him why the reception could not be held in his own house in Corrigbeg. He had his reasons for not wanting to hold it there either.

He knew from the beginning that his mother would not be happy that he was getting married. No matter who the girl was. But marrying a country girl would be worse than marrying a town girl. She always had an instinctive dislike for the country and especially country people. She somehow associated them with Fair Days in Corrigbeg, when they drove their cattle and sheep and horses, and God knows what, into the town, and left the streets an inch thick with sloppy cow dung. She never went out in the streets on a Fair Day because of her fear of the animals, and she made Vin Scanlon spend an hour after each fair was over, and the country people gone out of the town, pouring boiling water on the flag pavement in front of the house and shop, and scrubbing it down. She supervised from the door until the pavement was absolutely spotless.

Michael Joe had no particular complaint about the countrymen. They dealt with him, bought tea, sugar, flour and meal. And he often had a drink with them. Fair days were always good business days for him. He thought his mother would despise Ann because she was a countrywoman. A girl that should stay home under cows, milking them. A barefooted, fat, loud-mouthed woman, without grace or charm, with the mark of the dark bogs painted on her face. He thought his mother would think of Ann like this.

This prejudice of his mother he knew he could do nothing about. It would only make his marriage more difficult. But he made one attempt to try to get her to accept his marriage to Ann. Mrs. Shanahan invited himself and his mother to a dinner. Michael Joe extended the invitation to his mother one night after supper, just as he was leaving to bicycle out to Cloon, to see Ann. They had spoken very little to each other since he had announced he was going to be married. She was standing at the kitchen sink, washing the supper dishes.

'They're giving a dinner out at Shanahans' for you Sunday. And they want you to come,' Michael Joe said going at the matter directly.

She said nothing, but continued slopping away at the dishes, keeping her back to him.

'Will you come or no?'

'No. I will not. What do you take me for?'

' 'Tisn't a mud cabin they have.'

'Go on. Go on yourself. Leave your poor old mother alone. Go on let ye without me.'

'Listen to sense. No one is deserting you. I'm marrying that girl. Like it or no.'

'This is all the gratitude I'll get. After a life slaving away for you. Bringing a country oinseach into the house to take my place.'

'You never met her. You don't know what she's like. Ah, sure 'tis useless talking to you.'

She turned around and faced him. 'Did I bring you up without any respect for your mother? Any at all? Have you a heart of stone?'

'I have to think of myself,' he said sharply.

He knew he was hurting her, but he was driven to win his point.

He was vaguely aware that in this casual little scene, years of the past and years of the future were being settled. He was in a struggle, almost a fight. He did not formulate the scene in his mind that way, but all his instincts told him that something was being settled between them. For just one instant, the thought flashed across his mind that maybe he was even getting married to bring this struggle about, and to find out who would emerge the victor. It was madness to think that way. But her image was always with him. She was a dark shadow lurking at the back of his mind. He had to get rid of the shadow. He did not know how. He blundered ahead, as he was doing now, desperately holding on to his own hardness and detachment because if he lost it, she would triumph, and he had too much a sense of himself to ever allow himself to be dominated. He could never be a mammy's boy. So she would have to become a son's mother. He did not know how he was going to bring her around to accepting this role. He could plan no deliberate strategy. Did not even think it could be planned. A head-on clash was his way. Force against force.

'You don't think very highly of yourself to be marrying what you're marrying,' she said. 'Oh, if 'twas anyone else.'

'I'm leaving, now,' he said with his hand on the latch. He had jammed the tweed peaked cap firmly down on his dark head. 'And I'm bringing her in here. And I want no more insults thrown at her while I'm around.'

'Are you going?'

'I am.'

His ears almost pricked at the note of weakness, or weariness. He paused and gave her a chance to change her mind if she wanted to.

She turned from the sink wiping her hands on her apron, and drawing herself up. She was developing a stoop. The lipless, tight mouth twitched, then closed. She did not look at him, but behind him at the door he had half-opened.

'When is it to be? The dinner.'

'Sunday. I told you. They're giving it in your honour.'

'I'll go. On one condition. No dinner. I'll just take a cup of tea. A cup of tea. Do you hear? No more!'

'All right,' Michael Joe said, 'I'll tell Mrs. Shanahan.'

He was relieved that she had decided to come. It would smooth everything out for him at Shanahans'. He had imagined for a moment going out there and having to tell them that his mother wouldn't come to the dinner. John Thomas Shanahan would have drawn up on his dignity; Ann's mother would probably have accepted it. They would be hurt, though. That might even cause a breach in the engagement. Now that he was embarked on that, nothing would turn him aside. Married he was going to be, come hell or high water. He thought of it as simply and as single-mindedly as that.

Some of the shadow lifted. He began to see clear daylight ahead for himself. No complications. That's what he wanted. So he could enjoy himself. Everything was working out right, now, and things were going his way. That's the way he wanted life.

He took his mother out the following Sunday after second Mass, in Mickey Honan's Model T. Michael Joe sat with Mickey in front, with his mother alone in the back. He did not plan the seating arrangement that way, but he didn't want to sit with her. They might talk. And there was only one thing they could talk about now. And she would only attack him, in her way. She had the look about her now, of a woman drawn into herself, a black figure, completely shrouded in her heavy black coat, her face hidden under the wide-brimmed black hat. She wore no ornaments about her, and smelled of lavender.

The high tea was nervous and uncomfortable, and John Thomas Shanahan was the only one who seemed to be at ease. He orated away at Mrs. McCarthy. She watched him out of small, grey, sunken eyes. After the first introduction to Ann, she ignored her. Michael Joe was dying for a drink, but there was nothing but tea forthcoming. He began to sweat. The kitchen was shining, and hot, everything neatly in place. He took a huge mug of spring water from the white bucket on a stool near the back door, and lingered over it. Ann tried to help her mother with the table drawn up in the middle of the flag floor. The young brothers were not present. Probably sent out for the day, to be out of the way.

Mrs. Shanahan kept plying Mrs. McCarthy with hot buttered scones at the table. She ate one, and left the other untouched on her plate. She drank one cup of tea, though Mrs. Shanahan kept pressing her to 'have a warm'. John Thomas Shanahan talked about the town, and the debt the business of Corrigbeg owed to the farmers. They'd be nowhere without them. Mrs. McCarthy was impassive. She ate slowly, cutting her scone into little squares.

Michael Joe sat beside Ann, who couldn't touch a morsel. He wolfed down about ten scones. They were so delicately baked that one hardly made a good mouthful for him.

Mrs. McCarthy did not speak one complete sentence the entire time. Or a really distinguishable word. She nodded, muttered, made noises that sounded like talk. But that was all. As she was getting ready to leave with Mrs. Shanahan helping her on with her coat, John Thomas said loudly and heartily to her:

'Well, thanks be to God, we'll be having the two families together from this out.'

Mrs. McCarthy glanced at him, and then at Ann who was standing partly behind the big hulk of Michael Joe.

'Your daughter is a fine girl,' she said.

'There! What'd I tell you?' John Thomas laughed. 'And she won't come empty-handed.'

Michael Joe was surprised. His mother was bearing up better than he had thought. He put his arm around Ann in a burst of affection, and pulled her to his side. Ann hung her head and blushed.

'Ye'll get along like two peas in a pod,' Michael Joe said across to his mother.

'We will, I'm sure.' Mrs. McCarthy did not look at Ann as she spoke.

That seemed to resolve the whole day to Michael Joe's satisfaction, though it had been nerve-racking up to then. On the way home in the motor-car, he kept turning back to his mother, pointing out the beauties of the countryside to her, and telling her who owned the farms they passed, information he had found out from Ann. First, second, and third cousins of Ann's lived in many of the farms around.

If Michael Joe saw them as potential customers, he did not say. But he knew well the saying: 'Marry a country girl; marry her tribe.' Mrs. McCarthy was not very interested in the looks of the country. She was tired, and closed her eyes, resting after a great struggle.

Michael Joe was in such good fettle after the visit that he bicycled back out to Cloon that evening to press home his courting of Ann. They went for a walk in the meadows, in the moonlight. There was a light dew on the grass. Michael Joe was passionate. Ann was nervous, moody and silent, drawing back from Michael Joe every time he tried to kiss her. He was tolerant, and laughed, willing to bide his time.

'There's something the matter with you,' Michael Joe said after a silence.

Ann was only waiting to be asked. 'Your mother makes me afraid,' she said.

'That's only all in your head. She thought you were grand,' Michael Joe said. 'The more you know her the better you'll like her.'

'I don't know. I don't know.'

This had almost become a refrain with her, as if she were entirely bemused by what was happening.

'Ah, she'll be just like your own mother to you,' Michael Joe said. 'Don't think a thing about her. Put her out of your head.' He drew Ann to him and tried to give her a lingering kiss. She surrendered herself a moment, and then fought away from him, guilty at discovering that she could respond to his passion with a passion of her own.

'You haven't forgotten your promise?'

'What promise?'

'To make the pilgrimage to Lough Derg.'

Michael Joe doubled up laughing, and in the quiet, still night, his laughter carried far. Even the man in the moon appeared to be smiling.

'And that's what you're thinking about now. We'll go this minute if you like.' He had only a faint idea in his head what Lough Derg was like. He knew that a lot of people made the pilgrimage up to Donegal every year between June and August, to St. Patrick's Purgatory where St. Patrick was supposed to have spent forty days and forty nights praying and fasting. Beyond these facts, he knew nothing about the place, and what the pilgrims did there.

'We'll go next week,' Ann said. 'I'm dying to go.'

'Right you are,' he said taking hold of her again. He felt he'd never be able to restrain himself until the wedding.

Ann kissed him passionately after he had promised to go to Lough Derg.

25

THEY LEFT CORRIGBEG early morning the following Thursday to go to Pettigo, just across the border in Donegal. A bus coming from Listowel, in Kerry, a tour bus, stopped in Corrigbeg and picked them up. The bus was crowded mostly with middle-aged women, and silent, dour men. Michael Joe saw he was in for a black time. But he struck up an acquaintanceship with a tall, dark Kerryman, named O'Connor, who was making the pilgrimage with his wife. O'Connor kept him in stitches all the way up in the bus telling yarns. O'Connor's wife, a shy, gentle woman, talked with Ann. It was her third pilgrimage, so she was able to give Ann a preview of what was ahead. Ann was round-eyed listening to her. Michael Joe's laughter was the only laugh in a bus that had more the atmosphere of a ship of doom than a bus ride. Michael Joe thought the people on it were peculiar, as if they were all going to be hanged. He was glad he met O'Connor. And thought he was the best teller of stories he ever heard.

They got into Pettigo that evening, and stayed the night there in rooms with special rates for the pilgrims. He and O'Connor went off and had a couple of drinks, leaving the women together.

In the morning, Ann told him to eat a good meal because it was going to be his last for three days. Michael Joe didn't believe her. And for the first time, he really began to inquire what he had got himself into. Ann explained to him. A soft, deep radiance seemed to have come over her. Her voice was deep and rich. Michael Joe was amazed, and thought jokingly it must be the Donegal air.

Ann spoke in an intense whisper to him across the breakfast table in the hotel, as if she were confiding in him secret tidings of the Promised Land.

'We go to the landing. And then there's a boat across to the island. We'll see the basilica.' She lifted her eyes as if she was gazing at heaven. 'We'll have one meal a day. Black tea and a bit of toast. And an all-night vigil in the basilica the first night. And make rounds barefooted. Whether 'tis raining or no. And kneel on beds of stone. The penitential beds!'

Ann was so overcome she could not go on. Michael Joe stared at her open-mouthed.

'Great God, man, what have you got me into? Black tea and a bit of toast, is it, for three days?'

'That's all,' she said shyly. 'Offer it up. 'Tis all penance. Offer it up.'

He had never seen her so moved.

Michael Joe ordered another breakfast for himself.

A bus took them out again to the landing, from where a boat would take them across to Station Island.

A torrential downpour started, and a blustery wind blowing across the bleak moor which Michael Joe could see between the blasts of rain against the bus windows. He turned around to see if he could find O'Connor. He was in the back. His face was dark and serious. He was looking out of the bus window, muttering something under his breath.

'Did you bring an umbrella?' Michael Joe asked, beginning to panic.

'No one does,' Ann said smiling. 'The rain and wet is part of the penance.'

'Oh, holy God,' Michael Joe said. 'This'll be the death of me.'

They stepped out of the bus on to the landing and were drenched immediately. The boat was a big, oversized canoe, with huge oars plied by men who looked like Aran islanders. The boat was open. The rain poured down on them. Ahead of him, above the waves, Michael Joe made out the island topped with the dull silver basilica, looming out of the rain. The island and the basilica swayed; Michael Joe's stomach heaved. He retched up his breakfast over the side of the tossing boat. Ann put an arm around him. She was smiling blissfully, her hair soaked, the drops falling down her face. Michael Joe saw, in his sickness, that she was, at last, beautiful.

It was mad. The whole thing was mad. He was drenched to the skin, and cold. He'd get his death of pneumonia, so he would. He would not be in the better of this pilgrimage for the rest of his natural life.

The minute they got off the boat, a priest, standing in the rain, explained the rules of the island to them. No talking. Women and men in separate dormitories to sleep, the second night. All-night vigil tonight. Anyone caught doing unnecessary or frivolous actions, off the island immediately! Off with the shoes.

Michael Joe's feet were tender. The cobblestones were rough. One by one the pilgrims knelt in a bed of cobblestones, the rain and wind coming hard down on them, and held out their arms before a dripping image of the crucified Christ. Michael Joe forgot about Ann. He began to curse himself silently for coming. As he held out his arms before the cross, he was already beginning to feel that excruciating sensitiveness of his body which made him suffer for the next three days. His clothes were stuck to his skin; he shivered and his teeth chattered. He could feel goose flesh rising all over him. It was as if the very elements themselves were conspiring to make this pilgrimage truly a purgatory. A place or state between heaven and hell where the souls of sinners were purified of small sins of the body before they could enter heaven.

After the prostration in the penitential bed before the Cross, the pilgrims moved in out of the rain into the chapel basilica. But in the chapel the discomfort was even worse for him. While the rain was coming down on him outside, he resigned himself to it, but in the chapel, where he was sheltered, he became conscious of the wetness of his clothes against his warm body. A priest led them in prayers. Michael Joe could not pray. He glanced at the pilgrims around him. Faces full of dumb, patient suffering. Was he like them? They prayed. Their faces seemed to change as they prayed. The abjectness left, and was replaced by a sort of luminosity. Not the red glow of blood but the warmth of white heat. That was it! Their faces took on a look of white heat as they prayed. Michael Joe felt no white heat. Only cold cloth against his feverish body.

He could not pray. He was too conscious of his wet clothes.

Then the rounds began. Walking from grotto to grotto in his bare feet over the stones. His body was getting taut, his muscles clumped in his shoulders, his stomach tight and retching with the dry heaves as he stumbled along. The soles of his feet were cut and pierced. He could have lain down on the stones from exhaustion and pain, though the pilgrimage was only a short time under way. The other pilgrims were saying rosaries. He had rosary beads in his pocket and took them out. His hands shivered. The beads rattled. He tried to pray. But it was no use. He could not concentrate on prayer.

That night there was an all-night vigil in the basilica. Michael Joe began to pity himself. A priest led the pilgrims in communal prayer throughout the night. But there were also long periods of silence. The murmur of the prayers. It was like being in a hive of bees. What was he doing here? Why had he come? Ann! How was she bearing up under this crucifixion of the flesh?

Somehow he got through the all-night vigil without falling asleep. His body kept him awake. It was as if it were going through a fever, alternating flashes of heat and cold. Heat when his blood asserted itself, and cold when the dampness of his clothes penetrated and chilled his blood. In the silence of the chapel, images of his past life kept coming back to him. He could not pray. How could anyone pray? He saw Nell Cullen standing as she stood that day he went walking with her first, up by the Puffing Hole. Blue sky. The wind blowing her dress against her, and her long hair a riot around her face. The image brought back a rush of physical desire. The flesh was not yet dead. The buzz of the bees rose. He could not pray.

Only through images of Nell did he forget where he was and what was happening to him. He heard her laugh, many times. He accepted the images. Made no attempt to reject them. Was glad they came because he was able to forget himself for a time in them.

Holy Mary, Mother of God, pray for us sinners, now and at the hour of our death. Amen. The buzz of the bees.

And so, for the three days, it was the image of Nell that accompanied him in his rounds of prayers, the vigils, the silences, even in the men's dormitory when he had a chance to dry his clothes, and where he met O'Connor again. When they tried to talk, they whispered, and then stopped, as if energy were being wasted, or as if there were nothing really now to say. They were exhausted. The one meal a day, black tea and a few pieces of toast, gave no sustenance. Michael Joe drank the black tea to put warmth in him, but could not touch the toast. His stomach rejected it.

As the pilgrimage progressed, his body surrendered. He became numb to the stones, the penitential beds, the fasting, the ever-present rain and wind keeping him soaked and damp. The more his body grew numb, the more he thought of Nell. He was hardly aware of anything going on around him. He was always in a group of men, so he just followed them patiently and dumbly, and mechanically did what they did, while his mind wandered among images of his lost girl, hearing her talk and laugh. The Christmas night that he sat down to dinner with all her family. That night! He, the Judas, sat down and shared bread with them. That was a grand, warm night. And afterward, he had run away from her. Why didn't he stay? Why didn't he love her, and marry her? Oh, if she only had been pure. She had deceived him. She had pretended to be something she was not.

He would berate himself silently for having rejected her. Then he would berate her for hypocrisy. And then an image of her would come flashing back into his mind, always free, graceful, unutterably lovely, and laughing. The stars, the stars. Heaven. The woman before whom he was a clod. He would say that to himself. And then, no! He could have loved her if . . .

So the dialogue between self and soul went on in him. He wanted an answer from his images. He asked questions of them. But the girl only smiled and laughed, and played with him, as she had that first night long ago at the dance when he had met her, danced with her, and lost her into the night.

The pilgrimage was over. He was reunited with Ann at the return landing. He was abstracted and silent. She was radiant.

'Are you all right?' she asked him. 'Wasn't it lovely? I'm grand, now.'

'I don't think I have any body any more,' he said.

'Wasn't it lovely?' Ann whispered again, hugging his arm. 'Ah, I'm happy we came.'

Michael Joe tried to wake out of his stupor, and take a look at her. Her skin had turned lily-white, the powdery look gone. Her hair had straightened from the exposure to the rain. It floated wispily over her face. She held her head high, the slight stoop gone.

'It did you good,' he said, 'like a holiday.'

Ann squeezed his arm, and helped him into the boat, and she sat close to him all the way across while he stared blankly out at the slate-grey lake waves.

26

THEY WERE MARRIED at the country chapel of Cloon on a Saturday morning in mid-August. Mrs. McCarthy came down with a mysterious ailment a few days before the wedding. She had the doctor. He did not know what was wrong. He prescribed rest and medicines. Nurse Frawley was sent for and installed in a room in the attic of the house to attend Mrs. McCarthy. The plans for the wedding had gone too far for it to be postponed. When Michael Joe suggested to her that he might put it off, she insisted that he go ahead without her. She wouldn't be missed anyway. Michael Joe left the sick-room before he got bitter with her. He had thought everything was going to be all right. But he could see now that she wasn't going to surrender as easily as he had thought. He tried to put her illness out of his head. The doctor had said it wasn't serious. She was overworked, and getting old. The doctor thought it was a good idea to have a young woman coming in who would take some of the load of keeping a big house off her shoulders. Michael Joe looked at that side of the picture. Ann would be a help to his mother.

During the few weeks after the pilgrimage, Michael Joe was surprised at the calmness of spirit which descended on him. It wasn't that he saw the prospect of his life spreading calm and orderly before him: marriage, then children, being interested in his business, leading the decent life, regular and routine, of the average man in Corrigbeg. He did not have that kind of view of himself.

He wasn't thinking of himself at all. It was as if he were asleep, or walking around in a waking dream, watching a life going on that had nothing to do with himself at all. The calmness of spirit was more indifference to life than acceptance and clearness of view of it. He could not be touched by anything he saw. He courted Ann indifferently. She would even kiss him, lightly and tenderly, and he did not respond. She lost her timidity with him. He was having a new dark-blue suit made for the wedding. She picked the colour for him, and insisted on the tailor making a waistcoat. He agreed without a murmur, although he thought waistcoats were only for old men. She insisted on his going to Confession with her so that they could receive Holy Communion the morning of their wedding at the nuptial mass. He did. And they received at the little altar rails together.

Only at the wedding reception afterwards, in Ann's house, did Michael Joe begin to show some sign of real life again. The farmhouse was too small for the crowd, but the men spent most of the time out in one of the cow cabins where the quarter cask of porter was, so that the women had the kitchen to themselves. A fiddler and a concertina player came, and the dancing started. Michael Joe and Ann had to lead a Clare set.

Ann was not very good at dancing, and Michael Joe did not enjoy himself dancing with her. He was not very adapt at the céilidhe dances either. Modern dancing was his own style, waltzes, fox-trots, tangos, even a rumba. The céilidhe dances were a bit stiff and inhibited for him. And you didn't get close to your partner.

He got through the set with Ann in bad grace, tripping, making mistakes in the intricate figures, and stumbling around. It reminded him of that night at Blake's long ago, when he was drunk and had first met Ann, and had made fun of her on the floor. Now, though he was sober, he could not make his body keep time to the music.

After the dance, he went out to the cabin, and had a few drinks. He felt a little ashamed of himself because of the dance. He wandered back into the kitchen again. The atmosphere in there was beginning to warm up. He heard the high-pitched yells of the men, the cries of 'house, mother, and mind the dresser', and watched the fellows wheeling the girls, and the girls throwing back their heads, laughing, screaming half in fear and half in delight, the red blood flushing in their cheeks.

Then he danced a set with Ann's mother. It was strange. A small, wiry little woman, and he a big, dark man. She came up to him and put the request for the dance with him in the form of a challenge.

'My daughter isn't too light on her feet. And you look slow yourself.'

He laughed at her. 'I'd dance you into the ground any day, Mary Ann,' he said calling her by her first name.

The mother's eyes lit. 'Come on, you lumbering jackass,' she said.

He suspected that she might have taken a little port wine. She had never acted like this before. He responded to her in kind. The secret woman was coming out of her hiding place.

The fiddle and concertina struck up another set. Michael Joe put an arm around his mother-in-law.

She held herself straight and stiff, her greying head, hair tightly bound in a bun, high, not looking at him at all. Her small hand was light in his. And then she began to move to the music. Quick, light, formal, in perfect control of every movement of her body. Michael Joe hadn't been expecting anything like this. A charge of electrical energy passed between them. Instinctively, he knew he had to be on his mettle. This was dancing of a strange passion. Her face was like a mask of death, and her body was rigid.

Somehow, he did not know how, he caught the spirit of the dance from her. He willed his own body erect, held his head high. As he began to dance he felt taut as a fine wire stretched to its limits. But vibrating in the formal suspense of the dance. But that passion was replaced by another, a more subtle one, one in which he felt challenged to match the movements of the woman he was dancing with. He moved in the dance with her, restrained, free. His feet moving, more than the body, but that alive, too, pouring all its energy into the movement of the feet, and his feet challenging the woman.

Son-in-law and mother-in-law did not speak during the five parts of the set. It was a serious dance, to be concentrated on, and not ruined with talk. Michael Joe danced as well as she did, holding himself rigid yet moving with grace and sureness, the body obeying the feet. He executed each movement with her, perfectly. The people around the edge of the kitchen floor watched.

The climax was a wheel. He locked hands with her, and took her elbow and wheeled until he lifted her off her feet and she swung around him, screaming. The music stopped. And he came to a dead standstill, erect and rigid. She was laughing lightly. She melted against him for a second, and became the mother-in-law again. She ran a hand quickly across her forehead. Wisps of her grey hair had fallen loose. She looked up at him. He looked down at her, smiling, too, conscious that he was warm, and wanting to unbutton his waistcoat.

'I didn't think ye townies had it in ye,' she said.

Michael Joe smiled stupidly at her. He wanted to kiss her. He never had. Nor never would. He was very near to her for a split second. He wanted to thank her. Get down on his bended knees and thank her. He felt overwhelming gratitude to this little woman, whom he had barely taken notice of before, and whom he despised a little for the way she had kotowed to his mother that Sunday at the tea.

Ann came up. 'I'll hand you over now that I've seen you,' Mrs. Shanahan said.

Michael Joe was still bemused and speechless. Mrs. Shanahan went off.

'She used to be the best dancer in the parish one time,' Ann said.

'What happened? Why did she give it up?'

'Oh, when you get married . . .'

Michael Joe saw that Mrs. Shanahan had gone to where John Thomas, her husband, was sitting by the hearth and was standing behind the chair from which she watched the dancers for a moment, and then she bent and spoke to her husband, as if asking him if there was anything he wanted. He shook his grey head.

'You don't give up *all* the fun when you're married,' Michael Joe said to Ann.

He danced with her, but did not really enjoy it because she was not as good a dancer as her mother.

27

THEY WENT TO Dublin that evening to begin their honeymoon, taking a motor-car to Limerick, and the train from there to the city. It was the first time in the city for both of them. They stayed at the Gresham Hotel.

The honeymoon night was one of terror, fear of pain, nervousness, and shame for Ann. For Michael Joe it ended in frustration, and anger. In the early dawn, he turned away from her and slept, exhausted but not satisfied. They were unable to consummate the marriage. Ann was nervous. She cried. Michael Joe had to leave her alone. He was afraid she might get hysterical.

In the morning, when he awoke, she was not in the room. He got up and dressed quickly, in a slight panic. He did not know what she might do. Maybe she had taken the train back home. He had been rough with her the night before. He might have frightened her. He had frightened her, maybe. As he finished dressing, she came back into the room. She was smiling, and wearing the white hat with the veil that she had worn yesterday at the wedding. She had a black missal in her hand. Michael Joe sat down in the bed.

'Where in all that's holy were you?'

'I only went out to Mass,' she said gaily.

'To Mass!'

'Yes,' she said. 'There's a lovely small little chapel around the corner. Run by the Franciscans.'

Michael Joe said nothing. He was relieved that she showed no signs of strain from the night before, and seemed to be taking it in her stride. He decided to try and be nice and kind to her, and not tell her how mad he was that the first morning of their honeymoon she had left him and gone out to Mass.

'I was going to wake you up to see if you wanted to come,' she said. 'But you were sleeping so soundly. Snoring!'

'Was I!' he laughed. 'I didn't know I snored. You're finding out my faults already.'

They spent the day walking around the city. Michael Joe was tireless; he wanted to see the whole city in one day. He got into conversation in street corners with whoever was near him. He told them who he was and where he was from. And introduced the wife, as if he were an old hand at being married. He met a couple of fellows who wanted to take him for a drink. The horse show was over, but the spirit of the show still lingered in the city. He refused. The wife didn't drink. He was dying to go, but made the sacrifice for Ann's sake.

The movement and crowds in the city appealed to him. He marvelled at the tall buildings, and the old Georgian houses, and the huge shop windows. In Corrigbeg, the houses were only two storeys, and even those rare. When were these built? Who built them? The architecture impressed him, and he marvelled at the men who conceived and built such structures. He took open-mouthed pleasure in looking. The people he spoke to smiled at him, and he often bumped into people, walking along the pavement looking up at the tall buildings.

Ann grew exhausted early, and could not match his energy. The more she saw, the more silent she became, and withdrew into herself. The more Michael Joe saw, the more outgoing he became, and developed an insatiable appetite for information. He began to remember his Irish history. It came back in little dribs and drabs from his National School days, particularly the events relating to the 1916 Rising. He insisted that they walk to the General Post Office in O'Connell Street. He saw where Pearse, Connolly and Larkin and the rest of the brave fighters in 1916 made their famous defence. And the tricolour flag of the Free State now fluttering over it. From the General Post Office he dragged Ann over to No. 27 Pearse Street, where Padraic Pearse was born. Pearse, the greatest hero of them all, all those who had died.

He would hardly have stopped walking if Ann had not reminded him that they had not eaten. After eating, Ann said she had a head-ache and wanted to go back to the hotel. Michael Joe was disappointed.

'You don't have to stop with me. I just want to lie down a while,' she said.

'No. I'll stop,' Michael Joe insisted. 'We have plenty of time to be seeing things.'

'You will not. I can see you're dying to be out. And I need a rest.'

Michael Joe had to control his passion again. He took her back to the hotel, and then went out again himself.

He was in his element in Dublin, being alone, walking the streets, bumping into people, talking to them, and they were all willing to talk to him. Ah, what was Corrigbeg compared to Dublin! A graveyard. You'd hardly meet ten people on the street any day but Fair Day. He went down Westmoreland Street, and to O'Connell's Bridge, wider than it is long. He stood on the parapet and gazed down at the murky, strong-flowing waters of the River Liffey.

An image of the last time he had stood on the bridge of a river, with Nell, on the bridge of the Fergus, that rainy day he had taken her to Ennis, came into his mind. But he dismissed it. That was gone now. Tug boats on the river hooted. A barge carrying barrels of

Guinness went by. Men waved to him from the deck. He waved back, though they were tiny below him.

He got into talk with a fellow on the bridge. They went for a drink in a dark pub nearby. He bought a couple of sweepstake tickets from the fellow, and stood him several rounds of drinks. He wouldn't hear of the fellow buying. It was late when he got back to Ann. He was in royal form.

They went to the Abbey Theatre that night, on Michael Joe's suggestion. Paul Vincent Carroll's 'Shadow and Substance' was playing. Michael Joe thought it was great, and trembled with excitement at the tense moments, especially when the bleeding schoolmaster confronted the parish priest and defied him.

Afterwards, Ann wondered how a play like that would ever be let on the stage in Ireland. Michael Joe was so transported that he paid no attention to her. He kept going over parts of the play in his mind, sympathizing with the schoolmaster, the victim-hero, and wishing he himself had been there to defend him against the clergy and the jealous townspeople.

The marriage was not consummated that night either. Michael Joe was in a wildly passionate mood. Ann, again, was nervous, and unwilling. Michael Joe got rough, and she became afraid, and she begged him to give her a chance, and leave her alone for a while. He turned away from her but could not sleep.

The remaining two weeks of their honeymoon took the pattern of the first day. They walked together in the morning, Michael Joe restless, inquiring, trying to get to know as much about Dublin and its citizens as he could. As if they were foreigners. Ann listlessly and silently tagging along after him, embarrassed at times when she saw the smiles of the people he spoke to, and the half-ironical way they looked at Michael Joe and herself.

In the afternoons, she stayed at the hotel and slept. She let Michael Joe go out by himself a few nights, and he came home late, exhilarated and very drunk.

One night, during the two weeks, the marriage was consummated. Quickly, painfully, and, to Ann, shamefully. Michael Joe went to sleep immediately afterwards.

She continued to go to Mass every morning. And had to wait a few hours for Michael Joe to wake up. She spent these few hours longing to be back home again, as she was before her marriage, in Cloon, with her father and mother. But when

Michael Joe awoke she was caught again in the whirl of the city, for a time. He could never get enough of the city; it only made her tired.

Once, they went to the races at Leopardstown with a couple of friends Michael Joe had made. Michael Joe lost a couple of pounds betting. She was worried. He was throwing his money around everywhere, and would let none of his new friends buy anything. Oh, she longed for the honeymoon to be over, and to be back safely in Corrigbeg.

Michael Joe felt he could stay in Dublin forever. Here was a place to challenge a man. He fell truly and deeply in love with the city, and the life there. Though he was frustrated by Ann, he was able to ignore it, because the city itself compensated for whatever other dissatisfactions he had experienced there.

They returned home.

28

MRS. McCARTHY WAS up and well, and shuffling around the house. She took Ann under her wing immediately, and wouldn't let her lift a hand. 'You must be worn out with all that gallivanting around Dublin,' Mrs. McCarthy said. 'Rest your bones a bit.' Ann protested that she wasn't tired a bit, but was glad to get back. She hadn't really liked Dublin at all. She had really rested a lot. And if anyone was tired it was Michael Joe. But Mrs. McCarthy wouldn't allow her to help around the house, in spite of her protests that she wanted to. She spoke kindly to Ann, but firmly. Made tea for her. Suggested walks she could take so that the summer's sun would put some colour back in her cheeks. She needed to build herself up, she was so pale and thin.

Ann had no comeback to this kind of attention, so she submitted. Mrs. McCarthy continued to do the cooking, laundry, ironing and general housework just as she had before Michael Joe was married.

She did not, however, enter Ann and Michael Joe's bedroom which was down the corridor from her own, with one empty bedroom between them. This room she left completely to Ann's care. She did not tell Ann this, but intuitively both women understood that it would be so. Mrs. McCarthy would have liked to take charge of the room as she had in the past, but her own sense of delicacy prevented her. She could not bring herself to enter the room now, no matter how much she might have wanted to. And Ann, though she submitted to letting Mrs. McCarthy have control of running the house, yet might, in her own way, have resented this invasion of the one room in the house she thought of as hers from the first.

Ann was not the kind of girl to want much, or to demand much. But she did become attached to small things, and those she clung to, sometimes in abject terror, because if they should be taken away from her, she had no methods to prevent them from being taken, or to get them back when she had lost them. She felt vaguely that Mrs. McCarthy wished to keep her control over the house, and resented a new woman coming in. Ann did not want to cause trouble. She was awed and overwhelmed by the house at first, and was just as happy to let Mrs. McCarthy have complete charge of it. But she did consider the bedroom hers. And for a while, she lived in fear, lest Mrs. McCarthy should pry into it. She was relieved each day to find things exactly as she herself had left them, especially the bed made as she herself had made it. There were signs of love on the sheets in the morning which she herself covered over hastily. She often remembered that night at the Gresham in Dublin. And blushed.

She had time on her hands, and spent it in her room, sitting by the window looking across the street at the three or four houses she could see, and being impressed by their looks. They were all two-storey, slate-roofed houses, painted blue, ochre, yellow. Here she was, living in Corrigbeg at last, living in her own house, just as grand to look at as the ones opposite her, and married to Michael Joe McCarthy, one of the finest men in Corrigbeg. She was his . . . well, his lady. She dared to think of being married to him like that. She had come into the town from the country. A country girl in the town! She became almost breathless with pride, but nervous and a little afraid of her own pride, not trusting herself completely yet, and not being confident enough of herself, to indulge completely in her pride.

She never thought of Dublin, once she had left it. Sometimes, she opened the window of her room and put her head out to get a better view of the Main Street of Corrigbeg. It wasn't much to look at, two rows of wildly coloured slate houses on either side of a wide, tarred road on which travelled a few horses and carts, and one or two motor-cars. It was quiet, mostly deserted, and dusty. She liked it. The static, quiet quality of it. It was peaceful. She had always looked at it in the past from the outsider's point of view. She was just a country girl visiting her cousins, the Falanes. She was a stranger. But she wasn't any more. Behind the quietness of the town she knew that a mysterious life was going on—the things the townspeople did that made them look down on the country-people. She had only a vague idea what they were, but she was on the threshold. Whatever they did, it made them feel superior to countrypeople. And she herself wasn't proud of being country. She wasn't ashamed either; but she wasn't proud.

She spent much of her early days of marriage dreaming of the new life she had entered on. She did not dare, however, to go out on the Main Street alone, unless Michael Joe was with her, accompanying her to late Mass or taking her for a walk on Sunday afternoons, up to the White Strand or Spanish Point. She did not stay in the house all the time. Sometimes, she would go up to Falanes' to sit with Kitty, who had been her bridesmaid at the wedding. She went up to Falanes' by a back road that ran around behind the houses on the Main Street. The thought of going out on the Main Street by herself terrified her. She had a strange fear of what people would say. She was afraid they would see right through her. A certain sense of shame and embarrassment at her position of being the newly wedded wife and all that meant, kept her fearful of going on the street, exposing herself to the public gaze, as it were. She was never likely to meet anyone going up to Kitty Falane's by the back way, the New Line, as the road was known locally.

She and Kitty sat and talked. Ann questioned Kitty about Corrigbeg. She never had enough courage to question Mrs. McCarthy. Ann's questions were innocent. She was satisfied to know the names of all who were living in a certain house, their ages, where they came from, and so on. She wanted information. Kitty was interested in gossip.

'There's that Guard Mahoney up there at the Barracks. Don't let him ever get a chance at you. He's as horny as a goat.'

Ann blushed. 'Oh, Kitty. Stop that. I don't mean that. Those things aren't right to know. I only want to know who he is.'

'He's tall, dark and handsome. And even married women have to look out.'

Kitty poured out her heart about her own unfortunate romance to Ann, who listened, but hardly understood. If Kitty and her fellow were so much in love why didn't they get married?

'My fella,' Kitty would go on, half-laughing. 'You couldn't put a stir in him with a red-hot poker. Sure, half the time he hardly knows I'm here. Until he gets drunk. Then he comes around looking for me to take me for a ride in his car, maryah. They're no good. Men are no good.'

Ann was shocked. 'They are, Kitty. Sure, they are,' she said quietly.

And so the conversation would go on.

Ann did begin to blossom in the early days of her marriage. She was alone a lot, and had time to dream. She had no real responsibilities. And Michael Joe was attentive. More than that. He seemed devoted, and scrupulous to attend to her every wish. He was always asking her if she wanted anything. A new dress? New shoes? He bought her a box of chocolates a few times. He was even more attentive to her than during their courtship. And he was very passionate. He frightened her. She let him do what he wanted. But she cried out when he hurt her. But when it was all over, she was happy. She simply shut her mind to what was happening and tried to think of birds singing, or the fields at Cloon. Sometimes she even prayed when the pain became almost unbearable.

But, she was happy as long as she could forget about *that*. Michael Joe stayed at home with her every night, and they listened to the wireless together. Mrs. McCarthy always went upstairs, or went to the chapel at night, so that they were alone in the house. Ann would make tea for Michael Joe then, guiltily, and get a bit giddy from the music on the wireless. Michael Joe sat and seemed to enjoy her playing, teasing her, encouraging her, and calling her 'his little oinseach'. He would try to kiss her, and give her a rough with his heavy beard. She would scream. If he became passionate, and wanted to go to bed, she would insist on staying up until his mother came in. 'How would it look? If she came home and saw we had gone to bed?' Michael Joe couldn't understand that logic.

On Sundays they walked together to last Mass at half eleven.

And she was quietly proud to be walking beside this handsome man who spoke to everyone he met, and everyone spoke to him. He seemed to be getting jolly under the influence of marriage.

Mrs. McCarthy never accompanied them to the late Mass. She went to the seven, by herself, and spent the morning preparing breakfast, and cleaning up.

On Sunday afternoons, if the weather was fine, Michael Joe took Ann for a walk. Michael Joe spoke to the other married men and their wives and children who were out walking, giving but a curt nod to the boys at the corner of the street. Ann never spoke, preferring to let Michael Joe do the talking. She would not have known what to say anyway, even if she had wanted to say something. She stood shyly beside Michael Joe almost hiding herself behind him. It was all so lovely. Michael Joe booming away in his hearty voice inquiring after the health of this one and that one, commenting on the weather and whether it would hold up, now and then dropping a casual remark about Dublin and what he saw there, and its relation to the history of the country, and particularly the Rising of 1916, and the I. R. A. movement, much of which past was still fresh in the minds of many people in Corrigbeg.

Michael Joe's behaviour was beginning to instil a faith in Ann of the power of her own attractiveness. At the back of her mind, she had never been quite sure why he married her.

She was beginning to feel now that he really and truly loved her.

She was content. These walks began to make her feel she was taking her part in the life of the town.

One Sunday, Michael Joe wanted her to go to a football match down in Kilkee, and they could go to a dance at the Hydro Ballroom afterward. She didn't feel like it. What did they want to be going to Kilkee for? Wasn't Corrigbeg good enough for them? She would be content just to go for a long walk with himself beside her. That was what *she* wanted. Michael Joe did not press the suggestion.

There was one incident more than all the others that convinced her that Michael Joe was truly hers.

It was the first Fair Day in Corrigbeg since their marriage. Ann woke up one morning to the sound of cattle bellowing, sheep bleating, goats nannying, and what sounded like a thousand varieties of animal noises coming from the street below through their bedroom window. She got up and ran to the shutters and opened them. Below her in the street the fair was already in progress, and the men and cattle were already in the street. She felt sudden anger, and gripped the sides of the window shutters as if she would shut them again and blot out the sight of the fair.

Instead, she went back and woke up Michael Joe who had slept on in spite of the noise. He got up immediately. He had forgotten the fair. He should have the shop open already. This was one of his big days.

When he got downstairs, there was no breakfast ready for him. He shouted. Ann did not know what was up. Mrs. McCarthy usually had breakfast ready.

'Isn't my mother down, yet?' Michael Joe said.

Ann got nervous. And suddenly decided she'd make breakfast for him herself.

A boiled egg was the simplest. No porridge. She would be sure to spoil it. She bustled around and made tea and boiled an egg.

The tea wasn't strong enough and the egg was hard-boiled. Michael Joe didn't complain strongly. In a quiet voice he told her he liked soft-boiled eggs. She was sorry. Oh, my God. What would she do? She went out in the kitchen and said a quick prayer to Saint Jude, the patron saint of hopeless cases. Michael Joe drank the tea, but didn't touch the egg. He kissed her on the way out to the shop, and told her not to mind, but to go and see if there was anything wrong with his mother.

Ann went up and knocked timidly at the room door. She was trembling. In a sharp, firm voice, Mrs. McCarthy called out to her to come in.

The room was in darkness, except for streaks of light coming in through the closed shutters. Ann hesitated, not knowing where the light switch was, or whether to open the shutters or not.

'Will I open the shutters?'

'Leave them be. The switch is to your right.'

Ann found the light and turned it on. Mrs. McCarthy was lying on her back in bed, the bedclothes gripped tightly around her. Ann stared at her. She looked like a corpse laid out.

'Bring me a little toast. Lightly toasted now. Baker's bread. And draw the tea weak. Put them on a tray.'

'Yes, ma'am,' Ann said, and left.

She made the breakfast as best she could. Burned a few slices of bread before she thought she had toast to Mrs. McCarthy's satisfaction. Then she brought the tray up.

'Leave it on the table.'

Ann laid the tray down, and then stood beside the bed, waiting.

Mrs. McCarthy said nothing, but made no move to begin eating. Ann hurried out, closing the door because she thought that Mrs. McCarthy didn't want to get up and show herself while Ann was there. Ann couldn't understand why. The thought just occurred to her. And she acted on it.

Later on she went back up, and knocked.

'Can I take the tray?'

'Yes.'

She took the tray back down to the kitchen without asking Mrs. McCarthy what was wrong with her.

About midday, Ann's father came into the house. It was the first visit of any of her relatives to her house since she had been married.

'By God, you're holding up well under it,' John Thomas Shanahan said to his daughter. 'Isn't there anything on the table for a man to eat? What kind of a daughter are you at all? You'll have a couple of more in to you in a few minutes.' He rattled off the names of a few of her cousins from the country.

She wanted to cry, she felt so nervous. But she daren't in front of her father. She knew she'd get no sympathy from him.

She prepared a lunch of boiled eggs, tea, and bread and jam, for him, and hoped that none of her cousins would show up. She wouldn't be able to bear them. Coming tramping into the clean house with their hobnailed boots, caked with cow dung off the streets. And talking about cows and heifers, and goats, and spuds, and what not. And the price of everything. And what raps the Corrigbeg shopkeepers were, overcharging for everything.

'Haven't you any meat to lay before a man? What kind of a house is this you're running? No meat on the table!'

'I wasn't expecting you ... I ... I didn't think anyone was coming.'

'Well, they are! And you can expect a crowd every Fair Day from now on. Where's the mother?'

'Above in bed.'

'Hugh! I suppose she spends all her time in bed, now that she has you to dance attendance on her.'

Ann could not eat, herself. Soon after, a few more cousins came tramping in, and then Michael Joe came in for his lunch.

'Where's my mother?'

'She's in bed. I don't know.'

'Ah, well. I suppose she needs the rest. Let her stay.'

Michael Joe began talking to his country in-laws. Ann put eggs down in front of him.

'Eggs?'

'That's all . . . I don't know . . . there's nothing . . .'

Michael Joe let it pass. He was discussing the price of milch cows with her father, and what they were fetching at the fair. The cousins argued with the price John Thomas quoted. It depended who was selling and who was buying. They saw a farmer get twice that much this morning for a cow. Sell early before the price was set by the market.

Ann thought she had left all that talk behind her. She ran upstairs to her room. Michael Joe seemed to have forgotten about her.

She lay out on the bed and cried a bit. The voices of the men arguing continued downstairs. Then she heard them tramping out of the dining room and banging the door after them. Then she fell into a peaceful doze. It had been a strenuous and tense morning for her. The sounds of the fair below in the street would not let her fall asleep completely. She got up and closed the shutters, taking a quick glance down at the street with cattle, rump to rump, and men in their midst. Closing the shutters, she shut out some of the noise. She was able to doze better.

When she woke up she heard no more lowing and bleating coming from the street. It must be late in the afternoon, and the fair over. She felt relaxed, and did not get up immediately but lay in bed enjoying the peace.

She opened the shutters before going downstairs. The street was like a rutted, marshy bog road, covered with puddles of cow dung and the hoofprints of animals. She could smell the street through the window, and put a small perfumed handkerchief to her nose. Then she went downstairs.

Mrs. McCarthy was sitting in the dining room by the fire with her black shawl pulled tightly around her, staring into the fire.

Ann had forgotten completely about her, in her own confusion. She had had no lunch! Ann stood there, staring dumbly at her, not knowing what to say for her negligence.

'They ate?' Mrs. McCarthy said nodding towards the unwashed dishes on the table.

'Yes. My father . . . and . . .'

'Yes. I know,' Mrs. McCarthy said. She waved a bony, veined hand at the table. 'Get rid of them.'

Ann was glad to have something to do. She cleared off the dishes and washed them in the sink in the kitchen, and put them away in the cupboard. Mrs. McCarthy continued to huddle over the fire as if she was very cold. She noticed, however, when Ann was finished with the dishes. She got up and went out, opened the hall door and stood staring at the mud the men had dragged in along the hallway, from the street. Ann had followed her, and stood behind her.

'I'll . . . I'll clean it up,' Ann said. This was the mud brought in by Michael Joe, her father, and her cousins. She was embarrassed.

'The bucket is under the sink. And a strong brush out in the back hall.'

Ann ran to get the bucket.

She washed down the hallway, pouring bucket after bucket of water on it and scrubbing hard with the yard brush, until the concrete floor gleamed almost white. Mrs. McCarthy stood in the kitchen door supervising her. If Ann missed a cake of dung, Mrs. McCarthy pointed it out to her. Ann brushed the dirt and the water out into the pavement. Little beads of sweat appeared on her small forehead. Her body began to ache from the heavy brush, but she kept putting all her strength and energy into the scrubbing.

When she was through to Mrs. McCarthy's satisfaction, Mrs. McCarthy walked through the hallway and stood in the door looking up and down the pavement.

'Since we're at it, we might as well do this too,' she said pointing at the pavement.

Ann went in and filled another bucket of water at the tap. She began to pour buckets and buckets of water on the pavement. A few people passed by and glanced at her. Ann was ashamed for no reason that she could think. She was ashamed. Mrs. McCarthy stood in the hall door directing her where to throw the water. Ann did as she was directed. Finally, she began to douse the pavement in front of the shop, concentrating intently on her work.

'What in the blazes are you doing with yourself?' she heard Michael Joe say.

She looked up. He was standing in the shop door, his dark eyes glowering at her.

'I don't know,' she said in her confusion.

'Here, give me that.' He grabbed the bucket of water from her. He splashed it angrily against the pavement.

'Don't ever let me see you doing anything like this again out in the public eye . . . Vin! Vin! Come out here to me!' he roared.

Vin, knowing by the sound of the voice that something was up, came running out. Michael Joe handed him the bucket. 'Wash down the flags.'

He turned to Ann. She was smiling weakly, and breathing heavily from her exertion, but trying bravely not to show any weakness.

'Go on in home, now, and rest yourself,' Michael Joe said. Then he saw his mother standing in the hallway door. A burst of anger exploded inside him. He strode past Ann, and went up to her.

'She's not a servant girl,' he said to his mother. 'If I ever see her being used as one again, they'll be hell to pay around this house.'

Mrs. McCarthy bowed her head as if to look at the blank, cold pavement, shiny from the water that had been doused on it. She tightened the black shawl around her shoulders, and went back into the house with her head bent.

Michael Joe had ignored Ann in his anger also. He had gone past her into the shop. She stood in the wet cow-dunged pavement. At last, she felt, Michael Joe really and truly loved her. He had dared to cross his mother on her behalf. For her. He had done that for her! Then she was overcome with a sense of her own unworthiness. And then she felt a great flood of sympathy for old Mrs. McCarthy. She ran inside the house to look for her, and console her in whatever way she could.

29

FROM THIS POINT on, Mrs. McCarthy began to give up some of her control of the house to Ann. She complained of being tired. Ann was eager to help, and waited on her hand and foot, bringing her tea and biscuits to her bedroom, and consulting her in preparing dishes she liked. Mrs. McCarthy began to spend more time in her room, and when old cronies came in to see her, Ann always ushered them upstairs, when before they always talked in the dining room. Ann made it a point to always serve tea and cake to the visitors, even the most casual gossips who dropped in almost daily.

Mrs. McCarthy had always been a religious woman, rising early every morning to attend the eight o'clock Mass, hail, rain, or shine, and receive Holy Communion. She became even more diligent in the performance of her religious exercises now, going up to the chapel both morning and evening. Most of the time, she was accompanied by one of her cronies, other old women in the village whose main consolation in their late years was religion. It was a convenient way for Mrs. McCarthy to keep in touch with local gossip too, because the affairs of the town were discussed by the old women as they slowly walked to and from Mass in the morning, or rosary in the evening.

Mrs. McCarthy came down to the kitchen only to cook something special. On All Saints' Eve, she baked the apple tart. That had always been a tradition. Sometimes she made a currant loaf, or a sweet for after dinner.

Ann was a bad housekeeper. Her mother had never really shown her how to cook, or how to take care of a man's needs. She had let Ann help her only with the very minor household tasks, never with the essentials. It was as if she were preparing Ann to assume her role of lady in the town; and Ann was finding the role of housekeeper very trying. Michael Joe was often upset because his shirts weren't ironed the way he liked to have them. Ann put too much starch on the collars. If a clean pair of socks was not ready when he wanted them, he shouted. Sometimes, a lamb chop would be burned to a cinder. He would simply leave it on his plate and say nothing. Ann would get upset. He told her not to worry, but she could see he was angry just the same. Mrs. McCarthy would sit there listening to them, saying nothing, not interfering. Ann often had to consult her on how Michael Joe liked his food cooked. She would tell Ann not to spoil him, but cook it any way *she* wanted.

Though there were little moments like this, on the whole the early months went along happily for Ann. She felt secure in Michael Joe's love.

One night after supper when they had been married about five months, Michael Joe broached the subject of a coming Whist Drive to Ann. They had not yet made any public appearance socially, other than to be seen at Mass or Sunday walks. They had not attended any of the dances, or concerts, or the plays of the local dramatic society, or the moving pictures. Several times Michael Joe had suggested to Ann that they should put a stir in themselves and be seen out more often. But Ann had always replied that she was perfectly content to stay at home with him. What did they want to be going out for? There would be enough out without them. Michael Joe had never pressed her. His day was full in the shop, and he kept it open until eight or nine every night, and there was always a couple of the fellows in to see him.

Since he had married, many of the local bachelors and fellows idling round the village on the dole or doing odd jobs, began to drop in to him every day, as before they used to drop in to Kerney's. It was as if, by marrying, he was automatically elevated in their minds to the status of a sage. They came to him with their troubles, borrowed an odd ten bob which he willingly let them have, and listened to his advice and his yarns. He talked to them often of Dublin, but never in relation to his honeymoon. He spoke of it as if he had spent his holidays there, or visited it. Every day horses were discussed, and bets sent off to Ennistymon. Michael Joe became a leading handicapper. He got two papers, the *Irish Press* and the *Irish Independent*, and studied the form diligently in both papers. He soon became an expert in reading the form, and the lads who put down bets did not do so without consulting him first. He placed a few bets himself now and then. But he was not so much interested in betting as he was in studying the form itself, and being able to predict winners. Every evening, when he brought the papers into the house, the racing sheet was missing. He knew Ann would have no interest in it, and never miss it. He had kept it in a drawer pencil marked with the winners for the following day.

And so his life began to settle into routine, the routine of a substantial citizen respectable and married, with horse racing as his one aberration and passion.

He had decided that he and Ann should get out of their rut by appearing at the Whist Drive.

'You know well, Michael Joe, I know nothing about whist,' Ann said.

'There's always a first time in everything,' Michael Joe said.

They were sitting very domestically opposite each other before the fireplace in the dining room. Mrs. McCarthy had gone up to the chapel.

Ann was glancing through the newspapers. Michael Joe was restlessly puffing at a cigarette.

'Oh, I don't want to be learning cards,' she said. 'There's never any luck in the house they're in.'

'We're not opening a gambling house,' Michael Joe said. 'Look. I'll show you.' He got up and rummaged in the cupboard and found a pack of cards. He sat down at the table and shuffled them expertly with large soft hands.

'Come on. Pull over a chair. 'Tis simple to learn the game. You'll be able to put up a good performance when we go.'

'I don't want to learn. I'm content to leave that to you.'

Michael Joe's face took on a sudden, sullen look. 'Are we to stop in like this evenings for the rest of our lives?'

Ann was surprised and shocked at the tone. She felt nervous immediately, all the security of the past few months gone.

'Oh, well, I'll try,' she said sitting over to the table. 'But I have no head for cards. And I'll only be making a fool of myself in front of all the townspeople.'

'Yerra, you will not. 'Tis simple. Watch me.'

Michael Joe explained the game of whist to her. She let him do the talking, while she nodded her head from time to time and said: 'I see, now. So that's how 'tis done!' He explained the dealing, the bidding, the points, and how to keep score. She said that she thought it was simple once she heard him explain it. 'Twasn't hard at all. He dealt out a couple of dummy hands, cards face upward, and played all four hands, telling her why he led this card, why he threw that one. She sighed, and thought he was very smart to be able to play four hands of whist at once.

'Do you think you'll be able to handle it then Sunday night?' he said at the end of his demonstration. ' 'Tis no use going without you're knowing the game. They'll all be watching you.'

'I think so,' she said bravely.

On Sunday night she complained of cramps in the stomach, and had to send Michael Joe out to the Medical Hall for a bottle of milk of magnesia.

'Are you sure 'tisn't anything serious?' Michael Joe said, hovering over her as she poured out a tablespoon of the thick white liquid from the blue milk of magnesia bottle, and gulped it down, making a wry face from the aftertaste.

'Something I ate, I suppose,' she said. 'I'll take a lie down and 'twill go away.'

Michael Joe began to pace up and down in front of her. She held on to the bottle and spoon. She had a thoughtful, half-strained look on her face as if she were waiting for the cramps to come on her again.

'I suppose we might as well give up the Whist Drive.'

'Amn't I the good-for-nothing to be spoiling your fun?'

'You are not,' Michael Joe protested.

'Go without me,' she said suddenly. 'I won't mind at all. Sure all I'll be doing is lying down. Go on now.'

Michael Joe wouldn't dream of it. Going out without her. She insisted and insisted until they almost had a row. Michael Joe was afraid if it were anything serious he should stay home. Mrs. McCarthy would be down from the chapel, and she'd be there if anything was serious, Ann said.

In the end, Michael Joe left for the Whist Drive, after she had settled herself in bed with her rosary beads, and he had sat with her for a few minutes.

Michael Joe spent the most enjoyable night he had spent since coming home from Dublin. The Parochial Hall was crowded, about fifty tables. Everyone he met asked him where his wife was, and was he afraid to bring her out. He explained that she was feeling a little sick. Smiles and nods went back and forth. Michael Joe didn't get the joke for a while. But then it dawned on him that Ann might be going to have a baby. Someone said, 'More power to McCarthy. Faix, there, he didn't let the grass grow onder his feet.'

He was elated. But Ann didn't know. He wondered if she even suspected.

Going to have a baby! Going to have a baby! Going to have a baby!

The phrase kept echoing in his mind, above the chatter and the talk. He felt proud of himself. And he began quietly to hint at Ann's true condition to the people he spoke to, and made no attempt to deny their innuendoes, though he said nothing openly.

Kitty Falane was at the Whist Drive, without a partner. Michael Joe latched on to her. She was a good whist player, alert, with a good memory, and quick to size up a situation. Michael Joe whispered to her that Ann might be expecting, as they changed tables.

'You ought to be ashamed of yourself,' Kitty said.

Michael Joe beamed. He had always liked Kitty Falane. She was lively, and she pulled no punches.

'Yourself'll be making a move one of these days.'

'The man that'll get me that way'll have to work hard for it,' Kitty said.

Michael Joe played well. All-conquering. And the cards flowed his way. At one point in the Whist Drive, he and Kitty Falane were paired up against Canon Lyons and Doctor Healy's wife. But for the chatter between Kitty Falane and Mrs. Healy, the rubber would have been played in silence. Michael Joe won, because the opposition got no cards. It was not a match of skill. Canon Lyons rose from the table immediately the rubber was over, a wry smile on his pale face.

'That was rotten luck,' he said to Mrs. Healy.

Michael Joe smiled. He whispered to Kitty: 'Old ghost face is a bad loser.'

'Watch out. He'll curse you,' Kitty said.

'And be damned to him if he does,' Michael Joe said. He threw back his dark head and laughed.

He and Kitty won runner-up positions in the Whist Drive, and ten pounds. He walked Kitty home at two o'clock in the morning. It was cold. He felt hot, and his heart pounded. He was tempted for a moment. Kitty was a spirited one. But he smothered the temptation. And was ashamed of himself.

'You're a great player,' he said to Kitty as they walked side by side in the darkness. 'We'd make a great pair.'

' 'Twas a pity Ann couldn't come. But she had a good excuse. Ah, ye'er lucky. A child, already.'

He accepted her intention. Up at her door, he fumbled in the darkness and handed her a five-pound note. The old restlessness agitating him. The blood rising. Dormant for a while. Rising again. Rising.

'Your share of the take.' His hand touched hers. He pressed the money into it quickly, and set off at a lively step home. An old image came back. Rotten apples. Being pelted. Lying in the alley.

Ann was sitting up in bed with the light on, her hands folded on the multicoloured eiderdown, clutching black rosary beads between her thin fingers. Her face was drawn and haggard. Traces of tears were on her cheeks. She said nothing when Michael Joe came into the bedroom, but gave him a sorrowful, mournful, hurt look.

'Are you better?' he said lightly. 'I'm sorry I went. 'Twas nothing without you.'

'You stayed a long time,' she said.

'I had to. Kitty Falane and myself were the runners-up.'

A spasm of pain ran through Ann, and she gasped.

'What's up?' Michael Joe said, as if he had forgotten momentarily.

'I don't know, I don't know. It won't go away.'

'You'll go down and see Doctor Healy the first thing in the morning.'

Ann made him leave the light on all night. She sat up, gasping and vomiting. Michael Joe did not know what to do. He thought of calling his mother but it was too late. The pains and sickness had been attacking Ann ever since he had left her to go to the Whist Drive. He was sorry he went. He would never leave her alone again, he promised.

But he was exhausted, and lay down and fell asleep quickly, before he could stop himself.

In the morning, Ann had shadows under her eyes, and she looked ghostly. Michael Joe made her stay in bed. And he himself went down for Doctor Healy, who came up and examined her. Michael Joe went up to see her after Doctor Healy left.

He sat on the side of the bed looking proudly at her. She tried to smile but she was still feeling nauseous.

'Doctor Healy told me. But I half-suspected,' Michael Joe said. He beamed with satisfaction.

Ann said nothing. Her small mouth trembled as if she was trying to get something out. She hung her head.

'You aren't afraid now, are you?' Michael Joe said. He got off the bed and began to pace around the room. She looked at him, still unable to speak.

'Sure 'tis nothing,' Michael Joe said. 'Every woman has to go through it. You aren't the first nor you won't be the last.'

The processes of pregnancy and giving birth were just as much a mystery to him as they were to Ann. Neither of them had any precise idea of what actually went on. Doctor Healy had told Ann nothing, beyond the fact that she was pregnant; and he had prescribed some pills for her to take. She did not even know how the baby was to be born. She knew that she was sick, and that she must be looking a sight to Michael Joe with her vomiting and nausea. And, at moments, she felt so bad that she wanted to die. All the old wives' tales of the trials and tribulations of the woman who was going to have a baby began to revolve inside her head. Her panic increased. She did not know how long it would be before the baby would come, but it seemed to her that it would be born very soon.

Michael Joe really wanted to leave the room. But he stayed in spite of himself. He couldn't run off and leave her. She looked so pathetic sitting there in the bed clutching her rosary beads. As he paced up and down trying to think of something to say, Ann finally said:

'Send out for my mother. I want her to come in.'

'By God, I will,' Michael Joe said, relieved. He came over to the bed. 'I'll send Vin out right away.' As he looked down at her a sudden burst of passion swept through him. He could not control himself. He bent, and tried to kiss her passionately. She struggled.

'No . . . no . . . no!'

Michael Joe stopped. 'What's up? I'm your husband now, amn't I?'

'No. No. No more,' she said revealing in a single moment her deepest attitude toward their intimacy since they were married.

'No more! No more!' Michael Joe sat down on the bed, bemused. He did not understand. 'Holy St. Joseph, what is a man to do?'

'I'm going to have a baby. I can't,' she whined.

Michael Joe stood up. 'Did the doctor say anything about . . . about it?'

Ann was embarrassed. She didn't want to talk this way. She was feeling badly enough as it was.

'No,' she said.

'Well, ask him, in the name of God, before I have to be put in the asylum.'

As he was leaving, she said, 'Don't forget to send out for my mother.'

'No,' he said wearily. 'I'll send in herself, too,' he said referring to his own mother. 'And ask the doctor. Don't forget that.'

30

WINTER SET IN. It rained heavier, and the houses grew damp and cold. The mornings were frosty. Fires had to be lit in bedrooms to keep them warm. Hot-water bottles were put beneath the blankets, at the foot of the bed, so that feet could be kept warm throughout the night.

Ann's mother arrived from the country, and she and Mrs. McCarthy fussed over Ann for a day or two, prescribing warmth. A fire was lit in the bedroom, the hot-water bottle was kept hot all day while Ann was in bed, and special beef broth was made. Ann began to feel better.

Michael Joe had become caught up in the Christmas spirit, as was usual for him. This year, business was better than it had ever been before. Ann's family did all their shopping with him; and Ann's cousins, even to the fourth and fifth removed. He did not invite them into the house for a bite to eat, explaining Ann's condition. Drink was in order. Michael Joe was always a bit drunk by the end of the day from having to drink with the cousins and Ann's neighbours from the country.

He liked them. They were sharp-witted, shrewd people, and down to earth. And no nonsense about them. They liked nothing better than to bargain. They always accused Michael Joe of over-charging on the groceries, and tried to beat him down on the price. He would not yield. But always bought them a drink in the end. That salvaged their pride. To be able to outwit the townsman was their great glory.

And so Michael Joe was kept on his toes by these argumentative, aggressive countrymen. He went into the house only for meals, and ate them quickly and hurriedly, hardly speaking at all to Ann and his mother, who hovered over him, serving him.

As Ann began to get over the initial effects of her pregnancy she noticed that Michael Joe was becoming more and more irritated, the few times she did see him during the day. He criticized the meals she prepared, her wasting of turf to keep all the fires in the house going, and using up the coal for the range. He even criticized her for going to Mass every morning, which she had begun to do with old Mrs. McCarthy. What did she think she was doing? Trying to become a candidate for canonization? She was out of bed every morning and to Mass before he woke up. And she was usually asleep when he came in at night.

She worried just a little that he didn't talk to her, at least. Or drop in to the house sometime during the day, no matter how busy he was. She remembered his telling her to ask the doctor. And so, on one of her weekly visits to Dr. Healy, she thought she'd ask, in case Michael Joe should want to know. He never asked any questions at all now about how she was feeling.

She didn't know how to put the question to Doctor Healy. She had never got over the embarrassment and shame she felt the morning he examined her, that first time, in her own bed. Lying out naked. She had kept her eyes closed all the time, while he poked at her, and put the cold stethoscope all over her, and his cool hands pressed at her stomach. Oh, it had been mortifying. The thought always made her almost sick.

As the weekly visits went on, though, she began not to mind so much. And eventually, secretly, grew to like the cool touch, and the probing, and the quiet, soft voice, questioning.

The day she decided to ask him the question, after putting it off many times, he was sitting at his roll-top desk writing out a pre-scription for a mild laxative she would have to take. She had just finished dressing in a little room off the office, and hesitated, nervously twiddling with her chamois gloves. She had grown into the habit of dressing up a bit when she went to see him at the dispensary though it was only a short walk from her own house.

'Well,' Doctor Healy said, noticing her standing there, 'you're coming along nicely. Nothing to worry about. This is a little matter. Perfectly normal.'

He had told her, as her pregnancy progressed, that her hips were a nit narrow and the pelvis . . . but there was nothing to worry about. That would take care of itself as time went on.

'I'm going to be all right?' she said.

He looked at her quickly. 'Thin women are the hardiest in the long run.' He handed her the prescription. 'Give this to Mr. Lynch up at the Hall. And he'll fill it out for you.'

She looked at the illegible scrawl. Somehow, the whole mystery of her pregnancy was involved in it. But she had to ask a question. She bowed her head as if she were making a confession.

'Doctor, there's something Michael Joe asked me the other night . . .' She stopped.

Doctor Healy looked up. He saw she was blushing, and understood.

'Oh, that's all right. These things are perfectly normal.' He drew a ledger toward him on the desk, and busied himself writing in it.

'You can go on enjoying yourself without any fear. Of course,' he continued, laying down the pen and looking at her, 'some positions will be easier for you now than the usual one.'

'Positions?'

Doctor Healy drew a deep breath. He had been in practice a long time in Corrigbeg, and had been through this before, yet it always embarrassed him too, as if he had taken on what was in the air itself, in spite of his clinical attitude.

'There are *other* ways.'

'Other ways?'

He gave up. 'You should talk it over with Michael Joe. He'll be able to tell you.' He went back to writing on the ledger. He could never give detailed and direct advice in this kind of situation. He had been part of the people of Corrigbeg too long, born, raised, and had gone to school there. These matters were never discussed between doctor and patient. And, he suspected, not between husband and wife. He signed.

'Thank you, Doctor,' Ann said, and left hurriedly, glad to get it over. She had made the attempt.

She did not understand what the doctor was trying to say, but she could not escape the fact that he said it was all right to go on. She suddenly began to think as she walked back up home, of all the women who had died having a child. And, in her mind, she connected it with the continuance of the sexual act after the woman had become pregnant. It was dangerous, she felt, no matter what Doctor Healy said. He had been hesitant. He had not said anything about the number of women who died, and why they did. That thought haunted her. And she did not know what to tell Michael Joe if he should ask again.

But Michael Joe did not ask. Every night now, he was out somewhere. He never said where he was going, and she did not ask. Sometimes she would be lying half awake in the darkness, saying her beads to herself, trying to go to sleep. Sometimes she was not really asleep when he came home. She would smell the drink off him when he came into bed. She trembled. But he never asked. He fell into a deep snoring sleep.

But one night he did not sleep. She heard him climbing the stairs. There was a long interval between his taking each step, and his hands scraped along the wall outside the room searching for the door and the knob. She knew he was very drunk. She held her rosary beads tighter, and drew her knees up to her stomach. She remained this way as he came in and staggered around the room. He undressed in the dark, muttering to himself, and singing an occasional snatch of a song. He breathed heavily through his nose when he was not singing. The strong smell of drink floated to her nostrils and made her nauseous. She pretended sleep.

He lay still for a while after getting into bed, then he turned over and slapped her on the rump.

'Wake up there, you lazy thief,' he said good-humouredly.

She pretended to wake up. 'Don't wake your mother,' she said.

'I'll wake my mother,' he said, and grabbed her by the shoulders.

'Don't,' she said. 'I can't.'

'Did you ask Doctor Healy?'

'I . . . I . . . did.'

'And what did he say?'

'He . . . he . . .'

'Ah, dammit,' Michael Joe said. 'I know what he said.'

She felt Michael Joe tugging at her nightgown. She wrapped her arms around her stomach, remained with her back to him, and buried her face in the pillow.

When it was over, Michael Joe fell asleep immediately. Ann lay awake a long time, listening to the wind bansheeing through the telephone wires outside the window. Though she was cold she did not dare move over against Michael Joe for warmth. But soon, the heat emanating from his body warmed the bed, and she was able to stretch her legs out of her cramped position. Gradually she began to get warm from his warmth, and her feet touched his. But she still shivered.

31

THAT FIRST CHRISTMAS season after his marriage Michael Joe gave up all pretence of being a family man who had suddenly been domesticated by his marriage. He had tried to fit into the role of husband, but he began to be oppressed by the evenings at home sitting listening to the wireless or reading the paper, and the early-to-bed hours, and the Sunday walks. He was flattered and pleased by the image of himself in that role, fitting into the pattern of life in Corrigbeg, the pattern of the respectably married man. Whenever he felt oppressed by the role, he simply did not think about it, and satisfied himself mainly by telling yarns about Dublin to the fellows who came in to see him in the shop.

The Whist Drive had been the first break in the routine, and the competition and being in a crowd of people made him restless again to be out and doing something exciting. Ann's pregnancy had thrilled him at first, but when he discovered what it meant in terms of his intimacy with Ann, he was irritated, angry, and then downright hostile, though he could not say why. He could not talk it over with Ann. She was impossible to talk to that way. That night he had come home drunk, he was mad enough with her and the world not to care, but to go ahead and please himself. And he had. But next day he remembered the night before with a sort of cynical anger. He faced the fact that he had practically raped his wife. From somewhere in the distant past came an accusing voice. Was that it? Was that all he was capable of? He tried not to think about what was happening. He threw himself wholeheartedly into the spirit of Christmas.

A card addressed to Mr. and Mrs. M. J. McCarthy came from Nell and Seamus Larkin. The message on it was brief and impersonal: 'Our best wishes for a happy and a holy Christmas: Nell and Seamus.' The card was an image of the Manger scene, with the little Child lying on a bed of golden straw in a halo of white light, the Blessed Virgin in blue bending over the crib, St. Joseph, bearded and in brown, with a shepherd's crooked staff, standing behind her, and cows, donkeys and sheep peering out from the dark at the crib. A shining silver star topped off the scene.

Michael Joe always got the post in the shop from the postman. He brought the card in opened when he came in that night for supper. He threw it on the kitchen table saying to Ann: 'Here's a reminder from Mrs. Seamus Larkin.'

Ann was at the range frying liver for Michael Joe's supper. He liked liver, so she tried to have it as often as she could get it fresh from Butcher Downes.

Ann turned around and glanced at the envelope on the table, and then turned back to her work. She was in her fifth month now, and the child showed plainly in a round little bulge on her thin body.

'I'll read it later, when I have time,' she said.

Michael Joe picked it up and pulled the card out of the envelope, and read the message with mock devotion and sincerity.

'Oh, that was very nice of her,' Ann said. 'And we didn't send her any. I must do that right away.'

'Do no such thing,' Michael Joe said. He tramped heavily upstairs to wash himself.

When he was gone, Ann turned around from the range and picked up the card and stared at it for a long time. She grew misty-eyed at the scene in the Manger. The little Child had its tiny hands upraised to the Blessed Virgin as if crying to be taken out of the crib and nursed. Ann almost cried. She smelt the liver burning, and hurriedly laid down the card, and went back to cooking.

At supper, Mrs. McCarthy sitting with them, Ann timidly asked Michael Joe why she shouldn't send a card to Nell.

'Because 'tis all a fake. And we might as well be honest if we're going to be anything.'

'All a fake?' Ann cried. 'Christmas isn't a fake. What are you saying?'

'You know nothing about *that woman*,' Michael Joe said. 'You're an innocent compared to her. She's only mocking, sending that card.'

Ann gave him a perplexed look. 'She's a nice girl. She never would do harm to no one.'

'Nice girl how-are-you,' Michael Joe said. 'You can't see beyond your nose.'

Mrs. McCarthy had remained silent. She rarely spoke to Michael Joe now. Gestures of the mother and son relationship between them had vanished; they lived in the same house together, meeting but not talking and unable to tell what secret thoughts they had about one another, and were withholding.

'Yerra, whist, Michael Joe,' she said quietly. 'Let the girl's memory be in peace.'

Michael Joe gave her a quick look. 'We're all getting into the Christmas spirit, I declare,' he said. 'You changed your tune from a long time ago.'

Mrs. McCarthy bowed her head. She understood. Ann did not.

'There's no harm in sending her a card to wish her a happy Christmas. What harm is in that?' Ann said.

'I don't want us to have anything to do with them two,' Michael Joe said. 'We're well rid of them.'

Ann could not understand him. She knew that he had been great once with Nell Cullen, and it was rumoured that he was almost going to marry her. She had never heard why they broke up, and she had never asked. This sudden attack on a girl she looked up to, thought of as being an ideal, someone way above herself in every way, shocked her. Michael Joe was attacking someone she thought nearly perfect. And attacking her in a tone that frightened Ann. She was getting used to the fact now, that he was not the gay, light-hearted Romeo who teased her a lot, and liked to laugh and dance. Bit by bit, little explosion after little explosion, she was getting used to the brutal side of him. Street angel, house devil. But this attack on Nell roused her. In fear and trembling she tried to fight him, to preserve her own image of the ideal woman.

'This is the Holy Season of Christmas, I'd like to remind you,' she said trying to be firm.

'Ah, balderdash,' Michael Joe said. He had come on a burned piece of liver. 'Will you ever learn to fry this damn thing right?'

'I'm trying to say something to you, Michael Joe. Will you listen?'

Michael Joe made a motion at her with his knife and fork poised, a motion half of contempt, which she ignored.

Ann was getting angry at him. She trembled, and had to lay down her own knife and fork. It was as if her emotion were too great for her body to contain it.

'If she ever did any harm to you. And I doubt it. You should forgive her. Peace on earth to men of good will. Don't you take your religion seriously at all? The little Child . . . born on Christmas . . . he forgave . . .' She paused on the brink of incoherence.

'Ah, will you shut up. She was a whore,' Michael Joe said. He got up from the table, leaving his supper unfinished, and stomped out of the dining room.

Ann began to cry, quietly and softly, though she was nearly hysterical. It was as if she had suddenly found herself defending all womanhood, defending its highest type and ideal against the attack of a ferocious and maddened animal. A wolf. She knew somewhere inside her, with her instincts, that her defence was inadequate against the kind of attack she was faced with. There was a kind of despair in her breaking down. He had not seen. He had only used a filthy word. Thrown mud at her queen.

She cried at the table. Old Mrs. McCarthy rose slowly and came around and put an arm around Ann.

'There now, a leanna. Sure he didn't mean it, at all. Stop your crying now, and don't upset yourself.'

The old mother tried to console the young, pregnant wife as best she could, knowing in her heart of hearts that there was nothing that really could be said. And her own guilt lay heavily on her.

The next day, Ann left the house late in the morning, after standing in the hall door of the house and glancing next door to make sure that Michael Joe was not in the shop door and would see her going out. She went down to P. J. Harley's and bought a very big Christmas card, a bigger and more colourful Manger scene with the words of 'Silent Night' printed on the inside. She sent it off to Nell under her own and Michael Joe's signature, and a small prayer of her own that she made up on the spot: 'May the

Holy Divine Infant shine down his blessings on you and yours, and may He bring you a happy, holy, and blessed New Year.'

As she walked down the Main Street of Corrigbeg on her own, she glanced neither right nor left as she walked, and was saluted by no one. When she got home, she felt as if she had walked a hundred miles.

A few days later she had to go out again to buy a Christmas present for Michael Joe. She thought long over what kind of present she should buy him. She worked herself into a mood of forgiveness. She was willing to forget all the thing she said about Nell, and the other things too. Everywhere in the town there was festivity, coloured lights and decorations in the shop windows. Toys for children. She even went so far as to decorate the window of their own kitchen with holly and ivy, and made little cups from eggshells and wrapped them in silver paper so they looked like little silver chalices. Old Mrs. McCarthy helped her. Both of them together baked little sweetmeats and cakes, and Mrs. McCarthy showed Ann how to make a plum pudding for the Christmas dinner.

She was completely at one with the spirit of the season, the season of the Child. It was especially sentimental this year to her, because she was carrying a child too. Often, in her private prayers, she made the mystical association between the Child Jesus and the one in her womb, and vowed that he would be dedicated to the service of Jesus and the Blessed Virgin.

In such a mood, she forgot her anger at Michael Joe, and put out of her mind any thought of bitterness or fear of what he was bringing to pass around her. She wanted to give him a present which would make him feel like she herself felt, at one with the world. And she didn't know what would accomplish that trick. Finally, she hit on a prayer book. The idea came to her almost as an inspiration. It was the very thing. She would say nothing to him, but give him the gift. He would read the prayers inside, and then feel as she herself always felt in reading prayers in her own prayer book.

On Christmas Eve, Michael Joe came in late in the afternoon with two flat boxes, and handed one to Ann and one to his mother. He was smiling broadly, and smelled of drink. 'Here ye are, the two of ye. Happy Christmas,' was all he said. Ann told him to wait a minute. She ran upstairs, heavy though she was, and brought down the small box carefully wrapped. She gave it to him with tears in her eyes.

'What have we here, what have we here?'

He seemed to have forgotten the argument of the other night. Ann brightened. He opened the box, and he did not stop smiling when he saw the black prayer book resting in its box.

' 'Twas all I could think of,' Ann said.

Michael Joe gave her a kiss on the cheek. He did not take the prayer book out of the box.

'Yerra, you shouldn't have gone to the trouble for an old codger like me,' he said. 'I'm not worth it.'

His mother gave him gifts of ties and handkerchiefs, which she simply handed to him in their box, with a 'Happy Christmas'. Michael Joe took the box quickly.

'And many happy returns,' he said to her. There was an awkward silence. 'Well, I must be off out to the shop. 'Twould fall down without me. Scanlon can't turn a finger right.' He left quickly, taking both boxes with him.

Ann never saw the prayer book again.

He stayed at home Christmas Eve because not even Michael Joe would dare be seen out from his family on this night, unless he had a good excuse. He lit the candle in the kitchen window. And then buried himself in the paper, though he had read it from front to back already. Ann and his mother went to Confession together. Michael Joe didn't want to go. Neither of the women tried to persuade him. Ann wanted to, but she was at peace with him now, and did not want to bring on any disturbing note again.

All three of them went up in the dark to seven o'clock Mass on Christmas morning. Ann and old Mrs. McCarthy, the old woman in black supported on the arm of the young woman in dark brown, went to the rails at Mass and received Holy Communion together. Michael Joe sat restlessly looking around the chapel while they were at the rails. He used neither prayer book nor rosary beads at the Mass, and did not sing the 'Silent Night' or the 'Adeste Fidelis', and appeared indifferent to the Crib made of ivy and holly to the right of the main altar. Ann and Mrs. McCarthy went up and knelt before the Manger scene, after Mass, while he waited sitting in his seat watching the people leave the chapel.

He was late for his first Christmas dinner as a married man. He had gone up to Blake's for a few drinks with the boys, and had not felt the time passing until he heard the clock in the kitchen strike two. He finished his pint and bought a couple of Baby Powers' before he left.

When he got home, he insisted that Ann and his mother have just a little dropeen to celebrate. Ann had never touched anything stronger than a lemonade in her life. Mrs. McCarthy, of late, occasionally took a drop of brandy for her heart. The good-humoured argument about whether Ann should have a drop of whiskey or not helped to prevent a more serious fight over why he was late for his dinner. Finally, Ann let Michael Joe pour her a thimbleful with a lot of water in it. Mrs. McCarthy took hers neat, sipping it slowly.

Michael Joe stayed in the rest of Christmas Day. Ann and Mrs. McCarthy both took a rest after the dinner. He was left alone. He turned on the wireless. There was nothing but sacred music on from the BBC. He switched it off. There was no paper to read so that he could distract himself. He prowled around the house, and poked in a few cupboards. In one of them he found a book, *The Robe*, which he started to read. He gave it up. He could not go back to the time of Christ in his imagination. The story took no grip on him so he put it down. Then he went for a short walk down the back way, but it began to rain and he had to turn back.

Finally, desperate for something to do with himself, he went out to the shop and began to pore over the ledgers, making lists of his debts and his debtors. He lit a fire in the little room at the back, and eventually dozed on a chair, alone, there by the fire.

Now, alone, his mind turned back into the past, and the past was Nell. If he had felt deceived and betrayed by her in their living past, he was haunted by her now even worse, when she was no longer a living presence in the town. He didn't believe in ghosts, but whenever he closed his eyes and let himself relax, he could call her up in his mind as vividly and as fully as if she were alive before him. He did not indulge in this calling up of her image too often, or for long. A flash. She was there. He talked to her. And then he sent her away. Said no to her, rejected her again as he had in the past, and each time he said no, he knew he was being hard, bitter and cold. Once, he thought of forgiveness. Forgive . . . forgive . . . forgive. He laughed. He had no idea how to go about forgiving. The idea was totally alien to him. It had no reality. It was a word he had heard, but was without substance to him. How could he forgive? What did he have to do to forgive? He did not know, now.

32

AFTER CHRISTMAS, LIFE in Corrigbeg returned to normal. To the casual observer, Ann McCarthy's pregnancy was progressing as it should. She went to Mass and Communion every morning with old Mrs. McCarthy. She began to pick up gossip of the town from listening to the old women talk. She felt secure and happy in their solicitous remarks on the state of her health. Sometimes, they recommended that she take this or that herb. She paid attention to their recommendations; welcomed them. The old women had not yet accepted the drugs available at the Medical Hall. They cautioned her to avoid them. Ann enjoyed the attention. And, of course, going to Mass and Communion gave her that extra sense of security she needed. She had no exact idea of how her pregnancy would fulfil itself, or how the baby would be born. She had never been told, and had no knowledge, even now, of the physical details of birth, though she had been born and raised on a farm. Vaguely, she knew that the baby would have to come out of her stomach to be born. And she knew that giving birth would be an ordeal. That much she was sure of. The whispered remarks of the old women, their sympathy, and occasional stories they told in her presence of the hard time such-and-such a woman had made her fear what was ahead; but, it did not oppress her. She put her trust in God. And waited for her time in fear. But praying.

After the excitement of Christmas, life settled into its usual routine for Michael Joe, too. He got up when the women came down from Mass. If Ann addressed a question to him, he spoke as shortly as he could, ate hurriedly, and went out to the shop, which had already been opened up by Vin Scanlon. The only time he started conversation himself was to complain. If his eggs weren't boiled or fried right, he made bitter sarcastic remarks about Ann's not even having been taught to take care of a man. Ann was always tolerant. She had just been to Mass, and the overflow of religious emotion gave her enough inward courage to endure his moods without wanting to fight him back.

When he lost physical touch with her, he seemed to have lost touch with her altogether. She was disappointed that he never asked about her pregnancy. But even if he had shown any interest she would have been hard put to tell him anything. But Michael Joe was not interested. He saw the physical change coming over her, and the more she changed physically, the more of a stranger she became to him. He could hardly bear to be in her physical presence for very long. So he spent most of his time in the shop, except for meals.

In the shop, he was a different personality. He was neither moody nor critical nor complaining. Vin Scanlon and he got along well most of the time. Vin was a conversation partner when no one else dropped in. A clever listener, who knew all Michael Joe's vanities and catered to them, never attempting to steal his thunder, and laughing heartily at all Michael Joe's jokes and remarks.

Michael Joe was a good shopkeeper. He responded to every customer who came in, even if it was only a child on an errand for its mother, with a barrage of talk and good spirits. There was no pretence about his shopkeeper manner, the quick laugh, the inquiries after the health, his willingness to serve, his praise of his own merchandise, and his easy talk. He thought of his customers more as company than as money in the till. He was an easy mark for tick, again, and would give flour, or tea, or sugar without charge until the money came from England, or the pension came.

He had developed a special manner with women, and most of his customers were wives or girls. He was flirtatious with everything in a skirt that came into the shop. Even little girls. They were afraid of him. Sometimes he'd frighten them, and they'd run. But they always came back, half in love with their own fear. It was the same with the older women. He frightened them too with his boldness. 'Ah, 'tis well for you I'm a married man.' Or, 'I wish I was single again, as the song says,' he'd say giving a girl a bold look. She'd blush and get flustered. The married women would pretend to be insulted. But they came back again.

That was part of his daily amusement. The women never took him seriously, but they liked his flirting. It made him feel happy, too. He never had any intention of carrying his remarks beyond

208

a flirtation in the shop. In Corrigbeg, it would not be easy to step over the border of marriage without being a marked man immediately. There had been one known case of adultery in fifty years, and that had ended in the woman's going mad and having to be put away in the asylum. Such examples as that were remembered for a long time. They inhibited whatever inclinations might be present in the women or men of the town to commit adultery.

Michael Joe usually had other company in the shop than the customers. He encouraged the fellows idling around the town to drop in, so there was always someone in the snug at the back. Michael Joe kept a good fire in the grate, so it was always a good place for them to go on a cold, rainy day. The talk turned on horses, dogs, local court cases, football, and who was doing a line with whom. Sometimes, one of the guards from the barracks dropped in and regaled the listeners with stories of the inside on local petty crimes and arrests.

Michael Joe kept the shop open at night for an hour after the supper. Not, indeed, for the business. But fellows who were busy during the day would have a chance to drop in at that hour.

He was beoming a master at keeping the talk going. He read the *Irish Independent* keenly, and kept it hidden out of the way, so that it was not unusual for a fellow to drop in and say: 'What's new in the paper, Michael Joe?' And Michael Joe would give out with his version of the news, interlarded with his own opinions of everything from the Fianna Fail Government, the British Government, to the report of prices on the cattle market. His reporting of the news always led to a discussion and talk. He became a moderator and master of ceremonies in his own shop.

After closing up the shop at night, he would ramble up to the Parochial Hall for a game of snooker, cards or billiards, much as he used to do in his bachelor days. There he met the other shop-keepers of the town, and Tom Fitzgerald and Ed Donovan. He mixed equally well with these. The crowd that came into him in the shop during the day were the 'dole boys', drawing money from the government for idling. He was equally at home at the St. Joseph's club. He was appreciated there for his skill as a gamesman, as well as for the news he brought from the crowd who had dropped in to see him during the day. Not all shopkeepers in the town encouraged dropping in.

After a visit to the Hall, he would stop in a Blake's or any pub

—he was welcome in all of them—and have a couple of pints. He was beginning to get stout from the quantities of porter he consumed. If there was anything going on at the pub in the way of music, or singing, or good talk, he stayed late.

Ann was always asleep when he got home.

Thus, Michael Joe's early married life began to settle into a rut, and it seemed to the local people as if he were 'getting very settled in his ways' as they said when they gossiped about him. It was noticed that he only rarely appeared anywhere with Ann, usually at Mass on Sunday. That was all.

One Fair Day John Thomas Shanahan, Ann's father, was in the shop buying a month's supply of meal and flour from Michael Joe, and boasting of the price he had just made on five cattle. Michael Joe listened to him expound on the economics of the deal. He had bought the cattle six or seven months before when they were barely calves. Had turned them out to grass. Fed them hay now and then. Here he was now, getting ten times the price he had first paid for them. Michael Joe was interested. He had but a bare knowledge of cattle. Was there that much money in them? John Thomas Shanahan became cagey at that question. If a fellow knew what he was doing, when to buy, and when to sell, he could make a tidy nest egg.

Michael Joe had inherited from his father a ten-acre strip of land just outside Corrigbeg. His mother had signed the rights to the field over to him that day when she had transferred the bank account to his name. He had been letting this field to a local farmer and it had never entered his head that he could make use of it himself. The idea began to dawn on him now that he could enter the cattle business, and use the field for grazing the cattle. He approached the idea cautiously at first, because he knew well his own lack of experience could land him in trouble with the fast-talking, shrewd country farmers and drovers, who bought and sold as fast as greased lightning. He had often heard yarns of cattle being sold for a high price early in the morning and being bought back by the same man for a lower price late in the afternoon, if the fair had turned out to be cheap. And of course there was always the chance of buying cattle with the murrain or TB or something else he did not know about.

But in spite of the chances he knew he would be taking, he felt profoundly drawn to the idea. He did not consider entering the cattle business as a scheme entirely to make money. That was its main attraction only to begin with. That was what made him cautious at first. He did not want to lose money. It was a matter of pride, not really the money itself, because he never had been the type of man who thought of the acquiring of money as an end in itself. But it would never do for him to lose it. John Thomas Shanahan . . . what would he say if he heard his son-in-law was dealing in the cattle and losing money? This was the matter of pride that kept Michael Joe cautious. If he went in for the business, he'd make sure that it reflected on himself, and the reflection would not be bad. He'd make a good reputation at it.

The idea occupied his mind for the month after he had talked to his father-in-law. Ann's dowry of five hundred pounds had been deposited in the National Bank, and it had remained there untouched since their marriage. This would be more than enough starting capital for him. He would not have to consult her about withdrawing some of it. The account was in his name only. He would have to give the farmer who was renting his field notice. And the farmer might not like that. Especially with the spring grass about ready to come in. Then, he thought of the number of cattle he would buy. He thought he'd start with four or five at the most. Then, after that he'd see. Depending on how he made out, he'd see.

He said nothing about his plans to anyone.

The next Fair Day, the February Fair, he waited for John Thomas Shanahan to come in. He got up early, and opened the shop himself that morning, and spent a lot of time just standing in the door of the shop observing what was going on in the street. It had rained early that morning. Distorted reflections of men and cattle formed weird shapes on the wet street. Farmers driving cattle were still coming into the street in numbers. One moment the cattle would drive steadily and docilely, the next they were twisting and turning and charging and slithering, rising on each other, and then quieting down again under the shouts of the farmers and under blows from the long blackthorn sticks the farmers laid slashingly across their backs. The farmers and drovers moved among the cattle easily avoiding the jerking long horns. The street gradually became packed thick with animals, black Kerry cows, red and white shorthorns, bullocks and heifers, calves in high-penned, red-shafted donkey carts, an occasional bull, pigs, goats, sheep and even fowl.

Though Michael Joe had been watching this scene all his life, it seemed to him, that morning, as if he was seeing it for the first time. And it excited him. He waited impatiently for John Thomas Shanahan to show up.

When he finally did, Michael Joe, after a few brief questions on what way the fair was going, told John Thomas that he'd like to go out to the fair with him. John Thomas gave him a hard stare, full of questions he wanted to ask, and a little too in his look of a trace of suspicion. Was this son-in-law of his up to something? A potential competitor. He kept his peace, and asked no questions, but decided to watch this lad more carefully. He was town-bred and born and reared, but you never knew when one of them got the knack, and would pull the wool over your eyes in a deal before you knew what was happening to you. There were twenty pounds down the drain because you didn't watch out.

Michael Joe went out in the fair with him. He had on low shoes. Soon they got muddy, and the mud soaked into his shoes, so that his feet got wet. But he didn't mind. He was watching his father-in-law closely. John Thomas was buying a couple of bullocks.

He'd walk up to the bullocks, prod his fingers into their ribs, grab them by the ears to see what kind of reaction he would get, poke them in the rump with his blackthorn. Then, casually, he'd ask the owner how much he wanted for a particular animal. An argument would start immediately, because John Thomas would belittle the cattle, pointing out that they were as thin as rakes, that it would cost him a fortune in hay to get them fattened up for any market so that they would fetch a decent price. Then, with a banging of his right fist into his left palm, he'd make the owner one offer, and that was the only one, and God have mercy on him for making it, sure he should have more sense and walk away but sure he couldn't let any man be stuck with such cripples as those he was looking at. The owner would tell him to go look for another fool. A crowd would gather around the arguing, bargaining men. John Thomas made as if to walk away, and Michael Joe with him. A man stepped out from the crowd. 'Hold on a minute, there. Don't go away bitter.' The man tried to act as a go-between, between the owner of the bullocks and John Thomas. Offers were made on both sides. The difference was split. A luck penny was promised. Hold out yeer hands. The owner and buyer slapped. A bargain was made. The old farmers in the long black frieze coats and wide black hats, and the young men in the peaked caps, mackintoshes and leggings who had gathered round smiled when the bargain was made. Their faces, crude, bony, hard, and, even in the youngest, already wizened, broke into twinkling smiles, impersonal but happy. A ritual had been completed. A bargain had been made. Who had got the best of it would not be known until the end of the fair or the cattle market report in the evening from Radio Eireann.

The owner who had sold the bullock wanted to treat him to a drink. John Thomas was not a drinking man. But he'd have a lemonade. The owner spat into the mud, and turned away.

Michael Joe moved on through the fair with John Thomas. He bought a few more bullocks, always enacting the same ritual. Inspecting the cattle, making a bad offer, belittling the cattle, walking away, being called back, arguing, making offers and counter-offers, always trying to get the cattle as cheaply as he could, and then clinching the bargain with a slap of the hands.

'You have to watch out for them fellows,' John Thomas said once, 'or they take the eye out of your head and tell you you were better looking without it.'

Michael Joe had seen the ritual often before, but he had a personal interest in it now, and he paid more attention. The farmers and drovers had eyed him as he moved through the fair with John Thomas. He was not dressed like them. He wore his sports cap and tweed suit, white shirt, dark-brown V-necked sweater, and tie. Shopkeepers' clothes. And he had said nothing. A lot of the farmers knew who he was, but they still eyed him with suspicion. He was an outsider in the street of a Fair Day. What was he doing out of his shop? What did he know about buying and selling cattle? Michael Joe was not bothered by the attitude he sensed. When they did speak, they were over-polite to him. But he knew what that meant, and paid no attention to the 'Mr. McCarthy, sir'. They would 'sir' you to death, he knew. One minor incident occurred during the morning which made him laugh when he thought of it, though it almost made him look ridiculous before the countrymen. And if he got that kind of name, he might as well never set foot in the street of a Fair Day again. He would have to give up the cattle dealing before he started it.

He had been standing a little behind John Thomas listening intently to the turns and twists of a bargaining argument, and not noticing what he had his back to—a mistake none of the countrymen ever made. Then he heard a dry shout: 'Watch out there, Mr. McCarthy, or you'll get it.' Michael Joe moved quickly with that old football movement, the instinctive reaction and response of the athletic body when called upon. A cow behind him had begun to excrete. It came out of her rump in a green jet. Michael Joe got a few spatters on his suit. The crowd started to laugh. He had to say something fast, to extricate himself.

'More power to your arse, there,' he said to the cow, and laughed.

The farmers laughed with him. The vulgar response had been the right one. And no curse on the cow. If he had cursed her or got angry, he would have been the clown. The rejected clown, than which no figure would have been a sadder or more pathetic sight. A man who tries to make men laugh and they will not. Michael Joe had established himself in their community by making them laugh with him. He shared, somehow, their view of life because he had made them laugh. The remark had broken spontaneously from him. They would have recognized a deliberate cleverness or vulgarity. The vulgarity of clever men of a different kind from the men at the fair. A heady vulgarity that has not behind it the ease and acceptance of the vulgarity itself. Michael Joe's vulgarity was right for them. He was perfectly at ease with it. And so were the men around him. He ignored the cow-dung on his suit.

Soon after, he brought John Thomas into the house to Ann, for a bite to eat. He did not stay himself, and spoke only a few words to his wife. He went out into the shop for a minute. Vin Scanlon was busy, but able to handle the shop all right. Then Michael Joe went back to the fair.

The rhythm of the fair had slowed down since morning. It had started just before dawn when the shadowy forms of men moved among the shadowy forms of cattle, the grey light finally giving them outline and substance, and they had lifted their voices to bargain with the dawning of the day. At noon, the energy and freshness and keenness the farmers had at dawn had subsided. Early bargains had been made; in the early afternoon, the fever would rise again with the last flurry of bargains; then, around three o'clock, the street would be practically cleared of men and animals —quickly, as if the energy of buying and selling, having been spent, had evaporated into the grey sky, taking the men and the cattle up with it. Then the tinkers came along, drunk, and begging, fighting in the street. Sometimes, the farmers who had been drinking hard after each bargain during the day would begin fighting in the afternoon. The ashplants and the blackthorn sticks came down now on human flesh, and not on the animals. The drunken men fought out old family feuds, or new ones made that day: a slight insult, a half-crown held back from the price, no luck penny given—anything, any excuse for a fight. And so, men struggled here and there in the street, tinkers and their wives fought, verbally and physically, until the Civic Guards came and arrested them, put the tinkers in jail, and sent the farmers home to their wives.

Fresh fights were always breaking out until night fell, and the town was quiet again, except for the inside of the pubs, where a few farmers still lingered in the town, unwilling and not wanting to go back to their loenly farms and cottages out in the country, but taking advantage of their once-a-month freedom, and the companionship of Guinness and Jameson's, and of the other lonely farmers, to drain this day to its dregs.

Michael Joe came back to the shop when the fair had thinned out. He did not want to be seen walking around the town. It would look peculiar. But he watched the scenes of the waning fair from the doorway of the shop. A few drunken farmers were staggering around the pavement in front of Clancy's pub opposite him. They had their arms around each other and were singing a maudlin song, drawing the words out and the singing:

> I am a ramblin' hero, and love has me betrayed,
> Near to the town of Baltinglass, there dwells a lovely
>   maid,
> She's fairer far than Venus bright, and she's free from
>   wordly pride.
> She's my darlin' maid, her dwelling place is down by
>   the tanyard side.

Michael Joe enjoyed listening to the song and heard it out to the last drunken, moaning drawl, until the men who were singing practically fell on the pavement from the melancholy sentiment at the poor boy having to leave his love for America because of a cruel father.

The song put him in an extraordinarily happy mood, though it was sad. He went into the shop. It was dark and gloomy in contrast to outside. Michael Joe found himself blinking. He became intensely aware of the smell of the shop, snorting as he did through his thick nostrils. The air of the shop was heavy and musky from the smell of flour, meal, tea and spices all intermingled to produce an oppressive and heavy atmosphere. Michael Joe had spent the morning in the streets which had their own atmosphere. He had become used that morning to the smell of animals, and the fairly free sense of movement he had in the fair, though he had to be careful of horns, and stay clear of rumps. The gloom and heavy atmosphere of the shop hemmed him in. He had never felt that way before. He was brought up working in the shop. It was in his blood from as early as he could remember and was so much a part of him that he was hardly ever aware of it as having a separate existence.

This afternoon, he felt that way. The mood of the fair was gone.

He sent Vin Scanlon out to wash down the flags while he himself paced restlessly up and down the aisle of the shop between the counter and the bags of flour and meal, occasionally stopping to look out of the doorway. All down the street, the other hopkeepers were washing down the pavements getting rid of the signs of the fair. The streets would be cleaned in the morning. And the signs of the fair would be washed away for another month.

Suddenly he felt hungry, and went into the house. Ann was bent over the kitchen sink washing the pile of dishes that remained after she had fed all her cousins during the day. She was showing quite noticeably, now. She was wearing no make-up, and her face was haggard and wan as she turned from the sink to Michael Joe. He felt a rush of pity for her.

'I suppose you had a great crowd in from the country?'

'Wisha, nothing more than usual.' Ann wiped the perspiration from her forehead with a soapy hand. Michael Joe made no attempt to touch her. They stood away from each other speaking across the kitchen, and though there was kindness in Michael Joe's voice, it was not accompanied by any gesture of kindness.

'Do you want to eat or do you want to wait for supper?' Ann asked.

'I'll wait I think,' Michael Joe said, and went back out to the shop again. He was conscience-stricken. It had not occurred to him the type of burden, the extra work the fair would put on Ann when

216

she had to feed the crowd of cousins. And in the condition she was in. He felt responsible himself, as if it were he who had put the extra burden of work on her. She could hurt herself, kill herself with the work. And the child . . . he could be injured too. (Whenever Michael Joe thought of the child, he thought of it as 'he', never even admitting the possibility that Ann might give birth to a girl.) The whole image of Ann working and slaving away at the sink upset him. She was his wife, after all, and not the serving maid for her country cousins. He was by turns angry at her and sorry for her. Angry that she didn't protest, only dumbly went about doing the work. And then sorry because he would feel pity for any woman for having to put up with this kind of situation. There was no intimacy in his feeling for her. But he resolved to do something to alleviate the situation for her. He was horrified at the thought that if she kept up working like that, she might die.

When Vin Scanlon was finished washing the pavement and was back in the shop, Michael Joe questioned him whether he knew any girl who wanted to work as a maid, to sleep in and be there all the time to help Ann. A good strong girl. One that wouldn't be afraid to work. Vin Scanlon said he knew a girl. A Bridie Devine. Lived out at the Cottages. Michael Joe sent him to fetch her.

About an hour later, Vin came back with Bridie Devine. The girl was about twenty, medium height with wavy light-brown hair cut short and boyishly. It kept falling down over her forehead, and she had a habit of throwing back her head to get the hair out of her eyes. The eyes themselves were a limpid grey, with a wild, restless look in them; she never let them rest anywhere or on anything for long. The mouth was large but not full, and always seemed to be moving even when she was not talking. She habitually kept drawing in her breath and sucking at her lower lip. She wore no make-up, and her cheeks were a natural pink-red. She faced Michael Joe with a defiant, almost arrogant attitude. Michael Joe smiled.

'Are you able to do housework?'

'Would I be here if I wasn't?'

Michael Joe laughed. 'My wife is going to have a baby. You'll have to stop in with her. She isn't overly strong. She'll need a good strong girl like yourself to look after her. Are you willing?'

'What'll you pay?'

Michael Joe mentioned a sum. She nodded, satisfied, looking around the shop, restlessly flicking her eyes over the shelves.

'Come on in and meet the wife, then,' Michael Joe said.

They went in, Michael Joe preceding the girl. He appeared abstracted as if he were mulling over some problem that had struck him, that needed to be solved right away. He seemed to have forgotten all about the girl.

Ann was in the kitchen, at the range, making the tea for supper.

'Here's someone to help you,' Michael Joe said pointing vaguely behind him. Ann peered at the girl who was standing slightly to one side of Michael Joe, and already inspecting the kitchen with the flickering grey eyes.

'There . . . there was no need.'

'I didn't want you killing yourself.' Then, as an afterthought: 'Her name is Bridie Devine. She's from the Cottages. She can sleep up in the attic. She'll be around to help you all the time, then.'

The girl said nothing, but kept up her inspection. Then, her eyes rested on Ann, and paused there, in open curiosity at Ann's condition. She came forward to Ann then, her eyes on Ann's bulging stomach.

'You're going to have a baby?'

'I am,' Ann said softly.

'Hah,' Bridie said with a little laugh. There was somehow in the laugh the implication that Ann had let herself be caught.

'It isn't so bad,' Ann said.

'I'll never have any,' Bridie said. 'Men!' She tossed the hair out of her eyes.

Ann felt sympathetic towards her. Motherly.

'Can you stay?'

'I think so,' Bridie said. ''Tisn't bad.' Looking around the kitchen.

'I'll send Vin Scanlon out for your things,' Michael Joe said.

'Oh, wisha begorra, you needn't,' Bridie said. 'This is all I have, what's on me.' She was wearing a shin-length, dark-blue coat that was too long and too big for her. She had obviously got it from someone in the town.

Michael Joe left. Ann called thanks to him as he went out of the door, and reminded him that his supper was nearly ready. He went on out to the shop as if he hadn't heard her.

'We're going into the cattle business,' he announced to Vin Scanlon Vin looked at him surprised.

'What's that you say, Michael Joe?'

'I'm going to buy cattle and raise them for the market.'

'Oh, be the holy. That's great news,' Vin said. And paused. 'What did you think of her ladyship?'

'Her ladyship?'

'Her,' Vin nodded in the general direction of the kitchen. 'The gerrrll.'

'Oh. She'll do, I suppose. What have you up your sleeve anyway? Come on. Out with it.'

'Oh, nothing. Nothing. She's from the Cottages. A hard nail, I'd say.'

'Have you tried?'

'Ah, g'wan. I don't go in for that. I'm too young yet,' Vin said slyly.

The girl was standing in the doorway. 'You're wanted for your supper, Mr. McCarthy.' And she left.

'Don't let me catch you sneaking around the kitchen,' Michael Joe said. 'Do your sniffing outside these premises.' He took up the moral attitude seriously. There was many a house in Corrigbeg that had got a quite bad reputation because the master or the mistress of the house had exercised no control over the maid, and the lads of the town hung around there in the evenings and at night, like flies around a honey jar. He wasn't going to let the same thing happen in his house. So he had cautioned Vin.

When he went in to his supper, he cautioned Bridie herself in no uncertain terms. The three of them were seated at the table for supper. Mrs. McCarthy had stayed in her room all day, and her supper had been brought up to her there. Michael Joe was a bit irritated that Ann had asked Bridie to sit down to the table with them. She wasn't a member of the family. But he let that pass.

'Let you do your courting off the premises,' he said abruptly to Bridie. 'I don't want this place turned into a bawdy house.'

'Michael Joe!' Ann said.

They had not touched each other now for a long time.

'Never you fear, sir,' Bridie said. 'There isn't a man in the parish able for me. I've left my mark on a couple already. An' I can guarantee they won't come around again.'

'Well, you know the rule of the house, now,' Michael Joe said.

He was vaguely aware of his hypocrisy, but he settled his doubts about his sincerity by giving a little speech about law and order.

'We have to have law and order around the place,' he said

addressing the two women. 'There's houses in the town with their names dragged in the mud because of the bad conduct that goes on there. I need mention no names.' Ann did not know any houses like this. 'This has always been a respectable house. And we'll keep it that way.'

'I don't know what put you on your high horse,' Bridie said bravely. 'You need have no fear of me.'

'That's what I want to hear. Never let me hear any other.'

In her secret heart, Ann found his attitude strange. But she said nothing. In the short time they had been married, she had seen him change. If he wasn't distant from her, he was irritable. And now this. She agreed with what he said but was surprised to hear him say it. Found it embarrassing in front of 'poor Bridie' whom she had already taken an affection for, and pity on. The girl had nothing; a poor girl. Her family had a hard life there, she knew. Always on the brink of starvation. Ten or twelve of them living in a three-room cottage. The father and mother both drunkards.

Michael Joe left for the night and went up to the St. Joseph's Club where he played nap until midnight, with the other respectable shopkeepers of the town.

For the next few weeks, Michael Joe contented himself with laying plans for buying the cattle. He decided not to buy them at the Corrigbeg Fair. He was reluctant to let the people of the town know he was going into the cattle business. They'd know soon enough, and they'd talk about it. He wondered if he wasn't ashamed to be seen wandering the streets on a Fair Day poking at the rumps and hides of cows and bullocks, like any country farmer. He felt the weight of being a townsman. The townspeople looked down on the country farmers as unmannerly, vulgar. Hardly a cut above the animals they were so constantly with. And like them too, dangerous, unpredictable in temper, hasty, and likely at any time to run mad or fight if not controlled. Michael Joe was aware of this opinion, and particularly now. He would go about his first moves into the world of the fair quietly and unobtrusively.

He got up before dawn one morning, not waking Ann, and not telling her even beforehand, that he would be gone for the day. He bicycled in the dark to the fair in Kilmihil, about ten miles away. There, he stood alone in the square. There was no light except that daggering out from an occasional window where a man was up; small gas lamps at each corner of the square lit it up. Shadows of men and cattle began to move around him; the lowing and moaning and bleating of the animal world came to him out of the dark. In a strange way, he delighted in the noises, the smell, the heavy breathings, the sudden dampness, the low murmur of the voices of farmers, all coming at him in the pre-dawn darkness. He was not now the shopkeeper opening his shop, or entering it at nine or ten in the morning. And he wouldn't be facing the neat arrangements of groceries on shelves nor the weights and measures, today. He felt for the hundred and fifty pounds he had drawn from the bank. The bulk in his chest made him at ease in a moment of strangeness.

He had a slight touch of panic at the beginning of the fair, just before he plunged in and bought his first bullock. He almost wished he hadn't come. The uncertainty of whether he would make an ass out of himself bargaining with the farmers suddenly loomed almost like too much of a risk for his pride. Their shrewd eyes would soon discover his lack of experience, and once they discovered that, he would be a hare running from the hounds. He was a stranger in their midst, and to their ways. Between two worlds. The respectable world of the shopkeeper with its routine of public service run on fairly rigid laws of buying and selling, and fairly fixed prices for customers. A shopkeeper had to have a reputation for honesty. At the fair there was nothing but men bargaining over cattle, pitting wits against wits in a struggle for top penny in the market place. Any trick, any strategem was fair. Any means of blinding a buyer could be employed. The seller tried to hide faults, the buyer to find them. Michael Joe knew this. He was unsure. But the compulsion to enter the primitive world where he was thrown on his own resources, to rise or fall, was too much for him. He plunged.

By noontime he had bought five red shorthorn bullocks, and was feeling well satisfied with himself. He quickly got to know a few of the farmers the only way they could be known—to tangle with them in a hard bargain. 'Mister Stranger' they called him at first until he told them his name and where he was from. Some of them knew him vaguely, and the fact that he had a grocery shop in Corrigbeg.

'And what would a decent, clean-living shopkeeper be doing out in a place like this?' one of them said with a twinkle in his eye.

'One reason, and that only,' Michael Joe said. 'Ye can see for yeerselves.'

They shook their heads. 'And you to leave a nice, soft, cushy job behind the counter for slavery like this?'

If it was slavery, Michael Joe thought they were taking it lightly. They looked grim enough in their dark, wide-brimmed hats or checkered caps pulled down over their eyes as if to conceal them a bit, and the faces were one hardly distinguishable from another, grey, slate faces full of crags and nooks and wild tufts of moustache. Only when a sharp bargain was made, and darting remarks had passed, did the faces betray any kind of softness, and show distinctly. It was as if the owners of the bullocks, once they had seen that a man knew what he was about and could buy in the usual ritual, then only would they warm up to him. When the last slap of owner and buyer's hands had been made, Michael Joe often found himself getting a pounding on the back. 'I wouldn't let me mother have that bullock for that price. But . . . seein' who you are. Come on an' have a wet on it.' Michael Joe and the farmer would adjourn to the nearest pub. He had adjourned five times that morning, and each time the visit got longer and longer.

Michael Joe found out that with the farmers he had bought from, the visit to the pub counted as much as selling the cattle. There, in the semi-darkness of the pub, with a pint of Guinness in their hands, the farmers dropped the bargaining manner of the street, and talked the usual talk of men taking it easy in pubs. They were clubmen at home in the fellowship of their club, idling an hour or two away with their fellow clubmen. Though Michael Joe himself was a stranger to them, they knew the town of Corrigbeg like the back of their hands. And many of the people in it. And they inquired after such-and-such a one. Or told Michael Joe of adventures they had at the fair or football matches, there. And the fine women you'd see walking the streets there.

By noon, then, Michael Joe had 'a good load on', as the expression went. He had hired a blocker to drive his bullocks into a backyard of one of the shopkeepers until he would be ready to drive them home. Then he went out in the fair again and acted as a blocker, helping to make bargains for others, as he had been helped to make his.

The fair was never really at an absolute standstill. There was always some sort of a bargain going on, even if it was only a farmer buying a pair of trousers from the hawker who had set up his tent from the back of a lorry at the edge of the square. There was a sense of purpose and goal in even the slightest approach or greeting. When a man walked up to you you did not know what he had on his mind. He might let you know in a roundabout way that there was a milch cow somewhere in the fair he was interested in. Would you vet for him? Or make a bid, a false bid, to find out what the fellow wanted for her. Feints, darts and dodges. Name calling. 'Yerra, sure, that fella pisses agin the wind so he'll get his own back.' At times, in the bargaining, two men would get so fierce with each other with the hard names and the swearing that it seemed as if they would fight. But the blocker was there to make the peace and bring matters round to the main point, and off family background or the names of the Holy Trinity.

The time passed quickly for Michael Joe. The fair thinned out. Then he thought of the journey home. He sighed. And moved down the street to Lynch's pub, where he had left his bicycle; in the yard where his five bullocks. The grey day had held up on the rain so far, and the sky still looked as hard as slate. If he was lucky he would get home before the rain came. The street was one long puddle of cow-dung. He sloshed along. Then, ahead of him, he heard the voice of a ballad singer. It was a woman. A dark-shawled woman, the dark shawl over her shoulders, the dark hair, slightly matted, unkempt, uncombed. As he drew near, she seemed less a woman than a girl. The olive-skinned face and the sloe eyes. Streaks of dirt on the olive-skinned face. The voice was strong and harsh.

> If I was a blackbird I'd whistle and sing
> And I'd follow the ship that my true love sails in . . .

She could barely carry a tune. Over an arm hung a wicker basket in which could be seen framed holy pictures, paper flowers, and camphor balls. Michael Joe stopped to listen to her. He wanted to put off the thought of going home. Here was an excuse to postpone it for a moment. He only half-listened to the song. The girl was spare and lean, the lean look of the hungry tinker. Dark eyebrows over sloe eyes. She eyed Michael Joe. She was on the edge of the road, he on the pavement. A few children were lounging against the walls of the houses nearby, listening to her. Abruptly she brought her song to a close, and moved straight for Michael Joe.

'Hey, Mister, won't you buy a flower for the missus?' she wheedled, going into the begging act with her body, her eyes frisking him with curiosity, assessing, wondering if he were a soft touch.

'Wisha, girl, I have no missus,' Michael Joe said being funny with her.

'Ah, for the sweetheart, thin,' the tinker girl said to him, coyly, wheedlingly. 'Only a shilling, Mister.'

'A shilling! For one of them flowers. What do you take me for?'

The tinker girl smiled, displaying pure white, even teeth. 'You're a grand man. A grand man.' She sidled, her tartan skirts swinging, closer to him and touched his arm, looking up sideways at him.

Michael Joe laughed a deep belly laugh. 'Go on with your plámás. I'm after buying five bullocks, and haven't a ha'penny left on me.' He was going to make her beg.

'Mister, a man the likes of you is never without ease for a poor tinker woman.'

Michael Joe marvelled that the voice of the singer had been so harsh, but the voice of the beggar was full of grace notes of another kind, sensuous, lingering, half-wheedling, half-caressing. And that light, tentative touch on his arm. He was wearing a mackintosh, but the touch had gone home. The suppressed desire of months roused. Then he noticed for the first time that she was barefoot, the cow-dung clinging to her feet, caked there making shoes of mud.

'I'll buy you a drink if you'll come and sing a song for me,' he said laughing. The laugh was shaky.

'Ah, sure I couldn't,' she said glancing toward the pub. 'They wouldn't let me in.'

Michael Joe took the statement as a challenge. 'By God, they will,' he said. 'Or they'll hear about it from me. Come on.'

Michael Joe headed towards Lynch's pub, and she followed at a distance. The girl walked with that sliding, swishing motion, more of a dance than a walk, her head bent, the basket in her arm swaying to her walk, the walk of another race of women from warm climates, a walk that could never be entirely bred out of the blood and the muscles, not even by a damp, cold climate.

Michael Joe looked behind him as he entered the pub to see if she was following, and nodded at her, as if to say—brave it out.

He found a dark corner of the pub and made her sit down. The pub was crowded with drunken farmers doing their best to keep alive in the afternoon the excitement of the fair, but knowing they were fighting a losing battle. Michael Joe pushed through them to the bar and ordered two pints. He asked for a couple of sandwiches. Joe Lynch, the barman, had seen the tinker woman.

'She can't stop here,' he said nodding curtly toward the back. 'They're only trouble. Always a fight . . . fight.'

'I'm only feeding her,' Michael Joe said. 'A poor, hungry creature in off the street.'

Joe Lynch looked at him, the quick speculative look of the barman who trusted no one. No tick given. He drew two pints for Michael Joe, and handed him two sandwiches wrapped in white paper.

'Let her eat and be off, then. I want no trouble around here.'

Michael Joe felt truculent. 'You won't get any,' he said shortly.

He went back and sat down beside her. She had put her basket on the floor. Framed pictures of the Sacred Heart, small religious badges, rosary beads, camphor balls were mingled with the paper flowers. Michael Joe laughed as he glanced at the basket. Then he handed her the foaming pint, and took a sandwich from his pocket.

'There,' he said. 'Fill up on that. I don't know how ye keep up. Wandering around half-starved.'

She moved closer to him on the seat. 'May the Lord God, and the Holy and Blessed Mother, and the Divine Son, Jesus . . .' she raised the sloe eyes to the smoky ceiling.

'That's enough of that,' Michael Joe said. 'You can drop the act, now. What's your name?'

'Carty.'

'Carty!' Michael Joe said. 'Sure we must be related.' He laughed. She did not laugh, but showed her white teeth. In the half-darkness Michael Joe could see the shadowy outlines of her face, and feel the stirrings her body kept making beside him. She did not seem able to sit still. Her head, her face, her bare feet—part of her was always moving. He could not see, but heard and felt. He was warm and unloosed his mackintosh.

'Is Carty your name?' she said. The sloe eyes were looking at him more frankly and directly in the darkness. They had stopped playing the looking game, and had started playing the burning one.

'McCarthy,' Michael Joe said. 'From Corrigbeg.'

'You keep the shop there on the Main Street. Isn't that you?'

''Tis,' Michael Joe said. 'And you're wandering the streets barefoot, selling . . . this . . .' he said pointing down at the basket. 'How could we be related? I'm a shopkeeper.'

He was only making conversation. Anything to keep her near him. To spar with her. She knew, too. It was the sparring until they should come to grips, and have something resolved between them. The voices raised and shouting around them. Voices of men. And she the only woman's voice in the place. And he listening to her.

'We're related,' she said bringing her face close to his. 'I think we are.'

The secrecy of her. Michael Joe considered himself fairly hard-headed. He had had his one romance. One time he had made a fool of himself. Nell! The first time and the last. But this tinker woman, a tramp off the road, was opening worlds within him he had never suspected. It was not romance he felt. It was something darker. More secret. A place where there was light of a special kind, or the feeling of light rather than light itself. The feeling of light in the racing blood, rushing on, pulling a man anywhere. Out to sea. Sweeping all before it in a cruel rush. He knew he could not trust his hands upon her. Violence and cruelty, savagery . . . these feelings he found in himself, beginning sitting there beside her, trying to make her out in the semi-darkness. She was something and nothing. Did she know what she was doing to him? She burned. He could feel that.

His hand gripped the round glass of his pint, and he took a deep swallow to steady himself.

'And what do they call you?' he said knowing it was useless.

'Shuvrawn. Will I sing you a song?'

'Do,' he said. 'You aren't much of a singer. But I'll listen.'

She sang below the voices of the men, close to his ear, as if the song was for him alone. The voice was different again from the one she sang with in the street. She crooned at times; then a moan; was throaty, and droned like a small bagpipe, or cried like a gull. The voice ranged over sounds that Michael Joe did not know the human voice could make. She sang in the gipsy language—Sheldru; neither Irish nor English. Michael Joe did not understand what she was singing. But he did not need to. She pressed closer to him as she mouthed her song, and her sweet, porter breath blew over his nostrils.

There was something personal and impersonal about the song, both at the same time. He felt she was talking to him, singing it to him in what was like the voice of some animal or bird. The Sheldru gave the song that touch of darkness. But at the same time, he felt himself being drawn into a world where he could not recognize himself. A world where he was a wild, roaming animal, the world outside, her world where all rules and laws and order were gone, and he was only himself, as if he were the first man born into the world and without guidance, and thrown entirely on his blood and what it told him to do.

Was he drunk? The voice was close to his ear. Other voices in the background. Like but not. He wandered in darkness where there was only a female voice, calling, with noises that drove him almost to the pitch of madness.

Suddenly there was a silence in the pub, and a wild shout.

'Where is she? Where is the slut? The melting strap!'

The men parted toward Michael Joe and the tinker girl. The man was standing in the middle of the pub, a young man, blond and curly-haired, wearing a blue shirt open down the front to reveal a hairy chest. The sleeves of the shirt were rolled up on thick, bulging arms, short and hairy.

When the tinker woman saw the man, she grabbed her basket, and rose quickly, fear in her eyes, slightly cowering. The man made for her, grabbed her by the arm, and threw her toward the door. Michael Joe half rose, as if to go after her and protect her. The man turned on him, and shot a thick, hard fist at him, straight into the face, just as Michael Joe was half risen.

'You bloody bastard,' the tinker man said. 'Stealing my woman. Go home to your own.'

Michael Joe fell back on the seat. The tinker man turned around and ran out. No one dared lift a hand to touch him.

Michael Joe had two front teeth knocked out, and was bleeding profusely. Joe Lynch took him in the back, and they rinsed out his mouth with ice-cold water. Spatters of blood got on Michael Joe's mackintosh.

'You can't say but I didn't warn you,' Lynch kept saying to him. 'Warn you I did. But not a screed of heed did you pay. You can't trust them. Sure they're not civilized at all. Half savages . . . savages.'

Michael Joe said nothing in reply. His tongue kept flicking

through the gap in his teeth. Now that the first pain was over, he felt like laughing. A big, free laugh, to roar his head off. And he almost burst out with it. The spasms began in his belly. But at the last moment, listening to Lynch's talk, he controlled himself.

'The Lord have mercy on them,' was all he said, referring to his teeth in a sarcastic manner. Lynch thought he meant the tinkers.

'Don't be making any more trouble. They'd brain you if you go up to the camp after them. Honest to God. You'd get a tongs over the skull before you knew where you were. And be laid out. You'd better head off home.'

Michael Joe's mouth had stopped bleeding. He had swallowed some of his own blood, bland and tasteless. His lips had begun to swell, and his face puffed. In spite of the injuries, he felt calm and peaceful, without any anger, and without desire to seek revenge. In fact, he was happy in a strange way. That was why he wanted to laugh.

'I deserved what I got,' he said to Lynch, and began to button up his mackintosh.

He thanked Lynch for his trouble, got his bicycle, and went down to the backyard where his five red shorthorns were huddled around the gate, waiting to be let out. It was about four o'clock in the afternoon. The sky was still a solid slate of light grey, not rain grey, but enough to darken the light. It would hold this light for a couple of hours more. The spring days were getting longer.

As a boy, Michael Joe had occasionally driven cattle, helping a farmer at the fair for a few pennies. But that had been long ago. The cattle eyed him and scattered as he approached. He propped his bicycle against a wall, and opened the gate, and stood back. The bullocks charged. First one paused at the gate looking right and left nervously, then charged out on the road like a bull into a ring. The others followed. All of them stood in the road not yet having decided on a direction. 'Hup, there,' Michael Joe shouted. Some of them ran up the road, some down. 'Ye sons o' bitches, ye!' Michael Joe roared, and hopped on the bicycle after the few that had gone the way he did not want them to. But the bullocks were young and fast, and Michael Joe was not in the physical condition he used to be in. But for a few fellows that were loitering by the side of the road he might never have caught up with the bullocks. The fellows saw the bullocks running, and the man bent over the handle-bars of the bicycle, pedalling madly behind the bullocks.

They took in the situation immediately and stopped the bullocks, and turned them back. Michael Joe thanked them. They gave him a peculiar look. He noticed it. And laughed. His face was swollen. He wondered if they thought he had been gored by one of the shorthorns. He thanked them for their trouble. They were laconic. No trouble at all. Was he going far? To Corrigbeg. Their eyes twinkled in the red, bony, impersonal faces. They merely nodded, half smiling, as if they were in on a secret unknown to Michael Joe.

He drove the three cattle who had bolted back along the road, looking for the other two. The road ended in a large Fair Green, where he spied the other two cattle grazing. He tried to round them all together, pedalling on his bicycle like a trick bicyclist in a circus. Finally, he got them all out of the Fair Green on to the main road leading to Corrigbeg. A dog from one of the nearby houses took off after them, and they scattered, galloping, charging, shying. Michael Joe pedalled furiously again, trying to catch up to them. He was in a foul mood now, and could have slaughtered all five of them on the spot. Shot them, if he had his gun. And the blasted cur that was yapping at their heels, driving them wild.

Again he was helped out of his trouble by a few straggling men that were still around Kilmihil at the end of the fair. Again, the peculiar looks, the half-smiles, and the nods, as if they were withholding secret knowledge from him. He did not thank them this time. One of the men who helped him was holding a good, thick ashplant.

'How much for the stick?' Michael Joe said shortly.

'Yerra, you have so far to go, 'tis yours for nothing,' the man said handing him the grey ashplant. 'Lay it well into them.'

Michael Joe hopped on the bike, pedalled after the bullocks until he caught up with them, then steering the bicycle with one hand, he laid the ashplant across their rumps with the other, taking savage delight in beating them, and grunting as he beat.

The animals settled down into a herd, once they were on the main road. It was as if the sound and sight of the stick had calmed them down. Michael Joe kept them moving at a good gallop, spending his anger in his own pedalling and trying to exhaust the bullocks.

But they continued to run wild and stray whenever a by-road or boithrin crossed the main road. Michael Joe cursed them, walloped them, cursed himself for ever having taken up the cattle. His curses were those of a man driven almost to the verge of despair or lunacy, with just enough rationality left to utter strings of the vilest and filthiest curses that rose spontaneously to his bruised lips. The Holy Trinity, the Blessed Virgin, the Devil, and numerous saints were repeatedly mentioned on his tongue, coupled with references to the excretory functions. He thundered destruction and torment on the cattle many times. Tortures and pains of the damned. When he had them once again going the straight main road, he laid the ashplant mercilessly across their backs.

But he could not control them entirely. At the next by-road, they were off again, straying. Once, Michael Joe was so exhausted, he got off the bicycle and sat down on the side of the road, completely and utterly worn out. The cattle halted, and began to graze on the side of the road a few yards away from him. Two of them had turned down a by-road. They had stopped and were grazing too. He looked at them. They were malevolent. They had something in for him. *They* were torturing *him*. Playing games with him. Trying to kill him. Wear him out.

He was tired, every muscle was deadened, his nerves numbed, and his whole body felt like a ton of lead. He kept on his feet by sheer will-power. If he had sat any longer he would have fallen asleep on the side of the road, just like any other tired animal. The cattle raised their heads when he got up. They eyed him, but did not move. Such soft brown eyes! He had to cross a wall and circle a field to get in front of the cattle who had strayed, to chase them back on to the main road again.

The light was fading. It had held, but now was dying quickly. He'd have to get them home before dark, or they would wander off over the countryside, and he'd never be able to find them, and God only knows what bog hole himself might fall into. The threat of darkness renewed his energy, and he was able to get all the cattle moving at a good pace on the main road again. From time to time motor-cars passed in the half-light and the cattle turned back against Michael Joe. He raised the ashplant, swore at them shouting, and bore down on them with the bicycle. They turned against the car, skittering by it, rather than try to break by Michael Joe.

They scattered once more at a cross-roads about a mile from Corrigbeg. Michael Joe got off the bicycle and stood, watching them scatter. 'G'wan, ye melting sons of devils, ye. The curse of the Almighty down on top of ye. May ye fall over a cliff and break yeer bones.' The cattle had, in fact, turned down the road to the sea. It was now dusk. He was in half a mind to let them wander for the rest of the night, and even if they did fall over a cliff, he felt, now, that he would have suffered the loss without regret, and given up the cattle business for ever. He stood there in the lonesome road shouting after them. Then he calmed. Then he grew silently furious. They would not best him. He thought of them as his mortal enemies with whom he was engaged in a struggle to the death. And they would not conquer him. He'd get the best of them or kill himself trying.

He set off after them, and rounded them up again. By this time, Michael Joe had taken on the hang-dog, exhausted attitude of a beaten animal himself. He was breathing heavily through his bruised, puffed mouth. His thick shoulders heaved under the breathing. He gripped the ashplant as if somehow he was getting final strength to finish his journey from it. He had lost strength even to beat the cattle now, and did not roar or curse at them any more. The struggle had become silent. The man pushing his bicycle, the cattle rushing, skittering, stopping, charging, sometimes grunting, looking back at the man as if trying to estimate whether he would withstand a charge or not, and finally turning home obediently because the hunched, dark form kept moving toward them.

He got them into the grazing field, and bolted the latch on the iron gate. Light dark had fallen. He could not see them in the field as he leaned on the gate resting before making the final effort to get home. Were they phantoms that had suddenly disappeared? Were they there at all? He wished desperately that one of them would low or make some noise to convince him that what he had been through was real. Below him he heard the gurgling of the Cluanboney River, surging with water from spring rain. But no sound or sight of the cattle. He felt tired and lonesome.

His mother and Ann were sitting in the dining room at either side of the open hearth fire, Ann knitting and Mrs. McCarthy saying her rosary, when he got home. He stood at the dining room door and glanced in at them. Ann rose and suppressed a cry. She was coming to him. He waved a weary hand.

'I'm going to bed.'

He dragged himself upstairs with the help of the banisters. Ann followed him, and halted at the foot of the stairs.

'Aren't you going to eat?'

He did not answer. He entered the bedroom, took off his mackintosh, and threw himself fully clothed, in his dirty, cow-dunged boots, on the bed.

33

ONCE OR TWICE a month after this, Michael Joe went to fairs in towns other than Corrigbeg. Sometimes he took two or three cattle to the fairs and sold them for the Dublin or English market, and then bought younger bullocks to take home and fatten. He always made some profit on the transactions, but he spent whatever profit he made on drink. After selling cattle, he always adjourned to the nearest pub with the men who had been in on the bargain, and he bought drinks all around, never letting any of the other men buy any.

Soon he became a well-known and popular figure at the fairs in the county. He had a great following among the blockers, the fellows who did the odd jobs around the fair, driving the cattle into the lorries, or acting as middlemen in a bargain. He treated them liberally, and they spread his name so that there was always competition among them to give him a hand. Michael Joe noticed, and was flattered, and deceived because he wanted to be. Some of the farmers, however, made wry comments behind his back, some of those who would go to the pub and free-load off him. 'Ah, wisha, a fool and his money . . .'

Michael Joe was too taken up with this new life to consider whether he was acting foolishly or not. He learned to judge cattle well, made up his mind quickly when he wanted to buy, and stuck out for his own price always, once he had settled it in his mind. The farmers never found him a soft touch there. In the ritual of the bargaining, he was fierce, competitive, even arrogant. But when the bargain was made and he had got his price, he made up for the hardness of his attitude, by turning soft in the pubs where he took absolute command and ordered and paid for the drinks as if he owned the Bank of Ireland.

After the first experience with the cattle, he gradually learned how to drive them properly. The journey had been nightmarish, but he had learned how they behaved. The next time he drove them he instinctively knew what to do. He anticipated their moves, heading them off at the cross-roads, setting an even steady pace as much as he could, and speeding them up with blows of the ashplant on the rumps and shouts, when they approached a by-road where they could stray. He sensed them.

He also grew to love the ritual of the hand on the rump, feeling under the udders, and poking in the ribs. He inspected the bullocks he bought, carefully and elaborately, sometimes even grabbing a horn and parting the waxen snout to inspect the teeth. The farmers were impressed and grew to respect his judgment. When he was not trying to make a bargain for himself, he was helping another man at the fair make one.

The more friends he made, the more he drank. He became as well known in the pubs of the towns as in the market places. At a certain stage in getting drunk, he always demanded songs. If there wasn't a singer in the pub, he would send out for one. He would sit and listen quietly while the singer sang, his dark head tilted towards the singer. If he didn't like the song, he would tell the singer to stop, pay him half a crown and ask him to go away, and send in another singer.

The publicans humoured Michael Joe in this. He often became truculent over what he thought was a succession of bad singers. The publicans would persuade him to go upstairs and sleep it off. So it was that Michael Joe often did not come home from the fairs until the following morning. He rose in the early dawn and drove the cattle he had bought home. In the early morning the cattle were usually peaceful and tractable, made calm by the light after the darkness of the night. When he first observed this peculiarity of the cattle, he felt a great pity for them, and the knowledge brought him, in a strange way, closer to the animals, into almost personal touch with them.

He never met his tinker woman of the song again. Her husband, or her man maybe, had probably packed her in a cart and they had moved on up north. Michael Joe wanted to meet her. His inner ear always listened for her, and the dark eyes, set shallow in the dark, thick, fleshy face, took on a staring quality at times, at the approach of any tinker woman. He would stare and stare at the woman while she begged from him. 'A copper for the poor ould beggar, a copper, good sir. Ah, isn't it some girl will be the happy one with you beside her along the road.' Michael Joe always gave money. He would have liked to pass the time and talk to many of them. He would have liked to buy them drinks. But he remembered the first time. Sometimes he would ask them their names. There were many Cartys. He wondered if sometime in the distant past, his own family hadn't been tinkers, too.

When he got home after being out at a fair, he was quieter and gentler. Ann was growing bigger into her seventh month. He usually did not notice. But, one morning, he did. He asked her how she was doing. That was the only way he could express his curiosity. Ann was embarrassed. She turned away and busied herself with some little chore, and muttered something indistinguishable, like 'Fine, thanks,' as if she were a complete stranger answering a stranger's question. Michael Joe dropped the matter then.

She never asked him how he got the missing teeth, but he would often catch her glancing at his mouth with her small mouth parted, drawn back, as if in fear. The missing teeth gave his face an expression of comic brutality.

Michael Joe kept going to the fairs; he saw Ann less and less, and hardly ever saw his mother any more, either. She had taken to spending more time in her room since Bridie came, and Bridie brought her meals up to her there.

One morning when Michael Joe came home from a fair, as he was sitting at the table eating the breakfast Ann had prepared for him—she had sent Bridie out somewhere on a message—Ann broached a subject that was troubling her.

'There's something . . . '

He looked at her and smiled, showing the missing teeth. 'Is something troubling you?'

She was hovering over him at the table. At the turn of his face towards her, she turned away. 'There is.'

She sat down in the armchair behind him, and spoke to his back. 'I caught Bridie and Vin out in the back . . . in the cabin . . . '

Michael Joe did not answer for a while. Then: 'I warned him to stay away from her.'

'Our house will get a bad name.'

'Oh, we can't have that,' Michael Joe said severely. 'I'll have to talk to Vin. Give him the sack if he can't behave himself. Or her.'

'Oh she's all right otherwise,' Ann said. 'A great help. And great company. I'd blame that fellow of yours out in the shop.'

'I wouldn't put it past him,' Michael Joe said, rising from the table. 'We'll see what we can do about it.'

That was the lengthiest conversation they had had in some time. Michael Joe was genuinely indignant that Vin would try to pull a dirty trick like that on him, while he was away. Especially since he had warned him. Poor Ann must have been shocked. Michael Joe could hardly suppress a private smile. Though the incident might have its humorous side, he couldn't let it go on. It wouldn't do to have an affair like that going on in his house, and to have it get abroad in the town. He knew what the talk there would be. Soon, more fellows than Vin would come sniffing around after Bridie. Like a bitch in heat. And the reputation of his house would be ruined forever.

When there was a quiet moment in the shop, he spoke to Vin. 'I thought I told you to keep your hands off that one next door,' Michael Joe said referring to Bridie.

Vin looked at him slyly. 'It takes two to tango, there.'

'Never mind giving me any of your guff. Leave her alone, in the future. And if there's any more of that kind of thing around my house, the two of ye will be out on the street looking for jobs.' Michael Joe went behind the counter and into the glass cubicle where he kept the account books, and began going over them. He shut the door. Vin whistled quietly to himself in amazement. 'Mr. Cyclone, himself,' he muttered under his breath, and then looked around the shop for something to do before he should draw more of Michael Joe's thunder on him.

34

MICHAEL JOE DECIDED to stop at home one night that week instead of going up to the St. Joseph's Club or out to the football field to watch the team practise. He was beyond football now. A respectable married man, to be a father any day. Gone were the football days. But he still watched and took note of the rising stars. Became judicial and judgematical on them, much as he did over the cattle.

Ann was surprised to see him coming in about seven o'clock.

'I shut the shop early,' he announced. 'I think I'll stop at home tonight.'

'Oh,' was all Ann said.

Michael Joe went into the dining room and sat down and began to re-read the paper. He now paid just as much attention to the cattle market reports as he did to the racing results. Usually he would decide to go to another fair if he detected an upswing in the cattle prices.

The house was quiet except for the sound of Ann washing dishes in the sink in the kitchen.

'Where's Bridie?'

'Oh, I let her go out for a while. She wanted to see her mother out at the Cottages.'

'Wanted to see her mother, me ah!' Michael Joe said. He never asked for his own mother, knowing she was at the chapel. He read the paper for a while again. Then Ann came in and sat opposite him, and began to knit. She was working on a pair of white bootees for the baby. Michael Joe glanced up from the paper and saw her sitting opposite him, her small head bent over the thread, and the small hands working away clicking the knitting needles. She was wearing a white blouse and a black dress. Her arms half rested on her enlarged stomach. She had her short hair bound severely in a hair net.

He felt a burst of pity for her, and suddenly became aware of how much he had left her alone. He wanted to do something to liven up her life. That was it. To liven up her life.

He stood up. 'I'll be back.'

A disappointed look flickered quickly into her wan face, and then died. She watched him leave without saying anything.

He went up to Jackie Jones's and bought a bottle of port wine, and on the way down he went into Nugents' and bought sweets, chocolates and oranges. He came back into the house with his arms full.

'Here. Take a slug of that. 'Twill put heart in you.'

'Oh, Michael Joe. What did you do?' she said pathetically. She tried to smile. Her small mouth held the shape of the smile for a moment, then let it go, tried to hold it again, and then let it go again. She was not sure what he was doing, and did not really know how to respond to him if she ever really had.

He pushed the dark bottle of wine toward her. 'Come on now. Take a drop of this and 'twill bring the colour back to your cheeks.'

'Oh, I couldn't, Michael Joe.' She dropped her eyes to the white bootees on her lap.

Michael Joe put the bottle of wine on the table, and spilled out the contents of the bag of confections all around it.

'We'll have a quiet party,' he said.

He went to the cupboard and took out one glass, and poured a quarter of a glass of the ruby wine into it. Then held it before her.

'Drink this, in the name of God,' he said. 'You look like a ghost.'

She had clutched the half-finished bootees as if for protection.

'Ah, drink it yourself. I'm not much use for it,' she said.

'I didn't buy it for myself,' he said with a mock roar. 'Here, now.'

She took the glass.

'Go on. Go on. Drink it.'

She put the glass slowly to her lips, and took a sip.

' 'Tis lovely, Michael Joe. Thanks.'

He went out in the back and came back with a handful of bog deal and a few kippins, and built up a blaze in the fire though the late April night was not cold. He noticed that she had not touched the wine again.

'Come on, there. Down with some more.'

She gingerly raised the glass to her lips again, and took another taste, just about moistening her dry, pink lips.

'Ah, sure you're drinking like a bird,' he said pretending to be pained.

She laughed a little.

He put some of the confectioneries on a plate with one or two of the oranges and brought them over to the side table beside her. He took the wine away, and peeled an orange for her. All the while he talked, as he had not talked to her since before their marriage, telling her little anecdotes about what had happened in the shop that day, but nothing about the fairs.

'And there was old Moll with a pound of my best tea and a pound of my best sugar, and not a ha'penny to pay for them with. "I'll have a letter from England one of these days," she said to me. "You're getting that letter a long time, Moll," I said to her. "Ah, Misther McCarthy, sure the post do be slow coming from so far away," she says to me. "I'm glad 'tisn't from America the letter is coming, Moll, or 'twould never get here," I said.'

'Ah, the poor craythur,' Ann said. 'You shouldn't make fun of her. God knows, she hardly has a shoe to put on her.'

Ann was losing her fear. She loved to listen to him tell stories. He used to tell a lot of them to her before they were married. Harmless stories, hardly worthy of even the name of gossip. Funny stories with a comical verbal twist, such as the one he had just told her now. She chewed away at a quarter of an orange while she listened to him.

Mrs. McCarthy came in from the chapel, and stood in the dining room door.

Ann blushed, as if she and Michael Joe were two children that had been caught doing something naughty. Michael Joe got up.

'Come on in and sit down,' he invited his mother. 'I have a nice little drop of port. 'Twill do you good, a little drop.'

Mrs. McCarthy looked at him for a moment. Michael Joe was in an excited mood, and hardly noticed the look. What meaning it had, no one could say. Her face was a bony, waxen mask, hollowed now with age, ascetic from years of self-denial and self-restraint. Faintly watery grey eyes looked out at her son from hollow sockets. Then she turned to Ann.

'It isn't good for you in your condition,' she said.

'Ah, sure 'twon't do her any harm. Bring the blood back to her,' Michael Joe said.

'You'll ruin her, too,' Mrs. McCarthy said quietly, and left

That put a damper on Michael Joe's spirits for a few moments. But he recovered soon. 'She's getting old,' he said. 'Wait'll the . . . the . . . child comes. She'll get her second wind.'

Ann hung her head shyly. It was beginning to be a grand evening.

Bridie came swishing in a few minutes later. Michael Joe made her sit down with them though she turned away to go to her room in the attic when she saw the scene. Her restless eyes fastened on the bottle of wine on the table. Michael Joe noticed. He insisted she have a drop. But she refused, vehemently shaking her head. Michael Joe could tell that she was dying to taste it.

'Ah, don't force her if she doesn't want to,' Ann said.

'This is a celebration,' Michael Joe said. 'One drop won't hurt her.'

He poured her a little in the bottom of a tumbler. Bridie tasted it immediately, and sucked in her lips afterward. Michael Joe watched her keen delight. And laughed.

'Did you like it, Bridie?' Ann asked.

'Ah, sure, that's what the fly boys use to make you drunk,' she said with a toss of her head.

'Oh,' Ann said.

Michael Joe turned on the wireless, and twirled the knob to the BBC. Dance music from somewhere called the Palladium Theatre in London came over the air waves. It was a live broadcast, and after every group of numbers there was live applause. An M.C. kept repeating that everyone there was having a wonderful time. And invited those who had never been to the Palladium to come along and bring their sweethearts and have a jolly time. His voice seemed always on the point of breaking out into laughter.

'By God, we'll go there in our holidays sometime,' Michael Joe said to Ann. He had sat down in the armchair opposite Ann and was listening to the music, tapping his feet and keeping time. A new number began. He went over and turned the volume up a bit. '. . . cruising down the river on a Sunday afternoon . . . The birds above all sing of love . . .' A crooner sang in a sleepy voice. Michael Joe did a few turns around the room to the music, holding his empty arms out in front of him, and a comical smile on his face.

'The fellow invited us to the Palladium. And I'm going there,' Michael Joe said. He began to sing along with the crooner: 'Just two of us together . . . And we'll plan our honeymoon . . . Cruising down the river on a Sunday afternoon.'

Ann laughed nervously at his antics and turned away to look into the fire. Bridie was gazing at him with bright eyes. She was biting at her lower lip, and had finished all the wine he had poured for her.

Michael Joe stopped in front of Ann. 'Come on,' he said. 'Try a couple of turns.'

Ann looked down at her stomach in alarm. 'Oh, Michael Joe! Wouldn't I be the sight.'

He looked at her as if he had entirely forgotten her condition, and why he had started the little party in the first place. He seemed to be driving himself into a desperate kind of excitement, reaching for a moment of aliveness with her, and was willing to clown before her if he could achieve this end. He was so carried away by his performance that he forgot about the limitations for having fun that pregnancy imposed on a woman. For a moment he was irritated by Ann's refusal of his invitation. It was a little thing, but embodied in it was his memory of other occasions when she had not risen to his excitements, and had withdrawn, become defensive, too aware of risks, and not daring.

He suppressed his irritation. The band on the wireless had swung into 'April Showers', and the crooner was giving it his sleepy best again.

'Bridie there'll dance with you,' Ann said all of a sudden, as if she had suddenly discovered a way out of her own predicament.

Michael Joe swung over to Bridie. He seemed drunk though he had not touched a drop of the wine.

'Come on my girl, we're going to the Palladium,' Michael Joe said taking hold of her hand.

'No, no, I can't dance,' Bridie said pulling her hand away, and looking across at Ann.

'Oh, go on,' Ann said. 'He won't take a bite out of you.'

Michael Joe took hold of her again, and almost pulled her out of the chair. He put an arm firmly around her waist and swung her into the fox-trot.

The room was small, and once or twice they bumped against the side table and the chairs. After the first few turns, Bridie lost her awkwardness, the awkwardness of the maid dancing with the master, and she danced well with him. Michael Joe was awkward at first, too. It had been a long time since he had danced. As his body fell into time with the music and with the girl, he began to feel elated, and his powerful, thick-set body demanded energetic movement, more energetic and faster than the watered-down, civilized fox-trot. He began to swing Bridie crazily, increasing his grip on her. She had danced away from him, and the whole instinct of his body was to draw her near. She resisted. He whirled. Suddenly, he tripped over the leg of a chair, and both of them went sprawling against the table, Michael Joe falling forward on top of the girl.

She screamed laughing, and wiggled quickly out from under him, and then ran out of the dining room, and upstairs to her room in the attic. Michael Joe straightened up guiltily, and began to pull down his waistcoat and straighten out his tie.

'Ah, the poor girl,' Ann said. 'You frightened her.'

'... It isn't raining rain you know ... it's raining violets ...'

Michael Joe walked over to the wireless and shut it off. He was suddenly disgusted with the music.

'Ah, they don't have any decent songs any more,' he said to Ann.

He was trembling, and tried to hide it. He poured himself a glass of wine and drank it down as if it were water.

'I like them,' Ann said. 'They have nice words to them. And they're nice to dance to when you have the room.' She had taken up her knitting again, and was clicking away.

Michael Joe stretched himself fully in front of her, raising his hands over his head, and stretching his fingers out until they seemed like claws almost touching the ceiling over his head. He rose up and down three or four times on his toes, and then shook himself.

'I think I'll go for a short walk.'

Ann looked at him quickly, but then went on with her knitting. He took his cap from the back of the door, jammed it on his dark head, and left quickly.

He had started the evening and the celebration in all innocence, with the best intentions of livening up Ann's evening, and with some vague intention of making up to her for his own neglect. He had stumbled once more into the riot of his dark places, and into the old chaos of the blood. He had not sought the temptation, he told himself. The girl, Bridie, had come, and suddenly, when she was in his arms, he was caught. In his own home. He had read somewhere, once, that the call of the home will always triumph over the call of lust. Was it true? Home! What was home to him? What was there in the home that could help him triumph? Temptation was now in the bedroom in the attic over his own room.

He walked down the half-lit streets of Corrigbeg. The bland, shadowy forms of the houses on either side stood like dark sentinels watching him pass. Above him on the hill, the vague outlines of the chapel spread against the cloudy sky. Wild clouds blew over the face of the half moon.

In five minutes, he was out in the country, into the fields. They began almost at the doorstep of the town, and beyond them, the incessant roaring of the sea. The homes, the fields, the sea. Where did he belong? He knew, now, that it was not in the home. He had married Ann. What did that mean? It had to mean something to him. Back there in Corrigbeg was the house his father had passed on, and his father's father had passed on to him. How far back the McCarthys had owned, and lived, and were born in the house, he did not know. That house must mean something. It was not a house of darkness. Was he the dark one? Had it come to this? Would he make it a house of darkness?

So he questioned himself. All the time, his feet were carrying him out to his own land, where he kept the cattle. He crossed the sod wall into the field, and walked through it. The cattle were lying down at the far end, all together, huddled, chewing the cud, content together in the darkness. And here was the man, out walking at night, alone. They let him walk up and rub them in the dark.

35

ANN WENT INTO labour one morning in late May. A few hours before, she had lain in bed listening to Michael Joe fumbling around in the dark putting on his clothes, and then she heard him tiptoe out of the room. He was off to a fair somewhere. She did not know. She never asked him where he was going, and he never volunteered the information. After he left, she lay quietly in bed, praying to herself on the beads which she had hanging constantly around her neck now. In all her idle moments, she fingered them, praying to the Blessed Virgin to bring her safely through. She trusted deeply in the power of her prayer. And she had been going to Mass and receiving Holy Communion every morning. She knew the old superstition of the power the Eucharist had on a pregnant woman, and the blessings it brought to the as yet unborn child.

She screamed at the first onset of her contractions, though they were not strong. Old Mrs. McCarthy came in after the third or fourth scream. She knew immediately what was up. She went to the foot of the stairs leading up to the attic, and called to Bridie to get up, they had to take Ann to the Nursing Home. Bridie had not heard the scream. She was dreaming of a dark lover whirling her around a dance hall with a spotlight on them. They were winning some kind of prize.

She awoke to the noise, and quickly threw on a dress, and came down and into Ann's room. Mrs. McCarthy was sitting by the side of the bed. Ann had gripped the wrought-iron railing behind her head, and her small face was twisted in pain and fear. Her body jerked spasmodically under the clothes, and rose with the pain.

Mrs. McCarthy sent Bridie for a hackney to drive them down. Bridie ran out of the room fast, glad to be out of it.

Ann moaned and screamed all the way down to the Nursing Home in the car, though the journey only took a few minutes. Mrs. McCarthy sat at one side of her in the back seat, and Bridie at the other, each of them holding one of Ann's hands. Mrs. McCarthy lent her whatever strength she had, and tried to soothe her: 'There, now, a leanna, 'twill be all over soon ... all over soon.' Bridie sat terrified, holding Ann's hand hard.

Mrs. McCarthy sent her home after they got Ann into the Nursing Home, and told her to take care of the house, and tell Michael Joe when he got back.

Bridie had the house to herself all day. When she got used to the idea she went into every room and poked into all the cupboards and drawers examining the most private possessions of the family. She tried on some of Ann's dresses and flirted with herself in the mirror in the room. She took a hot bath and luxuriated in it, walking naked around upstairs afterward and not minding the chill.

In the afternoon, a messenger came up from the Nursing Home to tell her to pack some of Mrs. McCarthy's things, that she was going to stay overnight. They did not know down there how long it would take Ann to have the baby. She was having a hard time. This message made Bridie afraid. The last thing she'd heard leaving the Nursing Home was Ann's screams, and Ann crying for her mother. But when the messenger left, she helped herself to a glass of the port wine, and she felt better, almost like the lady of the house which she imagined she was. When Vin Scanlon came in from the shop for a bite to eat, she was on her uppities with him, and wouldn't let him touch her. She threatened to call the guards. He hadn't found her so unapproachable before, and couldn't understand the sudden change. She cleared him out of the house as soon as he had finished eating. She had work to do, she said. But she only wanted the house to herself.

News that Ann had gone to the Nursing Home had spread throughout the town. The old women who were her friends began to come to the door to inquire if there was any word yet. Bridie treated them haughtily. There was no word. She'd let them know when there was.

That night she stayed up late in the house by herself, listening to the wireless. She had another glass of port, and then put some water in the bottle so that the two glasses she had wouldn't be missed. She danced by herself to the music on the wireless. And dreamed. Since there was no one in the house, she decided to sleep in Michael Joe's and Ann's bed that night, and get up early in the morning before Michael Joe came home. Her own bed up in the attic was little more than a cot.

She awoke in the morning to the sound of heavy boots on the stairs. In a panic, she jumped out of bed, naked, afraid that Michael Joe would find her in his room and give her the sack. She liked her job. Ann was kind and never overworked her. Never bossed her. She just had time to get her dress up in front of her, before the door opened and Michael Joe came in, looking tired and weary. He stared at her for a few minutes, and she simply stared back biting her lower lip. Her face, flesh, and hair looked soft and warm in the morning light. Michael Joe was gloomy and sullen, and did not take in the situation immediately. He blinked at Bridie.

'Where's Ann?'

'Down . . . down at the Nursing Home.'

'And my mother?'

'She's with her.'

Michael Joe was silent for a few minutes, still looking at her. Then he lumbered across the room, and tore the dress out of her hands.

'Don't hit me,' she pleaded. 'I meant no harm. 'Twas no harm to sleep in your bed. No one else was here.'

He laughed, showing the space between his teeth. Then he advanced towards her, and she backed, crouching against the wall, putting up her two hands to protect herself. He forced her hands away and drove his full weight against her backing her to the wall. She whimpered. And then he was pressing his lips hard and biting down on hers. She whimpered now in a different way. And bit him back.

'Hahhhhhh,' Michael Joe said. The hands that had all day yesterday poked and felt the cows, now curved around Bridie's firm breasts. She made no attempt to stop him. As he stroked, she leaped, winding her legs around him. Then Michael Joe backed to the bed, carrying her.

And they began their bout of love. Michael Joe did not take off his clothes. He fumbled and cursed a bit. Bridie whimpered. He kissed her. Then, quickly, it was all over, he burying his teeth in her neck, and she crying out not to be hurt.

He lay beside her breathing heavily for a while until his passion had subsided. Then he dragged himself out of bed, and, turning away from her naked in the bed, straightened himself out.

'Come on. Get out. We'll have to get down and see her.'

Bridie slid out of bed trying to cover herself with her hands.

'I don't want to.'

'I said you'll have to.'

The two of them walked down the pavement together, Bridie on the inside of Michael Joe. Several people stopped to ask Michael Joe how Ann was. He mumbled something. They whispered words of sympathy and encouragement to him. It would be over soon . . . Bridie looked at the shop windows while they were speaking.

Nurse Nagel opened the front door of the Nursing Home for them and led them down the long dark hallway, and into the kitchen. The air was sharp with the mingled odours of ether and disinfectant. Piercing screams and cries from a woman undergoing labour came down from upstairs.

They entered the kitchen. Bridie took in everything at once, the row of nappies stretched on a line across the kitchen, the big pots of boiling water on the range, a row of medicines and syringes on a side-table. Nurse Nagel waved them to sit down. The kitchen was hot. Neither of them did. She shut the door.

'Keep the noise out.'

Bridie moved back toward the door as if instinctively drawn towards it for a quick getaway, or to hear the screaming from upstairs.

'How's Ann?' Michael Joe said dully.

'Ah, the poor girl. A hard time . . . a hard time,' Nurse Nagel clucked. She was a large, full-bosomed, fleshy woman.

'She isn't . . . bad, is she?'

'Nothing worse than thousands of women every day all over the world. She's in good hands though. Don't worry, now.'

'How long . . . ?'

'Ah, a little over twenty-four hours now . . . there's nothing can be done. 'Twill be over soon, though. She's nearing her time.'

Michael Joe looked around the kitchen, but nothing in it seemed to focus his attention.

'Maybe she ought to go to the hospital. I want no expense spared. She'll have to have the best.'

Nurse Nagel gave him a withering look. 'This isn't the first case of its kind I've handled. Doctor Healy is here. The best thing for you is to go up home, and I'll send up for you when the time comes. Your mother is with her. She'll be all right.'

The clapping of a bell sounded urgently, and a faint scream came through the shut door.

Nurse Nagel moved quickly. 'Take my advice and go up home.' She hurried out of the kitchen.

Michael Joe looked at Bridie. Her face had paled, and was set in a mask-like stillness. Her lips were dry, and the mouth shut tightly.

'Come on,' he said touching her on the shoulder. 'This is no place for you.'

When they got home, Bridie threw herself into an armchair without even taking off her coat. Michael Joe touched her face.

'You're cold,' he said. 'Will you have a drop of port wine?'

She shrugged.

'Aren't you going to talk to me at all? Are you blaming me for everything? For that down there too!' He pointed through the walls in the direction of the Nursing Home.

'Go 'way,' she said. 'I don't want to see you. She's in terrible pain.'

'All right, I will. I'll go away.' He made for the door.

'Don't,' she said. 'Stop!'

'Go out! Stop in! Great God, what do you want me to do? What difference does it make, anyway, where I go? We have to wait'.

Then he found himself on his knees before her. 'Jesus Christ, don't be like this,' he said. 'Don't hate me. That makes everything worse. I couldn't help it.'

'I don't hate you,' Bridie said. 'I'm not thinking of you, at all.'

'Jesus,' he went on, 'Ann is down there in bloody agony, and she might as well be in Timbuktu, as far as I'm concerned. Isn't that a terrible thing to admit?'

' 'Tis. We're lick alike. We did a terrible thing. If I have ... a ... baby.'

He took her hands in his. They were cold. He began to rub them between his own.

'I think you're a grand girl. Isn't that a terrible thing to be saying too? If you have a baby, I'll bring it up. I'll pay for it. I won't let you down.' His hands sought her thighs.

She got up, and ran out of the room. 'I'm a bastard!' he shouted after her. 'But I won't let you down.' He heard her running upstairs, and almost went after her. The sound of footsteps coming in the hall stopped him. He straightened out. A woman came asking for Ann. He told her the child wasn't born yet, and shut the door in her face. Then, after sitting down a few minutes to collect himself, he went out to the shop.

36

FRANCIS MICHAEL McCARTHY was born around midday of that bright, blustery May day. A May child. His mother was profoundly moved that he was a May child. The month of the Blessed Virgin. Her rosaries had borne fruit.

It was said in Corrigbeg that Michael Joe McCarthy drank

steadily for three days, and visited his wife and child only when he was drunk. No one in the town condemned him for this. It was a matter of amusement. After all, the first child, and a son at that.

At the same time, another piece of gossip was whispered around. The McCarthys' girl, Bridie Devine from the Cottages, had run off and left them in the lurch at such a terrible time. Wasn't she the out-and-out slut. No gratitude.

But old Mrs. McCarthy rose to the occasion. She took charge of everything. Wasn't she the remarkable woman? No one could believe that a woman her age had so much energy left. She was up and down between the Nursing Home and the house every day, and spent all the time she could with Ann helping her take care of the baby. Ann's mother came in for a few days, too, but she had to go back out to the farm again for the cutting of the turf.

Mrs. McCarthy and Ann together decided on the name. Ann wanted Francis after St. Francis of Assisi, because he loved animals, and they followed him around everywhere, and he could tame them. In the dim recesses of her mind, he had always been a bright image. If she had had a girl it would have been named Mary. But the boy was Francis. Mrs. McCarthy suggested Michael as the second name, for Michael Joe. Ann thought that was lovely too.

Ann had a visitor early one night. Nurse Nagel opened the Nursing Home door, and there was Bridie Devine standing there looking defiant but frightened. ' 'Tis you,' Nurse Nagel said looking down her nose at her. She had heard that Bridie had left suddenly without giving any notice. What a slut!

'I want to see Ann ... Mrs. McCarthy,' Bridie said.

'And what business have you with her?'

Bridie did not answer.

'Well, come on, then.'

Nurse Nagel led her upstairs. It was nearly seven o'clock in the evening and Ann had just finished feeding the baby, and it was back in its crib, crying. A small light was burning in the room. It was in gloom and shadows, and smelled of medicines and disinfectants. Nurse Nagel turned on the full light, and Ann tried to pull herself up in bed. Nurse Nagel rushed towards her, and made her lie back, propping her up with pillows. Then the nurse took up the crying baby, and brought it downstairs. Ann watched her go with a pained, worried expression on her pale, hollowed face.

Bridie had barely advanced beyond the door. She was gripping her hands in the shape of a doubled fist, in front of her. Her eyes moved restlessly around the room like a trapped animal.

'Oh, is that you, Bridie?' Ann said wearily. Mrs. McCarthy had told her that Bridie had left the house.

Bridie stood where she was. 'I'm going to England,' she said.

'He always cries after he's fed,' Ann said.

Bridie suddenly let her eyes rest on Ann. 'Was it terrible?' she whispered.

Ann closed her eyes and rested. For a moment, she looked like a corpse laid out on the bed. Then she opened her eyes again.

'We all go through it sometime,' she said. 'Welcome be the will of the Almighty.' She raised her eyes. 'Thanks be to God and his Blessed Mother for bringing me through my trial.'

Bridie came forward slowly toward the foot of the bed as if drawn toward it by a magnet, keeping her eyes focused on Ann.

'Where . . . how . . . how did it come?'

Ann turned her head away in the pillow and gazed at the wallpapered wall. Ann could not really have answered Bridie's question in any detail. She had been put to sleep for the birth. When she woke up, she was presented with a clean baby wrapped in a white blanket. She had only the vaguest idea of what had happened.

'You'll find out for yourself some day,' she said to Bridie in a hollow voice.

Bridie was terrified. 'Oh, my God, I'm sorry,' she said, gripping the wrought-iron bars of the bed.

'You have no cause to be sorry.'

'I have . . . I have.' Somewhere in Bridie's mind there was a distinct connection between Ann's pains in childbirth and her adultery with Michael Joe. 'I'm going away,' she went on. 'And I'll never come back. To England. I'll go to America. That's far away. And I'll never trouble you again.'

Ann did not know what she was talking about, or what she was trying to say. She was tired and wanted to sleep, or if Nurse Nagel would come back with the baby, she would stay awake. She loved to look at the cradle and him in it.

'You were no trouble, Bridie. You were always a great help.'

'You don't know . . . you don't know . . . will you listen?' Bridie said. 'You'll have to forgive me before I go. You'll have to forgive me.'

'Forgive you?' Ann was now looking at her. Bridie was leaning forward over the foot of the bed toward her.

'Michael Joe and myself. We did something wrong. We did something wrong. I'm sorry.'

The truth penetrated to Ann and she felt herself grown suddenly numb, like a block of ice. She had no very vivid image of what Bridie was trying to tell her. Vaguely, she realized that Michael Joe had done some horrible thing with this girl. She was not shocked because she had no real sense of the actuality of what had happened. Nothing really had happened as far as she could truly realize. Bridie had said . . . something wrong . . . something wrong . . . herself and Michael Joe. It was to the words rather than any real sense of the actuality behind them that Ann responded. She withdrew. Closed herself up, and did not hear any more as the girl went on pleading and muttering incoherently at the foot of the bed something about forgiveness . . . forgive me . . . forgive me . . .

Nurse Nagel came back in with the child asleep. Ann, with a burst of energy, pulled herself up in the pillows.

'Give him to me,' she said, ignoring Bridie at the foot of the bed.

Nurse Nagel turned to Bridie. 'You'll have to go now. Talking too long only upsets her.'

Bridie left the room. She had grown calm, almost truculent when Ann did not respond to her plea. She threw a look at the two women as she left, as much as to say: 'Damn ye all, anyway. Ye can lick my arse.' She swaggered out of the room.

'That's a bould one if I ever saw one,' Nurse Nagel said.

Ann stretched out her thin arms to hold the sleeping baby. Nurse Nagel placed him in them, carefully. Ann pressed the blanket to her thin body.

Later on, Michael Joe came in with the smell of drink on him. Nurse Nagel also let him in.

'That slut ye had working for ye was in here a while ago,' she said.

'Bridie? Bridie visited Ann?'

'I should never have let her up. Her kind should be kept in their place.'

Michael Joe knew instantly what had happened. If he had had an excuse, he would not have gone up to see Ann. But here was this eagle-eyed mountain of flesh watching him.

'Ah, sure, she means well,' Michael Joe said. He went on up the stairs to see his wife.

The room was in semi-darkness with the small light burning at a corner table. Michael Joe stood at the door, hesitant. There was no stir in the bed which he could see in the gloom.

'Anyone awake?' he whispered, and almost laughed at the sound of his own voice. It was as if he found his doom upon him, and thought it ridiculous.

'Go home,' Ann's voice answered.

He had taken off his cap and was holding it in his hand. He put it on. It seemed like a gesture of defiance. He did not jam it on his head. Let it rest on the black waves, half cockily. He searched around in his mind for something to say. Could think of nothing. And left without seeing Nurse Nagel.

He went up to Blake's and began drinking, celebrating the birth of his son.

37

ANN REMAINED IN the Nursing Home an extra week. She had a relapse. Mainly nerves, Doctor Healy told Michael Joe when he inquired. He did not go down to visit Ann any more after that night. His mother was all the time down there. Ann's mother came in again. And her father visited once. Michael Joe's absence wouldn't be noticed. It wasn't expected of a man, anyway, that he should be up and down to the Nursing Home where his wife was lying in. So he had no fear that his not visiting Ann would look odd. But he did catch Doctor Healy in the street one day, and asked him when Ann would be coming home. Then the doctor explained hastily to him about the nerves. Michael Joe simply nodded, as if it was all a matter of the mysteries of a woman's physical condition after she had given birth.

When Ann finally did come home, she and old Mrs. McCarthy put the baby's cradle in Ann and Michael Joe's bedroom, and turned the bedroom into a nursery. Old Mrs. McCarthy took complete charge of that operation while Ann sat in a wicker chair by the fire in the bedroom with the wrapped baby in her lap.

The dressing table was covered with a linoleum cloth and Ann's medicines were arranged on it, with all the baby's powders, vaselines, and cloths. The drawers of the dresser were emptied, all Michael Joe's things were packed into one, and the rest were used for the baby's nappies and clothes. A white enamel bucket for the nappies was placed behind the door. Old Mrs. McCarthy and Ann gave the child its first bath at home, together, though Mrs. McCarthy handled the baby, while Ann watched and handed her towels.

Michael Joe slept three nights in the bedroom. After that he couldn't stand it any longer. There wasn't a night but the baby cried for hours with colic, and Ann and Mrs. McCarthy walked the floor with it while Michael Joe tried to sleep. At six o'clock every morning, Mrs. McCarthy marched right into the room, and the day began with herself and Ann giving the baby a bath. There was a constant smell in the room that Michael Joe couldn't stand though he did not mind the smell of a street on a Fair Day, or did not notice that he himself often smelled of cattle, now that he began to be around them so much.

In the end, he moved upstairs to the attic, which Bridie had vacated. There, his night's sleep was not interrupted, and he could stay in bed until a decent hour in the morning.

Most of his contact with Ann, then, was through his mother. She never came downstairs. Took all her meals upstairs, served by Mrs. McCarthy. Michael Joe ate alone. He would ask his mother how Ann was, and she would answer in just as perfunctory a manner as Michael Joe had asked. He wondered if Ann had told her about Bridie. He never found out. He was being closed off from them. Once, he made an attempt to talk to Ann, sticking his head in the bedroom door to ask how she was. She answered in a dull, toneless voice that she was getting along all right. There was no invitation to talk in her voice. He withdrew.

For a while, Michael Joe was just as well pleased that she remained up in her room, and did not want to see him. He hoped that she might come to her senses soon, and see that the end of the world hadn't arrived, and their life might return to normal again. He thought she might get over the shock in time. Why wouldn't she? Ah, she'd forgive him as time went on. She couldn't hold out forever. He thought he knew her well enough. She wasn't the kind of woman to harbour a grudge against him for long. She was too religious. He hoped that her religious emotions would finally sway her into forgiving him.

At the end of Ann's first month at home, no break seemed to be forthcoming. She continued to live in the bedroom with the baby. Michael Joe was further irritated by all the bills he had to pay. The doctor had to be paid, the Nursing Home and Nurse Nagel. But that was nothing to what came after. The baby had to have this, that, and the other thing. A new pram had cost him twenty pounds. Ann also had to have special things. A day did not pass but his mother came out to the shop to him for money to buy some medicine at the Medical Hall that Ann had to have. She never told him what the medicine was for. Only that Ann needed it. After a while, Michael Joe was beginning to think that Ann must be running a hospital upstairs with all the medicine she bought at the Medical Hall. Day by day, the old women of the town trooped in and went upstairs to visit Ann. His house was becoming a home for the aged.

One day, his mother bustled into the shop as usual and asked for money. He was waiting on a customer, and paid no attention to her until he was finished, and the customer had left. Then he turned to her.

'What is it this time?'

'Ann needs a little something from the Medical Hall.'

'What's wrong with her at all?'

'Never mind what's wrong. She needs the medicine.'

'I'm shelling out of my pocket for it. I'm entitled to some explanation. Ye'er doing nothing but making mysteries up there, the both of ye.'

'You'll have to deny yourself now. You have a wife and child. They have to be sacrificed for. You'll have to deny yourself.' His mother spoke with some sense of triumph, as if this was a lesson that she herself had not taught him, but that life itself was finally bringing the bitter lesson home to him.

'Look here,' he said. 'I'm fed up with all this nonsense. And damn mollycoddling.' He strode past her, and out of the shop, into the house.

Ann was sitting in the wicker chair by the fire in her room, breast feeding the baby. When Michael Joe burst in on her without knocking, he stopped at the sight. The baby's pink face was pressed against the small white breast which Ann was holding to him. The little jaws were working fast. Ann was gazing down at the baby. She half-rose, startled, out of her chair, when she saw Michael Joe. She took her hand away from her breast, and the nipple fell out of the baby's mouth. He began to search the air, seeking the nipple.

Ann drew her blouse over her breasts.

'Look,' Michael Joe said, 'you're hiding away long enough. You have nothing to be ashamed of.'

Ann tried to say something. The baby began to cry. Then Mrs. McCarthy came in.

'Get out of here,' she told her son. 'You have no business here.'

Michael Joe turned to his mother. 'I'll be master in my own house,' he said. 'And be damned to ye women.'

Ann had begun to croon over the crying baby. Michael Joe stopped at the sound of her voice. It had a strange note. Something he had heard somewhere before. Half whimper, half croon. But he went on.

'You'll be down at the dinner table tonight. And bring *him*, too, before he suffocates in this room. And get all this stuff out of here. There's plenty of room in the house. That's my final word.'

He pounded out of the room.

They all ate dinner together that night, in a strained atmosphere, where the two women got out of having to talk to Michael Joe by paying all their attention to the baby.

Ever since Francis Michael was born, Ann, his mother, felt that she was suffering from some incurable disease. The relapse of weakness which she had suffered after his birth and which had kept her in the Nursing Home longer than normal, began to worry her when she got home. Doctor Healy had not told her what was wrong with her, beyond a bout of nerves. She had not asked him. She sensed he was being evasive, and was reluctant to give her disease a name, or give any details. He prescribed pills he said were iron supplements to her diet. She had noticed her hair was falling out. It had never been heavy or luxuriant. The iron pills were for the hair. Then he prescribed a red liquid to relax her, to be taken before she fed the baby. Before he let her go home, he pronounced her in good health, and progressing normally after her heroic struggle.

She did not believe him. He was keeping back something. She could tell by the way he whispered about her to Nurse Nagel outside the room door where she was lying in. But she didn't dare ask him any details.

She had put Bridie's visit out of her mind after Bridie left her, and was not even thinking about her at all during Michael Joe's visit. All she had been conscious of then was Michael Joe himself, his huge, dark hulk, and the odour of cow-dung that her keen nose had been picking up about him for a long time, but was even more sharp now, here in the Nursing Home, rising above its smell, which she liked. She had not really seen him because of the semi-darkness of the room. And that had made his presence more terrifying to her. When he spoke that one time, she felt her whole body drawing in on itself, drawing in around her stomach. When he left without a word, she felt herself relax in proportion to the receding of his footsteps lumbering down the stairs.

She relied on old Mrs. McCarthy for physical and moral support. Ann was terrified to handle Francis Michael herself. But old Mrs. McCarthy was efficient and sure-handed. Ann let her do practically everything but nurse the baby. Mrs. McCarthy would sit beside Ann while she nursed, never really watching, often praying her rosary, and always ready to take the baby when he needed to be patted during the feeding. Ann did not mind her dependence on her. She did not know what she would have done without her.

Ann did not tell Mrs. McCarthy the suspicions she had that she was suffering from an incurable disease. That much she kept to herself. But old Mrs. McCarthy must have suspected something. She kept track of all the medicines Ann had to take, and made her take them at the right times. An unspoken bond grew between the young and the old Mrs. McCarthy over the medicines. The taking of the medicines brought back the memory of sufferings over and done with, but never to be forgotten. Ann had undergone the great trial of womanhood. It was understood that because she had a 'hard time' she had suffered more than most women. Mrs. McCarthy's fussing over the medicines, and her almost fanatic devotion to the baby, was partly an acknowledgment of this fact. Both women knew it. Ann was acknowledged as the suffering mother, and she, in her turn, acknowledged her need of old Mrs. McCarthy, who had been through it all before.

After she had come downstairs, and life began to resume somewhat of its normal routine again, she began to worry more distinctly about what kind of disease it was that she had. She had time on her hands to worry. Michael Joe came in only for his meals; he was out every night, and she was asleep when he came home. He never disturbed her. Old Mrs. McCarthy did most of the work around the house. They had a woman come in twice a week to do the washing.

She began to read. First the serial love stories in the *Irish Independent*, and then romantic novels in English she found in the cupboards of the house, and then religious books—lives of saints and martyrs, accounts of miracles, and so on. As she read, Francis Michael was beside her, rocked to sleep in his pram.

One day she read an advertisement in the *Independent* about a two-volume set of books called *Medical Information for the Home*. She sent away for the set surreptitiously, and watched the postman every day for fear he would bring the parcel into the shop to Michael Joe.

When she got the set, she spent the long evenings poring over its pages, not even neglecting the copious and elaborate illustrations of the human anatomy, male and female. She kept the books hidden in the bottom drawer in her bedroom, not even letting Mrs. McCarthy see them. The naked and detached manner in which the human body was treated, thrilled her secretly, though she thought the illustrations profane, if not dirty. She read in this two-volume set every night, when old Mrs. McCarthy had gone up to her nightly visit in the chapel. She absorbed the details and remembered in detail what she read, though she never communicated her new knowledge to anyone. Her daydreams were often centred around her medical reading, and disease became a mystique.

She decided that she had a weak heart as a result of the labour in childbirth. That remained her essential ailment for a long time, kept quietly and secretly to herself. She lived with her flutterings and catchings of breath and did not tell a sinner's soul. As her reading and rereading progressed, she began to develop symptoms of whatever particular disease fascinated her, developing a variety of post-pregnancy ailments from sore nipples to painful menstruation.

Doctor Healy had to be called in often to visit her. She enjoyed the visits. He always prescribed some medicine. Since she herself knew what was wrong with her, she always checked in the book to see if Doctor Healy had prescribed the right medicine. When he did not follow the book, she distrusted him, but could not change the prescription because it was written in Latin.

Every month, Michael Joe had to pay a fair-sized medical bill, along with bills for special things for the baby. Now he paid without a murmur. Ann had at least come downstairs, and was seen out again. Appearances had to be kept up. That was all he wanted now. It was a small mercy, and he was thankful for it. Matters could have developed worse. Ann could have talked about himself and Bridie. But of course she couldn't. That had to remain within the four walls of the house. If the gossips of Corrigbeg got a hold of that, he would be a marked man from then on, and the house would always be spoken of in whispers, and would cast its shadow on the Main Street, a haunted house. And Michael Joe did not want that. He still had some pride left. So he paid the medical bills without questioning.

As early as three months, Ann began taking Francis Michael to chapel with her. She sat in the pew with him in her arms, having wrapped him well in blankets. The little fellow usually slept. She thought this almost a miracle, a good sign already, that he behaved so well in the chapel and didn't disturb Canon Lyons praying, or the people. She was able to pray herself. It gave her a peculiar mystical joy to be murmuring her prayers over the sleeping form of her infant son. Old Mrs. McCarthy would also be murmuring beside her—the voices of the two women praying for the child.

When Ann had been churched—the purification after the birth— she had prayed before the altar of Our Lady, next to the main altar, and had dedicated Francis Michael to her eternal service.

The only time she went abroad in the town was to chapel, carrying the bundled-up baby.

Her life became centred around her medical reading, the child, and her religious devotions. She read the medical book several times over. Gradually, her knowledge began to creep into her conversation with the old gossips who came to visit Mrs. McCarthy. They became her friends; their conversation became her conversation. The old women usually had piseóg cures, traditional cures handed down from generation to generation of women by word of mouth. Cures with herbs from the fields as their basis, and spices: ginger to make you sweat; black pepper for the shivers; unsalted butter for burns; black tea for almost anything. Ann began to value these biddy early cures almost as much as the ones she found in her book. At eleven months, little Francis Michael caught his first cold. The old women suggested a red flannel blanket with a sprinkle of vinegar. Old Mrs. McCarthy said the cure was infallible. Ann tried it. And it cured the child of his first cold. And that was what Ann always used to cure him of his colds while he was growing up, making new red flannel petticoats to fit his growing size.

The only time Michael Joe ever really saw his son was when he came home early from a fair, drunk. He would insist that Ann bring the child down. The first time he had asked, Ann put up an argument. Michael Joe looked very excited, was humming little snatches of song to himself, and even acknowledged herself and his mother with a few comical remarks. 'Holy Marys' he called them. And he hoped they always said an odd prayer for himself. Michael Joe managed to make the last Mass every Sunday, but had not been to Confession and Holy Communion for a long time.

'Bring the lad down so his father can have a dekko at him,' Michael Joe said. 'Sure he must be suffocated up there. And the two skirts here,' he nodded at Ann and his mother, 'don't give him much fresh air either.'

'Oh, Michael Joe, the poor craythur is asleep. I can't wake him.'

'He'll have to get used to waking out of his sleep if he's to get on in this world,' Michael Joe said. 'G'wan up and bring him down.'

Ann did not want to cross him. He was in a rare humour, and for a moment life seemed good again.

She went upstairs and brought down the baby bundled up. She handed the bundle to Michael Joe.

'Yerra, off with the wraps there so we can see what he's made of.'

Michael Joe threw off the blanket. Ann nervously picked it up.

'Be careful, Michael Joe. He's only a baby.'

Michael Joe caught the baby around the waist with his big fat hands, and raised him over his head.

The baby was healthy looking, round-cheeked, dark-eyed, but pale. He had a broad forehead like Michael Joe's but the mouth was small and sensitive looking, like the mother's. The baby frowned at the suddenness of being hoisted in the air; then his natural vitality took over, and the baby laughed.

'Hah!' Michael Joe laughed up at him. 'You're a brave lad, here.' He raised him up and down a few more times, taking real pleasure in the gurgling laughter of his son. Then he threw him a bit higher, and caught him. Ann almost fainted.

'Give him to me! Give him to me!' she said fiercely, reaching for the child. Michael Joe held on to him. When the baby saw his mother reaching for him, and heard the tone of her voice, he began to bawl.

'There, now. You see what you've done.' Ann said.

Michael Joe tried to get the baby to stop crying, crooning and making faces at it. The baby only cried harder. Ann tore the baby from him. For an instant, Michael Joe looked bemused. Then he got angry.

'Ah, ye've spoiled him already. Blast it all.' He stamped a foot. Ann took the baby upstairs.

Michael Joe glanced across at his mother. 'What can be expected? Two of ye mollycoddling him morning, noon and night.'

'I won't make the same mistake twice,' she said.

'Ah, God, I don't know what to do with ye,' he said. Then he went out to the shop.

That was one of the few attempts Michael Joe made to have contact with his son. The two women took pains that the child would not be around when he was in the home, so that the child would not be upset. Michael Joe showed no real interest in seeing him after this incident.

At a little over two years old, Ann had taught Francis Michael to make the sign of the Cross, and to utter a child's version of the Hail Mary. She would make him perform for the old women who came in to visit. She would crouch behind him, hold him by the hands and encourage him, the dark curly-haired boy with the lineaments of his father plainly reproduced in him, to recite the Hail Mary: 'Haymary . . . fugrace . . . lois with thee . . . blessthoumong womn . . . bless foot thy woojesus . . . holy Mary, mothr god, prayforus sin . . . now, hourofdeath . . . amin.' Then the little boy would quickly make the sign of the Cross.

The old women applauded, and praised him to the skies. They'd never seen the like. A two-year-old able to say the Hail Mary. God only knows what he'd be doing next. Ann tried not to smile too much.

Many of them wanted to kiss him, as they might kiss a holy or a sacred object, in the hope that the sanctity would rub off on themselves, and bring them good luck. Secretly, they thought he had the makings of a saint. They would get in on the ground floor. Ann practically cried with pride after they left. She hugged him to her. And soon, she was teaching him the 'Our Father', driven to make him perform more difficult tasks by the praise, and by the fame she knew her little son was acquiring in Corrigbeg through the gossip of the women.

At three years, he could follow her on the rosary, at which she and old Mrs. McCarthy would coach him before he went to bed at night. Old Mrs. McCarthy told him stories of the little baby Jesus, how much he loved his mother and how good he was to her.

At four, Ann used to get Francis to run her messages to the Medical Hall. She'd send him out for a bottle of this or a bottle of that, making him repeat over and over again the names of the medicines because they were strange and difficult for a little boy to pronounce. Sometimes, he would not be able to pronounce the name of the medicine right, and he would burst into tears. Then she would write it out for him in a little note, and wrap the money in the note. Francis Michael grew to love the ritual of the messages to the Medical Hall. Some of the bottles were pretty, and caught hold of his fancy, and he began to save them—the blue milk of magnesia bottle, and a golden-brown one for some kind of pills, and one with a dropper were especially attractive to him. He kept his cache hidden in a far corner of the backyard, away from where anyone would find it. Ann knew he was collecting the bottles. It gave her a strange thrill of pride.

At five, whenever anyone asked little Francis what he would like to be when he grew up, he would bury his head in his mother's skirts, clasp her around the thighs, and refuse to answer. Ann would pry his arms loose from around her, laughing nervously and saying that it was only the shyness that had come over him of a sudden. She would coax little Francis, telling him to be a brave boy and stand up straight and turn around and answer. She would wheel him slowly around to face his audience. Shyly he would lift his head, and in a half whisper say, 'A priest.' The women listening would be delighted. The child was only confirming his early promise. What else could you expect from a child that could say the 'Hail Mary' at two, and the 'Our Father' at three, but that he would want to be a priest? They fondled him while his mother held him to her. Then, when the praises had been exhausted, and her little boy already elevated nearly to the rank of sainthood, Ann would tell him to run out and play. He paused once outside the dining room door to hear what his mother and the women were talking about. He heard her say: 'Oh, it must be the damp weather we're having that brought on my sciatica again. I didn't sleep a wink last night with the pain in my side. I think I'll make a novena for it.'

The boy ran outside, and as he played he kept wondering what was wrong with his mammy. He usually played by himself in the backyard. His mother considered him still too young to be playing on the streets of Corrigbeg with the roughies of the town.

38

OLD MRS. MCCARTHY died when Francis was seven, the week before he was to receive his First Holy Communion. Indirectly, it was this that caused her death. She and Ann spent hours every day teaching Francis his catechism. The moment he came in the door from school, old Mrs. McCarthy would hurry downstairs, and she and Ann would sit in the dining room with Francis between them, asking him questions out of the catechism. If he failed to answer, he was set down at the dining room table to get by heart the answer he had failed to give. His mother and grandmother were kind, but insistent. He would be the best boy going up for his First Communion, would know the catechism backwards. On that they were determined. The boy was obedient, tried his hardest to please his mother and grandmother by learning the catechism. He learned most of it word for word under this constant tutoring, and was in the running for the catechism prize at the school, which would be awarded by Canon Lyons. The two women were driving the boy a little harder in preparation for the examination. The moment old

Mrs. McCarthy heard his footsteps in the hall coming in from school, she came downstairs. One day in her hurry, she tripped and fell down the thirteen steps, and lay unconscious at the foot, a black bundle of clothes. Ann screamed. Francis simply looked. Ann took hold of him and ran outside, screaming, to the shop, and managed to convey to Michael Joe that something was up inside. He and Vin ran in together. Michael Joe carried his mother upstairs though he knew it was dangerous if she had any broken bones. He sent Vin for Doctor Healy. He could not bear to see her lying in a heap at the foot of the stairs, and so he carried her up and laid her out in the bed. He did not try to determine whether she was alive or dead, or touch her at all beyond laying her out on the bed. Then he sat down in a chair, and waited for the doctor to come.

It really did not occur to him that she might die. She would not die. She had been there always, as far back as his dimmest memory could carry and beyond. She was as present to him and as natural as light in the morning and darkness at night. She would always be present somewhere in him. The best of him was her, he thought. And he had been a bad son. Not paid her enough attention. He was not struggling with her, now. He should have paid more attention to her. Forgive him. He spoke to her image. He did not really see her as being outside him, at all.

And so he waited calmly for Doctor Healy to arrive.

She battled for two days and then died in the night. The old women of the town, her cronies, gossips, those with whom she had been walking up and down to the chapel, preparing for death with them, were with her at the end. One of them called Michael Joe in when they could see she had taken a turn for the worse. She had begun whispering his name, as she had whispered it many times during her dying moments. He came in. She seemed to recognize him for a moment; her eyes were bright; then they glazed. Michael Joe knelt down by the bed, and dropped his dark head on the eiderdown, listening to her laboured breathing. He wanted to speak to her. One of the old women took him by the arm, and led him out.

Canon Lyons was called, and he came and administered the last rites of the Church. Afterward, on his way down from the sick-room he stopped in the dining room where Michael Joe was sitting with Ann and Francis. Ann held Francis in her lap, though he was a seven-year-old and almost as tall as herself now. She kept asking him questions from the catechism to keep his mind off what was going on. Michael Joe was silent, his head buried between his hands.

Ann jumped up when she saw the Canon at the dining room door. Michael Joe stayed sitting.

'Come in, Canon, come in,' she said getting flustered and grabbing hold of Francis by the hand.

'Is this the little fellow we hear so much about?' Canon Lyons said, coming in. He tousled Francis, and tipped his chin and looked long into his face. 'Ah, he's a grand little fellow, a grand little fellow.'

'How . . . how is she?' Ann said.

The Canon pursed his lips. The lean face, mask-like, impersonal, said: 'No hope, I'm afraid, no hope. Ye might as well know the truth.'

Michael Joe stood up. 'No hope?'

The Canon turned to him. 'I'm afraid that's so. But she'll die in peace, anyway.'

'Die in peace,' Michael Joe mumbled.

'She won't have a worry on her mind or a stain on her soul,' the Canon said driving home his point. Then turning to Ann and the boy: 'We'll be seeing this little fellow at the rails for his First Communion. Ah, he'll be a grand man.'

'Yes, Canon,' Ann said bowing.

She walked the Canon to the front door, nodding and bowing all the way, making Francis salute him as he left.

Michael Joe remained sitting in the dining room.

Old Mrs. McCarthy never once asked to see Ann or little Francis.

The old women laid Mrs. McCarthy out in the traditional fashion, in her own bed, surrounded by candles, her wax-like hands joined on a crucifix; a plate of snuff was laid on a table near the bed. There was no ólagón, but the body was never alone until it was taken out of the house. The old women sat around and prayed. All day visitors came, knelt beside the bed where the corpse was laid out, said a prayer, and then went downstairs to the dining room, where Ann and Michael Joe sat with Francis between them, and offered condolences. The round-faced clock over the mantelpiece in the kitchen had been stopped at the moment of her death.

Before the body was taken out of the house for its short journey

263

up to the chapel, and from the chapel to the graveyard next day, Michael Joe and Ann and Francis went into the room to say a last farewell. Michael Joe went in first, and knelt by the bed, bowing his head in his hands. Ann led Francis by the hand in after her. The little boy gazed as if transfixed at the corpse on the bed, staring at the hands. Ann put an arm around him, kneeling down beside him. She let go of his hand a moment to cross herself. He screamed.

'She moved, she moved!'

Ann hurried him out of the room. Michael Joe started out of his trance at his son's scream, and stared too in terror at the corpse. He was alone for a minute, and then backed out of the room, away from the bed, still staring at the corpse, as if he expected it to rise up against him. He went into his bedroom, and took a quick slug of whiskey from a bottle he kept there.

Ann took Francis downstairs. He was whimpering.

'Hush, hush, there, a gradh, there's no harm . . . no one will harm a hair of your head.' She took him into the dining room and enfolded him in her arms. 'Your grandma is dead. She can't hurt you.'

'Will you save me if she gets up?' he asked through his tears.

Ann kissed him over and over again, passionately.

'I will, a gradh, I will.'

'Didn't she take her medicine, Mammy?' he asked suddenly.

Ann could not answer.

'Will you always take your medicine, Mammy?'

'I will, I will, asthore,' she said tenderly, and began to stroke his fair face.

At that moment, Ann knew that there was only one thing she really cared about in life; and that was her son. And for him she would live and die.

39

AT TEN YEARS old, Francis was made an altar boy. He quickly got a reputation for being the most diligent, punctual and well behaved of all the altar boys. He had learned the Latin of the Mass and the rituals with the same diligence that he had learned his catechism. Ann, though she could not pronounce the Latin very well, coached him as she had coached him in the catechism. Francis had a firm, clear boy soprano's voice. He would sing out the responses of the Mass so well that he could be heard in almost every corner of the chapel. Ann tried to attend every Mass he served, and watched him carefully on the altar. She had made the surplice and the soutane he wore: red trim on the black soutane, and elaborate lace trim on the surplice. She always made sure his surplice was starched stiff and gleaming white.

In all Ann's training and bringing-up of the boy, she never consciously tried to put any distance between himself and his father. She had dedicated him from the beginning to the service of the Blessed Virgin Mother, and all the pains she had taken with him were only to make sure that his steps did not stray from that path. She did not want him to be like his father. That much she admitted to herself. It pained her when people commented on the physical resemblance.

Michael Joe noticed the way she was bringing the boy up, but did not interfere. He was too taken up with his own life. Sometimes Francis wanted his attention. The day he had been made altar boy, he came running into the shop after school and shouted at Vin: 'Where's my Daddy, where's my Daddy?' Michael Joe was in the back with a couple of fellows who had dropped in to see him, and he heard the little boy shouting. The fellows had been talking about the very open private lives of some of the actors of a travelling show that was then making a week's stand in the town. Michael Joe tipped them the wink to shut up the minute he heard his son's voice.

Francis came running into the snug at the back and was about to blurt out whatever news he had for his daddy, when he became shy in the presence of the fellows staring at him.

'Well, what's the fuaster?' Michael Joe said in a kindly way from his chair by the fire. He did not get up.

Francis blushed, and began hopping from one leg to another. He tried to talk but could not bring out what he had to say in a clear manner.

'Well, go on, spit it out. No one here'll take a bite out of you,' Michael Joe encouraged him.

'I'm going to be Canon Lyons' altar boy,' he finally got out. He hung his head as if he suddenly became conscious of a shame attaching to what he had to say.

'Ah, be the hokey, that's great news,' one of the fellows said trying to set the young lad at ease.

'He'll have all the girls looking at him now above in the altar. Sure, the poor ould Canon won't get an eye from a girl in the place,' Michael Joe said.

Francis began to look around him seeking a way to escape. Michael Joe got up and came over to him, and stood before him. He stared at his son a minute, contemplating him. All the old images of Canon Lyons had suddenly come back to Michael Joe, and in the light of them, he contemplated his young son, who would now be his servant at the altar. The boy was aware of the strange look his father was giving him, and he wilted under it.

'I'll be inside the rails,' he said lamely.

'Well, g'wan in and tell your mother,' Michael Joe said. 'She'll be delighted to hear it.'

Francis ran out of the shop, and indoors to tell his mother. He had been so excited at being chosen as an altar boy. Delirious. Lifted into the clouds. He could not imagine anyone else not being as excited about his news as himself. As far back as he could remember, he had wanted to be an altar boy, inside the rails, dressed in a surplice and soutane, helping the priest at Mass with the eyes of the whole parish on him, singing out the responses to the priest in Latin that hardly two people in the whole chapel understood. And his mother watching him.

His mother was so delighted with the news that she made him a special sweet of strawberry jelly for dinner that night. But his joy was not entirely complete. Somehow, he had imagined, with the intense imagination of the young which blots out everything else but the object of their passion, that his becoming an altar boy would make his father as happy as his mother. He saw that his father did not care. That troubled his joy. He wanted his father to say that it was great that he had become an altar boy. The incident was small, but the wound went deep. He became dimly conscious also, of some real difference between his father and his mother. Something shadowy. He could not name it. His mother rejoiced and his father did not. Why...? Why...? Why...? He troubled about it for a while. But soon forgot in the excitement of the actuality of being an altar boy, and serving Canon Lyons at Mass.

When Michael Joe came home drunk from the fairs, Ann cautioned Francis to stay out of his way. He had the whole back garden to play in, and it was no time to stay around the house watching his father and the state he was in. She didn't want Francis to be seeing a bad example. When the boy heard that his father had gone to a fair, he prepared himself for the worst. It was as if, when he came home from school, the house would somehow have changed. His father was home from the fair... and drunk... keep out of his way. He blew his father's drunkenness up into fantastic proportions. He could see his mother's fear, and feel it. It communicated itself to him. But since he could not see the object that caused it, he made up a monster in his mind.

Since his mother died, Michael Joe was always fighting drunk when he came home from the fairs. It was as if his mother's death had loosened the last civilized inhibitions that he had, and the beast surfaced with drink. He'd shout at Ann over nothing. He'd make up excuses to fight with her. She sat there passively listening to him. Never daring to answer him back. He'd call her names about her ability as a housekeeper. Then attack her family. Then her intelligence. Then her religiosity. But he was never physically violent with her.

Sometimes Francis would creep to the back door where he was playing by himself, and he would hear his father shouting. He imagined that he was attacking his mother.

One night, Francis, whose bedroom was next his parents', woke up to hear his mother crying out in the next room. His father had come home drunk from the fair, that day. When Francis heard his mother crying out he thought she was dying. Something was happening to her. And he blamed his father. The crying out continued as if his mother were in great pain. He began to sweat, then he felt his own body grow stiff, as if he were a piece of iron or a piece of wood. He thought his heart had stopped; and his breath. Then he heard his father say something; the voice was strange; it sent goose flesh through Francis. He could not hear what his father said, but then he heard his mother shout out: 'No...no...no...Michael Joe...I can't, I can't. Stop it. You're hurting me.' Francis was going to jump out of bed and run up and call the Civic Guards. Then he heard the bed creaking in the next room, creaking, creaking, creaking. Was the house going to fall down? Then, suddenly, everything was quiet. Was his mother dead ... dead?

He hardly slept the rest of the night. He lay out, stiff as a board, his arms rigid by his sides.

Silent tears streamed down his face from time to time, when he realized that he was helpless to aid his mother.

Next morning he was up early and waiting. Finally, his mother came downstairs. There was no mark on her. He observed her while she made the fire. Not a mark on her. He had expected her to be black and blue all over.

'You aren't hurt, Mammy, are you?' he said.

'Wisha, no love, what'd hurt me?'

He pondered while he ate breakfast with her. Then, she sent him off to school.

'Run off to school now before your father gets up. He'll be in a bad mood today, I'm afraid.'

His mother's cries kept ringing in his head all day at school.

40

When Francis was twelve, a girl fell in love with him, the little draper's daughter down the street, Maidie Hogan. The little girl came to the door one evening after school, and knocked. Ann went out and answered. She was surprised to see the dark-haired little girl standing there, and didn't really know whose child she was.

'Is Francis in?' the girl said boldly.

'He's . . . he's . . . he's doing his lessons now,' Ann said.

'Tell him I want him,' the girl said.

'You want him?' Ann paused. 'What do you want him for?' she said in a kindly voice.

'I want to give him this,' the girl said holding out a piece of lined notepaper she had torn out of her exercise book.

'Can *I* give it to him?'

The girl gazed frankly at Ann, sizing her up, as if she were an opponent. 'Well,' she said. 'I suppose.' She handed the notepaper to Ann.

'Good-bye now,' Ann said and closed the door.

She leaned against it, and clutched the notepaper to her bosom. Then she opened it and read it:

> Dear Francis,
> You are my boy now.
> Love, Maidie Hogan

Ann went into the dining room and sat down. How long had this been going on? Why hadn't Francis told her about it? She was a slutty little girl. A brazen one. Ann didn't know what to do. There was no one she could turn to for advice. She muttered a few quick prayers for spiritual guidance. Then she shoved the note inside her dress.

The next morning, Ann could not get up. A sudden attack of lumbago came on her. Michael Joe came into Francis' room and told him to go up to Mrs. Twomey and ask her to come down and take care of the house, his mother wasn't getting up.

Francis dressed quickly and went up for Mrs. Twomey. Then he went up to see his mother. He suspected his father. The voices had come back to him. He knocked at the door. His mother's voice sounded in pain.

His mother was lying straight out in the middle of the bed, with her hands folded across her stomach, outside the clothes. She had two pillows propping up her head, and her face was waxen. She looked like Grandma McCarthy had when she was dead. Francis couldn't talk.

'Come here to me,' Ann said.

Francis slowly made himself walk to the side of her bed. She fondled his hair. He wanted to run away.

'What'll I do?' he burst out.

'Oh, sure I'm not going to die,' she said with a little laugh. Then as an afterthought: 'Go up to the Medical Hall and ask the chemist for a bottle of Sloan's Liniment.'

'I'll say a prayer for you, Mammy,' he said, and ran out of the room.

For the next few weeks, until his mother was up again, he spent the days in constant fear that when he came home from school she would be dead. He ran all the way home, and went up to her immediately he came into the house. And he stayed with her until supper time, and then went up after. His father was in a bad mood. Francis stayed out of his way.

He offered up every Mass he served for his mother, and made a special novena to St. Francis, who was his saint.

In the evenings when he sat by his mother's bedside, the smell of medicines in the room, she talked to him. She told him about her girlhood in the country, out in Cloon. She told him about the little stream near their house where she and her brothers used to catch fish barehanded; and how they all went barefooted in the summer, saving hay in the meadows, and catching bees in jam jars in the dusk of the long summer evenings. She talked on and on about her childhood, weaving a spell around Francis with the magic of strange adventures that befell her as a child in that wild country thatl ay beyond Corrigbeg. It seemed to Francis that nothing ever happened to himself half as exciting as the things that had happened to his mother.

'But for you, Francis,' she said once, 'I wouldn't be getting better as fast.'

'I'm not doing anything, Mammy,' he said. 'I want you to be better.'

'So you can go out gallivantin' around the town again. Is that it?' she laughed.

'I don't want to go out. I want to stay with you,' he protested.

And he had given proof of his devotion while she was sick. Enough to satisfy her that there was nothing serious in the note that girl had brought to the door. She burned the note in the fire in the bedroom without ever showing it to Francis.

One evening, Francis came home from school and there was no one in the kitchen or the dining room. He threw his satchel on the kitchen table, and ran upstairs, and burst into his mother's bedroom without knocking. His mother was lying naked on top of the bed. Mrs. Twomey was bending over her, and she had an iron in her hand and was pressing it on cloths on top of his mother's back. Francis took in the scene in precise and minute detail, the white body stretched out, the bottom, and the white thin legs extending, wide, out from it. He did not at first glance associate the sight of the body with his mother. Then she spoke.

'Who's there?'

' 'Tis only Francis,' Mrs. Twomey said.

Ann sprang up, clutching the bedclothes around her. 'Cover me up, cover me up!' she screamed at Mrs. Twomey.

Francis ran out of the room.

'Did he see me, did he see me, do you think?' he heard his mother say to Mrs. Twomey.

'Ah, sha, what if he did itself?' Mrs. Twomey said.

Then he heard his mother moaning: 'Oh, Mother of God, what'll I do? What'll I do, at all?'

He mooned around the rest of the evening in the backyard, and did not go back up to see her. Every time he made up his mind to, he was suffused with a sense of shame. He had never realized his mother looked like that. The image of the naked body kept flashing into his mind. He kept trying to keep it away. But it would never go. He did not want to see it. But yet it kept coming back.

He waited until after supper to go up and see her. Then it was dark, and she had the shutters shut, and the small lamp lit in the room. He pretended nothing had happened, and she did too. She questioned him about school that day. The whole incident was forgotten, except when she put out her arms for him to come and kiss her good night. He hesitated. She noticed, but did not let on. He kissed her brusquely, and left. Ann was worried again, worried just when she had felt secure.

One morning, soon after that little incident, when Ann was up and well again, she asked Michael Joe to stop a minute as he was leaving the dining room to go out to the shop. She had continued to worry about Francis. He had become quieter than he usually was, and mooned about the house not watching her, but she felt she was being watched. She often noticed him staring at the picture of the Madonna and Child which she had hung over the dining room table, staring with his pen in his mouth when he ought to be reading his lessons or writing his exercises.

She didn't know what was up with him. She began to think that maybe she had not got to the bottom of his 'romance' with that Maidie Hogan girl. She had never really questioned him about it at all. Maybe it was more serious than she had imagined. There was something secretive about the quietness that had come over him. Every time she asked him a question, he seemed embarrassed, and couldn't look at her. He was concealing something from her. Could there be something really *bad* going on between himself and that little girl? Could a boy of twelve . . . oh, he couldn't! That would be unthinkable. Still, she didn't know anything about boys. Even when Francis was a tiny little fellow and she would be bathing him . . . oh, she couldn't bear to think of what she saw. What could you do with a boy? She could never talk to Michael Joe about it. But if Francis was that way as a baby, God knows what he might be now, at twelve. Oh, she was confused. And tortured. With no one to turn to. She had to say something to Michael Joe. That was why she asked him to stop a minute.

He turned around surprised. 'What is it, woman, in the name of God?'

'Francis . . . Francis is behaving strangely of late.'

'I haven't noticed anything strange about him,' Michael Joe said, and made as if to leave the room.

Ann was driven to coming to the point more directly than she wanted to. 'There was a girl dropped in a note saying she loved him. Hogan the draper's daughter.'

Michael Joe turned back, a broad smile on his face. 'Well, good heart to the lad. I was beginning to think . . . but, sure the breeding will out.'

Ann's face set. The hesitance and awkwardness left her. It was as if she had been lashed by a whip, and some inner source of strength had been struck, which helped her to rise to resistance.

'Listen to me,' she said, 'and don't give me any of your dirty talk.'

The past lay between them in a flash, called up at the moment of conflict, ready as a weapon. Michael Joe knew it was there. And Ann, who had always held it in readiness, now used it, though nothing was openly said. Michael Joe's pose was stripped. He gave her a hard stare.

'Leave the lad alone,' he said. 'Stop pushing and poking into his affairs every two minutes of the day.'

'That girl . . . they're doing something *bad*.'

'That little girl!' Michael Joe threw back his head and laughed. 'Sure she still thinks 'tis made to pee out of.' He intended the vulgarity as an insult. And Ann knew it. But she ignored it.

'It's Francis I'm worried about.'

'Leave him alone. If the two of them are up to anything, 'tis only natural. Let it take its course, woman, and keep your nose out of it.'

'You have no interest in his welfare at all! You never had. You don't want to help him in trouble.'

Michael Joe bent close to her, and let fly again, compelled to be vulgar with her.

'What do you suggest I do? Tell him keep it in his pants, and not to be showing it around to every little girl in the town. Is that what you want?'

Ann sat calmly letting him talk himself out. She seemed suddenly to be able to transcend herself. The fear, the fright, and the quiet terror she sometimes felt in the presence of Michael Joe, was gone.

'I want him to go to college,' she said.

'Send him away! To college. Are you out of your mind entirely? I never went past the eight' class myself, and I'm none the worse for it. College how-are-you! A gentleman Jim she wants to make of him.'

Ann clasped her long, pale hands together. Both hands intertwined to the shape of a big fist, pointing at him from her lap.

'When I came into this house,' she said with quiet ferocity, 'I brought five hundred pounds. I have some claim to that money still. And, God knows, I haven't spent much of it on myself all these times. That is to go for his education.'

Michael Joe sat down opposite her and lit a cigarette, and blew the smoke at her. 'That money is long since spent,' he said coolly. 'Did you think 'twas going to last forever?'

'Don't you make anything in the shop? Or at your fairs?'

'I do more business than any other ten men in the town,' he said leaning towards her.

'Then you have the money to send him to college. I'll tell you,' she said leaning toward him, like a little bantam hen, 'I won't give you a minute's peace either *outside* this home, or *inside* it till the day I die, if you won't consent.'

Michael Joe knew what she meant. She *had* left him alone, and because she had done so, he had left himself alone, had not tortured himself with guilt, but pushed the past into the past.

'Couldn't he go to the Christian Brothers?' Michael Joe said, trying now for a compromise.

'I want him to go away,' she said.

'Ah, damn it, have it your own way, then,' Michael Joe said, rising and leaving her.

That evening Michael Joe was sitting by himself in the snug at the back of the shop, unable to read the paper. He had not gone in for his supper, as a gesture of rebellion. And he was determined not to go in. He had lost a battle. She had beaten him with unfair weapons. If the incident with Bridie became known . . . and she'd tell . . . she didn't care about herself, he saw. She had no self-respect. That she had lost, if she ever had any. And there was much more she could whisper, more intimate matters, things at the very core of their married life that never could be spoken.

There was a knock at the door, interrupting his musings. Francis came in.

' 'Tis you!' Michael Joe said in anger. 'What do you want?'

'Mammy wants you to come in for supper.'

He was about to answer roughly, and frighten the boy. He always seemed to be frightened when he spoke to his father. Then Michael Joe had a sudden thought.

'Come in, come in a minute, 'til I see you,' he said in a kindly way.

Francis came in hesitantly, and stood with his hands by his sides, like a soldier on review, a few paces from his father.

'Come hether to me. I won't take a bite of you,' Michael Joe said.

'Yes, sir,' Francis said.

'I suppose you know your mother wants you to go to college?'

'Yes, sir.'

'You wouldn't want to stop home and be in the shop with me. We'd have great times, here, together.'

'I don't want to go to college, sir,' Francis said.

Michael Joe brightened. Ann had reckoned without the breeding telling in her son. He was a McCarthy. What would he be doing going down to a school infested with priests teaching out of books!

'Didn't I know, didn't I know you'd have a mind of your own,' Michael Joe murmured to himself. And then to his son: 'I'll take you to a fair, one of these days.'

'I want to stay home, sir,' Francis said.

'Home?' Then Michael Joe saw the truth. The lad didn't want to go to college because he wanted to stay home with his mother. And then he went a step further. He'd send the lad to college, after all. That would be it. A neat little trick, after all. That would keep him out of his mother's way. Everything was working out well, after all.

'I'm afraid you'll have to do what your mother says,' Michael Joe said, pretending to be disappointed. 'Come on, we'd better go into supper before 'tis cold on the table.'

41

AND SO FRANCIS MICHAEL MCCARTHY was entered at St. Ronan's College for Boys between the ages of twelve and eighteen. And his father and mother both rejoiced that he was going to school there.

Ann was quietly proud. She had won her victory over Michael Joe. For a time, it made her softer and more approachable. It almost seemed as if the dark, brooding atmosphere of the house was going to lift, and once more the two of them could walk abroad in the sun of a Sunday afternoon. Michael Joe never proposed the walk, and Ann did not know how to make a move that would bring them closer together. She could not forget the past. She was not jealous that Michael Joe had betrayed her with Bridie. Rather, it made her afraid of Michael Joe. She couldn't bear his touch; and she was always afraid when he was around her.

But a certain lightness and gaiety did come over her when she was preparing to send Francis off to the college. She was extravagant in buying what he would need. Only the best suits, shirts, ties, boots—everything bought new. As a going-away present from herself, she bought Francis a set of silver-backed toilet accessories—a hand mirror, a hair brush and a clothes brush.

Michael Joe never complained at the outlay of money. He made Ann out a draft for fifty pounds on the National Bank, without a murmur. She spent that, and he did not complain when she asked for more, though he did make a sarcastic comment. 'Making a toff out of him entirely?' he said to her. She gave a small laugh. Michael Joe was smiling. 'We can't let him down there in rags,' she said. 'He'll be able to hold up his head with the best of them.' Michael Joe looked indulgent. The house brightened for a moment, and possibilities were opened. Neither of them explored. Neither of them knew how to, now.

That September morning when Francis was leaving to go down to Ennis, Ann would not go down in the car. She said no, she wouldn't go. Michael Joe tried to persuade her. Again, a moment opened up possibilities, but Ann refused to stir outside the house. She would not dress up and get in the car and accompany them down to the college. Francis did not try to persuade her to come. When Michael Joe and Francis were gone in the car, she went up to the chapel, and spent most of the day there grieving, prostrate before the Tabernacle, trying to cure her loneliness by talking to the Presence there.

The journey down to Ennis in the car was the first time that father and son were ever really alone together for very long. Francis was quiet, serious and stiff-mannered, and looking all polished and shiny in his new navy-blue suit, new boots, new shirt, new everything, even to his underwear. He was stockily built; Michael Joe in miniature—thickset, dark-haired, a determined facial expression. He was lean whereas Michael Joe was fat. Already there was a touch of the ascetic about the boy, the sign of a strong will keeping whatever was within him well under control.

Michael Joe soon discovered that he had nothing much to say to Francis. That did not worry him. He was proud of the way the lad looked, and felt that he could hold his own among the best that he would meet at St. Ronan's. The old McCarthy blood would out, now that the lad would be away from his mother. Breeding would tell. Michael Joe was secure in that thought.

He made sure the boy had enough money, and gave him a couple of pounds to keep him in pocket money until he came home at Christmas. He advised him never to rat on anyone. That was the one rule he should remember—never to spy on his companions, never to betray them no matter at what cost. Keep that rule in mind and he'd get along all right. Francis listened with a certain deliberate air, as if forcing himself to listen.

'Will you do that now for me?' Michael Joe ended his advice.

'Yes, sir', Francis said.

Then Michael Joe talked to Mickey, the hack, who was driving the car.

They had a long discussion about the All-Ireland hurling final to be played that week, and then went on to discuss possible winners for the St. Leger at the Curragh. Both of them forgot about the boy in the back seat. He did not mind; he was trying to imagine what St. Ronan's would be like, having already forgotten about his mother and his home.

Michael Joe delivered Francis over to Father Quigley, the Dean of Boys, said good-bye to him with an expansive, man-to-man handshake, then hopped quickly back in the car and told Mickey to step on the gas.

He made a day of it in Ennis, by himself, that day. Dinner at the Old Ground; drinks with friends he knew there since his football days. One of them, Jack Quinn, now owned a sporting-goods store which he ran along with a bar. He wondered what brought Michael Joe down to Ennis. 'Putting the son over to the college.' Jack thought that was great, and wondered why Michael Joe hadn't brought the son out to the town for the day. The thought hadn't occurred to Michael Joe. He muttered something about letting the lad make a clean break. Then, he bought a pair of brand-new football shoes for Francis, and had Jack Quinn deliver them out at the college.

As the day wore on, Michael Joe got drunk, maudlin, and finally sentimental. Old memories of another day in Ennis came back to him. And Nell. He went over to the bridge of the Fergus and gazed down over the bridge to the murky flowing waters. Tears came into his eyes. Ah, if it had only been Nell's son he was bringing down to the college today, ah, if it were only . . . the two of them, Nell and himself, would be here. Nell wouldn't be the one to stop at home. Ah, if it was only Nell's son.

In his sentimentality, he forgot all other feelings about Nell but that he had once loved her. He felt no guilt either that he was rejecting his own son in the name of an old and lost love.

42

FOR ANN, NOW, the house was a dark, damp, gloomy cavern without the presence of her light. She left her son's room exactly as it had been; made the bed and aired the sheets for a while every day, waiting for his return for the Christmas holidays. She did not know how she would pass the time until then. Sometimes, she lit a fire in his room and sat beside it, writing him the weekly letter, a long, meandering letter full of religious sentiments, new prayers she had clipped from religious magazines, new novenas her gossips had passed along to her, and her thoughts on the lives of her favourite saints, of which St. Francis was the chief. She always included a religious picture, bought at P. J. Harley's, with the letter. Now and then, she would eulogize one of the local priests for a sermon, or an act of charity he had done. In this way, she indirectly expressed her own hopes for her son.

She never wrote him gossip though she knew all the news of the town from the old women who visited her every day. She considered that a son who would one day be a priest was above that sort of thing.

She was most of the time alone in the house. When the silence and the emptiness made her afraid, she would put on her coat and dash up to the chapel, and prostrate herself before the Tabernacle. There she felt peace and security.

The house had whispers for her. It spoke of old Mrs. McCarthy, dead, but her ghost haunted the dark corridor upstairs. Ann was sure she had heard her shuffling footsteps, several times. Ann never dared enter her room. She sometimes thought she saw Mrs. McCarthy coming back to haunt her, shaking a crooked, white, bony finger at her, and accusing her of something. And then, again, she imagined she saw the figure of the old woman shuffling around the house, looking for something. What had she lost? What had she lost? Ann was terrified. She felt that Mrs. McCarthy's spirit was not at rest, so she had a series of Masses offered by Canon Lyons for the repose of her soul. And a High Mass on the anniversary of her death, which she attended by herself, dressed in black. Michael Joe seemed to have forgotten his mother's death.

Often, Ann sat half-praying, half-dreaming her winter nights away by the fire in her son's room, indulging in images of him appearing on the high altar above in the chapel, radiant in golden vestments, his arms extended in a blessing which enfolded the whole congregation in an embrace of divine love.

Michael Joe's life was not changed in any way by his son's departure for college. He had made the right move in getting the boy away from his mother. That was that. He had no other sentiment about his son's absence.

He rarely stayed home at night, and he always came home late when he went out, having spent his evening drinking or playing cards at one of the local pubs.

He was always restless in the house, using it as a place to eat and sleep in, and not as a home. It was as if the house haunted him, and he feared its living image and the images of the past that it evoked in him.

He kept out of the house as much as he could.

In the shop, he always had distractions. Idlers around the town always dropped in to talk. Vin Scanlon was there to listen if no one else was there. Travelling salesmen came by. Customers, especially the women, stopped for a chat when they bought something. His warm manner was always attractive, though none of them wished to be burned.

Once or twice a month, Michael Joe drove his bullocks to the fair, where he found the excitement he was looking for, among the farmers and drovers and buyers from Limerick and Dublin bargaining for cattle, drinking after clinching the bargains.

And, sometimes, when darkness had fallen after a fair, Michael Joe knew where to go for a woman with whom he could bargain for something else.

One morning, as he was rising from a silent, quick breakfast with Ann, who always hurried down from her morning Mass to prepare it, she spoke to him as if trying to detain him a little longer, to have his presence a few moments, hear his voice addressing her, much as she feared it.

'I had a letter from Francis,' she said.

'Wisha, did you, now?' Michael Joe said. 'That's grand.' His curiosity was aroused for a moment. But he did not know how to let her see it, without giving himself away too much. The habit of hiding himself from her for so many years had put one more barrier between them. He waited for her to go on.

'He's getting on grand,' she said.

'And why wouldn't he? He's a McCarthy, isn't he? And they always got on with the crowd.' He stood in the door of the dining room, waiting to see if she had any other news from his son.

'He says the priests are very nice to him. One of them told him the other morning he was the best server he ever had.'

Michael Joe scowled. 'Tell him from me to mind his football, and not get carried away with nonsense.'

Ann dropped her eyes, and gazed into her cup of tea.

'Well, I must be off out,' Michael Joe said, stretching.

'Wouldn't you . . . wouldn't you write him a line?'

'Me! Is it me writing letters? You'll take good enough care of that end of it,' he said sarcastically, and left.

He thought for a while after going out to the shop, that maybe he should drop a line of a letter to his son. The lad might need a bit of advice, stuck down there among all those priests. He had half a mind to write. But he picked up the *Irish Independent* and forgot the letter in poring over yesterday's racing results.

That first Christmas holiday when Francis came home from college, Ann saw that the work she had begun with him as a little boy was now showing the proper signs of developing. The priests in St. Ronan's, she was sure, were taking up where she left off. He went to Mass and Communion every morning during the holidays, always carried with him the thick, hard-backed missal, beside which her own prayer book was only, she thought, a few pages. He explained to her that he was able to say every prayer from it that the priest was saying above in the altar.

Ann nearly fainted.

What went on at the altar, what the priest said up there, had always been beyond her. Now, her young son was initiated into the mystery. He had come far already, in the short time he had been away at school.

During the holidays, the sacristan at the chapel told Ann to send Francis up to help him build the Crib, and decorate the altar for Christmas Mass. Francis went up immediately, and spent some time of almost every day for the rest of his holidays, helping the sacristan. On Christmas morning, when Ann prayed before the Crib, she remembered as she prayed that her son's hand had helped to build it. And Francis had served at the Christmas morning Mass, his boy's voice piping out the responses in loud, clear Latin. And his mother listened, forgetting all the Christmases of the past in her present joy.

Michael Joe went to last Mass on Christmas Day. He had been out late the night before. He was late for Christmas dinner, as usual, and slightly drunk. He had brought home a few Baby Powers', and tried to make Ann have a drink. And wanted Francis to have a well-watered-down whiskey, too.

'I'm a Pioneer,' Francis said. 'I took the pledge.'

Michael Joe was in good humour, so he joked with him about taking the pledge.

'You won't be able to touch a drop for life. Look at what you'll be missing,' he teased Francis.

'Michael Joe!' Ann said.

'I don't care,' Francis said. He pointed to the Sacred Heart badge on the lapel of his coat. 'I swore an oath. And I won't break it. No matter what.'

Michael Joe ignored the defiance. 'Yerra, wait a while, me young boyo. You'll come in here to me some night on top of your head.' He laughed.

'I hate drink,' Francis said calmly.

'Ah, well. Good luck, then,' Michael Joe said, tossing of a half one.

He put the boy's hatred of drink down to his youth. The blood would tell later on.

Michael Joe never asked Francis to work in the shop when he was home on holidays. He had Vin Scanlon to help him always, and he knew that he'd be a lot more easy with Vin around, who knew his ways, than having his son there. Francis would drop in occasionally, dressed in a dark suit, and carrying a book or a missal in his hand. The atmosphere of the shop changed when he came in. If there were fellows there talking to Michael Joe, they hurriedly took their leave, after a few polite words to Francis. Vin Scanlon would put on a sudden show of work, and leave Francis and Michael Joe alone. Michael Joe would become uneasy, and try to make the best of his son's visit. But he felt his style was cramped. The boy wasn't old enough yet, for them to start talking man to man. All Michael Joe could do was be polite to Francis. He was hoping that Vin Scanlon and Francis would get along. Vin might be able to show him some of the ropes. But when Michael Joe spoke to Vin about it, Vin offered no help.

'Ah, he's a grand lad. A grand lad,' Vin said. 'Sure he has nothing to learn from me. They'll learn him everything at the college.'

'Ah, you're a bloody weasel, Scanlon. Take the lad to a dance, some night. Up to Lahinch. Ye'll be away from the town. Don't worry about the cost.'

'Ah, sure he wouldn't be seen out with a working lad the likes of me,' Vin said.

'I'll give you a fiver if you take him up to the Falls Hotel one night,' Michael Joe said.

Vin was tempted. 'No, no,' he said finally. 'He'll go with his own.'

Michael Joe did not know what that meant. But he wanted to forget about the problem, suddenly.

'Ah, we'll give the lad his head. He'll come around in his own good time,' he said.

Then he told Vin a dirty story he'd heard the night before.

Michael Joe felt that, in the long run, it was better that Francis did not hang around the shop too much, or come with him to the fairs, until he was ready for it. He'd have to be grown up then. Only when he was grown up would he understand. And when that

ay came, father and son would face the world together, man to
ȵan. Until then, he'd have to give the boy his head.

As Francis progressed in college, he began to spend less and less
me at home during his holidays. He was always off visiting fellows
ⱴho were in school with him in other parts of Clare, Limerick, or
ȉipperary. Michael Joe was just as well satisfied not to have him
ȼound. And the lad was making friends. That would stand him in
ood stead later on in life. Ann was more lonely than ever. But
ȵe was consoled when Francis told her that all himself and his
ȼiends did was make retreats, go on pilgrimages, visit monasteries
ɳnd take bicycling tours to visit various priests around the country.

Francis never invited any of his friends to Corrigbeg. There
ⱴas nothing of interest for them, there, he said. Ann agreed with
ȵim. The less she saw of him, the more mysterious he became to
ȵer. And the more she saw that her early training was bearing fruit.

43

MICHAEL JOE FOUND out that Francis wanted to become a priest
the summer he came home after completing his senior year at St.
Ronan's. Ann told him at breakfast one morning. Francis had not
told her definitely, but she suspected, and could not withhold the
news from Michael Joe. They were sitting across from each other
at the breakfast table. Francis had gone to eight o'clock Mass.
Ann waited until Michael Joe was well under way with his breakfast, and then told him directly, not beating around the bush.
Michael Joe did not answer her for a few minutes, but continued
eating.

'So he told you for a fact that he had his mind set on it?' he said
finally.

'You always knew that's what he wanted to do with himself,'
Ann answered toying with a piece of toast on her plate.

'I did not! Ah, every boy wants to become a priest at some time
in his life. Until a smart lassie gets a hold of him. And he finds out
'twasn't for ˙tirring the tea in his cup he got it.'

Ann blushed and blessed herself. She took a nervous sip of te as if to give her strength for what was ahead.

'He isn't interested in girls.'

'Balderdash!' Michael Joe muttered, drawing his fork across th yolks of three fried eggs on his plate. He shovelled down a mouth ful of egg. 'Never had a decent chance to be anything else in thi house,' he muttered.

'Now, that isn't true,' Ann said. 'He had your example tc follow if he wanted to. No one put him up to it, if that's what you think.'

In defence of her son, she lost her fear.

Michael Joe stopped eating for a minute and gave her a long hard stare as if he would like to eat her up.

'Before the poor lad could walk you were taking him up to the bloody chapel. You had him saying the Haily Mary before he could talk. You don't have to think much about where that leads to.'

He cleaned what remained of the egg yolk off his plate with a crust of bread.

'Are you blaming me because he wants to be a priest?' Ann said.

'I am,' he said. 'I never thought... I see it now. But blast it, he's a McCarthy still.'

'What are you going to do? You can't change his mind now.' Her fear was coming back. She did not know what power he had. He had some power she felt, and she did not know how much he could or would do once he began to exert it. She had roused him, now.

'Tell him when he comes in I'll want him in the shop today.' He lumbered out of the dining room.

Ann sat alone at the breakfast table sipping tea, and now and then nibbling on a piece of cold toast. She waited for Francis to come in from attending the eight o'clock Mass. She did not know how Michael Joe could be handled. She trusted Francis to have some solution. In thinking about her son, she forgot about Michael Joe.

Across from her she had laid out his place for breakfast. He received Holy Communion every morning at Mass, so did not eat until he came home. She sat there now, not minding being alone, waiting for him to come in. The house was no longer too large and empty for her.

As she sat there at the table, images of how her son would look as a priest floated into her head, and filled her with warm satisfaction and a sense of someone present. Her fears vanished. The image was vague, without substance, filled with colours of vestments, murmurings of Latin, a priest presence making mysterious signs and movements on a velvet flower-bedecked altar, moving in incense, raising a golden monstrance, muttering blessings of the Eternal over people's heads. The images of her son as a priest would always give her strength, she knew, and would always make her feel that her life had been worthwhile, after all.

Then Francis came in, interrupting her dreams. The physical likeness to Michael Joe had become more pronounced as he had grown older, the same bluntness and directness of presence, the almost truculent, determined manner. But the dark eyes were calm and cold. There was a tightness about the mouth, a restrained, lean, wilful expression about the face which seemed completely his own.

'Is my breakfast ready?' he asked, as soon as he came in the door.

Ann rushed out from the dining room, brushing back the wisps of greying hair from her forehead.

'Wasn't it the quick Mass?' she said. 'Who was it? Father Garvey?'

'Yes, Mother,' he said.

Francis called her 'mother' now, and not 'mammy'. Ann knew he was growing up when that change occurred in the last year.

Francis crossed the kitchen and went upstairs without glancing at her. She watched him go up the stairs, as a little dog watches the master leave and cannot follow. She bustled into the dining room and prepared his breakfast.

She had the hard-boiled egg on the plate beside the egg cup when he came down. She waited for him to sit down, then poured his tea.

'You wouldn't care for a plate of porridge, now?' she said. 'I have it made. Your father had some.'

'No, thanks, Mother, the egg is enough.'

'I don't know what use it is to go starving yourself. Are you fasting again?' She longed to get more details of his life, especially the religious exercises he did. He never talked about them, but she knew he fasted and made novenas.

Francis drank the glass of water, taking small sips and swishing it around in his mouth before swallowing. He had a large Adam's apple, and it rose and fell slowly as he sipped. When he finished, he spoke. Ann was leaning towards him.

'I'm not fasting, Mother,' he said flatly.

'Don't try to hide from me,' she said, bullying him gently. 'You have an appetite as good as your father's. And here you are with only an egg and a piece of toast.'

Francis concentrated on topping his egg. 'I eat enough,' he said.

Ann was silent for a few minutes, and let him eat.

'You're sure . . . of your decision?' she said, after a while.

He looked at her calmly. 'I am.'

Ann sighed with relief. 'You haven't any doubts now, have you? You're sure *that's* what you want to be.' She didn't dare mention the word priest. That would have betrayed too much of her feelings.

'Everyone doubts, Mother,' Francis said, as if he were quoting from a sermon he had heard. 'You can never tell if you're worthy or not.' He bowed his head as if he had suddenly become aware of the over-pretentiousness of his statement.

Ann was impressed. Her son was becoming a more and more mysterious person to her every day. She observed him while he ate. He cut his toast into small squares, and masticated his food slowly and deliberately before swallowing it. He took small spoonfuls of egg.

When he was through eating, Ann gave him his father's message.

Francis let the news sink in before answering. 'I promised Father Garvey to play golf with him today.'

'He was in no mood this morning,' Ann said quietly.

'At his grouching again?'

A charged but subdued intimacy fell suddenly between them, both of them conscious of their antagonism for Michael Joe, and united in it, but unwilling to express it more directly, to elaborate on it, because guilt held them back.

'No worse than usual,' Ann said.

'You told him my decision?'

'I did. He didn't like it.'

'I've applied for All Hallows, Mother. I'm going up there in September whether he likes it or no.'

'Whist, there, asthore, whist. He's still your father. Give the news a little time to sink in.'

286

'I haven't time,' he said. 'I've applied already.'

Ann laid a restraining hand on his arm. 'He's going to have to pay your way, asthore; we'll have to come round him, somehow. With the help of God we'll manage it. Don't cross him.'

Francis had never considered the economic side of his vocation. That he wanted to be a priest filled his mind with images of himself already as a priest. That a trivial matter like money to pay for his further six years in the seminary could stand in his way, irritated him. It was so trivial to think of money when other, more profound, more elevating thoughts were constantly in his mind.

'Isn't he grateful at all that God sent me the call?' Francis said.

Ann shook her head. How could she explain. 'Don't cross him,' she repeated, 'don't cross him. Go on out to the shop. Do what he says for a while. We'll manage him, with the help of God.'

Francis wiped his lips dry with a napkin, and then rose. Every move he made seemed deliberate, planned and willed. He made a slight gesture of the hands to his mother, palms extended upwards, to indicate his resignation.

The news that Francis wanted to become a priest sent Michael Joe into a rage. As he went out to the shop, he glanced up at his name above the shop door: M. J. MC CARTHY, chiselled in inch-thick concrete letters, as if they had been put up to remain forever. If Francis became a priest, the McCarthy name would die out in Corrigbeg, forever. Michael Joe's name would be removed from over the shop door, and another man's name would be put up there. That would make Michael Joe turn over in his grave. The end of the name. The McCarthy name brought to the end of the road by a son who wanted to be a priest.

Michael Joe shook a clenched fist up at the name. 'By God, never,' he muttered. And then went into the shop. To think that he had spent all that money on the boy's education, and all it amounted to was this. This was the fruit of his mother's training. He hated Ann in his heart for having distorted the boy's true inclinations. To be like his father.

In his rage, Michael Joe began planning for battle. He had lost the first round six years ago, when he had consented to letting the boy go to college. That was blind of him. But now his eyes were fully opened. The name would not die. He vowed that. The McCarthy name. He'd fight for it now. Anyone taking a look at his son Francis, would know he never was intended for the priesthood. A strapping young lad like him. Built like a stallion, God knows. He should be out servicing the women of the county, and forget about the priesthood.

But how to win his son away from his vocation? How could that be done? The years he had neglected Francis rose before Michael Joe. He should have interfered in the lad's upbringing. Why didn't he? Why didn't he? He shouldn't have left his bringing up to Ann. Should have fought sooner.

A mistake, a mistake. But it wasn't too late yet to do something about it. After all, somewhere in the lad his own blood must be at work. Francis had Michael Joe's blood running somewhere in his veins. And that blood had little liking for the priesthood. Michael Joe would have to call up that blood in his son, somehow. It was there to be called up. Of that he was sure and certain. And when it rose up, the lad would kiss good-bye to any ideas he had of becoming a priest.

Michael Joe pinned all his faith, now, in the power of his own blood sleeping, unaroused, in the veins of his son.

He would battle Ann and the Church for possession of his son, placing all his faith in the power of his blood to assert itself in his son. His own life was at stake; the tradition; the future generations of his own flesh and blood who would carry his own name and image down the years. In this fight, he felt he had the best ally a man could have, his own blood.

When Francis came into the shop, Michael Joe and two fellows from the town were at the counter, reading the *Irish Independent*.

'Tommy Lonergan was up on her,' Michael Joe was saying. 'No wonder she didn't finish in the money.'

'I thought she'd give me a better ride,' one of the fellows said.

'Carrying that weight over eight furlongs? Nothing doing,' Michael Joe said. 'No staying power.'

'Good morning,' Francis said above the voices.

'Ah, Francis. There you are. I never saw you come in. You ate your breakfast, I suppose?'

'Just finished.'

'Always eat a hearty meal in the morning. There's a long day ahead. And you might need the nourishment. You can never tell.'

'Yes, Father,' Francis said.

'You know the lads here, I suppose?'

'Morning.'

'How's yourself?' one of the fellows said.

'Well, thank you.'

'Look at that for manners, will you?' Michael Joe laughed.

'There's a college education for you.' Then he got an idea.
'We're trying to pick a couple of winners for the day. Here, take a
;awk at these.' He pointed to the probable starters at Leopards-
own for the day. 'See if you can pick a winner.'

Francis remembered his mother's words of caution. He glanced
.t the newspaper.

'There,' he said. 'That one'll win.'

Michael Joe leaned over his shoulder and spelled out the name:
Amor Vincit. 'Great God. what sort of a name is that for a horse?'

'It means "love conquers", Francis said.

'Amor might conquer but I don't know will he win the race,'
Michael Joe said.

The fellows laughed. Michael Joe took a look at the horse's
breeding and form.

'Not bad. The dam won a race or two in her time. And the
sire threw a couple of winners. Maybe you're right after all,'
he said, turning to Francis.

'The spit of the father,' one of the fellows said. 'Can pick a
winner blind.'

Michael Joe beamed. The fellows left thanking Francis profusely
for the tip.

'But I only picked him out,' Francis protested.

'He has the form, too, the form.'

The chance was a golden one for Michael Joe. He began to
build up the purely chance selection by his son, until he made it
a thing of the blood.

'You have it in you, I can see. Some people are born with it. I've
picked more winners in my time than any other man in Corrigbeg.'

' 'Twas pure chance,' Francis said.

Then Michael Joe calmed down. 'I've a small job for you to do.
I'm no hand at it myself.' He lifted the false top at the end of the
counter and went behind it. Francis followed him.

'I'll be glad to do it,' Francis said. 'But I promised Father Garvey
a round of golf this afternoon.'

'Golf, is it! Golf!' Michael Joe said. 'Ah, begorra, times have changed. In my own day, 'twas football. A good man-to-man game. None of that chasing a medicine pill around the sand, for me. I played a couple of great games in my time. See this collarbone, here?' Michael Joe pointed at the old shoulder that had been injured. 'Knocked out in a game with Quilty once. Ask around the town. There's many around that remember that match. One of my great ones.' He sighed. 'But, I suppose you have your own taste. As long as you have a sport, you take after your father.'

Michael Joe entered the glass cubicle where he kept the account books. Francis entered after him, calmly observing his father, and wondering about the sudden garrulousness.

There was barely room for both of them to stand, one on either side of the vacant high chair, in front of the desk, with the thick ledger open on it.

Michael Joe explained to Francis that he wanted him to write letters to a few people in Corrigbeg who owed him big bills. He gave Francis a handwritten list of about forty names.

'That many?' Francis said.

'Wisha, do what you can. And have your game of golf. You can finish the rest tomorrow.'

He left Francis alone with the ledger, and went out in the shop. Vin Scanlon was sweeping around in the back. He gave Vin the day off. His son was going to help him today. 'Breaking in the colt,' Michael Joe whispered to Vin.

Michael Joe heard a tapping on the glass of the cubicle. Francis was banging on it with the handle of the pen, and beckoning him to come in. He went in.

'What should I put in the letters?' Francis said.

'Yerra, anything will do,' Michael Joe said. 'Remind them that their lawful debts should be paid up. That's all. But don't make them mad or they'll never pay.'

As he was talking to Francis a young woman came into the shop.

'Watch this,' Michael Joe said, tipping him the wink.

He went out and weighed flour for the young woman, flirting all the time with her, and overdoing it. Michael Joe whispered something in her ear. The woman laughed loudly, and shifted her weight in a small wiggle. Michael Joe put an arm around her and gave her a squeeze. She drew back hurriedly from him, glancing at the front door for fear anyone would come in and catch them. Michael Joe said something to her again. A peal of woman's laughter rang through the shop, and penetrated through the glass cubicle. Francis tried not to watch, but he did.

Michael Joe came back into the glass cubicle and handed Francis a slip of paper.

'Enter this down under O'Shea.'

'That one.'

'Her husband is in England. She's a great sport. I'll let you take care of her the next time she comes in.'

Michael Joe left the cubicle with a large smile on his face.

Francis worked furiously trying to frame letters of credit until he heard a motor-car pull up outside the shop, and saw Father Garvey walk in, and shake hands with his father. He jumped down off the high chair and went out into the shop.

'Emigration is ruining the population,' Michael Joe was saying.

'Oh, things are being done. Things are being done,' Father Garvey said, nervously clasping and unclasping his white hands.

'Not nearly enough. Not nearly enough. Isn't that a fact, Francis?' Michael Joe said turning to his son.

'We're going out for a round of golf,' Francis said.

Ann came flurrying in the door.

'Ah, Father Garvey,' Ann said breathlessly. 'Isn't it nice of you to pay us a visit.'

'He isn't stopping, Mother,' Francis said. 'We're going out.' He moved towards the door. 'Are you coming, Father?'

'I have dinner just ready . . .' Ann said.

'Well . . .' Father Garvey said, at a loss for an exit line.

'Some other time, Mother,' Francis said.

Michael Joe grabbed Father Garvey by the arm as he was leaving after Francis. 'A couple of good, fiery sermons from a young lad like yourself would have the lads stirring about their proper business,' Michael Joe said. He tipped the wink at Francis retreating through the door.

'I'll see what I can do,' the young priest said.

Ann went to the door of the shop, and watched her son drive off with the priest. Then she turned on Michael Joe.

'How dare you? How dare you insult the priest?'

'Yerra, good God, woman, you don't know what's going on at all. Isn't there any dinner coming up around this place? Or is it all for the priests?'

Ann ran out of the shop.

Michael Joe was very satisfied with his morning's work. He had seen signs in the boy. Good signs. He was willing to learn the business. And a bit of a sport, like Michael Joe himself. Michael Joe didn't doubt that he himself would have been a good golfer if he took up the sport. Maybe he would. He and Francis on the golf links. Not bad. Not a bad image, at all.

Next day, Francis came back into the shop again, and continued writing the letters of credit. Michael Joe dropped into the cubicle often to find out how he was getting along. And to chat with him. He was interested in the game of golf. Was Francis good? Father Garvey? Was it hard to learn? He wasn't exactly fishing around for an invitation to play. But he would have considered it if it came. It didn't.

He got a brilliant idea, himself. A master stroke. On one of his drop-in visits to the cubicle, he asked Francis if he'd like to come with him to a fair in Corofin, the Monday of the following week.

'Go to a fair?' Francis said, puzzled.

'Yerra, man, yes. You haven't ever been anywhere if you haven't gone to a fair. I'll tell you what I'll do. I'll make you a present of a couple of bullocks. And see what you can get for them.'

'I wouldn't know how,' Francis said. 'I haven't the faintest notion how to go about . . . selling bullocks.'

'Neither did I,' Michael Joe said. 'But I learned fast, let me tell you. One of them country fellows would take the trousers off you while you weren't looking. And tell you you weren't naked.' Michael Joe toned down his imagery for his son.

'But why do we have to go to Corofin? There's Fair Days here in Corrigbeg, just as well as in Corofin.'

That stopped Michael Joe. He had never sold cattle in Corrigbeg of a Fair Day. Kept off the streets altogether. He kept his fair activities outside the town. What the locals didn't know wouldn't trouble them. And he could not explain to his son why he would rather go to a fair with him outside Corrigbeg. That would mean he'd have to tell too much. And he didn't think Francis was ready for that yet. When the son and the father were sinners, then they could both talk.

'Ay, maybe 'tisn't such a good idea, after all,' Michael Joe said, dropping the subject quickly, and leaving.

A few nights later, at the supper table, Michael Joe brought up another idea he had been mulling over in his mind.

'A couple of us are going to the Galway Races,' he said. 'They'll be a great day there. We have room for one in the car.'

Francis was silent.

'Oh, 'twould be a grand thing for him to go,' Ann said, giving Francis his clue.

Michael Joe was surprised, and welcomed the unexpected support. 'A day out never hurt a man. Will I count you in, then?' he asked Francis.

'Wouldn't there be room for *two* more?' Francis said looking across at his mother.

'Ah, go on. Sure what would the likes of me be doing at the Galway Races?' Ann said, flushing with pleasure at this proof of her son's loyalty.

'Your mother wouldn't enjoy it,' Michael Joe said. ' 'Twould only tire her out. All that walking. We'll be gone all day. You can tell her about it when you come back.'

'Ah, that would be grand. Just grand,' Ann said.

'Well, all right,' Francis said. 'But under one condition. We don't stay out all night. I have to be up for Mass next morning. We'll come home early.'

'Never fear,' Michael Joe said. 'Never fear there. You'll be the boss in that department.'

Michael Joe stayed at home that night, he was in such good humour.

44

MICHAEL JOE SHOVED a five-pound note into the breast pocket of Francis' coat that morning, before they started for the Galway Races.

'There,' he said. 'Make sure you put that to good use. We'll have a couple of winners today, as sure as my name is Michael Joe McCarthy.'

Francis did not touch the five-pound note.

On the way down in the car, Michael Joe lorded it over the other fellows in the car. He had the card for that day's races, and he began assessing the form of the horses in all eight races. The fellows argued with him, but he beat them down with solid information. He had studied the form well, these past few days, in preparation for his own performance.

The only comments Francis made were to correct mispronunciation of horses' names, especially one Michael Joe had great trouble with. A horse with a name in Irish: Teacht Agus Imheact. Francis pronounced it for him, and told him it meant: Coming and Going.

'By God, he better be going if he has my money on him,' Michael Joe said. And then to Francis: 'Your learning is coming in handy after all.'

Francis was once again able to supply information about a horse called 'Mayor of Casterbridge'. It was the name of a book by an English writer named Hardy, he told his father.

'Ah, they oughtn't to let a horse with that kind of name run in an Irish race,' Michael Joe said.

When they arrived in Galway, they went to Lynch's Hotel and ordered breakfast. Francis had his usual boiled egg and toast. Michael Joe accused him good-humouredly of wanting to starve himself. But Francis couldn't be persuaded to eat any more. Michael Joe ate enough for three men, because, as he said, there was a long day ahead.

After breakfast, Michael Joe suggested they adjourn to the bar to fortify themselves for the day ahead.

'I'll sit in the lobby, and wait,' Francis said.

'Yerra, no one but women sits in the lobby,' Michael Joe said. 'Be a man. Come on with us.'

Francis went with them.

The bar was a dark pit, packed full with shouting, arguing men, jostling, standing shoulder to shoulder, face to face, and back to back. Michael Joe pushed ahead, cleaving a path through the crowd, like an old Irish warrior, striding on to the battlefield through the ranks of his men.

He shoved his way to the bar.

'What'll it be, lad?' he shouted back at Francis.

'Lemonade.'

'What? What's that you say? Sure they have no lemonade in these premises.'

The other fellows put in their orders for half-whiskeys.

'You wouldn't care for something stronger?' Michael Joe shouted back at Francis.

'I'm a Pioneer,' Francis shouted at him.

' 'Twould do you good to forget Father Matthew and the Temperance Society for one day,' Michael Joe said. He ordered a lemonade, and was embarrassed when the barman cocked an eyebrow at him.

Michael Joe tossed off a couple of half ones, and then got in a conversation with a bowler-hatted man standing next to him at the bar. They argued about who would win the Galway Plate. The bowler-hatted man had a tip.

'God Almighty, sure there's tips floating around all over the place,' Michael Joe said. 'If you listened to them you'd go mad. The form is the only thing that counts. And the breeding.'

He looked around for Francis. He was gone. Michael Joe tossed off his whiskey, and left the bar.

He found Francis in a corner of the lobby, watching the crowd milling around him, the shifting, swelling crowd. The bar had overflowed into the lobby.

'Ah, here you are. I didn't know where you went. Look them over, look them over. It'll be a great day. A great crowd. And a fine day. Thank God.'

Francis glanced sharply at him when he heard the 'Thank God'.

'Come on. We're going out to the racecourse,' Michael Joe said.

They rode out to the racecourse in a bus. All the way out, Michael Joe argued with fellows in the bus. Form and breeding. Form and breeding will always tell. Never mind yeer tips.

Michael Joe and Francis headed towards the grandstand. Michael Joe stopped at one of the hawkers' shows where fellows were throwing cork balls at a clown in a white conical hat, whose head, bobbing and shrieking, was stuck in a canvas frame, about thirty feet away from a marking line. Michael Joe insisted on throwing a couple of balls. He made Francis hold his coat, and then drew back a thick arm to throw the balls at the dodging, shrieking clown. He missed all three balls. The crowd encouraged him. 'Stand back there, and give Tony Galento a chance,' someone roared. Michael Joe bought three more balls. Fired. And missed again.

'Ah, God be with the old days,' he said taking his coat from Francis. 'The ould aim isn't what it used to be. I was a great sport in my time.'

'Rooooollllluuuuuuppppp . . . rooooolllluuuupp,' the hawkers shouted. 'Put your money down. Take yer chance. Hit the human target. Ten bob the winnah.'

'I used to be one of the great footballers in Corrigbeg. Ask around, they'll tell you.'

'Yes,' Francis said.

Michael Joe put an arm around him as they walked towards the grandstand.

'Some day I'll tell it all to you. Some day. When we have a moment's peace and quiet.'

Francis eased out from under his arm. Michael Joe became absorbed in watching the horses cantering by with their jockeys up.

'Look,' he said, grabbing hold of Francis. 'Take a look. Look at that little dwarf of a fellow up there on the chestnut. Look at the chestnut. The ears. A horse runs with his ears. Did you know that?'

'No,' Francis said.

'They're like fairies up there,' Michael Joe rhapsodized. 'Great heart. Guts, it takes. Guts. For the horse, too. And the poor jock, with hands the size of a child reining in a horse ten times his weight and size. A bloody miracle. A miracle.'

Michael Joe went over to the bookies and began placing bets.

Himself and Francis watched the races from the grandstand. At the beginning of each race, Michael Joe was quiet. But as the horses took the last jump into the stretch, he came alive and began to roar. A fierce, bull-like roar, repeated and repeated in time to the rhythm of the tired horses' hooves. 'Come on, lad, come on, come on.' He began to pound Francis on the back with excitement. The jockeys whipped on the horses, the whips rising and falling on the horses' flanks. Three or four horses were without riders. A woman shrieked: 'Come on, Red Rover, coooommmme oooooonnnnn.'

At the end of every race, Michael Joe adjourned to the clubhouse bar to refresh himself, and work up enthusiasm for the next race. And then the final-stretch drama was enacted all over again: Michael Joe shouting, roaring with the crowd; tired horses plodding to the finishing posts, being whipped on by marble-faced jockeys leaning forward on their necks, delicate hands slashing in silken fury.

Michael Joe enjoyed every minute of it. He was having a lucky day too. The form and the breeding were telling.

On the way back from the racecourse, in the bus, a man played the accordion. Michael Joe insisted on giving a song, 'Courting in the Kitchen'. After the song, a drunken woman swayed over the gangway to him, and sat on his knees, and kissed him.

Francis was sitting next to Michael Joe on the inside. He looked away.

'That's the son,' Michael Joe roared at the woman.

'Wisha, God bless the craythur, he's the spitting image of yourself,' the woman said. 'Let me give him a kiss.'

She threw herself on top of Francis. He raised his arms to protect himself. The woman drew back.

'He hasn't your manners, though,' she said to Michael Joe.

'A little encouragement. And a quiet spot. That's all the lad needs. Then the breeding will tell.' Michael Joe defended Francis.

When they got back to Lynch's Hotel, Michael Joe made for the bar, and tried to drag Francis along, but he begged off. He'd see him there in a few minutes.

Francis went out in the street. Pale, lemon-coloured light of a watery sunset was shining on the city. Men were milling around on the pavement and street, slowing down cars. A little down the street, a crowd had gathered. Francis heard shouts coming from there. He went down to investigate.

Two men were drunk, and swinging wildly at one another in the middle of the crowd, and encouraged by the crowd. 'I'll kill you. I'll slaughter you with me bare hands. And ate your guts,' one man was shouting at the other. 'You son of a whore, I'll tear your heart out your gullet.' And they attacked each other, swinging, biting, kicking, like animals. Blood streamed down both their faces.

Francis left the crowd. He was sick, wanted to vomit. He must get his father to go home.

He went back into the bar, and shouldered his way through the tightly packed bodies.

He found Michael Joe sitting on a half-barrel of porter, surrounded by a crowd of fellows, and orating to them. He had a pint of Guinness in his hand, waving it like a conductor waves a baton. Michael Joe saw him first.

'Well, look at what the wind blew in. Here's the son.' He introduced Francis to the fellows.

'I want to talk to you,' Francis said.

'Fire away . . . fire away,' Michael Joe said. 'We're among friends. All pals at the Palace, eh?'

'I want to go home,' Francis said.

Michael Joe gazed down at the pint of Guinness in his hand, as if pondering his son's statement, and the tone of it. He willed himself sober. He rose, and took Francis by the arm into a dark corner of the bar. Then he turned around and faced his son in the semi-darkness.

'Your mother tells me you're thinking of going on for the priesthood?'

'I've applied to All Hallows. For the African Missions. I want to go to Africa to bring the faith to the savages.'

Michael Joe laid a hand on his shoulder, and took a long, bleary-eyed look at his son.

'You're my only son,' he said, sentimentally. 'The only son I have. Who'll carry on the name, I ask you? Who'll carry on the name?'

Francis glanced around him. They were being ignored.

'I have the vocation. I can't ignore that, no matter what.'

'No God is that cruel to demand this kind of sacrifice from you,' Michael Joe said. 'You have a duty to your father . . . and mother.'

'No duty comes before duty to God,' Francis said. 'Our highest duty is to God. You know that well.'

'You're determined to go your own way then?'

'I'm determined.'

'You're so son of mine,' he said. 'G'wan home if you want. I'm staying.'

Francis turned his back on him, and walked away, out of the bar.

He went out in the car, and sat in it, waiting until his father would come out. He prayed for himself, to ask God to give him courage to persevere in his vocation. He said many Our Fathers and many Hail Marys. After he had prayed a while, he dozed. And his sleep was easy, untroubled.

He woke up to the noise of pounding on the window of the car. It was light dark outside. Light from the shops plastered the pavement. Francis saw a man pounding at the window of the car. He put his face to the window to get a better look. His father was ending down trying to peer in through the window. Francis hardly recognized the face; it seemed bloated, soggy, ashen, a paper face that had blown against the window.

'Is anyone in there?' Michael Joe shouted.

Francis tried to answer, but couldn't. He pressed his face against the window of the car. Michael Joe peered at him, and blinked a few times.

'I'm looking for my son,' he shouted. 'Where is he? Where is he?'

Again, Francis could not answer. He was physically unable to form the word 'here' in his throat.

Michael Joe stumbled away from the window of the car, and pawed his way along the car to the front. Then he sat down heavily on the front bumper. The car bounced from his weight. He stared drunkenly at the gutter in front of him.

'Are you ready to go home?'

Michael Joe blinked at him. 'Home? Home?' He grabbed Francis. 'We're going somewhere. There's someone I want to show you. Someone I want to show you. You're not my son. I'll show you your mother.'

Francis thought he had gone mad, and decided that the only thing he could do was humour him.

They rounded up Mickey the Hack, and the other fellows, and packed them in the car.

'To the Silvermines. I want to show my son something there, a minute.'

The fellows didn't object. They were drunk, and singing, and sang all the way to the Silvermines. Michael Joe did not sing.

The Silvermines was a small town like Corrigbeg. Michael Joe made Mickey the Hack stop, and got out, and asked a fellow in the street the way to Larkin's.

'The bank manager's?'

'Who the hell do you think I was asking for?' Michael Joe said.

'Down the end of the street, there,' the fellow said, backing away.

Michael Joe staggered back into the car, and gave instructions where to go.

The car stopped in front of a two-storey, slate, blue-washed house; the lower storey, to the left, had the gold letters of the National Bank of Ireland lettered across the windows.

'Come on,' Michael Joe said to Francis.

They got out. Michael Joe staggered up to the blue door, and pounded the brass knocker, pounding, pounding.

'Stop, Father, stop,' Francis said. 'You'll disgrace . . .'

The door opened. Nell was standing there. She had an apron around her waist.

'I brought him,' Michael Joe said. 'I brought him to you. Your son. Here he is.' He grabbed Francis and pushed him into Nell's arms.

The passing years had matured Nell into a model image for a bank manager's wife. The fair hair, that had been once long and wavy, cascading back over her shoulders, was now trim, neat, short and blonde. Obviously dyed, or tinted. She had filled out. Before she had tended to thinness and litheness, now she was solid, a substance of buxom flesh, though she was still not fat. The face had grown not quite sharp, but tight, precise, sallowed by pancake make-up.

She wore a dark-grey serge dress, sober-looking, proper-looking, that fitted her tightly. Her hips and buttocks rounded firmly through the dress.

'Well, isn't this a surprise?' she said, drawing back from Francis, but letting a carefully manicured hand rest on his shoulder, and gazing at him out of the grey-blue eyes. A slight smile played around the firm mouth.

'Look at him,' Michael Joe said. 'He wants to desert me. Going off to the priesthood. Running away. He's no son of mine.'

'Come in. Come in,' Nell said, drawing Francis by the arm. 'Seamus is out. And the girls and boys. Ye'll have a cup of tea, surely?'

'We won't be delaying,' Francis said, embarrassed.

She led them into a parlour off the hallway. It was well appointed, and tastefully done. Light colours on the walls. A piano. Mahogany sideboard gleaming with silver. Thick, plain rug on the floor. Comfortable armchairs and sofa. Tiled fireplace. Decanters of liquor. Family pictures, enlarged, framed with gilt on the walls. Over the mantelpiece, a large picture of the Sacred Heart, pierced through, and dripping blood.

'Well, now. Won't ye sit down,' Nell said. ' 'Twill take me only a minute to have Mary put the kettle on.'

Michael Joe threw himself into an armchair, and sank into it

He looked up at Nell. His eyes were blinking sharply, as if they were trying to focus properly on her.

'He's your son,' he went on. 'Your son. I want you to stop him, for me. He'll stop for you.'

'Oh, Michael Joe. Try to pull yourself together now.' Nell turned to Francis. 'How's your mother now? Ah, sure I remember her well. We were always good friends.'

Francis did not know who Nell Larkin was.

'I don't know . . .' he said.

'Oh, sure that's right. How could you? I used to be Nell Cullen. An old flame of your father's there,' she laughed. Though her tone was light, she seemed to summarize in that phrase her own attitude towards the past.

Then Francis seemed to pull himself together. 'I'm sorry for bursting in on you like this,' he said. ' 'Twas his idea. I couldn't stop him.'

Michael Joe was beginning to droop in the armchair. He roused at his son's words.

'Stop him for me, Nell. Don't let him go 'way from me.'

Nell crossed the carpeted floor, her high heels flicking precisely.

'Now, Michael Joe, we'll have a cup of strong, hot tea. And we'll talk about it then. Seamus should be back soon with the children.' She rang a silver bell for the maid.

Michael Joe staggered to his feet. 'You won't do anything for me?'

'Oh, Michael Joe. Be sensible. There's nothing I *can* do. If the boy wants to be a priest, I'd think you should be proud and happy.'

'I want none of your damn hospitality, then,' he said, and charged out of the parlour.

Nell started to go after him. She stopped in mid-movement. For a moment, her hands were outstretched, and her body leaning forward, as if she were performing, awkwardly, a movement in a dance. Then she stood erect again, and looked at the carpet.

'That's it, I suppose,' she said. 'What can I do?' And then she had an idea. 'Come back and visit us, some-time, now you know where we live,' she said to Francis. 'I have a boy your age. And a girl a little bit younger.'

'Thanks,' Francis said. 'I might some-time. I'd better get him home.'

'Don't be too hard on him,' Nell said. 'Be kind. That counts for a lot. Especially for a priest.'

If Francis had stayed, remained with her to listen to the stories she might tell him of the past, the reserve and shell she had wrapped herself in through the years might have fallen away for one evening, and the telling of the lived past, sorrowful though it was, might bring the old warmth and gaiety back.

'Was he in love with you?' Francis said.

Nell went over and kissed Francis on the cheek. 'Go and look after him,' she said.

Then she turned her back on Francis.

45

MICHAEL JOE STAYED in bed most of the next day. He sent Ann out to the shop for Vin Scanlon. Then, he sent Vin up to Blake's for a half-dozen Baby Powers' whiskeys, and told him to let no one see him bringing them. He drank them, while he was in bed.

But toward evening he grew restless, and got up. He refused to eat and went out of the house, and turned up to the Puffing Hole, driven by some obscure compulsion to visit it.

He took a short cut across the fields and meadows. It was late, shadow-filled evening. Trams of hay, the hawthorn bushes on the walls, the birds, all things in nature threw shadows, and Michael Joe's shadow mingled with the shadows from nature. He was trying desperately not to think, to forget what had happened the day before. Francis would leave for All Hallows. There would be no one to carry on the name. No son. The end. He had to keep moving, walking, staggering.

As he was crossing a field running beside the cliffs, he suddenly heard a pounding of hooves behind him. He turned around and saw Sexton's red bull bearing down on him, with horned head lowered. He knew the field had a dangerous bull in it; warning signs were posted all along the walls. But he had not noticed them. He had not really watched where he was going.

He began to run, calling on his body to obey, to respond to the energy which fear had released. And, suddenly, the shoulder he had injured long ago, began to ache. In the old days, the days of his football glory, when his body was at its finest trim and mettle, it had always answered the pressing occasion. The bull bellowed and charged. Michael Joe ran, but he could not gain on the distance between himself and the wall he was running for. His shoulder ached.

Then he felt himself being run over by the animal, and the sharp horn digging into his side somewhere. Then, as he felt himself being raised aloft, excruciating pain pierced through his whole body. He felt the hot breath of the animal, snorting, pawing. He fell to the ground, and doubled himself hedgehog fashion, hoping to protect himself. He was not afraid. His mind had cleared, so that he could see the fat shape of the bull, the dark, curly, red bulk, hear the snorting, the half bellows, taste his own blood in his mouth, smell the strong animal scent of the bull, and, as the bull raised him aloft, feel the hard horn, the deep fat along its back as he was thrown over.

As he lay on the ground, waiting for the next charge, he heard the yapping of a dog. He looked up to see the bull charging at a little black and white fox terrier who was yapping around the bull's heels, and distracting it. Michael Joe began to crawl across the remaining distance to the wall, and dragged himself up, and over the top, letting himself roll down into the ditch at the other side.

He began to moan, but then became silent, lying spread-eagled in the deep grass of the ditch, the grass spattered with his blood, and the blood seeping out of his body into the ground.

The sea sounded in his ears. Ah, it had been long ago, that sea sound, when it had been friendly. What had brought him to the pass he was in? Here he was dying, alone, in a ditch. Was it punishment for something? From someone? The pounding of the sea shook the cliff around him. Yes, God, he was guilty. And images of the past flashed through his mind to torture him.

The words of Canon Lyons came back to him: 'I see ruin and destruction in your face.' But he hadn't destroyed anyone, had he? Images from his past with Nell rose up—the night he tried to make love to her and Canon Lyons had spied on him. No, no, that wasn't destruction. What could he do? He loved Nell. He wanted her.

And then he thought of Seamus Larkin. No, no. He had meant well to him. He saw himself striking Larkin the night of the dinner at the hotel. And that blow came back to accuse him.

The images came and went, flashed, blotted out, and were succeeded by other images. Always images of Nell, Ann, Seamus Larkin, and Francis. Images blooded with the lives of people whose lives had crossed his, and with whom he had struggled.

Then he saw his mother. At last she came too, as if she had been so far away, and had to come from a long distance, and was late in arriving. He saw her feeding him that Christmas morning when he had come home drunk. Nourishing him back to health. And he had denied her, too. Along with the rest.

Forgive, forgive, forgive, he pleaded with the images.

He saw that he had sinned against all of them. Why had he married Ann? He knew he did not love her. He always knew.

And did he love Nell? Why did he deny the thing he loved? He ran away from the light into darkness.

He groaned now. No longer moaning. Moaning was for the physical pain. And the groan was for his life.

He wanted forgiveness. He wanted to be forgiven before he should die. But the images flashing and floating in and out of his mind could not forgive him.

He thought of God. He did not know Him. The religion he had seen had obscured God from him. He had never spoken. He groaned for something to be that would forgive him. He tried to pray: 'Our Father . . . Who art in heaven . . .' He could not go on. The prayers were meaningless to him now, at death's threshold. But he did not want to die unforgiven. Who would forgive?

His deepest desire as he lay there in the ditch was to create a Being, a God who would whisper to him from out of the falling dusk, above the crashing of the sea, that his sins against the people he knew had been forgiven.

He could not create that Being.

Two lovers who were wandering by heard his groans, and saved him. He was rushed to the hospital in Ennis. He had lost a lot of blood. Transfusions were given. He was in a coma for a while. But then, the instinct to live triumphed. The animal saved him, that had almost killed him.

He survived and was brought home. Ann nursed him back to health. And he submitted to her ministrations. He grew quiet.

nn was no longer afraid of him. She bossed, bullied him, and he
tered no word of complaint.

Francis was frequently by his bedside before he went away to
ll Hallows. He read from devotional manuals to Michael Joe.
ichael Joe did not really listen. The sound of the voice was enough.
e was comforted by it. Accepted his son's religious half sermons.
That else could he do? He had called for a voice himself. And there
ad been no answer.

The voice of his son was better than darkness.

46

MICHAEL JOE WAS still confined to bed, recuperating, when
rancis left to enter All Hallows. Ann had supervised all the prepara-
ions for her son's departure. The last month had been an exciting
 one for Ann. And she had blossomed under its demands. Her pale
kin had deepened to a creamy yellow, and her face had filled out.
She had begun to eat more since she was eating alone with Francis.
She gave off, now, a faint odour of eau-de-Cologne, and had taken
to using a light-coloured lipstick.

Herself and Francis went to Limerick on a shopping spree,
to buy the new wardrobe Francis would need at All Hallows.
She went off to a hairdresser while Francis was being measured
for a black topcoat, black suit, and soutane. All her life she had
been trying to keep the curl in her straight, sparse hair. The hairdresser convinced her to let her hair have its natural set—a lot could
be done with straight hair. Ann came back from the hair dresser
to the tailor's, with a new hair style, and looked ten years younger.
Francis did not remark on it. But he kept glancing at her when he
thought she wasn't looking.

While Francis and Ann were in Limerick, Nurse McGuire
took care of Michael Joe. She was shocked at the change in him.
He had lost weight, and the face was ashen. He would neither joke
nor flirt with her.

'A fine strapping man like yourself. And not a stir out of you

in the bed. God knows, what is the world coming to at all?' sh
said to him.

Michael Joe smiled weakly at her. The two missing front teet]
gave a pathetic turn to the smile. He turned his head away fron
her, to the wall, and dozed off.

Ann went with Francis to Limerick, to see him off to Al
Hallows. She sat proudly in the back seat of the hackney car, with
his luggage, while he sat up front with the driver, looking ver)
handsome in his new black suit, white shirt and black tie. His black
wavy hair glistened with brilliantine.

Soon after Francis left for All Hallows, Michael Joe was able to
get up and come downstairs. And, as soon as Ann thought he was
able for it, she began bringing him up to the chapel with her for
visits in the evening, and to last Mass on Sundays, letting him take
her arm, and walking slowly so that he would not have to exert
himself too much.

He got his strength back rapidly from the exercise of walking
to the chapel, and was soon in the shop with Vin, and holding
court in the little room at the back, with whoever dropped in.
He always answered questions as to the state of his health, per-
functorily: 'Grand. Grand. Fit as a fiddle. Right as the mail.'

He began keeping a can of Guinness in a tea-chest beside the
fireplace in the snug, and drew on it from time to time during the
day. When he had emptied it, he sent Vin up to Blake's to have
it filled again.

In time, the gossips caught on to the significance of Vin Scanlon
and the can, and they could tell the state of Michael Joe's health
by the number of times Vin and the can appeared in the street on
any given day. Bad days, he went up and down four or five times.

Ann heard about the can. And she had a talk with Michael Joe
one night, in bed, before he fell asleep. He did not go out, now.
Went to bed early, mildly drunk, and slept late in the morning.

'I think you ought to make the First Fridays,' Ann said. 'In
thanksgiving. 'Twas a miracle you were saved. A miracle.' Ann
was sitting up in bed, had the light on, thumbing her beads.

'A miracle?' Michael Joe mumbled.

'You could have died from the loss of blood up there in the
ditch. I don't know that you're thankful enough. God in his mercy
above saved you from a cruel and lonely death.'

There was silence for a few moments except for the rattling of the beads.

'Lord have mercy on me,' Michael Joe said with a sudden burst of religious fervour. He crawled out of bed, over Ann, and knelt by the side of the bed, burying his head in his hands. He began to moan out loud, thumping himself on the chest:

'Lord have mercy on me . . . Christ have mercy on me . . . Sacred Heart of Jesus look down upon me.'

Ann paused in her rosary to watch him.

'Come on, now, poor craythur. Put out the light, and come on to bed.'

She put out a gentle hand, and stroked his greying head.

And so, Michael Joe, moments of fervour brought on by fear when he thought of his narrow escape from death, or when Ann reminded him of it, thought he had found God. But the moments did not come often. And he always had the can of Guinness in the shop.

Michael Joe decided to sell the cattle. They had been the indirect instruments of many of his sins. He would get rid of them, give them away for practically nothing, make a sacrifice of them, the cattle, for his sins.

Himself and Vin went to an early December Fair in Ennistymon, shutting up the shop for the day. He sold all five bullocks to the first jobber who made him an offer. He made no attempt to go through the ritual of bargaining. The jobber made a tentative offer, way below what the cattle were worth. Michael Joe said for him to take them away out of his sight. Vin protested. 'Let them go, let them go,' Michael Joe said, waving at the jobber. 'Good luck with them. They're good cattle.'

Michael Joe spent the rest of the day getting drunk with his many friends at the fair who were delighted to see him on his feet again. Toward evening, as he was stumbling along the street, leaning on Vin's arm, they passed a tinker woman singing at the side of the street. Michael Joe paid no attention to her. She stopped singing and began to beg from him.

'Mr. McCarthy . . . kind sir, the dacent man . . . the fine man.'

Vin Scanlon told her to be off or he'd hit her a skelp.

As Michael Joe got drunker, he began to introduce Vin Scanlon to his friends, as his son.

'Thish . . ish my son . . . my son . . . Michael . . . Mick . . . aren't you Mick, my son?' he'd say to Vin.

'I am that,' Vin would say, laughing.

'A grand lad . . . a grand lad . . . proud of me.'

Vin hired a hackney to take them back to Corrigbeg.

When Francis came home from All Hallows on his holidays, Michael Joe gave up the drinking while he was at home. But Francis did not bother him. He did not spend much time at home. He stayed at St. Ronan's a lot, his old college. Here, he was able to be with the priests all the time, sitting with them, walking with them, hearing them and asking them questions.

Ann complained once to him that she didn't see much of him any more.

'Do you not know that I must be about my Father's business?' he said quoting scripture to her.

A frown puckered her small forehead. And she did not understand what it was he had said to her.

47

FRANCIS MICHAEL MCCARTHY was ordained to the priesthood at All Hallows College in Dublin. He was destined for the African Missions in the Belgian Congo. Ann and Michael Joe attended the ordination at the college. Michael Joe stayed sober, watched every moment by Ann for fear he might disgrace herself and Father Francis before half the assembled bishops and clergy of Ireland.

There were fifteen other young men ordained besides Francis. After the ordinations, the parents of the newly ordained priests assembled in the tree-lined quadrangle of the college, and knelt on the brilliant June grass to receive the first blessings from their priest sons.

Michael Joe knelt beside Ann. His face had grown flabby, and had that bluish-purple colour of meat about to go rank. He wore a white handkerchief in the breast pocket of his dark-blue suit.

Ann had made him wear it, arranged it in the pocket for him. He did not object.

Father Francis blessed his mother first, placing his white hands on her head. She kissed his anointed hands after the blessing, and remained with her head bowed, ashamed to let her son see the tears of happiness in her eyes. She was saddened somewhat by the thought that soon he would leave her for the Belgian Congo.

Michael Joe bowed his head and shoulders for the blessing, bowing down almost to the earth. His son's white hands cut the sign of the cross over him, he muttered the Latin, then imposed the white hands on the dark, grey-flecked head.

'*Pax vobiscum*,' Father Francis muttered.

Michael Joe remained kneeling and bowed after the blessing until Ann touched him, and he looked up.

Also from Brandon

ARANMEN ALL
Tom O'Flaherty

Tom O'Flaherty, older brother of Liam, was born and reared on Inis Mór, the largest of the Aran Islands, and his stories bring to life the world of Aran at the turn of the century. Almost every page is dominated by the sea, with its harvests of fish, seaweed and the flotsam and jetsam of shipwrecks, and with its constant threats of storm and drowning. There are stories, too, about eviction, land war, emigration and return. Indeed, Tom O'Flaherty showed in his writing the concern for social, economic and political conditions which was to lead to him becoming a political activist in the USA.

Tom O'Flaherty, whose brother Liam was the author of *The Informer, Famine* and many other books, left Ireland in the early years of the century for America. A socialist and republican, he was a comrade in the US of James Larkin, John Reed and James Cannon. Writing fluently in both Irish and English, he contributed to newspapers, including *An tÉireannach*. He returned to Ireland where he died on Inis Mór on 10 May 1936.

192 pages; ISBN 0 86322 123 8; paperback £4.99

Books by Bram Stoker

"Elegant reprints... The jacket illustrations are particularly good." *The Irish Times*

THE LAIR OF THE WHITE WORM

This extraordinary horror story, filmed by Ken Russell, features an enormous primeval serpent which dwells in a maze of deep caves and which can transform itself into a seductive noblewoman. Bram Stoker's last novel, it echoes with resonances of both his most famous creation, *Dracula*, and his remarkable first novel, *The Snake's Pass*; it has the authentic touch of the master of horror and suspense.

Bram Stoker (1847-1912) was born in Clontarf, Dublin. In 1876 he moved to London where he became manager and secretary to Henry Irving.

160 pages; ISBN 0 86322 124 6; paperback £4.99

THE SNAKE'S PASS

First published in 1890, *The Snake's Pass* is Bram Stoker's first novel and the precursor of *Dracula*.

"In this book, set in rural Ireland in the last century, the 'gombeen man' (moneylender) provides a representation of evil every bit as powerful as that of the later creation, Dracula." *Cork Examiner*

"The theatrical sense pervades all his writing but perhaps it is clearer in his first novel, *The Snake's Pass*. The tale is charmingly and exciting told... and, as for the story line, it is simply crying out for TV dramatisation." *Irish Independent*

256 pages; ISBN 0 86322 119 X; paperback £4.99

DRACULA'S GUEST

"Stoker was writing for a new and largely British public but his imagination and his risk-taking were purely Irish, a fact he never tried to conceal... These uneasy tales are to be enjoyed as much for their storytelling as in the gothic imagination of their creator. Recommended." *Irish Independent*

"Bram Stoker is still the popular master of the late 19th-century gothic absolute... The potency of his tales lies in the claustrophobic horror mixed with shafts of brilliant, ironic description." *City Limits*

160 pages; ISBN 0 86322 120 3; paperback £4.99